Also by Isabel Cooper

THE NIGHT BORN

ISABEL COOPER

sourcebooks
casablanca

Published by Sourcebooks Casablanca, an imprint of Sourcebooks
P.O. Box 4410, Naperville, Illinois 60567-4410
(630) 961-3900
sourcebooks.com

Printed and bound in Canada.
MBP 10 9 8 7 6 5 4 3 2 1

To Pedro Wrobel, who once played my inspiration for all good-hearted noblemen in fancy clothes.

Part I

Call: What was the First Betrayal?
Response: *Gizath, secondborn of the younger gods, slew his sister Letar's mortal lover by ambush and deceit.*

Call: How many times was he a traitor in that action?
Response: *Three, for he was false to Veryon in the attack, to Letar in believing himself right to do so, and to the better self he had been before he struck the blow.*

Call: What was his fate?
Response: *He was cast out beyond creation, where he nurses his hatred for mortals.*

Call: Does he still seek to harm us?
Response: *Always.*

—Litany of Letar's Blades, Part I

No, I must dispute the conclusions of my learned—I will not say biased, though it's known to all that his mother was from Criwath—colleague. It is true that we in Heliodar, by good fortune and geography, were able to preserve ourselves from the worst of the storms: it is a fact that my countrymen thank the Lord of the Wild and the Golden Lady for each day. Nor would I wish to be thought unsympathetic to the great devastation others faced. Letar has taken many souls into death, and each is mourned. But I will maintain that it is good fortune, nothing more. Thyran, the creator of those storms, may be the foulest blot on our fair city's history, but nobody can imagine that he bore any love for the land that bore him. I submit this: he had no scruples when it came to killing his bride, her paramour, and ten servants. Why would he be more merciful to his city than to his own house?

—The Honorable Baniki Yansyak, speaking at the Midsummer Debates, Year 55 after the Storms

Chapter 1

SHE WAS GOING TO DIE.

Yathana would have reminded her that everyone was going to die. But Yathana was leagues away, where the spirits that charged the magic of each Sentinel's sword-spirit went to rest after exhausting themselves channeling the gods' gifts. That burst of magic had left Branwyn with temporary metal skin and an absence at the back of her mind—which was normal—while facing a horde of malformed, malicious creatures.

That had become normal, too, over the last few days.

Now the twistedmen came on, pouring through the shattered gate of Oakford. They swarmed past the colossus of warped bodies that shambled across the yard, a moving charnel construction that held their leader, Thyran.

Branwyn knew the name, a shadow from the past given horrible life. She'd glimpsed the man himself, but her more immediate concern was his army.

Together, they formed a writhing mass of oversized claws and skinless-seeming red flesh. Some looked as though their faces were melting. Others had the beaks of birds, full of teeth and traps for the unwary who viewed them too closely.

She threw herself at them. Talons screeched as they ran along her arms. Black blood hissed in the air. The enemy never became individual bodies, simply one entity with lines of vulnerability: a leg here, a neck there. Branwyn carved a path through the shifting wall of flesh, Yathana slicing away what obstructed her.

Hallis's voice rose above the shrieking of Thyran's troops, yelling the signal that Branwyn had been waiting for.

One of the beaked creatures had caught her by the wrist when the word reached her. It yanked her forward, opening its mouth too wide. The shifting gray presence within had entranced more than one of Branwyn's companions to their death—but now the sigil on her forehead let her mind turn the charm as easily as her metal skin turned claws. She spun into the monster's grip, let Yathana's edge take its head from its shoulders, and then, when she'd made a half circle, started running.

She wasn't alone. A dozen others, soldiers stationed at Oakford and half-trained peasants who'd stayed to face the siege, kept pace, leading Thyran's troops on. They raced for the middle of the shattered town, where archers hid behind piles of rubble and the ground concealed a dozen sinkholes.

The twistedmen followed. Arrows did take some, and others stumbled, becoming easy marks for the archers' second volley or simply having to slow down, letting Branwyn and her companions gain a few precious feet of space.

More to the point, they had followed, away from the rest of the troops, away from the walking abattoir that carried Thyran. Branwyn saw the construct off to the side as she turned to fight. It lurched onward, crushing the wounded beneath its rotting feet, and Amris var Faina, Thyran's foe from a hundred years before, charged forward to meet it.

One of Thyran's wizards raised its boneless hands and sent a bolt of icy power screaming toward Branwyn. She threw herself sideways to avoid it, crashed against a pile of rubble, and staggered backwards, slashing out at a twistedman that was grabbing for her.

She regained her footing in time to see Katrine, her fellow Sentinel, and Sir Olvir, an earnest draft horse of a man who served the god of justice, rush Thyran's mount from behind. It staggered as two swords sank into the backs of its knees; in that instant, Amris leapt with all his strength. His blade hit the center of the colossus.

Then three of the twistedmen were on Branwyn—an arrow

had taken out the wizard, thank the gods—and she turned her full attention to them.

Yathana pierced the rib cage of the first with her usual ease, the metal of a soulsword divinely sharp even when the inhabiting spirit wasn't present. One of the soldiers jabbed the second in the side with a spear—not a fatal wound but enough of a distraction that Branwyn had time to yank her sword free and plunge it into a more vital organ.

She simply slammed her head into that of the third. Its gaping maw sought purchase on her face for a futile second before Branwyn's full weight hit it, knocking it backwards and into a hatchet that had only cut firewood a few days before.

For a few heartbeats, the world was clear around her. The construct had collapsed into a pile of corpses. The air was heavy with blood and smoke, much of it acrid. Darya, who was immune to poison, had led a squad of the twistedmen into a building and then set fire to a nasty packet of herbs.

Branwyn inhaled deeply anyhow.

There were still too many of the twistedmen, she realized. Only eight of the people she'd led still remained. She knew that she had only a few more minutes until she became flesh again, with the enhanced strength and skill of any Sentinel but no more.

And Thyran rose from the mountain of dead meat glowing with sickly fire. Olvir and Katrine stood below him. They'd been helping Amris to his feet, but now all three were still. Branwyn saw Darya start running toward them and knew that she herself was too far away to possibly intervene.

She was going to die.

Everyone was going to die.

There was nothing to say to the soldiers around her. There was nothing to do but face her death as bravely as she could. More twistedmen were running toward them already. Branwyn braced herself, lifted Yathana—

—and saw the twistedmen freeze in place, staring at the same multicolored radiance that Branwyn glimpsed from the corner of her own eye as it surrounded Katrine, Olvir, and Amris. Thyran's flame froze, too, when it struck the shimmer, and then went hurtling back at its creator.

They had a moment. Branwyn didn't know why, but she knew they'd better use it.

She broke into a run, crossing the distance toward the nearest still-distracted twistedman, saving her breath but shouting a battle cry in her mind.

From beyond Oakford's walls, she heard the clear, sonorous sound of a war-horn.

Reinforcements had arrived.

Chapter 2

Star Palace of Heliodar, five months later

"MADAM BRANWYN ALANIVE, LIAISON FROM CRIWATH."

The better part of the name wasn't hers, but Branwyn stepped forward.

The polished marble floor of Heliodar's Star Palace was smooth beneath her boots. She moved slowly as much to avoid a humiliating slip as she did to lend the proper ceremony to her entrance. All eyes fastened themselves on her.

There were sixteen in all. Four belonged to the footman who'd announced her and the scribe in the corner, a weary middle-aged functionary. The other six sets were all from Heliodar's High Council, the assortment of strangers that her mission depended on impressing.

Branwyn bowed low, studying the faces that regarded her from the dais as best she could. Reflexively she categorized their owners by likely physical threat. Three—a fox-featured, dark-haired woman; a plump councillor in spectacles; and an oily man in more concealing, plainer clothes than the others—were negligible to average: healthy but unused to physical work, and with no evidence of any experience in combat. The one in a purple surcoat, with gray hair and a similarly gray mustache, bore himself like he'd been trained for war at one point, but his age would work against him in a fight. Seated next to him was a man of about Branwyn's thirty-odd years and, as far as she could tell while he was sitting down, roughly her height, whose sleeveless russet-colored doublet showed arms that tended toward sinew rather than bulk, but that were firm and clearly muscled all the same.

He'd be a quick one, Branwyn judged, and his dark eyes were keen. He and the footman would be the ones to watch, assuming that the latter had taken some lessons to go with the silver-hilted sword he wore.

A lifetime of Sentinel training sorted her opponents in a heartbeat. It took longer for her to remember that none of that applied.

Her fight wasn't physical this time. The sixth member of the High Council, the one in the gold circlet who looked like a skeleton with half an ounce of flesh stretched over it, had more power than any of the others in the chamber. Even he, High Lord Rognozi, had no absolute authority.

The marble beneath her feet, and the earth that lay below it, were foreign ground in more than one sense. Branwyn spoke with more conscious awareness of each breath than she'd needed in any fight over the last fifteen years.

"My lords and ladies," she began, voice coached to a pleasing cadence and words long since memorized on her journey. "I come with these messages from King Olwin."

With a gesture she knew to be smooth, she proffered two sealed letters. The contents would repeat her message and confirm her identity, provided that the council didn't think she'd murdered the real Branwyn Alanive on the road and taken her place.

The footman, resplendent in a purple coat with gold braid, took the letters from her and transported them the entire twenty feet to the platform where Heliodar's rulers sat. Branwyn waited.

She felt overdressed in her wool gown and bronze torc, and not in terms of finery. Most of Heliodar's council wore gemmed circlets, rings on many fingers, and an assortment of silk and velvet that would have made tailors and courtiers in Criwath weep with envy. They wore the silk thin, though, and the velvet slashed open. Rognozi's violet and silver brocade was long-sleeved and his only ornament was the circlet, but age and frailty likely played a part there. Branwyn didn't know what lay behind the long, plain black sleeves and high collar of the oily man, but even his clothing was far thinner than she would've expected in the Hunter's Month, midway through autumn.

She should have expected it, though. Heliodar, out of all the human kingdoms, still had the magical strength for fireless heat, as well as for the pure white globes of light that illuminated the council's private audience chamber. Those who had power generally weren't shy about showing it off.

Rognozi opened the letters with a silver knife and a shaking hand. He read slowly while Branwyn waited, ignoring the way sweat was making her back itch.

"Likely their war," the fox-faced woman whispered to the mustached man, confident that her words wouldn't carry.

Normally, she would have been right, but Branwyn had gotten her minor blessing from Tinival, god of justice and truth, when she'd been reforged as a Sentinel. The whisper and what came after reached her ears clearly, as on an unfelt wind.

Their war. She stifled her response.

"Good to have real word instead of rumors," the lord with the mustache muttered in response.

"Official word, at any rate," said the woman.

The ostentatiously plain one was eyeing Branwyn as though she were a dog that might bite—or had just not been house-trained. The one in spectacles was blinking, frowning either in nervousness or perplexity. The youngest was simply watching, his pale, narrow face alert. He wore a bronze circlet on his shoulder-length dark hair, unlike Rognozi's gold or the others' silver: Branwyn wasn't sure what that meant.

Criwath and the Order had been able to tell her very little. Heliodar, being the least affected by the winters that ravaged the world, needed few Sentinels, and those who went there didn't have much to do with the nobility. The High Council and King Olwin carried on sparse correspondence, as became countries that were neither allies nor enemies, and what few traders went between the two didn't often meet with the city's rulers either.

Finally, Rognozi folded both letters and handed them back to the footmen, who put them on a small table to the side of the dais. "I'm convinced of your identity, Madam Alanive," he said, which should have made Branwyn wince, had she been a more honest person, "and the message you bear is dire. Say it now, please, so that we can all hear at once."

The moment was upon her.

"Thank you, my lord," she said, and drew a deep breath. "I come to beg the aid of Heliodar, in an hour when Criwath's need might become that of the world."

"The war?" It was the youngest lord, who leaned forward in his chair as he spoke. "The Skinless Ones?"

That sounded like another name for the twistedmen, the ordinary—if one could call them that—forces arrayed against humanity. Certainly it described them well enough.

"Just so, my lord, and worse. Thyran the Traitor, Thyran Bloody-Handed, has returned." Before any of the seven could reply, before the startled gasps from around the court could turn into murmurs of speculation and disbelief, Branwyn continued. "I saw him myself, in the siege of Oakford, and I'll swear as much before any knight of Tinival. The man who broke the world walks it again."

———————————

She was the most interesting thing to happen all day—all bloody year, if Zelen was being honest.

The pageantry of council sessions always appealed to him: the rolling words of the ceremony, the smell of incense, and the rich colors of tapestries and stained glass and clothing. He came away feeling as though good had been done, and despite his tenuous position, he'd helped accomplish it often enough that he didn't entirely dread the meetings or reporting on them to his father. The family very rarely issued instructions to him, and mostly it didn't offend Zelen to carry them out when they did. Some meetings were actually exciting.

Until Madam Alanive's entrance, this had not been one of them. The year was winding down, and the business at hand involved reports of winter supplies—necessary but dull—preparations for the Festival of Irinyev—much as they'd been every year—and toad-like Marton rambling about the Problem of Vice in Our Fair City for the fifty-third time.

Then, this woman. New. Terrifying in the news she'd brought: Thyran, servant of Gizath the Traitor God, had almost conquered the world a hundred-odd years back. He *had* started years of storms, blizzards that had damaged even Heliodar badly and had reduced the more northern landlocked kingdoms to famine and cannibalism. He, his storms, or his armies had also unleashed a fascinating assortment of monsters on the world. Just before the storms had reached their peak, he'd vanished. "Died," all of Zelen's tutors had said, but they'd never mentioned how. When Zelen had gotten old enough to read for himself, he'd discovered that nobody knew.

If he was back, with an army... Zelen saw the blood drain from his fellow councillors' faces and felt it leave his own. Nearsighted Starovna raised their joined hands above their head, parted them in a circle, and rejoined them at their heart, the sign that invoked the Four Gods for protection. Kolovat smoothed his mustache.

Marton was the first to speak. "What proof, madam, do you have of this?"

The woman didn't seem surprised by the question, nor as irritated as Zelen would've been—though, granted, she didn't have ten years of dealing with Marton to get her back up in advance. She faced the assembled council with her shoulders straight and her chin high: serenity, thought Zelen, but no trace of arrogance.

He also thought that bad news had never come in such a lovely form.

Madam Alanive was as tall as most of the council, as tall as Zelen himself or taller, with broad shoulders, round hips, and hard muscle showing beneath the sleeves of her tightly laced gown of blue wool. Her eyes were a slightly darker blue than the gown's summer-sky color, her hair rich gold and pulled back into a simple knot, her features square and strong boned.

Along the hem of her gown and the cuffs of the sleeves ran gold embroidery in patterns of knotwork diamonds, and opals shone from the ends of a bronze torc at her neck. The woman wore no rings, and the torc was too broad, and too open at the front, to be used against her. Her skirt was neither very full nor very long, and the boots she wore under it were polished to a sheen, but still boots.

That might have been normal dress in Criwath, but Zelen suspected it was more significant, and he wasn't surprised by the woman's reply.

"I was present at Oakford when he attacked, my lord," she said. Her voice was low-pitched and precise, every syllable clear. "I witnessed his magic at work. The man himself, if he is a man, was recognized by the soulsword of a Sentinel there, among other signs."

The soulsword made sense. The Sentinels, odd creatures that they were, each carried a dead person's spirit in their sword, usually one with some expertise in battle or magic.

"Sentinels," Starovna said, more to their fellow councillors than to Branwyn, "generally know their business where such things are concerned."

"After a hundred years," said vulpine Yansyak, "even a spirit could be in error."

"And the Sentinels have their own…agendas, you know. I

know little about them or their training," Marton said, proud of his ignorance, "but they're not precisely human by the time they take the field, and even assuming good intent"—which his tone implied would be foolish to do—"gods know what sort of faults in perception or judgment that leaves them open to."

Branwyn Alanive listened quietly, without a dramatic change of expression, but Zelen saw her jaw tighten. He felt for her: he wanted to throw inkstands at half the council on a regular basis, and he wasn't generally pleading for help in a war.

"It seems to me," he said, leaning back in his chair and drawling in a manner that had always infuriated his father and older brother and did much the same to Marton now, "it doesn't matter much whether the Bloody-Handed himself has made an appearance or not. The lady's speaking of a damned large army on the Criwath border, with at least one magician who's Thyran's equal in power. Unless we claim Olwin and the rest are imagining *that*, it sounds as though the rumors are true, and we have a problem."

The other five glanced at each other. Kolovat and Starovna were nodding, grave. Yansyak was chewing on her lower lip. If Thyran wasn't leading the army, she was too polite to say in front of the visitor, maybe whoever it was would be content with Criwath. Maybe it wasn't Heliodar's fight. Marton was tapping his fingers on the table, considering a number of issues, none of them likely matters Zelen wanted to hear about.

Rognozi surveyed all of them and then lifted his thin hands.

"Enough," he said. "Madam Alanive, you have stated the premise of your case and stated it well. We've asked those questions which come to mind, and you've answered. This matter deserves more consideration than that we can give in an afternoon's audience. We will take it up again…" He considered, glanced at the faces of his subordinates, and then said, "Two weeks hence, at noon."

This time, Branwyn's dismay was far more evident. The others might not have noticed the tension in her shoulders or the widening of her eyes, but her quick inhalation nearly echoed in the room. "My lord," she said, taking a step forward, "I don't wish to question your judgment, but the matter is urgent. The border holds for now, but there's no knowing when Thyran's next attack might come or what he's doing in the meantime."

"All the more reason for caution," said Starovna, with the same lack of passion they'd used to support Branwyn's claim.

"As you say," Rognozi agreed. He addressed Branwyn again, a perfect formal blank that Zelen knew from experience was utterly immovable. "Madam, your passion speaks well for your cause. But if the matter is an urgent one, so too is it weighty, and I will not see our blood spilled in haste. The schedule stands."

Branwyn, without Zelen's experience, nonetheless clearly had caught on to the futility of arguing. "As you say, my lord."

Only then did Rognozi allow himself his dry version of sympathy. "Where are your lodgings?" he asked.

"The Leaping Porpoise, my lord, near the harbor."

"I would house you as befits an ambassador," said Rognozi, "and my wife would welcome the company."

Knowing Lady Rognozi, Zelen was sure that was true, but Madam Alanive wasn't. He recognized the struggle on her face as she battled between not wanting to impose and not wanting—or not daring—to decline an offer from the high lord. "My lord is too kind," she finally said.

Rognozi gestured to one of the footmen. "You will tend to her belongings." Not bothering to get an answer, he turned back to the room at large. "The hour comes for us to take our leave," he said, the first step in the closing rite. Servants began circling the room, putting out candles.

Kolovat stood, the amethysts in his circlet catching the light, and walked to stand at Rognozi's right. "In the name of Poram's might and the power of creation."

"In the name of Sitha's craft and the webs that uphold civilization," Starovna chimed in, walking to the left-hand position.

Marton positioned himself beside Kolovat. "In the name of Tinival's justice and the truth we all must seek." As always, Zelen tried not to roll his eyes.

"In the name of Letar's healing," said Yansyak after a few quick steps to the furthest left of the room, "whether that be union, vengeance, or death."

Zelen and Rognozi stood at the center, eldest and youngest, and finished in unison, "May the gods favor that which we've done here and guide us in the world outside."

Chapter 3

There were certain difficulties, Branwyn was learning, with being an actual guest in a social sense, rather than a paying customer, seconded soldier, or half-welcome visitor boarding until she could kill the appropriate beast and move on. Chief among them just then was the fact that, while the rest of the court's inhabitants seemed to know precisely where to go after the closing rite, she didn't, thanks to Lord Rognozi's generosity, and thus stood in the middle of the room like a lost duckling. Many of those present, councillors and servants alike, gave her a minute of scrutiny, but none approached.

If diplomacy hadn't been involved, Branwyn would have found the nearest servant and made inquiries, but her briefing had been not only lengthy but foreboding. *There are more layers in Heliodar's etiquette*, Adept Consus had said, *than in a Silanese feast-day cake, and any of them can be a weapon for an enemy. Don't provide it.*

Branwyn surveyed the room, noting points of entry—official and less so—possible hiding places for traps or assassins, stained-glass windows in complex rose patterns that glowed red and blue even in the afternoon's subdued light, thick tapestries with soaring dragons and dancing long-limbed stonekin, and furniture that appeared far too heavy to break over a foe's head, even for her.

Yathana's absence from her side left her off-balance. Branwyn thought—prayed, really—that she'd disguised the soulsword enough that the servants who moved her wouldn't gossip, but there was no way of knowing—and she missed Yathana's presence regardless. The spirit had grown up in Heliodar, for one thing, before she'd joined the Blades, the militant priests of the Dark Lady, and she might have had useful notions about the situation.

Gods knew Branwyn didn't. She stood, tried not to look too lost, and examined the stained-glass windows. Their designs were the gods' symbols, repeated and joined in patterns: a golden spider for Sitha, a green pine tree for Poram, a blue sword for Tinival, and, for Letar, red droplets that could be blood or tears, or both.

The craftsmanship was lovely, and the scenes on the tapestries were fascinating, but neither was likely to be any help. Perhaps, Branwyn thought, she should go assist the servants down at the Porpoise.

Then she saw Verengir turn from a diffident conversation with the mustached lord and head in her direction.

Standing and in motion, he confirmed her earlier impression. The doublet framed a figure narrow at shoulder and hip and fell just far enough on Verengir's thighs to encourage speculation. What Branwyn could see of the man's legs between the hem and the top of his dark-brown boots was clearly lean and well maintained: his burgundy hose left little room for concealment.

A belt with a bronze buckle in the shape of a topaz-eyed lion held a money pouch, a bronze-hilted knife, and a matching sword. The council got to go armed; Rognozi didn't, likely for the same reasons he didn't wear jewelry, and neither did Marton nor Starovna, but the others wore swords of various lengths.

"Madam Alanive," he said with a sweeping, flourishing bow, one leg stretching back behind him. "Forgive me if I presume, but you look as though you'd welcome assistance."

"I suspect I would, my lord Verengir," Branwyn replied. "Am I meant to strike out on my own, or follow the high lord like a stray kitten, or—" Over his shoulder she saw Rognozi stroll out of the room, deep in conversation with a man she didn't recognize. "Ah." She bit back a curse. "I suppose that eliminates one possibility."

Verengir glanced behind him and chuckled, but kindly. "I

thought so. Rognozi means well, unless he has reason not to, but it's probably been a generation since he's had a guest who doesn't know the way to his house. And it's Master Verengir, or Zelen. I won't be the heir except under truly unfortunate circumstances."

"Branwyn, then," she said, and held out a hand.

Habits died hard, and she wouldn't have been sure what else to do in any case, but she was still a little startled when Zelen took her fingers lightly in his, bowed again, and touched his lips lightly to her knuckles. "A pleasure, Branwyn."

Her hand tingled at the contact, and the rest of her body wasn't far behind. "Likewise."

"Would you care for an escort, or simply directions?"

"An escort," she said, "if you have the leisure."

"Oh," Zelen replied, "I expect I can manage it. I didn't come with a carriage, but I can hire one easily enough."

"I'd prefer to walk, if you've no objection. It'd help me learn the city better, and I've spent about an aeon sitting lately."

"A trouble I know well. Shall we?" He offered a crooked elbow, and Branwyn took it.

A pit of vipers, Yathana had said about the Heliodar court, never being averse to clichés. Branwyn wasn't prepared to say that she was wrong, but a few of them did have lovely scales and hissed very prettily.

Impulsive gestures had their flaws, and the downside of offering his arm to Branwyn when they were still in the council chamber was that they had to part when they reached the Star Palace's outer hallway and footmen brought their cloaks. It was not the most elegant moment Zelen had experienced.

Branwyn's cloak was thick black wool, lined and trimmed with gray and brown fur, and an inch or two shorter than her gown: practical, again. She started to reach for it before the footman put it on her, bumped his hand in the process, and grinned awkwardly. "Apologies."

"Sickeningly helpless, aren't we?" Zelen said when another man in livery had helped him into his red brocade cloak. "I promise I do know how to dress myself, rarely as I may call on the skill."

Laughing, Branwyn took his offered arm again, though with a carefulness in her movements that made Zelen sure she spent little time in such a position. He would have wagered as much even before: her skin was smooth for a warrior's, but the marks of sword and bow were still there. She smelled mostly of the mint-scented soap common to the better sort of inn, but slightly of leather and metal as well. "I admit, I'm not used to servants."

"And that," Zelen said, "is probably the other reason Rognozi left you. He expected that your retainers would get directions. His man probably spent a few minutes trying to find them."

"I'm sorry to hear it," said Branwyn. "I hope it wasn't inconvenient for him."

"No, he'd give up quickly enough. Rognozi was born and raised when nobody would travel alone, that's all. Not even a soldier."

A glint in her eyes and a slight tilt of her lips showed that Zelen had guessed right.

The gilded magnificence of the Star Palace gave way to the gardens. Trees blazing crimson and gold in autumn colors lined the pathway toward the gates. Beyond them were bare flower beds and rosebushes where the last petals of the season spread blood-red on the ground, casualties of the rain that had slackened to an unpleasantly damp mist.

"I hadn't heard the name Thyran since I grew too old for tutors," Zelen said.

"Mostly, neither had I," said Branwyn, and sighed. "That's part of what I'm up against, of course. Even the worst—or best, in a way—of necromancers couldn't raise a man a hundred years dead, and the council knows it."

"Then what happened?"

She gave Zelen a look that felt as though she mapped every inch of his face, then said: "He never died."

They came to the garden gates, where the trees parted and fanciful wrought-iron and silver bars allowed a view of Heliodar's shining many-colored roofs. A few still stood half-fallen-in, and there were gaps that didn't appear in paintings from a hundred years before. Zelen had gone all his life without really calling that to mind, and now his attention was drawn to the absences, the scars that still lingered.

"The general who faced him set off a spell and took them both out of time," Branwyn went on once they'd passed through the gate. "Then, one of Thyran's more historically minded surviving minions discovered his whereabouts and how to break the enchantment. He didn't get a wonderful reward for his pains, but he succeeded."

"A hundred years of sleep didn't improve Thyran's temper, I take it?"

"No."

They took the road down, though not very far. Rognozi's mansion sat just below the palace on Ravens' Hill. Zelen searched vainly for a comment with wit to it, abject fear not being quite the thing to show to a woman one admired, short-foundationed though that admiration might be.

Thyran. At eight, Zelen had dressed up as the man—well, in principle, though it had mostly been a matter of black cloth and injudiciously applied raspberry jam—to try to frighten his sisters. He'd gotten a slap from Alize that had made his ears ring, and another from his nurse. After his father had heard the news, Zelen had slept on his stomach for a week.

A son of Verengir did not use that name lightly.

"I can understand why," Branwyn said into the silence, bringing Zelen back to the present. "Not only does it sound unlikely, but nobody would want to believe it. I didn't."

"You mentioned other signs."

"Ah. Yes. It gets a bit complicated," she said. "Too much so, I thought, to explain at the end of the council session, with all of you eager to go about your business. It seems that Amris var Faina didn't precisely die either."

"*General* Faina?" Military history had never been one of Zelen's strong points, but he'd read enough. The man had stopped Thyran at the end and supposedly died in the process.

"I can swear to that too."

She spoke with a patience that embarrassed Zelen. "I trust your account," he said hastily, though he hadn't been sure he did before. "But you have to allow a man a bit of shock. Has Letar gotten tired of visitors?"

Branwyn laughed. It was a quiet, smooth sound and incongruous with the sharp, dark humor in her face. "I wouldn't blame Her for it, but no. Faina's lover became a soulsword after he died. The soulsword and his Sentinel found Faina and brought *him* back to the present day. Faina was the one to recognize Thyran."

"And the, er, soulsword recognized Faina?"

"Just so. It's a strange story, I'll grant."

"Certainly not what I was expecting to hear today."

"Nor any of your fellows, I noticed." She gazed ahead of them, to where green-painted roofs sprouted over another set of gardens: the first signs of the high lord's mansion. "I don't blame them for not believing, or not wanting to. Nobody did at Oakford either."

"You may find it worse here," said Zelen gently. "This is where Thyran came from, after all, and where he learned to dedicate himself, and we've never been able to find out how. Bit of an old wound, you understand."

"And nobody did? Find anything out?" Branwyn kept surveying the landscape.

"I'm sure the priests tried to learn more when it happened, but the city's largely spent the last hundred years trying to forget he ever existed. Particularly the nobility."

"You seem to be one of the exceptions," she said, directing that sharp scrutiny at him once more.

They'd come to the gates to Rognozi's gardens, and a pair of footmen stood there, giving Zelen no excuse to provide an escort further. "Well," said Zelen, "I'm not precisely a paragon of my house and position. Ask the rest of my family."

The evaluation she was giving him took on a hint of curiosity, maybe even confusion. "But you're their representative on the council?"

"Ah, well, they don't think highly of that either." He bowed with the skill he'd learned along with walking, but more attention than he usually bothered putting in. "Welcome to Heliodar, Branwyn. I hope we meet again soon, and outside the court."

Chapter 4

"WELL," SAID BRANWYN UNDER HER BREATH, AND THEN caught herself. She'd waited until she was on the path between the footman-guarded gate and the mansion ahead of her, and she'd declined the aid of Rognozi's servants to walk all of five minutes, but still there was no point maintaining telling habits, particularly when they served no purpose: she didn't yet have a soulsword to hear her.

Well, she thought silently instead, *he seems fascinating*.

The intrigue was tactical as well, not just the allure of Zelen's lithe physique and big brown eyes, though as she'd stood facing him by the gate, she'd been keenly alive to his proximity. His expression when he'd spoken of his family, one of pain that long custom had polished into amusement, had made Branwyn wince for him.

She wondered at his motives for providing information: a bored lordling's excuse to spend more time with a comely woman? Tweaking the noses of a family he clearly wasn't fond of? A genuine desire to be helpful? Gods knew, Thyran was threat enough to scare any who believed, but assuming good intentions too easily was precisely the sort of amateur mistake Branwyn wanted to avoid, even if she was, in truth, an amateur at court politics.

Her thoughts took her through a hedge-crowded garden and up a set of broad stairs to the entrance of a wide three-story house, painted a silvery gray and sprouting peaked green roofs at every possible angle. All of it was wood, suggesting that it had been destroyed, or partly so, in the great storms after Thyran's first defeat, then rebuilt to be warmer than stone. That spoke of some practicality, roofs aside.

A short man in elaborate pale-green livery answered Branwyn's knock and inclined his head respectfully. "Madam Alanive?"

"Yes, thank you."

"Welcome to Rognozi. Please follow me to your rooms." He glanced past her, then added, "We have quarters for any attendants, if..." His voice trailed off, both polite and expectant.

"That's very thoughtful, but I have none."

"Very good, madam." He didn't let on if it wasn't, precisely, but his expression went tellingly blank. At a guess, the man was some thirty years younger than his employer, but unescorted travelers were still not the norm, particularly those from as far off as Criwath.

Branwyn followed him into a hall full of radiance, despite the dark walls: magical lights reflected off of tall mirrors every few feet. The floor was bare wood, relatively unpolished, which she thought was likely another concession to Rognozi's age.

"What a lovely house," she said, and earned a smile from the footman or butler or whoever he was.

"My lord's family was fortunate enough to save much of what they had before the storms," he said, "and he and my lady spared no effort or expense in restoring much of the rest."

"A noble endeavor," said Branwyn. "A friend of mine has made quite a study of life before, particularly of the art and comforts of that era." Darya mostly did that by dragging jeweled goblets and gold candlesticks out of ruined cities, but there was no need to go into detail. "Now that you mention Lady Rognozi, should I make my presence known to her?"

"There's no need. My lord and lady will meet you at dinner, but that won't be for a few hours yet."

He wasn't trying to condescend, but Branwyn heard the unspoken *of course* sprinkled liberally through his speech. She couldn't really object. Chances were good that she'd have ended up sounding the same, had he asked her to explain half her duties. Besides, she was too relieved that she'd have an hour or two to herself, with no need to try to remember the manners she'd learned in the far past and brushed up on in extreme haste. The meeting, and speaking to Zelen, had given her information. She wanted a chance to consider it and put it into what order she could manage.

She thought she'd gotten the councillors connected to the names Olwin had provided. Rognozi and Verengir had distinguished themselves. Yansyak was the red-haired woman, Starovna wore spectacles, Kolovat had the mustache, and Marton dressed plainly for reasons that Branwyn wasn't certain she understood yet. There was a great deal that she wasn't sure she understood.

The Order had sent her because of her gifts, because of all those who'd seen Thyran face-to-face, she was the easiest to spare, and because she was calmer and a touch more polished than many other Sentinels.

Branwyn still thought she made a poor diplomat and an even worse spy.

———————

"You give the impression of being less desperate to reach sanctuary than usual," said Altiensarn, the upper four of his copper-furred tentacles lifting and lowering in a polite greeting. "Did the meeting go so well, or has healing lost its charm?"

"I wouldn't say well, exactly. Interestingly. The world might be ending." Zelen hung his cloak on a peg by his office door, where it looked amusingly ornate against the plain gray stone. As was usual when he arrived after a council meeting, he suspected that he did too.

Altiensarn blinked, third eyelids sliding smoothly back and forth over gold eyes. "More so than usual?"

"That sounds dangerously philosophical." Zelen ran his hand through his hair, mentally lifting off the weight of the circlet. "The rumors are true. Thyran's back."

Over the years, Zelen had gotten to know his partner in healing decently well and had developed more of a sense for waterfolk moods than the average human. Altiensarn didn't obviously panic, whether that was natural or a habit learned by being a large furred being with a tentacled face among humans who tended to misinterpret sudden movements. All of his tentacles went still, though, and beneath them his voice, deeper than the usual chirping rumble, clicked out a series of sounds that Zelen would've wagered were prayer or profanity.

"More or less, yes," he said. "There was a woman—military envoy from Criwath. She didn't get much chance to describe the situation, but it sounds as though things there are in a damned bad state."

"As would only be natural," said Altien. The outer two of his tentacles waved slowly, and then he said, "But you and I can only tend our own sections of the reef. Does this news put different tasks in front of us?"

"No." Zelen gave his partner a nod of acknowledgment as he sank into his chair and started taking off his doublet. "How has the afternoon been?"

"Relatively calm. We had one elderly man with a cut leg, three pregnancies to inspect and one to end—"

"Ourselves, or did we have to send them to the Mourners?"

"The woman wasn't far advanced. Herbs and supervision sufficed."

"Thank the gods." Letar's power could stop growth in the womb, but, as when it stopped any other growth, it was difficult for the host to endure—and ending a pregnancy so far gone was usually an emotional affair. That day, of all days, Zelen didn't want to make the journey to the Threadcutter's Temple to check on a patient. "Sorry, please continue."

"A young man had a stomach illness that might easily have been bad meat or good wine, and there's a child with a fractured arm in the chamber of rest. She came in perhaps ten minutes ago. I gave her dragon-eye syrup and was waiting on you, as you know my opinion regarding human bones."

"Ludicrous unbendy mysteries, yes." Zelen undid the final button of his doublet and pulled on a plain linen smock to match Altien's, the thick fabric blessedly warm. He did what he could for the clinic, with fires and the help of an elderly wizard who could be bribed with court gossip, but it was always colder than the palace, which said much.

"I believe 'inflexible' was my term."

"I'm sorry. I'll take better notes next time," said Zelen. Passing his partner, who'd poured his entire seven feet into a too-small chair, he took the left door out of their shared study.

The little room he entered was the warmest in the building, and he shut the door hastily behind him so it would stay that way. Inside, a narrow cot in front of a fire held a girl nine or ten years old, one arm in a neat sling. Despite his protests, Altien could manage some basic principles of human skeletons. She opened glassy hazel eyes at the sound of the door, but didn't move.

"You," said Zelen, "look like you've had a damnable time of it."

She giggled, a good sign. It was hard to laugh when you were in overwhelming pain, and if she sounded a bit less than fully present, it meant the syrup was doing its work. "Mitri dared me to walk the roof," she said, and wrinkled her nose. "And I can't even get him back for it proper."

"Oh, I don't know," Zelen said, sitting down at his worktable. Altien had prepared all the essentials: straight lengths of wood, wide bandages, and a bowl of plaster. "My sisters would say, so long as you have your wits, you can take as much vengeance as you want. This next bit might hurt, I'm afraid—yell if you want. Altien's heard worse, half of it from me."

The arm was small and the break a thin one, the sort common

in children. Zelen pressed, then pulled, picturing the lines that he knew by heart. The coiled muscles stretched, letting him draw the bones beneath straight and true. The girl gave several sobbing yelps, almost hiccups.

"That's the worst of it," he finally said, reaching for splints and bandages, "and you did sterling work. Here." He passed a handkerchief toward her.

The child made a delighted sound—bright-red kerchiefs went excellently well with painkillers, Zelen had found—and mopped her eyes. "Really?"

"Mm-hmm. I've heard grown men yell like hunting dogs in full tongue for much less."

"Huh!" she said, sounding obviously satisfied. Then, with the careless backtracking of children and those not quite with their wits about them, she added, "It's not because of my arm I can't get back at him; it's because of his brother."

"What about his brother?"

"Not around no more," she said, the remnants of tears gradually leaving her voice as the memory of pain vanished and distraction occupied her. "Mitri's mam thinks he was stolen away. *My* mam thinks he tumbled down a well someplace."

Either was possible, Zelen absently thought, dipping and then wrapping cloth. The streets at Heliodar's border were hazardous places for children, though accident was more likely than kidnapping. "I take it they've searched."

"Oh, yes. My mam and da were out half last night."

"Was that when he vanished?"

"So people noticed. When he didn't come back for dinner," said the girl. "Mitri says he bets Jaron ran off to sea, but who'd take him? He's not but eleven and skinnier than me. But I don't want to say it. Even if he did dare me. He didn't mean for me to fall."

"You've got a good head on your shoulders," Zelen said, "whatever your arm might be doing just now. What's your name?"

"Tanya. M'da's Jan the Wheelwright, lives at the corner of Old King's Road and Snakebend," she said, with as much confidence as any baroness Zelen had ever heard announce herself.

"I'm sorry about your friend, Tanya, and your current misfortune."

"Thanks," she said. Zelen, absorbed in his work, couldn't see her face, but there was a preparatory sort of silence about her. He half anticipated her next subject. "You know a lot about the gods?"

"I've studied a little," he said. "I'm no priest."

"Nah. Priests are always busy. I guess you are too, but—"

"But I can talk while I'm busy."

"Do you think Letar will let him look back at Mitri and his mam sometimes? If he's dead, I mean."

"I don't know the Dark Lady's will," Zelen said slowly, pulling a curtain over old pain for the sake of his patient, who asked earnestly and innocently, "but all I've heard makes me believe She would, if he wanted to. She's kind, in Her way."

"Oh," said Tanya, and closed her eyes again. "That's good."

Chapter 5

TANYA WAS STILL SLEEPING WHEN THE BANDAGES TURNED firm enough that Zelen could release her arm. As usual, he had to admire the young's ability to sleep in whatever situation they found themselves. The syrup doubtless helped, but Zelen had taken a bit of it himself now and again, and he doubted he would've been able to drift off with one arm held in the air.

He rose and started to reroll the leftover bandages while he walked toward the office. There was always another use for them. The stiffening mixture didn't keep well, sad to say, but the ingredients didn't cost too much, and with luck there wouldn't be a rash of broken bones in the next week.

Altien was still seated behind the desk, making notes. His handwriting was careful, small, and scratchy, better than Zelen's, although his diagrams were inevitably round where they should be straight and vice versa. "The girl's father is in the receiving room waiting for word," he said, "and there's a small crowd of young people outside the clinic. I invited them in, but I surmise they fear being given tonics or possibly washed."

"I'm constantly tempted, I admit. Sticky creatures, children."

"Humans' are, yes. But I suppose you can't help it."

Zelen was chuckling when he went out into the receiving area, which itself relaxed the man sitting there: a dockworker, broad shouldered and large bellied, with dark skin like his daughter's and gray-specked hair. "It was a terribly boring sort of an injury," Zelen told him. "Tiny fracture, young bones, should be back at all her old mischief in a few weeks. Try to be more complicated in the future."

Jan the Wheelwright actually laughed then, as Zelen had intended, and a few more worry lines disappeared from his forehead. "Forgive me, sir, but I don't think we will. Though I've no doubt Tanya could manage it, if any of 'em could."

"She seems the sort. Brave girl, likely more than is good for her," he added sympathetically. "You can take her home now if you're up to carrying her, or wait a bit for her to wake up."

"She's not so heavy," said Jan, rising from the long bench that rested along one wall.

"No." Zelen dithered briefly between concern and respect for privacy, then came down on the side of the former. "She mentioned that a friend of hers was giving you all a bad time of it."

"Jaron. Mmm." Tanya's father sighed. "No trace of him. He'd reached the age to argue with his mother a bit, so he *could've* run off, but…"

There was no need to finish. Heliodar had no shortage of abandoned buildings and old wells, nor of predators. Being forcibly taken aboard a merchant ship or a fishing boat as a dogsbody was the most pleasant possibility.

"Would another set or three of eyes help?" he asked. "I've a bit of time on my hands."

"Might," Jan said, slow and cautious. "And I'm sure the lad's parents would thank you for it. As would I. Best tomorrow, though, when there's light enough. You know where we're at?"

"Tanya mentioned."

"Then thank you twice, sir," Jan said. Reaching into the battered pouch on his belt, he produced a small cloth sack of coins, likely copper swordfish, the smallest and most common currency. Zelen didn't try to give it back but didn't examine it either. If the payment covered the ingredients that went into Tanya's cast, he'd feel fortunate. If not, it wouldn't be the first such episode.

"Fair night to you," said Zelen, and opened the outer door.

Five youths of various ages and degrees of grime were gathered there, watching in wide-eyed suspense. They weren't watching him or the door any longer, though, whatever they might have been doing when Altien had spoken to them. A shining black carriage across the street, harnessed to a pair of immaculately groomed gray horses, had commanded all their attention.

Zelen knew the driver's russet-and-gold livery. He knew the coat of arms on the door. If he hadn't recognized those, he would have known the three men who emerged, and particularly the figure in the center: tall, slim, dressed in unornamented black and gray clothes that cost a month's wages in this part of the city. His hair was platinum blond, but his face was otherwise very similar to Zelen's own.

The children didn't miss the resemblance. They stared at Gedomir and the guards, then back to Zelen. The coach and the liveried, armed men were clearly the more fascinating picture, but the knowledge that one of the clinic healers had a relative his age, likely a brother, and a rich brother at that, was clearly striking a few of the older ones as interesting.

"Gedomir," said Zelen. "I hadn't known you were coming to the city."

It took all of his self-control to keep from swearing.

———————

It seems you played a few cards right, a familiar mental voice said as the butler opened the door to Branwyn's room. *I can't enjoy a room like this as I once did, but it's a much finer view than the inn.*

Yathana was lying across the foot of Branwyn's bed, three feet of straight, razor-edged steel in a scabbard covered with midnight-blue silk, with thin golden chains connecting small amethysts and garnets. Her hilt appeared gold too—a thin layer of gilt did wonders—and the eye-sized fire opal in the center of her guard was now flanked by two chunks of amber on the quillons and another on the pommel.

Seventeen years of partnership had given Yathana's normal form time to sink very deeply into Branwyn's consciousness, and even after two months of practice, the additions stood out whenever she had occasion to examine the soulsword. Adapting to the shifts in balance had come more easily, praise the Four.

"It looks wonderful," she said to the butler, though she really hadn't even noticed the room save for marking a window opposite the door—real glass, not shuttered, and framed by heavy rose-pink curtains. "Thank you."

"The maids will have put your clothing away"—he gestured to a tall oak chest in the corner—"and there's a rune by the window. Trace it, should you need anything."

"Thank you," Branwyn said again, and hesitated, not certain if she needed to give him a more formal sort of dismissal. While she was considering the matter, he bowed and left her.

You aren't doing too badly, said Yathana, as usual speaking with a crispness that suggested autumn leaves underfoot. *He thinks you're a country bumpkin, of course, but then, they all will.*

"I noticed," muttered Branwyn. "Though I'd have thought carrying you around—"

You could be a rich hayseed. Many are. And we're not being observed. The maids did search your clothing, but no more than I'd have expected.

"I suppose I'd do the same, in their place."

I'd bloody well hope so.

Branwyn sat down on the bed, which was covered in a snowdrift of white cloth, surrounded by thick red curtains, and big enough for a small scouting party, if not a full army. A small crystal orb on a low table beside it gave off faintly pink light as well as heat, though most of the latter came from a fireplace opposite the wardrobe.

It *was* a nice room, certainly the best she'd ever been in. Branwyn yielded to impulse and threw herself backwards onto the excessive mattress.

They will, however, probably get suspicious if you start jumping on it.

"I haven't done that since I was twelve."

I never know when one of the living will revert. How did things go?

"They're understandably reluctant to believe, and I suspect there's no common opinion among them. They haven't decided." The canopy was a solid wash of red above her. Branwyn focused on it. "It's not a refusal," she added, as much to herself as to Yathana.

How long are they going to make us wait?

"Two weeks."

Sitha's arse, they haven't gotten a shade less self-interested since I died, have they? If Yathana had still had teeth, she clearly would have been grinding them.

"Olwin said they'd be slow to act," Branwyn pointed out, forcing herself to try to agree with the arguments she was making. She'd need patience. It was best to start developing it now. "So did you, if I recall correctly. Two weeks might give me a chance to make our case more thoroughly, and perhaps Thyran won't move in that time."

Or the time it'll take them to move the armies out, if they do see reason? It'd serve them right if the Twisted were crawling up their backs by the start of winter. Dark Flame, why have you and your family decreed that we always need the most inconvenient, irritating bastards to help us get anything done?

"That's a fair amount of railing at the gods for a priestess."

The Blades can't expel me. I'm dead.

"I never would have expected the dead to gloat so much."

Yathana chuckled, reluctantly. *Ah well. We have the opportunity we have, I suppose, and with the gods' favor, Thyran's still nursing his wounds from that odd knight you befriended. Do we have any likely targets here?*

"Rognozi, though he could've offered his house out of simple politeness. Starovna," she added hesitantly, still trying to attach names to faces, "the one with spectacles, gave us credit for good judgment, which was flattering, but then spoke in favor of caution. Verengir made a good point on my behalf—that Thyran's identity was second to the threat of an army and a sorcerer—and escorted me home, but he doesn't hold the lordship, and I don't know precisely how much influence he has."

That family was always a reclusive lot. Simple country purity and healthy living. Very tedious.

"This one doesn't seem to be. Healthy, yes," she added, remembering the muscles on his bare arms.

You don't need me to caution you, said Yathana, who could read Branwyn easily. *Seducing him might not be a bad idea, though, tactically.*

"A bit obvious, isn't it?" She sat up and began to unlace her boots. "Do you think any of the nobility would spill secrets in bed, particularly to an unknown quantity from Criwath?"

One never knows.

The first boot came off, and Branwyn found herself eager to change the subject. "How much *have* things changed?"

Not as much as elsewhere, from what I've seen. Ironic, I know. But—

The sword's inner speech took on a serious, thoughtful aspect. Branwyn didn't pause while she took her second boot off; she'd long since learned to listen while taking care of mundane tasks. She sharpened her inner awareness, though, and prepared a special place in her memory for whatever came next.

There's something wrong in this city, Yathana said. *Possibly across the entire region. I don't know whether it's a change or not, but it's there. It's not very blatant, as far as I can tell, but it's extremely wrong.*

Chapter 6

"I hope I'm not intruding," said Gedomir.

He stood in the office and, as usual, stood *out* in the office. Every detail of his appearance said that he didn't belong there, and his countenance emphasized it. The plain wooden desk and cheerful red cushions on the chairs, the similarly colored wooden shelves of books and scrolls, and the thick curtains, fashioned from leftover and garish gold-and-blue velvet—all might as well have been new forms of insect, for all that Gedo had seen them before.

Altien, a new arrival since Gedomir's previous visit to the clinic three years ago, had gotten a startled look, then a barely polite nod, from the Verengir heir. The two had responded with equal practiced politeness to Zelen's introduction before Altien had excused himself for the evening.

"No," said Zelen, "I was just finishing. I can't say I expected you, of course."

"There were a few business affairs to manage—nothing that you need to be concerned about, naturally. I'd been intending to return to the house, but I know that you allow the servants a remarkable degree of latitude and employ very few," Gedomir said, "so when your butler said that you were occupied here, I feared that they might not be prepared to receive a guest."

"Considerate of you," said Zelen, trying to make himself believe that it actually might have been. "But I'm sure they'd manage. You don't exactly demand luxury."

"Luxury, no. Correctness, yes. You appear...well," Gedomir

said, glancing between Zelen's smock and the folded doublet on the desk. "And keeping interesting company."

"I must have written about Altien. Can't easily match his skill, or his dedication."

"If that's your judgment, of course you know these matters better than I do. I suppose it would be good to have an assistant with your tasks here—one without other duties to occupy him."

"Altien's a partner, not an assistant. Fully as good as I am in most areas, and better in a few others. We do get a few nonhumans in here from time to time, you know." Zelen stacked up his final paper and pulled his tunic over his head, ignoring the way Gedomir dramatically turned his back. "Remarkably insightful about the dangers of the sea too. Literally lifesaving, when the fishing boats or the ships are out."

"I'm sure," said Gedomir.

"How are the family?" Zelen asked, rather than pressing the issue.

"Well." Gedomir sounded far more approving. "Mother and Father are aging, of course, but still strong, and Hanyi's taking her place as a help to them."

"Alize settling into married life?"

"Yes, to the best of my knowledge. No word of issue yet, alas."

"It's only been a year. Besides," Zelen said, "getting an heir or three is really your responsibility, isn't it?"

"Oh, yes. Mother's spoken of a few appropriate candidates, though I haven't heard any names."

"Better you than me, though I'll look about for you if you'd like. Kolovat and Yansyak both have single daughters, if I'm not mistaken."

"Mother has it under control. And not Yansyak. That line—"

"Tinival's...justice, Gedo." He caught the oath at the last second, made a quick substitute for the anatomical term that he'd been going to use, and still knew without seeing the man his brother had grimaced. "That was a hundred years ago."

"And we're still paying."

"Not for Yansyak's part in the affair. Infidelity's common enough. Most people don't kill in response, much less murder an entire household and try to destroy the world. Speaking of Thyran…" In conversation with anyone else, Zelen would've been surprised it had taken him so long to think of the day's news. His brother had a way of diverting his mind.

"I heard as much this evening," Gedomir said. "The woman's story—the woman herself—seems interesting. She came alone?"

"From the sound of it, Criwath's forces are pretty well occupied at present."

"If her tale's reliable."

"We could easily demand that she swear it to one of Tinival's knights. She has sense enough to know that."

"I heard she offered, yes," said Gedomir. "I also heard that you talked with her a fair amount and provided her with an escort back to the high lord's estate."

"You have very accurate sources," Zelen said, and opened a desk drawer. He kept a set of ruby-colored glasses in there and a bottle of half-decent wine. Usually he drank with Altien after a hard day, but now he knew he'd need help keeping the conversation from turning into the sort of flaming row he and Gedomir had often had in their younger days. "I'm surprised you even need my report. Drink?"

"I haven't started indulging, no. What do you know about this Alanive creature?"

Zelen poured and sipped. "Very little so far. She's clearly done service in the army, or as a warrior, even if she's stuck in diplomacy now. Smart, well spoken, from what I've seen, but a king would hardly send an envoy who wasn't."

Rather lovely, he added, but silently.

"You could likely find out more," said his brother. "That might be quite useful."

"Oh, yes. I'll use my astounding seductive abilities to uncover all Criwath's state secrets, shall I?"

The burst of sarcasm got only a raised eyebrow from Gedomir. "Nothing like that, I'm sure. Only cultivate an acquaintance, form impressions, and add what you discover to your letters. Father and Mother would be grateful for the knowledge."

He didn't have to say that it was barely any effort compared with what a younger son owed his family, or remind Zelen whose funds kept him fed, clothed, and housed, the clinic running, and wine in the glass he was holding. Those lectures had taken place years ago and hadn't only come from Gedomir.

"Getting to know her won't be a chore," Zelen admitted, "and I doubt she'd share knowledge with me if it was truly secret. Very well." He tossed back the last of the wine. "And now perhaps I'll make an early night of it. One of the children here went missing, and I've offered to help search tomorrow."

"Ah," Gedomir said. He paused in consideration, brow furrowed, then added, "Take Nislar along when you go. I won't need two bodyguards before I leave, I'm certain, and he might be of some assistance."

Gratitude warred with shame for his former thoughts. "That's kind of you, Gedo."

"Oh," Gedomir said, "we each serve in our proper place."

———

A low table held a small white bowl and pitcher, with enameled pink roses and blue dragon-eyes twining across both, as well as a towel and a cake of soap. Branwyn crossed to the table, poured out water, and silently began to wash.

Action helped to settle the mind, so long as the action itself wasn't thoughtless or impulsive. So Branwyn's teachers had said, and she'd found it to be true before. This was no exception. By the time she shook off the last water droplets, the first question was on her tongue.

"Why haven't the priests sensed it?"

The Four Gods' servants had powers themselves. Priests of the elder gods Poram and Sitha served in a more peaceful capacity, for the most part, but Tinival's knights could tell lies from truth when they had the chance to administer an oath. Letar's Mourners mostly sensed wounds and disease, but the Blades, her extremely militant order, were generally fairly sensitive to Gizath's power. Given that Yathana had been one before, Branwyn assumed that Gizath was the source of the wrongness.

I don't know, said Yathana. *I've been wondering that myself. Death gives us perspective that even the Threadcutter's priests don't have while they're alive. Maybe that's it. Or maybe having lived in the city so long makes them blind to the wrongness.*

"Or," said Branwyn, sitting back on the bed, "it could be that they're aware but can't change matters? Heliodar was the site of the greatest betrayal since Gizath's. That might echo, without any way to stop it."

More a missing limb than a bleeding wound? Branwyn could feel the soulsword contemplating the possibility. *It could make sense. I'd rather not assume.*

"Neither would I." She rubbed the bridge of her nose. "If this were any other mission, I'd go and ask. Maybe I should—they certainly wouldn't willingly give us away." It probably wouldn't be the end of the world if they did either. Being a Sentinel wasn't illegal, nor did it change her mission or her status as Criwath's military envoy. Marton wasn't the only one to find the Order off-putting, though. Branwyn's job would be easier if the people she spoke to didn't worry that she was one bad day away from cannibalism.

A known Sentinel would also be a target, whether from active corruption within the city, if it did exist, or from people worried that she'd get in the way of more mundane agendas. That might happen regardless, but Branwyn would far rather her enemies underestimated her if so.

Not deliberately, said Yathana, *but priests are mortal and temples are human organizations. An acolyte who hasn't learned discretion or discipline, or someone whose mind isn't always what it should be, overhears, a patient sees you entering and leaving and puts the pieces together... there are no guarantees. I could tell you stories.*

She had, a few times, though not specifically to that end. Branwyn, who'd known priests only from a distance and from the Forging until she was fifteen, had once been shocked by the realization that the temples weren't smoothly functioning monoliths any more than the Order was.

Not worth the risk, I'd say, or not worth seeking out. If you end up having a private moment to speak with one of the Dark Lady's servants, do it, but don't go to the temples without an excuse. Besides, if they're blind from a life here, there's not much they can do to help us.

"I'll be sending out messages tomorrow," Branwyn said, "setting up meetings, but I doubt I'll be called on to meet people immediately. I could go out and learn more about the city, especially the parts that I won't see while I'm drinking wine with the council members."

That, said Yathana, *sounds like an excellent place to start.*

Chapter 7

DESCENDING FROM THE HILL TOWARD THE BAY THAT FLANKED Heliodar in the east was, in a way, familiar to Branwyn. Most of the fortresses where she'd been quartered had themselves been the center of fortified towns. Concentric circles were common, with farms outside the town walls in places where the countryside was safe or people were bold. Heliodar was constructed along the same basic lines.

Size did make a difference, though, as the dancing girl was rumored to have told the high priest. The scale of Heliodar multiplied the unexpected turns where a straight street ran into a building and changed course, shifted segments so that a district of recent wealth bordered one where formerly grand houses fell into disrepair or desperate battered cleanliness, and generally presented buildings to Branwyn's stunned vision like marching ranks of an army. She was beginning to make out differences, though, to know the faces above the raised shields and readied pikes, which had seemed impossible on her trip to the Star Palace and almost inconceivable when she'd made her way from the city gates to the Porpoise.

The inn was her first destination on an afternoon radiant with sharp autumn sunlight, a familiar landmark and one that she could excuse returning to. The Rognozis, at dinner the night before, hadn't acted at all surprised when she'd mentioned going back to explain and settle her accounts, though the round-faced and merry Lady Rognozi had offered the services of a messenger instead.

"Thank you," Branwyn had replied, while eating roast pigeon

with more care than she'd ever given food before, not to mention more utensils, "and I'm certain they'd do a wonderful job, but I'd best attend to it myself. I'm a bit overcautious about inns after my journey, you understand."

"I do indeed," Lady Rognozi had said with a click of her tongue. "Why, I remember a spring when I was a girl, journeying from no farther than my family's estate—three days by coach—and..."

The story that followed had involved larcenous innkeepers, drunken footmen, and a game of chance that Branwyn found impossible to understand. It had made her laugh, though. It had, more importantly, more or less settled the question of her errand the next day without suspicion, and provided some distraction from the subject of her mission.

Neither of the Rognozis were old enough to remember Thyran's War precisely, nor the start of the Great Winters, but they'd grown up feeling more of the effects than most. Lord Rognozi's father and three of his siblings had perished then, he'd said. Lady Rognozi had simply gone silent, which Branwyn was already recognizing as odd for her, at the mention of Thyran, and neither of them had eaten very much.

She was inclined to think well of them, as much as she could let herself think well of any living soul in Heliodar yet, particularly those in the nobility. She was also inclined to believe that her absence from the house that day was a relief for all parties.

Branwyn certainly felt more herself in the lower city. Physically, it was much less enjoyable, but it was a trip back to a world on her scale—a world where she at least felt mistress of whatever she might encounter.

The great houses gradually shrank, as did the gardens in front of them, and the iridescent coating on the roofs—the shine that had given the Star Palace its name—became small patterns or disappeared entirely. Down near the water, the large buildings were warehouses, the streets were twisted and narrow, and many of the inns, shops, and houses were patchwork, made or repaired with materials from other buildings that had been destroyed during the Great Winters. The tavern where her third conversation ran dry, for instance, had a foundation of gray rock, then became half red-brick and half smooth, gray wood.

Inside, it was a tavern much like most other half-decent examples of its type: dark, quiet during the day, and smelling strongly of cheap wine, which was one of the better options. The bartender was happy enough to talk, but all of her stories sounded fairly normal: her nephew's apprenticeship as a smith, how much she was anticipating an upcoming festival, the rumors of war.

"But you'd know, hmm?" she asked, refilling Branwyn's wineglass. "Criwath, by your accent. How bad is it?"

"Bad," said Branwyn, recalling the siege of Oakford, the smell of fire and mass death. "Or it was. The twistedmen retreated, but I'm certain they're planning their next move, and even far away from the front lines, everybody's on edge. Uneasy. How are matters here?"

"Eh." The bartender shrugged, her tan shoulders a striking contrast to the light green of her chemise. "Folk talk, but that's all. Worst that's happened here this week is a fight over cards—one of 'em got knifed in the side, but I hear his friends got him to Verengir quick enough. The Mourners didn't even have to waste their strength."

The name was a firework on a quiet summer night. Branwyn's head didn't actually jerk, she was fairly sure, but it was a near thing. "Verengir?"

"Mm-hmm. The lord's younger son. He—and one of the waterfolk now, though gods know why they want to be messing about with humans—run a place down near the market, healing with herbs and needles and whatnot. Handsome lad," she added. "If I weren't married, I'd not mind having him see to a few of my problems."

The waterfolk, Yathana put in, *might have a different view of the city from most. Worth meeting. And worth finding out what your councillor is doing down here, if he's the same man.*

"A lord's son as a healer?" Branwyn sipped her wine, which was sharp and a touch spiced. "Was he disinherited?"

"Not at all—well, he's on the council, and he wouldn't be there if the old man had cast him off, stands to reason. Some say he had his heart broken and does good deeds to forget, and others that he did something real wicked and this is penance."

"What do you think?"

"I dunno. But he doesn't act wicked. Or heartbroken."

Getting thanked for being useless was enough to break a man's heart.

Chessa, the missing boy's mother, had been past the point of weeping or rage. When Zelen sent Nislar back to his brother's servant and presented the bad news, her thin face had only shown weary numbness. "I'd not had much hope," she said, a phrase Zelen suspected covered more than the last two days. "Thank you for trying, m'lord."

He wished she'd slapped him.

There would be no comfort in his house, just Gedomir, who'd likely find a comment or two to make before he left for the country. Zelen couldn't predict whether the subject would be Chessa's child-rearing—and by extension that of nearly every family near the docks—the hope that other children would profit from this sad example of recklessness, or the better ways that Zelen himself could spend his time. He doubted he could sit through any of them with equanimity, and so he turned toward the clinic.

He was in sight of the flat-topped little yellow building when he saw another figure approaching it. The afternoon shadows were growing long, and the person was wearing dark clothing, so they blended well. It took another few feet before he could tell that the figure was an athletic woman with a sword at one hip, and he was nearly at the clinic itself before he recognized Branwyn Alanive.

"Poram's balls, what are you doing here?" was the first thing he said.

Her cool blue gaze reminded him that he'd had manners once. "Following the path of a rumor," said Branwyn mildly. "I'll admit it's fairly nosy of me, but I didn't realize I'd be intruding."

"It... No, you're not... Well..." In the strictest sense, no, she wasn't. The streets were public and the clinic welcomed all during its hours. In a slightly less-strict sense, as Branwyn had said, she was prying, and he certainly hadn't anticipated her presence. She didn't jar on his nerves after the surprise, though, as Gedomir had the night before. "I'm not very good company now, I'm afraid," Zelen said, which was the core of the issue.

Branwyn gave him a long examination, one that took in his matted hair, the shallow scratch on his forehead from trying to crawl under a broken staircase, and the dirty, torn state of his plain clothing. "You certainly look more disheveled than you did when we met before," she said, "not to mention more exhausted. Can I buy you a glass of wine, or would you rather go find a bath and a few hours of sleep?"

She spoke matter-of-factly, as though she met with filthy, tired, slightly battered people every day. It took a moment for Zelen to remember where she came from and then realize that she probably *did*, or had, and that the people in question been much worse off than he was. "I've a bottle and two glasses in my office," he said, "and Altien's still on duty for a while. Care to join me?"

"That sounds wonderful." It was very likely that she was being kind, but she was also kind enough to give every evidence of sincerity. Had Zelen been a better man, he never would have seized the opportunity.

Had he been less exhausted, or Branwyn less kind, he might not have felt any guilt about it.

"You're well set up here," she said when she followed him indoors. Her eye traveled over cushions, bookshelves, and chairs. "Nicely insulated for winter, I'd imagine, with the curtains, and plenty of reading material."

"None of it exactly sensational, I'm afraid," he said, struck by her assessment so soon after Gedomir's. "Give one of the chairs a try. I can almost promise they won't collapse."

"That does set my heart at ease." She sat carefully.

Under the yellowish magical light of the office, Zelen saw that her tunic and breeches were a dark charcoal gray, not quite black, and her shirt was nearly the same deep red as the wine he poured. The sword at her belt, gilded and gemmed, was the most ornate thing about her that day.

"It takes courage," he said, "to wander about carrying a weapon like that—not to mention making the trip from Criwath."

Branwyn glanced down at her waist. "For a soldier," she said, "obvious wealth is as much a defense as it is a lure. Some figure that I have to be good to carry it so openly."

"And others?"

"They learn."

Zelen didn't doubt it. He drank, settling into his accustomed chair, letting the walls of the office close in around him, familiar reassurance with one new element. Courtly manners suggested he ask how she was liking the city, or the Rognozis. Gedomir would've wanted him to pursue the subject of the trip.

"How old were you," he asked instead, "when you left home?"

Immediately, he feared it was a misstep. Branwyn's lids dropped, half veiling her eyes—home might not have been a place she'd wanted to think of—but then she spoke without pain or anger. "Thirteen, more or less. Why do you ask?"

"I was on my way back from searching for a boy. I'm"—he drank more wine to get the words out—"fairly sure he's not trapped or injured in the city. As sure as I can be. We could always have missed a place, couldn't we? But the locals looked, my people and I looked, and we went as far as he was likely to go, playing. Nothing."

"How old is he?"

"Eleven. Not large for his age," he added, remembering what Tanya had said.

Branwyn considered the facts. "His age doesn't rule out running away to take up the sword," she said eventually, "but you don't, no offense intended, have much of an army here. He wouldn't have had to run away to join the city guards, would he?"

"No, and they're not bloody likely to take him either," said Zelen. Despite the situation, the image made him smile, but it was brief. "There are estates in the country where he could've hoped to be taken on, though, or ships."

"You'd know more about that," she said. "This is the closest I've ever been to sea."

"Really?"

"There isn't much coast in Criwath," she said, which Zelen knew. He simply couldn't imagine life without the sound of the waves at night, or when he had to go out to the country, the chance of a salt breeze when the wind was in the right direction. "I was never sent to places where there was."

She traveled a fair bit then, and not—or not always—of her own choosing. Olwin might have sent her as an envoy elsewhere, even before Thyran's return. Zelen noted that as he watched her drink the last of her wine. There, he could tell Gedomir at least one thing his brother probably hadn't known. "The ocean's treacherous, even here," he said, his thoughts circling, sharklike, back to where they'd started. "Most children here know well not to play on the docks, but…children know many things. There comes an age when you start wondering if they're all true, maybe testing that."

"And such exploration doesn't always end well," said Branwyn, picking up the thread.

"No." Zelen's family would likely have said it had ended poorly for him. He disagreed—but he'd survived. "So there's one more possibility. Nothing to be done about it if it's true, of course. I'll have a word or two at court—perhaps he did go to one of their houses."

"If he's on a ship, it'll come back."

"Poram willing," Zelen said. It was more hope than conclusion, but still the day sat less like a stone in his chest. He remembered when he'd first seen the ocean, the ever-shifting nature of it, the sun on the water like a golden road or one of Sitha's spiderwebs, and considered telling her about it. Then the hourglass on the desk caught his eye, and Zelen sighed. "I don't mean to rush you off, but duty will call very shortly."

"Mine as well," Branwyn said. She set her glass aside and stood up. "I'm sorry I couldn't be of more help."

"Whatever help there could be," Zelen told her, "I think you were."

Chapter 8

ROGNOZI'S PARLOR HAD BECOME INTIMIDATING IN THE COURSE OF two days.

Ever since Zelen had joined the council, he'd waited there for dinner every few weeks, or taken sherry on more casual occasions. The house as a whole had put him more at ease than the one where he'd grown up, though that wasn't a very high bar to jump.

Now he had a curiously dry feeling in the back of his throat. He couldn't sit still, but kept crossing one leg over the other, then reversing them.

Having a purpose was not good for his state of mind, even when that purpose was pleasant, and only one of his qualified.

Damn Gedomir, he thought uselessly, *and damn Father too.*

"Zelen Verengir," said Lady Rognozi, sweeping into the parlor in a cloud of rose scent and bouncing gray curls. "Dear boy, you grow more handsome each time I see you."

Zelen, who'd made the lethal mistake of sitting in one of the upholstered chairs, struggled to free himself from its all-enveloping yellow cushions. "It's joy in seeing you, my lady, of course," he said, and finally won his liberty enough to stand and bow.

"That's a well-polished turn of phrase if I've ever heard one," she responded, "but I'll take it, with thanks, nonetheless." A toss of her head set the pearl drops in her ears swinging. Then, theatrics over, she descended into a chair, arranging lilac skirts around her. "Make a well-preserved woman happy and tell me this visit isn't about council matters. Petrus is at the Golden Lady's temple and likely to be there for hours yet."

That was good news for Zelen, but he was sincere in his reply. "I hope all is well."

"As it ever is. At our age"—she spread her hands, rings flashing—"one gives considerable thought to the gods."

"My nurse said we should do that at any age," he replied, "but I'm afraid I'm as bad about that as about following most of her teachings." That wasn't sincere, quite, or it didn't get at the whole truth, but the rest of it wasn't suitable for light conversation. He moved on. "In any case, I'm here on a purely frivolous matter. A friend tells me that Elena Drazen is tremendous in *Spirits of the Air*, and I'd thought to ask you both, and your charming guest, to join me at the Falcon tomorrow."

Lady Rognozi lifted perfectly groomed eyebrows. "And should my lord and I be unable to attend, will your heart be broken?"

"Of course."

"You're a dreadful liar," she said cheerfully. "But given the motive for it, I'll forgive you and summon the real reason you're here."

"Ah." Hearing her deduction felt like missing a step in the dark. "I don't... That is..."

Lady Rognozi pulled a silk rope next to her chair. A young woman, her dark clothing plain but in good condition, opened the door. "Please tell Madam Alanive that Master Verengir is calling on her," she said. "In the Yellow Parlor."

The maid bobbed a curtsy and left, leaving Zelen in the jaws of peril.

"Sitha bless us, Master Verengir," the lady said with a charming giggle that took at least another twenty years off her age, "you'll be blushing next. There's nothing to be ashamed of—she's a lovely young woman."

That was slightly less insight than he'd feared. In theory, having Heliodar's most blatant matchmaker on his side was an advantage.

"She'll be returning to Criwath before long, remember," he

finally said. It was the only objection he could muster, short of revealing what Gedomir had asked him to do.

"How very star-crossed. But she'll be *here* for Irinyev's festival and the ball."

"Is she going?"

That would be an opening. Dancing naturally led to conversation and there were always plenty of places in the ballroom, or in the gardens outside, for exchanging confidences—or other activities. One could easily lead to the other.

"Of course. I've made her an appointment with my dressmaker already. I'm sure the results will be breathtaking—not that what she has currently isn't quite striking, but she wasn't expecting to dance."

"I imagine she won't lack partners," Zelen said, trying for neutrality.

"Imagine indeed!" The lady laughed. "I'm only glad that... Well, she could do much worse than you for a...let's say a *friend* in the city, you know."

There was that missing step again. "I'll do my best," he said, and reminded himself of what he'd told Gedomir: Branwyn would doubtless keep any real secrets hidden, no matter how friendly the two of them got.

Zelen toyed with the embroidery on the chair's arm, tracing the outline of a bluebird.

Lady Rognozi added softly, "And there's always after the war. Four grant that it be soon."

"She's raised the subject with you then?" Zelen looked up.

"More so with Petrus, but a trifle, as much as was in good taste over dinner. That was sufficient." Lady Rognozi closed her lips tightly.

"I'm probably risking the same sort of conversation," Zelen said, "though I'd be in for it regardless, since I'm on the council. Do you think we should throw in with them?"

"My dear, I wish I knew," she replied. "Petrus wants to help, I know, but he fears that we're all falling for a ruse—not that Madam Alanive or even Criwath is deceiving us, necessarily, but that they're being deceived. Or all might be as Madam Alanive says, but sending our army may still be unwise tactically."

"In which case, he wants us to wait and see what happens?"

It was the most neutral way he could phrase the question.

Lady Rognozi had been in the city's highest circles nearly as long as her husband, though, and her understanding was obvious. "He might. Or—there may not be a wise path. War is very much beyond me, and I am very glad these decisions aren't mine to make."

"I don't know if I'd want them," Zelen said.

For once, Lady Rognozi didn't even try the polite reassurance: oh, his family certainly listened to him, and clearly he had their trust, and so forth. She was paler than usual that day, Zelen noticed, and the lines on her face lay very lightly. Behind them, she looked young and frightened.

Zelen thought he more than likely did too.

They were still staring at each other when Branwyn walked in.

So they have sense enough to be afraid, Yathana observed. *Speaks well of them.*

Branwyn couldn't respond to the sword, which Yathana knew very well and took shameless advantage of, but she agreed on both counts. The subject Lady Rognozi and Zelen had been talking about was obvious, unless there was another dire threat Branwyn hadn't heard of or an assassin was after them both. The older woman was fully as grave as she'd been at the dinner when Branwyn had explained a little of her mission, and Zelen's jaw was set.

It was to both of their credit. Fear had shadowed all who'd been at Oakford ever since Amris and Darya had come with the news of Thyran's return. Branwyn couldn't remember a day since that she'd gone without feeling that twist in her stomach. Often it came in ambush from nowhere, when she'd managed to distract herself for a while from the matters she couldn't yet change.

She'd had a couple months to accustom herself. The blisters, so to speak, had burst and healed and calluses had mostly formed in their place. To everyone in Heliodar, Branwyn knew, her news would be a fresh wound.

"My apologies," she said. "I was told—"

Both of the room's occupants turned toward her with undisguised relief. Zelen bowed, though with far fewer flourishes than he'd done on their first meeting, and Lady Rognozi forced a smile. "No, no, you're quite welcome. It's I who should… I fear I'm in a bit of a brown study today."

"I'd be surprised if any of you weren't," said Branwyn, "and I'm sorry for that."

"Please," said the lady, "come and have a seat, and think nothing of it. In the end, it's likely better to know." She did a better job of smiling the second time.

Branwyn perched on the edge of an extensively cushioned yellow chair, mate to the one Zelen was sitting back down in. She met his eyes and was pleased to find them steady and clear.

"And," he said, with enough cheer to further increase Branwyn's opinion of him, even if it obviously took him some effort, "you've sent the fellow packing once already, haven't you? Army and all."

Branwyn spotted an opening. She struck, balancing her words carefully. "We did, yes." *See, you'd be allying yourself with a competent force.* "But we still need help. We used a few maneuvers he wasn't prepared for, and he'll be more wary in the future. My superiors believe we should strike as hard as we can as soon as we can, so that we give him no chance to recover, or to…acquire…more troops."

The process by which Thyran's greater creatures, mortals transformed by hosting demons within them, created the twistedmen and the other foot soldiers of his army was singularly unpleasant. Branwyn thought she'd disturbed Lady Rognozi's life enough for a few days.

Zelen appeared curious but, perhaps for the same reason, didn't inquire. "Of course, he could be expecting you to do just that."

"That's possible," said Branwyn, "though I wish I could say otherwise. But surprise isn't the only element in war. I'm given to understand that there are circumstances when the most obvious move is still the correct one."

"You're more versed in the subject than I am," Zelen said. "And I fear we're in grave danger of boring our hostess."

"Not at all," said Lady Rognozi, who'd regained some of her composure while Zelen and Branwyn talked. "But I'm given to understand that Zelen came on a considerably less serious mission. Are you free tomorrow, or must you meet with that tedious Marton?"

"Not until eight," Branwyn said, "and thank you for the warning, my lady."

"Oh, he means well, I'm certain."

"I'm not," said Zelen. "Would you care to join me at the sort of play he'll most definitely not approve of?"

"Yes—but would that affect my chances of convincing him?"

Lady Rognozi and Zelen laughed. "He'll only think I'm a bad influence," said Zelen.

"And it will delight him to try and save you," the lady added. "Particularly as it's overly late for Petrus and me to lend an air of respectability, I fear."

Zelen narrowed his eyes at her, and she looked completely innocent in return. Once again they shared a mannered world of safety and scandal, a world Branwyn could only half grasp: a tune where half the instruments were strange. If it was hard to play, it was easy to listen and admire.

Promising, said Yathana.

The sword wasn't wrong. Even if Zelen was, from what he'd said, unlikely to know vast diplomatic or military secrets, he might be able to tell her about a scandal or two. Advantage was advantage, and all knowledge was useful in the end.

"That sounds wonderful," Branwyn replied.

"Then, by your leave," Zelen said, standing up, "I'll take mine, and call for you at four. My lady, a pleasure as always, and please give my best to your husband."

He did better with the bowing that time. Branwyn and Lady Rognozi both watched as he left. It didn't seem entirely likely that the lady paid as much attention to his taut backside as Branwyn did, but then again, maybe so. She was elderly, not dead or blind.

"He's a charming young man," said Lady Rognozi, which could have been evidence either for or against Branwyn's assumptions. "I'm glad that you've caught his eye. Petrus and I are beyond the age when we can entertain you as you deserve, I fear."

"Oh, surely not," said Branwyn.

Now there's *a line with a few meanings*, said Yathana. *Pity we didn't come here twenty years ago.*

Branwyn would have had to be ten years older, too, she thought, and tried not to imagine the possibilities, particularly when Lady Rognozi spoke again. "You're very kind, and I know you're not here for pleasure, but I would hope that you can find the liberty to enjoy yourself. I certainly would argue that you've earned it."

This is where she puts a hand on your knee.

The lady did no such thing. "And I believe it does Zelen good to hear perspectives from outside the city," she added, while Branwyn thought profanities at her sword.

"His family has him here most of the time, don't they?"

"Oh, yes. The older ones keep to themselves, out in the country.

There was a bit of a tragedy when Zelen was a child, and some credit that for their reclusiveness, but they weren't fond of the city even then." Lady Rognozi shrugged, clearly mystified by any such preference. "There are a few of the best families who feel that way. The joys of hunting and riding and so forth."

"That view is common in Criwath," said Branwyn, amused, "though I've found Heliodar delightful so far, and I've never been overly fond of hunting." Having to survive that way had taken much of the charm off the experience, though she knew plenty of Sentinels for whom that wasn't true. "I'm sorry to hear he's known loss."

"I wouldn't think Zelen himself remembers—he couldn't have been more than three—but I'm sure the family was affected."

"If I may ask, what happened? I wouldn't want to step on any sore spots unknowingly."

"There was a fire, and five or six of the family were killed. Lord Verengir's sister had just given birth, and neither she nor the babe… Well, it was all very sad." The lady sighed. "I remember one of their most trusted servants ran off with valuables afterward too. Adding insult to injury, we all thought, and what a horrible man to take advantage of those circumstances."

Silver will get you gold he played a part in them. I'd like to know what these valuables were too.

Branwyn wouldn't have objected to knowing that either. The man could really have just been opportunistic, as Lady Rognozi said, but Lady Rognozi hadn't spent twenty-odd years dealing with monsters and sorcerers, or lived her life fighting Gizath and his followers. She also hadn't heard Yathana talk about sensing corruption. "I'll tread carefully," she said aloud.

"Do," said Lady Rognozi, and Branwyn knew she was earnest. "I'm certain he feels more deeply than he lets on, you know."

You could say that about most people with rank or money in this city, Yathana weighed in, *and probably half without either. The place is a maze of knives. You don't get through it without armor.*

Chapter 9

"I CONSIDERED HIRING A CARRIAGE," ZELEN SAID, "BUT THEN I recalled you saying you'd spent too much time sitting, and you hadn't even begun talking with my fellow councillors at length. Still, if you'd like—"

"No," Branwyn said. "Thank you. You're entirely right."

She smiled as she took his arm and they walked down the steps together. When her liaisons had been longer than a drunken night or two, they'd been smooth, businesslike affairs, where all parties knew the score well in advance. Men rarely tried to impress her— she had no influence over their rank or pay, and Sentinels were uncanny enough that their admiration didn't give most people any particular pride. Having one try to do so romantically sent a bit of fresh energy through a mind weary from negotiation.

So did the way Zelen had regarded her when she'd come to meet him. On Lady Rognozi's guidance, she hadn't dressed as elaborately as she'd done at court—no skirts or jewelry, and she bore Yathana on a silver-buckled belt—but the white doublet and hose of doeskin clung to her figure in a way Branwyn knew was flattering, and the dark-purple shirt set both off to good contrast. She knew the light in Zelen's whiskey-brown eyes when she'd appeared, and enjoyed it.

He was worth admiring, too, in dark blue-green, black, and white. His arms were bare again, a convention that Branwyn was coming to appreciate more and more, and his head was unornamented, as it had been when he'd come to call the day before, but large pearl buttons floated on the winter sea of his doublet. A ring on one hand shone with blue fire in the sunset, and a topaz winked from the opposite ear.

"I constantly feel," Branwyn said, "as though I'm walking through a jewel box."

"I can't imagine that's a complaint."

"Only envy, I suppose, and feeling a little like a country cousin. Which I am, in most respects."

"Don't let the shine overawe you too much. Jewels are cheap here. We still deal with the waterfolk and the stonekin, and there are some advantages to that. This"—he gestured to the topaz in his ear—"might bring as much as a good set of boots, if I found a dealer who felt generous."

"You sound as though you've tried."

"Oh, well. A man gets in over his head now and again."

Even if his family could buy and sell armies? I don't believe it, said Yathana.

Branwyn might not have either, except that there was the clinic. She'd recognized washed and reused bandages and well-scrubbed walls with paint starting to peel. The furniture in the office had been sturdy and cushioned but scuffed, and there'd been a yellowish tinge to the lighting there, not the pure white of the palace or the Rognozis' house.

"I hope you found a way back to shallower water," she said.

"I excel at finding the shallows. A lecture or two from my father isn't so much of a price in the end."

They were heading away from the palace and the mansions that Branwyn had visited, but in a different direction than that which led to the Porpoise and the city gates. The buildings were large and bright, but the gardens had disappeared. People passed in groups, often laughing, often at least tipsy.

"Have you been to many plays?"

"A few," said Branwyn, "but never in a theater. We had traveling players through a few times a year when I was a girl, and the temples put on the religious ones now and again." She recognized the change of topic, but let it go and gave him an impish look. "I was Jyllan for the midsummer festival when I was eight. I'm told I changed into a very credible hawk, though I think most of *that* credit goes to the man working the curtains. And the hawk."

Zelen laughed. "Trained?"

"Stuffed and on a stick. But a marvel of taxidermy."

"An honor for any girl to transform into, I'm sure."

"Oh yes."

"I'm surprised you didn't go on the stage for life."

Branwyn supposed she could have, technically: at thirteen, the children that the Sentinels raised and trained could leave the order and take up other lives, though always standing ready to assist in other ways if needed. She'd never even considered it. "It's not as much of a living in the Northern Kingdoms," she said, "and besides, I have other talents."

The Falcon loomed up ahead of them, a round stone building that took up the whole street, with its insignia not just on a sign but on banners outside the front doors. Every window shone with magical light, and voices within rose and fell in a vast hubbub.

Inside, she got to sit next to Zelen on the cushioned bench, his thigh hard and warm against hers and his nearness turning her skin extraordinarily sensate, so that each brush of their shoulders made her heart leap. A few times she heard a hitch in his breathing, too, and once or twice he shifted his weight in a way that made Branwyn sure he wasn't a stranger to her feelings.

It was a mark of the play's quality that she remembered any of it.

The story was a lighthearted one. A merchant's three identical daughters kept getting mistaken for one another. One was secretly marrying the gardener, another was joining the army against her father's wishes, and a third was studying magic. There was another pair of wizards, rivals, one of whom was in love with the merchant, and their familiar spirits who kept bungling matters through not understanding mortals.

Branwyn laughed a good deal, as, silently, so did Yathana, and the end came almost too soon for her.

"I don't know much about wizards in private employment," she said as they walked back. "How much of that was exaggeration?"

"Not very much, given the right wizards—and the right employers," said Zelen. "Plenty of people compete through them, you see, like they do with tailors or cooks."

"Do you have one?"

"No," he said. Their steps against the stone blended, and his arm was firm in her grasp. "My family was never much for luxury, and I have other ways of getting in over my head, as I mentioned."

That might have led to an advantage, except that Branwyn suspected he didn't mean gambling, women, or intoxicants. She tried another path, one likely to be more fruitful. "They don't strike me as much use in, say, combat."

Zelen blinked. "No, they rather aren't, not that I've gone to any effort to test the matter. I suppose the guard does employ some, but most private magicians are there for heat, light, amusing illusions, and all that sort of thing. You've mostly known them in the army?"

"Yes. A few of them were extremely valuable at Oakford." One, Tebengri, had been her lover for a few nights, before they'd gone back to Criwath to study the ramifications of what they'd seen and done in the battle. "They had to adjust fast—but all of us did."

"One hears rumors," said Zelen. "But I never knew how much to believe. Creatures that would make you their puppets if you looked in their eyes, for instance—"

"Their mouths," said Branwyn. "But yes, they exist. A mage I know said that Gizath not only governs treachery, but can turn any bond against the things it joins. Slavery, or turning your will against itself…could have been either in that case. I don't know how far they've gotten in studying it."

The brown hedges of Rognozi's garden hulked up around them, strange shapes in the twilight. Branwyn looked away from them and from her memories and up at Zelen, who was grimacing. "Forgive me," he said. "Not much of a subject for a pleasant night out."

"It won't be one it's easy to avoid in the days to come," Branwyn said, "and I brought it up as much as you did." She took a long breath, smelling the night air, rich with woodsmoke, and the warmer, smokier scent of Zelen. They were here, at this moment, and alive, without any immediate threat to either status. If it was important to remember the war, it was also vital not to forget that.

"But," she went on, sliding her hand down to grab his, "if you are feeling remorseful, you could always make up for it."

She sensed Yathana departing for the place between worlds where she went on such occasions.

"Ah?" Zelen stepped forward, taking hold of her shoulders lightly. "And how might I do that?"

"Distract me," said Branwyn, and pulled him into a kiss.

———

Shadows of his past and devils far away fled from Zelen's awareness, having begun their retreat as soon as Branwyn took his hand. There, in the shelter of autumn-blighted plants and evening shade, he stood with a beautiful woman in his arms, and all moments except that one could go to hell.

Branwyn had a patient nature, he discovered. The sweet pressure of her lips was insistent, but unhurried, seeking rather than forceful. She explored, she learned, not with the cautious daring of an innocent but with the interest of a master jeweler examining a likely purchase, or a smith testing the balance of a sword.

The object of her scrutiny couldn't match jewels or metal for impassivity. It was mere heartbeats before Zelen was groaning into Branwyn's mouth. He fought back the urge to pull her lush body against his or to return her kiss with bruising force, because he sensed a challenge in her slow investigation, some balance of power that would shift if his control broke.

Also, it was damnably, torturously erotic.

If slow was what the lady wanted, he could manage slow. There were his hands on her shoulders, for instance, and he could slide them down, taking in soft doeskin and hard muscle and then the even softer roundness of her breasts. He could cup, there, and skim his fingers back and forth, until Branwyn made a husky, wordless noise. Layers made it harder to navigate by feel, but he traced small circles with his thumbs and felt her nipples stiffen.

Her grip on the back of his head tightened, becoming almost painful before she seemed to realize she was pulling his hair and let go. The hand in question moved down his back, leaving a trail of sensation that spread through Zelen like fire on flash paper, and settled on one hip, letting Branwyn curve her fingers over his arse. A step forward on her part brought their bodies together. Her kiss demanded now, rather than seeking to learn, and Zelen was oh so eager to give her everything she would ask—and to suggest a few additions if her list ran short.

The top silver button on her doublet was between his fingers when the bell in the tower rang.

"Ohhell." It was one word, almost a whisper, and the very frustration of it made Zelen's cock pulse in response. "Eight?"

"I think," he managed. He had to free his mouth to speak, and the side of her neck was long and golden, so Zelen started kissing his way down from her ear. "Seems—mmm—a reasonable hour to be."

But then Branwyn was stepping back. "Then I have to go meet with Marton," she said, "and come off as respectable when I do." As if it would help, she tucked a strand of hair behind one ear and smoothed down the front of her tunic. "Pyres take the man."

"I couldn't agree more," said Zelen. Gods, he *ached*.

Branwyn's eyes gleamed blue in the fading light. "You could if you had to give him your attention after this," she said. "We'll meet again. Soon, I hope—and thank you."

She leaned forward for a brief kiss. Then she turned and was gone, a graceful white figure that vanished into the shadows. Zelen leaned against a hedge and seriously considered performing indecent acts in the high lord's garden.

Chapter 10

Duty had often been taxing and frequently dangerous, but Branwyn didn't think it had ever been so thoroughly annoying.

Zelen's kisses had left her thoroughly roused, and she'd had no chance even to satisfy herself. A hasty series of adjustments to her hair and tunic, and she'd gone back out again. For a while, every step she took, every brush of fabric against her thighs or breasts, every motion of the carriage, was a reminder of the too-short interlude in the garden.

Dining with Marton and his family did serve as a very effective cold bath.

They ate in an ostentatiously unornamented room: sober, dark walls and furniture, no mirrors or jewels, and far more space than any ten people needed, let alone the six at the table. The knives and spoons were silver, as was the candelabra. The plates were very thin bone-white porcelain—probably twice what precious metal would have cost, and far more breakable.

Marton, his wife, and his older daughter all wore heavy wool, with high collars, long sleeves, and no color brighter than gray. His younger daughter and her husband were slightly more daring, he in light brown and dusty green and she in a lilac dress that actually showed her arms to the shoulder. Her father kept glancing her way and shaking his head, making Branwyn feel sorry for the woman.

"How do you find the city?" Lady Marton asked as they sat down.

"Very pleasant, thank you. Everyone has been most hospitable, particularly Lord and Lady Rognozi, and the city itself is fascinating. I only wish I had more spare hours to spend exploring it."

"I'm pleased to hear it," said Marton. "I've done my utmost to promote forms of pure and healthy occupation, and I allow myself to hope that such seeds have fallen on fertile soil. I'll dare to take your sentiments as confirmation."

Healthy, maybe, snickered Yathana. *Plenty of fresh air and exercise.*

Branwyn took a hasty sip of wine. It was heavily watered, but that was as well. She had the feeling she'd need to control her reactions. "That must have been quite the endeavor," she managed.

Apparently it was. She learned more details of Marton's promotion of virtue, over the next hour, than she ever could conceive of wanting to know, though that did free her from having to make conversation.

Even the food was…virtuous. The majority of it was bread and boiled vegetables, without spice or butter. There was also what Branwyn thought had been a chicken, though it too was boiled and flavorless. Lady Marton asked if she'd heard of Kalara Meraniv's theory of food and consciousness, and when Branwyn admitted her ignorance, helpfully explained it. Meat, apparently, tended to—and here the lady actually dropped her voice—"excite the senses inappropriately, if eaten without moderation."

Oh, said Yathana, *so that's what's been wrong with you.*

As meals went, Branwyn had eaten worse, but that had been in the field, where how long food lasted and whether or not she could find it at all had been much more important than how it tasted. She'd eaten *better* at cheap roadside inns and in the houses of peasants who lived mostly on bread and porridge and saw whole cuts of meat once a year. Expensively bad food was a new experience.

"And that," Lord Marton said, branching off a rambling statement about the Temptations of Youth that Branwyn hadn't really followed, "is why I welcome your news and the opportunity you bring us."

"If you'll pardon my asking," Zelen said, moving a smooth piece of polished aventurine ahead three spaces on the marble board, "what do you think about this war in Criwath?"

Altien gave the question, and the board, a long evaluation. He sipped from his goblet of wine in the meantime, tentacles curling delicately around the brim. "For my people, if there's any chance Thyran has returned—and it sounds from what you say as though that chance is very great—then we must begin preparing. There's little we can do to assist directly. I'm no warrior, and we fare poorly when we go too far from the sea. But we can protect ourselves and supply a few needs, and with forewarning we can make a place for any who seek refuge, in case the worst does happen."

"Do they know?" Zelen asked, startled by the immediate action in the answer. He'd expected depth—he'd never known the water-man to be shallow—but as a matter Altien would contemplate while he talked, not one he'd already fully thought through and come to conclusions on.

"I've written messages home about the situation," said Altien. "I assume others of us here have as well. I suspect that Criwath has sent an envoy to my people, too, and to the dwellers-in-earth. It's what I would do, if I were a king facing such a threat."

Zelen eyed the board. His yellow and green pieces had taken half the neutral territory. Altien's lapis and garnet ovals were making a complicated pattern on the outside. "And for us? Humans here?"

"I couldn't say. Thyran is unmistakably a threat, and will remain so. There's no ocean that can polish his edges to smoothness. If Criwath wants to strike now, that might be wise." The tentacles lifted, expanded to briefly show Altien's gold-colored beak, and then fell again. "But I'm no tactician."

"Obviously," said Zelen, gesturing to the board.

Altien made the clicking sound that was his laugh. "I couldn't say if it would be best to put all your forces behind an attempt to eliminate the problem now. If it can be done, it seems wise—but those from our city would be going blind over unfamiliar ground, and if Criwath is wrong, our soldiers might be more useful in the city's defense. But then, Criwath's generals likely anticipated that."

Zelen picked up his goblet. It was mostly empty. "I don't know why I bother with the question," he said, leaning back in his chair. "Father will make the decision, and damned if I've been able to change his mind in thirty-two years."

"You bother because you wish you could," said Altien. It was a dispassionate statement, with no more emotion than he used when describing injuries: *attend, the patient has a knife in his side here*. "And because when your father does make the decision, you hope to justify it to the council and, more, to the envoy you admire."

"I did warn her. And she doesn't seem the sort to hold it against me."

"So you hope." Altien sent five pieces, mixed red and blue, forward on the sides. "What sort of a person is she?"

"Beautiful," Zelen said immediately, then realized that he sounded young and dangerously close to writing insipid poetry, and cleared his throat. "Clever, or interested, or likely both. I was never bored, talking with her—and I wasn't talking the whole time either."

"I wouldn't have said it."

"Poram's arse you wouldn't."

"Go on."

What was he going to tell Gedomir? It was wise to begin lining up those facts. "She's been in the war for a while. I'd wager she was a soldier of some sort before that. High-ranked enough to talk with the army's wizards, but that's to be expected if they're trusting her as a diplomat. I almost wonder if she's nobility traveling under a false name, or born on the wrong side of the blanket."

"Why would she disguise herself? Humans generally take pride in noble birth, from what I've seen, and listen more to those with such advantages."

Zelen picked up a polished citrine star. "We do," he said, "but we're also more cautious around them. She might want to keep us off guard. And nobility from another country, a country we haven't always gotten on with…"

"There could be resentment."

"She could be a target." He put the star down with a click, uncertain if the space he'd chosen was tactically sound but not inclined to care. "If you wanted power over Criwath, or favorable terms, you could do worse than take one of their more valued people hostage. It'd be hard for them to strike back during a war."

Altien sat still, six-fingered hands motionless on the edge of the table. "Is that common?"

"Not common, but it happened occasionally, from what I've heard." Zelen poured himself more wine. "The Great Winters, and after, rather cut down on official visitors."

He wanted to believe that in their aftermath, having faced down the common foes of Thyran and twisted nature, people would have moved beyond such practices. More, he wanted to think that nobody would seek such an unjust advantage against a country Thyran was actively menacing.

Almost two decades in the council meant he couldn't really convince himself.

———————

"I'm glad to hear it," Branwyn said carefully, "but I would welcome hearing more of your point of view. It might inspire me when speak to your fellows, after all."

She even smiled. *Masterful bullshit*, said Yathana.

Marton smoothed his oiled hair. "Why, only that war bri

out the finest qualities in our youth, of course. The discipline of combat allows them to rise above animal instincts and seek greater purpose."

Branwyn, who'd been in Oakford the night before the siege started and the day after it ended, stifled her reaction with bread.

"It instills camaraderie, besides," Marton added, "and inspires heroism," and Branwyn's amusement deflated.

She'd seen both. She'd seen their aftermath too: the weeping, the blood. Branwyn remembered a girl, no more than sixteen, cradling the gutted corpse of her friend. The Mourners had pried it away eventually. There'd been no herbs to spare on calming her down.

Camaraderie. Yes.

She got the bread down while Marton kept talking.

"I know," he said, in the tones of one making a very generous concession, "that I met your initial agreement with skepticism, Madam Alanive, and for that you have my deepest apologies. It was a hasty reaction to the source of your information. While I cannot fully approve of the Sentinels, I must grant that their...way of being...is necessary in the world we now inhabit, and they're not given to falsehood as such. Having had the leisure to consider the issue—"

"You believe that a war would do Heliodar some good," Branwyn said, managing not to sound entirely flat.

"Father doesn't welcome war," said the younger daughter quickly, "not as such. But presuming that it's ongoing—"

"Just so. The gods," said Marton, inflating his chest like a horse resisting a saddle band, "provide crucibles in which to shape the young people of our land for worthy causes, instilling in them a sense of pride and of loyalty to their homeland, and diverting their thoughts from the idle pursuits that lead to rank debauchery. So they have led you to us, to bring us to this moment of noble decision, and I have every confidence that we shall prove worthy."

He continued in that vein for a while—what seemed like a

long while to Branwyn. She nodded and smiled in the right places, uttered vague but complimentary sentiments in others. All the time she thought of Zelen, who wasn't precisely a *young* man, and of those more wide-eyed with faith in what people like Marton said. She imagined them marching off to fight skinless horrors and mind-warping evil, full of conviction that this would be an uplifting experience and that they'd come back better and nobler for it.

Criwath needed the soldiers. If Darya, Amris, and Gerant were right—and Branwyn had no reason to doubt that they were—the world needed the soldiers. The consequences of failure were a slaughterhouse, where desperate people killed and fed on each other or even worse. Thyran hadn't succeeded before. This time, he might.

It was good that Marton was on her side. Branwyn told herself that throughout the end of the dinner and through the final goodbyes, when she gave Marton and his family a courteous bow and expressed her ideally sincere-sounding hopes that they'd meet again.

"Let me off here, please," she told the carriage driver a few minutes into the ride.

"Are you well, madam?"

"Yes." No. "Yes. The walk will do me good, though."

Something, Branwyn thought, *had damned well better.*

Chapter 11

GEDOMIR SNORTED. "SHE'S A CAREER SOLDIER, SHE KNOWS details about Oakford, and she's persuaded at least Lady Rognozi that the matter is serious? I would have expected far more after a week, given your…abilities."

"We haven't exactly spent the whole week together," Zelen responded. He leaned back, his chair on two legs, his feet on the desk of his private study, and a goblet of brandy in one hand. It was a comfortable position. More to the point, it irritated Gedomir. Zelen saw a muscle twitch under his brother's right eye every time he took a sip. "She's had others on the council to meet with, and it'll be suspicious if I'm always on the Rognozis' doorstep like an abandoned kitten."

He'd had his duties as well, but it was better not to mention them. Gedomir was skeptical enough about the clinic when it didn't get in the way of what he wanted.

"Can you arrange to be there in the future, when she speaks with the others?"

"Possibly, sometimes, if I can find out when and where and if I know the people well enough that I won't be called out for it, or thrashed by a pair of footmen for being an impudent young wastrel. And I still might find out no more than I have already." Zelen saw his brother's expression darken. "Have you considered," he pressed on, "that the lady might have neither dark secrets nor a hidden agenda? Sitha love us, Branwyn's asking for help for her kingdom, not plotting to undercut you on the whitefish trade. I can understand disagreeing, but—"

"Naive as always," Gedomir said. "What if the council should agree and propose the assistance in the form of a tax that would ruin us, or a levy of all able-bodied citizens under forty? Or what if this is Criwath's plan—lure our military might, or our treasury, off chasing phantoms, then overtake us?"

"Why would they now?"

"Because they can, fool." Gedomir sighed. "Don't mistake me; her cause may be just, though I suspect Criwath doesn't have the capacity to properly judge such a threat, and we may all agree in the end. If we don't, and if disagreement must turn to action, it's better to be fully prepared. That is where you come in."

"It's wonderful to know that you have a use for me." Zelen took another sip of brandy, relishing the burn more than the taste. He couldn't find a flaw in his brother's argument, not then—perhaps it was the way all true heads of houses thought. The others on the council had never spoken to him about it.

"Your attitude doesn't become you," said Gedomir. "Particularly not when I *had* been going to tell you that, if the autumn ends well, we may be able to find extra money in the household funds for that charity house you operate."

As usual, outrage at the customary tactics warred with a tenacious vestige of shame for being so ungrateful to his family, with more and newer shame—for feeling the old sort and for knowing the bribe would work—the inevitable winner. "I'm sorry," said Zelen, trying to sound less truculent than when he'd been nine years old and speaking with a missing front tooth. "That's kind of you. I'll see what I can manage by way of invitations, though I really can't make any promises."

"I didn't expect any." Gedomir pulled on one of his gloves. He hadn't taken his cloak off: the visit was a swift one, an afterthought to his primary business in the city. "Out of curiosity, what would you recommend we do?"

"Help them, of course. I've no notion of tactics in the middle of a forest, and I'm certain plans would need to be made, but that's a matter for specifics—the generals could discuss it. We have wizards and soldiers, neither doing very much." The words came more heatedly than Zelen would have expected. "And it's an army of Gizath's creatures attacking human lands. How could we *not* see a just cause there?"

"Ah." Gedomir's mouth twitched in what, on a more frivolous man, might have passed for a smile. "You would have served the Dark Lady well, Zelen."

———

"I'm afraid I don't have the time to be fitted properly," Branwyn lied and, more truthfully, added, "but I'm certain that a seamstress of your skills can work from this dress's measurements."

She handed a folded bundle to the woman, who took it with a cautious expression and shook out the blue wool gown that had served Branwyn at court and a number of formal dinners. For a miracle, neither she nor anyone else had stained it yet, but Lady Rognozi had gently made it clear that Branwyn needed more.

"The fabric's a bit thick," the seamstress said after making a lengthy comparison between Branwyn and the dress and pinching the wool between thumb and forefinger, "but if you're willing to try on the other once I make it, so I can adjust it properly, I can manage. What are you thinking for the ball gown? I'll tell you now I haven't got much left, this close to the festival, but there's some rose-printed gold silk that would suit you nicely."

"That will be fine," said Branwyn, "thank you. When it comes to the cut, though, I'll need sleeves to the wrists and a long skirt."

The seamstress was one Lady Rognozi recommended. She was, therefore, used to dealing with the vagaries of the nobility and used to maintaining an appearance of calm neutrality. Only a few seconds of unblinking regard gave her away.

That and Yathana's opinion. *She's not sure whether you're a raw-meat-eating barbarian or one of Marton's sort, except that Marton and his lot wouldn't go dancing unless it was at sword point.*

"You can make the neckline low and the dress tight," Branwyn added, stung at the comparison, "and cut out as much around the stomach and back as you can while maintaining the fit. I have scars on my arms and legs, though, that I'd prefer to keep hidden."

That was, in most senses, another lie. The reforging did leave its marks, and Branwyn's were on her limbs, but they weren't as easily explained as most scars would have been. Branwyn had picked up a few of *those* on her back and sides, even with the quick and thorough healing that Sentinels gained. The prospect of showing them in a ball gown didn't disturb her at all.

You're both lucky, said Yathana. *Trying to disguise Rowan's hair, or, gods help us, Vivian's face, that would be a job.*

Branwyn knew it, and knew as well that it had little to do with luck. Her comparative skill at diplomacy had played a part in getting her sent to Heliodar, as did her blessing from Tinival and the fact that she'd been on hand to witness Thyran's attack, but another, larger factor was the fact that clothes could hide the marks of her reforging.

She could make everyone believe that she was entirely human and nothing more—at least as long as all went well.

Evening was falling in vibrant shades of rose, gold, and violet. A few stars were out, low above the city's roofs, when Zelen followed Lady Rognozi's instructions to the dressmaker's on Flaminia Street.

He paused in front of the shop, where a plaster dummy wearing a butterfly-print gown smirked at him despite its lack of features. Lady Rognozi had been fairly confident regarding his timing, but she was a woman who took a while about her wardrobe. It would be just his luck to be too late—or perhaps the will of the gods, thwarting his more underhanded, if still likely harmless, motives.

When he tapped on the door, a boy with a spotted complexion and arms an inch too long for his otherwise good attire answered. "Buying for a…lady, sir? Has she been here before? You'll have to know her figure pretty well otherwise." He winked.

"Rather hoping to meet one here," Zelen said.

The boy snickered. Zelen would have, too, twenty years before. "We're not that kind of establishment, m'lord, but I have heard—"

"That's to say," Zelen interrupted, "I was hoping to find one of your customers here. A blond lady from Criwath, my height or so, blue eyes… Oh, thank the gods," he said, as Branwyn stepped out of the back room, bowing to the seamstress, *before* Zelen had to try describing her figure to an adolescent.

"It's always wonderful to be appreciated," said Branwyn, turning toward him with a startled smile, "but I don't believe I've done much to deserve it."

"You can't imagine how untrue that is. Good evening," Zelen added, and bowed.

"Good evening," said Branwyn. Her smile lingered and turned curious. "You were looking for me?"

"I was. Lady Rognozi said you'd still be here."

"That explains the method, but not the motive," she teased.

She was dressed plainly, in the same dark clothing that she'd worn at the clinic and the Rognozis' house, but it was much less plain now that Zelen had explored the form beneath it. The devilish glint in her eye didn't help his composure, nor did the quirk of her lips. The shop boy was going to start snickering again soon.

"I'd like to take you to dinner," he said, abandoning all preliminaries. "There's a place a quarter hour's walk from here that I think you'd enjoy."

Chapter 12

ZELEN'S FIRST THOUGHT, WHEN BRANWYN TENSED AND dropped her hand from his arm, was of robbers. Even as he drew his sword, he concluded otherwise. They weren't in the part of the city the larger gangs claimed as their own, and no small band of ruffians would have gone after two fit, relatively young, and well-armed people.

Also, the people who'd been following them were silent. Robbers would have demanded money, and drunks out for blood sport would have gloated. These just advanced, the dark mass splitting into individual armed forms.

With a grace that Zelen wouldn't have credited if he hadn't seen it, Branwyn swiveled on one foot, turning her side toward their assailants. A *twang* cut through the air, and then a light object clattered against the stones where she'd been standing.

Facts flashed across Zelen's awareness as single words: *crossbow* and then *assassins*.

Running wouldn't help. The city watch was few and far between, nothing to pin his hopes on, but anything was worth a shot. "*Murder!*" Zelen shouted at the top of his lungs.

Then he threw himself forward, coming in low to the ground and whipping his sword toward the ankles of the closest adversary. The killer sidestepped, but barely, and then Zelen was in among them, where darkness and close quarters gave him the advantage. The assassins didn't want to hit each other, but *he* was perfectly content to kill every damned one of them, if he could manage it.

Seven against two meant he had little hope there either.

He turned in time to catch a club on his upper arm rather than the side of his head. The pain was instant and breathtaking. Zelen struck out half-blindly and felt flesh give way before his blade, drawing a hiss from the man it was attached to. As his vision cleared, he pressed the advantage, stepping forward to block a lunge, then whipping his sword sideways and up across his foe's chest.

A *clang* came from his side in the darkness, then the beginning of a startled cry, and finally a gurgle. The voice was low, totally unlike Branwyn's. *Thank you, Mistress of Flame*, Zelen managed to pray silently before coming around, back to the wall, to cut into the knee of a club-wielding woman.

The strike took the woman down, as Zelen had known it would: she curled up shrieking on the ground. The crossbowman fired again. Zelen hiked a knee into the groin of another assassin—the man he'd wounded first, with the cut on his chest bleeding copiously but apparently not enough to keep him down—and glanced over his shoulder.

Branwyn pulled her blade from the chest of a dying man and leapt sideways as another club came down. Zelen's heart froze. He knew she wouldn't make it, but he couldn't watch. His foe was recovering, another man was coming in with an overhand slash, and Zelen had to turn back, raising his sword in his own frantic defense.

A series of grunts and cries meant Branwyn had escaped grievous harm. In his gratitude, Zelen had no leisure to consider the ring of metal on metal he'd heard before they started, a noise without any apparent source.

———

A crossbow bolt hit Branwyn in the neck.

It bounced off, of course, but the impact closed her windpipe briefly, causing a deeply undignified *ulgk*. More importantly, the man in front of her gaped, and there was a gasp from behind him that meant the wretched crossbowman had likely seen the deflection, too, despite the darkness. There was a flurry of movement in that direction, *not* coming toward her.

She would have sighed if her breath hadn't already fallen into the rhythm of the fight. When the man in front of her tried to strike, a swing made slightly wild by his surprise, Branwyn caught the blade, stepped in, and whipped Yathana across *his* jugular. She sprang past him toward the fleeing crossbowman, but one of his friends was in the way, trying to break her skull again.

That blow was easier to sidestep than the one that had hit before, praise Poram's darkness and Sitha's stone. Blunt impacts hurt, even in Branwyn's metal form, and the muscles on her left side were soon going to start feeling the hit she hadn't been able to dodge.

Her circular kick to the woman's elbow missed the joint but connected with a *crack* nonetheless, and from there it was only a smooth unfolding of her body to plant Yathana in her foe's stomach and carve a path upward.

The crossbowman had fled, though, and that was far from ideal.

Three of the assassins were dead, another down and curled in on herself, and one fled. As Branwyn turned from her new position, Zelen ran the sixth through. He winced as he did so, but did a good job of it, and neatly ducked to avoid the long knives of the seventh. That brought Zelen within the assassin's guard, which he took quick and thorough advantage of: a solid punch to the stomach, then a sword hilt to the temple.

"Your sense of range is excellent," said Branwyn, after the man crumpled and she peered around to ensure that no more were coming. "Are you hurt?"

Zelen's face was whiter than usual and his lips set, but he shook his head. "I was about to ask you the same," he said, and then frowned, examining Branwyn with an intensity that made her glad of the darkness and his unaltered vision. "You gave me a rotten few moments there, you know."

"I'm well," she said, "but sorry. I'd imagine they were after me, unless you have more enemies than I was aware of."

"No," said Zelen. "Politics can be ruthless, but it hasn't been deadly here in longer than I've been alive. Besides, I'm not much of a target."

He bent to the man he'd just felled and felt his neck. The heartbeat there was steady. Later, the fellow might well die—knocks on the skull could do that—but for the moment, there was little that needed doing. Zelen rose and went toward the woman he'd crippled, who'd fallen silent and still when he'd been too busy to notice. Blood pooled under her leg, but she still lived as well.

The fabric of his cloak didn't tear easily; he had to take his knife to it.

"Here," said Branwyn, coming up behind him and holding out her hands. "A shame neither of us brought bandages."

"Dreadfully negligent. What night on the town is complete without a bit of bloodshed?" Zelen passed his cloak to Branwyn, who drew it taut and held it for the blade. He cut a long strip of the fabric, then knelt down again and began to bind the assassin's leg. The darkness was no friend to his endeavor, but he managed.

"This is nothing new for you, is it?"

"Bandaging, or doing it without a light in an alley when I've just escaped death? At the risk of ruining my reputation, I'll give very different answers."

Branwyn laughed, soft and smooth as always. "I was thinking the former," she said, "though I'm no judge of your life. I've seen less skill from healers who've spent years at it—less from a few Mourners, in fact."

"I'm sure you say that to all the men," said Zelen, "but I thank you." He tied the knot and got to his feet. The others caught his eye then, the ones beyond his reach.

The world smelled of blood and offal. He'd never before seen any of the people in the alley, but four of them had been people and no longer were. Zelen bowed his head. "Queen of the Dead, Mistress of the Flames, Letar, Who Is the End of All, we give these souls into your governance." He still knew the words by heart, he discovered, and Branwyn joined him. "May their evil perish with their flesh, and may you in your evenhandedness best use what good remains."

"So it is, and was, and shall be hence," Branwyn added at the end, and shrugged when Zelen glanced at her. "A local variant, I expect. Thank you. That was kindly done."

"It was what I could do."

The pleasant tension from before the attack was gone. Branwyn was as lovely as ever, even bedraggled, but Zelen couldn't have thought of pleasure in that alley, and she gave no indication of doing so either. Her hand lingered on Zelen's as she returned his cloak, though, smoother than he remembered and oddly cool. He suspected that the fight had thrown off his perceptions.

"Have you killed people before?" she asked.

"No. Seen them die, yes, but never at my hand." The weight of that was coming toward him, the dust of its progress already visible from the walls of his mind. "You?" he asked, and then recalled her obvious skill and felt idiotic.

But she shook her head. "Not people, until now. If I hadn't been used to other creatures, I might have thought to try and spare these. Ya—a friend of mine would say that was stupid, and she might be right. It's certainly pointless to regret now."

"I don't believe you have cause to regret," said Zelen, and, on impulse, put an arm around her waist. "You likely saved both of our lives. And you were splendid doing it."

"I'm sure you say that to all the women," she echoed, "but thank you. And now—" She glanced at the wounded. "Where does one take captured assassins in this city? My information fell woefully short in certain respects."

Chapter 13

TINIVAL HAD A SHRINE CLOSE BY, WHICH WAS FORTUNATE. Branwyn was beginning to feel her bruises even before she and Zelen picked up the surviving assassins, and carrying a decent-sized man a few city blocks didn't help matters.

It did render her thoroughly conspicuous. She could only be glad that the transformation had worn off by the time they reached any decent lighting, and that Zelen knew the way.

For a man who was entirely human, too, he'd fought quite impressively, and she hadn't been lying about his skill at healing.

The company was even more valuable. At the end of the prayer, Branwyn had looked from the dead to the two that Zelen had managed to leave alive, and remembered all the comments about Sentinels that she'd never quite been supposed to overhear. *Half a step from murderous at the best of times* had been one, and *Well, they have to satisfy their urges, don't they? Gods know they're useful, but…*

But.

The man on her back was a dull pain, deadweight despite not technically being dead. The streets were dark, but those people in them stopped to stare regardless, and most backed away.

Have you killed people before?

Not people.

The twistedmen and the rest of Thyran's creatures were buds from greater beings, fusions of demons and the people who'd gone over to the Worldbreaker's banner of their own will, spawned with all their progenitors' hatred. Branwyn had slain other things in her life—outright demons and creatures transformed by sorcery—and she'd never regretted it. She'd wondered, at times, whether they were as irredeemable as the Adeptas said, but she'd always met them when they were preying on her charges, and they were too dangerous for her to even consider being less than lethal.

More to the point, she'd simply never considered it. Twistedmen and monsters were more trouble than they were worth where interrogation was concerned. Gizath's human forces were more often the business of the Blades, and letting them talk was usually deadly. If you came face-to-face with an enemy, you struck to kill. So Branwyn had been trained, and so she had lived, and until she'd seen Zelen fight, any alternate path had never been more than a vague philosophical concept.

That had made her good at what she did, and what she did was the life she'd chosen. Branwyn couldn't regret it. All the same, she kept the memory of Zelen's face when he said *You were splendid* close, and the remembered feeling of his arm around her made a strengthening contrast to the weight of the unconscious man on her back.

The streets were darker than they had been before, and Branwyn had learned to treasure light where she found it.

———————

"You bring strange gifts, Master Verengir," said the knight on duty. He was one of the stonekin, tall and lean with glittering sky-blue streaks in his dark hair.

Zelen knew him slightly, partly from holy days but mostly from occasions when their separate business had taken both of them to the Temple of Letar at the same time. "Well, I was passing a dark alley, Lycellias, and I thought of you," he said.

Walking had given him some composure back. It had helped more to have a quartet of squires take the wounded away, back into the interior of Tinival's temple. Zelen knew a Mourner was stationed there: the assassins would live, if divine might could aid them.

"Had they your murder in mind, or did you prevent another's death?" Lycellias asked.

"I'm fairly sure we were the targets," said Branwyn, "but how did you know?"

"Had they been footpads, they'd have gone to the guards. Had it been a brawl, you'd have involved no authorities. Therefore…" He spread his hands. "How did it come to pass?"

They told him. Lycellias listened with complete, attentive calm, and as always, Zelen wondered how he managed such stillness while wearing plate mail. He couldn't have done it, and while he was on the slender side for a human, the stonekin was far narrower in the shoulders and hips. Perhaps it was a blessing of Tinival.

"Some few days may pass before they can speak, if they wish to buy their lives in such a manner," he said when Zelen and Branwyn had finished their story. "Should that be the case, I assume you'll wish to know what they say."

"You assume well," said Zelen. "Send a note to my house and I'll come hear from you. If you think I should hear the story direct from the assassins, I'm willing, but the day I start doubting a knight's accuracy is the day I take to the wilderness and grow a beard."

Branwyn snickered at the image, and even Lycellias's thin lips curved up. "And you, lady?" he asked.

"If you don't mind fetching me," she said, glancing at Zelen, "it might be better to go through you. I'd rather my hosts not know about this."

"A courteous guest," said Lycellias. "Or a suspicious one. The first quality is kind, and the second likely wise."

"I suppose so." Branwyn's chuckle was only an exhalation and had no real humor in it. "I wish I could say that the Rognozis would have no motive to kill me, but I suspect every noble family here could have reason. Granted, if they did want me dead, I'm not sure why they'd hire outside help. They could simply poison my dinner and say I'd fallen ill."

"That would still make people suspicious," Zelen said reluctantly, "and a run-in with a lot of thugs might not. Or not as much. There'd be rumors either way, but if I wanted you dead, a few assassins could be a better option, on the balance."

"I'll keep that in mind," Branwyn said. A smile flickered on her face, appearing and disappearing in a heartbeat. "Lady Rognozi *was* the one who suggested the dressmaker's. It's likely we were followed from there, if not before, assuming I was the target."

"She made no secret of where you were, though. Granted, she knows me"—Zelen decided not to mention the lady's matchmaking agenda—"but she doesn't have a very suspicious nature, and the servants might have told a caller where you'd gone. Unless you'd told them not to."

"No," said Branwyn.

Lycellias cleared his throat. "Speculation may serve little purpose now," he said, "when more knowledge will likely emerge within a few days and may counteract any conclusions you reach. Your homes would serve you well in the meantime. Rest may provide new avenues of speculation."

And he had his duties to attend to, Zelen read between the lines, and didn't need two outsiders cluttering up the temple.

"Excellent points," said Branwyn, apparently reaching the same conclusion. She bowed. "Thank you for your assistance."

"The Silver Wind calls, and I rejoice in answering. Do either of you feel the need of an escort?"

"Not for me, thank you," said Zelen. "How many squads of assassins can be lurking about on one night?"

"The night in question has a great deal to do with the answer," Lycellias said. "Yet I think your judgment sound. May Tinival shield you on your journey."

It was a silent walk back to the hill where both the Verengirs and the Rognozis lived—silent between Branwyn and Zelen, at any rate. The city supplied plenty of noises, of the sort Branwyn was familiar with but only just getting used to on a grand scale, and she was careful to note and identify as many as she could.

Zelen had probably been right about the likelihood of more assassins, but *probably* rarely saved lives.

"Do you have a story prepared?" he asked as they approached the Rognozis' gates.

Branwyn hadn't ever needed one before. "I suppose a tavern brawl would reflect poorly on my diplomatic image."

"That depends on the audience," Zelen said with a chuckle that warmed her despite both the chill and the situation. "But I'd blame a runaway horse, if I were you. That sort of thing happens from time to time. Say you got out of the way, nobody was hurt, throw in a smashed-up fruit cart if you like. Details tend to help."

"You sound as though you've provided a few alibis before."

"In my wayward youth."

"I'm thankful for your waywardness, then."

"I'd planned to be considerably more wayward," he said, making a wry face, "but I fear this isn't our evening."

"No." Battle led to lust more than occasionally, but that was in the immediate aftermath, and usually in the flush of triumph. After hauling wounded people through the streets, then talking over who in the crowded city might most want her dead, Branwyn wanted only a hot bath, a soft bed, and darkness. From the lines around Zelen's eyes and the slump of his shoulders, she suspected he felt the same. "Another time."

"I'll hold you to that," said Zelen. Once again he took her hand and kissed the back, but this time he held it for longer. "And I'll send word when I hear from Lycellias."

Chapter 14

"THEY GAVE US LITTLE ENOUGH, I FEAR," LYCELLIAS SAID.

One of the sword-marked doors led to a short, wide hallway of polished maple. A plain door off of that opened onto a small but airy room where two couches faced each other across a golden-red wooden table. Lycellias sat on one, Branwyn and Zelen on the other. The news surprised none of them.

"Can't expect a person to give their name and address when they hire killers," he said, "damned disobliging as it is of them."

"No," said Branwyn, "but I'd cherished hopes of a description."

Lycellias nodded. "So too had I. But the prisoners each said that the person who sought them out was cloaked and hooded. Beneath the hood, they both said, the face was unsteady. It shifted constantly so that they couldn't speak definitely of any feature."

"Did they get any sense of a figure? A voice?" Zelen asked.

"Tall, they said, with neither breasts nor curved hips that they could make out. A cloak hides much, of course, and much more can be done with binding. They did say that the person spoke with refinement and, indeed, that they acted fastidious—always standing, touching nothing in the place where they met, and so forth. The voice, they said, was low."

"Well," Zelen said, "we've eliminated most people who aren't at least the wealthier sort of merchant."

"The Rognozis seem unlikely as well. She's too buxom for binding or a cloak to have much effect, and his age would be obvious even if his face was enchanted," Branwyn added.

"Unless," said Zelen, "they used an agent. That means the rest of it's no good either. Plenty of people with resources who came up from the docks, you know."

"An agent would yet be a beginning," Lycellias said. "The place of the meeting is known to us now as well, and there may yet be more to find there."

Lycellias made a good point. "Fair," Zelen admitted, as if a knight could be otherwise. "Sorry for jumping straight to despair. I've chased too many cold trails lately, if that's the phrase I want. Never been much of a hunter."

"Which quarry do you speak of?" Lycellias asked.

"A missing boy down at the docks. No trace of him, and we turned over every rock we could find."

"Ah. We'd have been of little aid then, and the child's kin would have known it."

It was true. The knights were wonderful when you knew the scoundrel you wanted brought to justice or had a specific innocent at a specific place who needed defending, and they were top-notch at determining whether or not an alleged scoundrel actually deserved that name, but the Silver Wind didn't help when nobody knew who was to blame for a crime nor whether one had even taken place. Neither did any of the other gods.

Branwyn echoed his thoughts. "Knights for judgment and defense, Blades for dark sorcery, Sentinels if monsters are involved—"

"Much luck you'd have finding one," Zelen said. "I think it's been ten years or more since the Order sent any of their people to Heliodar."

"—but for those who've merely vanished, mortal vision is the only recourse. It's a pity."

"Searching for lost things, if they were tied enough to the one who sought them, was one of the Traitor's powers," Lycellias said. "That was long ago, before he was the Traitor, before even my grandfather's day. The art has left the world, or gone beyond the reach of mortals."

"I hope it's gone beyond the reach of Gizath's people now, too," said Zelen. He didn't much care for the notion of anybody being able to find him or what he wanted hidden through sorcery. Imagining the Traitor's minions with the ability made his flesh crawl.

"Nobody's seen evidence of it in the war. Or the histories from before the winters." Branwyn mentally paged through old books. "I think that he lost that influence during his fight with Letar."

Lycellias nodded. "The wounds from that battle were to the world as well, and not only the physical."

The Battlefield was northeast of Criwath. Nobody knew the precise location because nobody with any sense wanted to go to the place. It was where Gizath had killed his sister's mortal lover and where Letar had, in turn, tried to kill him.

"Unfortunate in many senses," said Branwyn. "A way to track our quarry magically would be very useful—but then, it's possible that trying to kill me wouldn't have been enough of a tie. I'm assuming they *were* trying to kill me, by the way."

"You were the target, yes."

"So I'd figured. The butler at the Rognozis said that a man had come with an urgent message for me and been directed to the dressmaker's." Branwyn rose from the couch. "It's rather comforting for everyone, or should be. I only have to survive the next week or so, and I'll leave this unknown enemy frustrated."

"Gods willing," said Zelen. He'd spent most of the previous night asking them for exactly that.

Such prayers were pointless. None of the Four could prevent mortal evil, not directly. Zelen hadn't forgotten that, but he hadn't been able to stop his petitions either. The people he'd killed had weighed on his spirit and his own closeness to death had shaken him, but he would have endured either a million times rather than watch that club coming down toward Branwyn's skull.

Outside, a wide square stretched between the temples to the north, clerks to the east, crafters to the south, and inns to the west. It had been mostly empty at night, but in the middle of the afternoon, as the year wound toward harvest and the Festival of Irinyev, it was an ocean of people.

The shining carriages of lords, with matched horses and jingling reins, passed peasants' mule-drawn carts full of cabbages and the heavily laden ponies of trading companies. Shops sold bright glass jewelry, herbs from the high mountains of Silane, and amber from Kvanla, the most common port of ships that went out from Heliodar.

The people were mostly locals: largely dark of hair and eyes, pale-skinned, covering as little and wearing as many trailing ribbons as was practical. Some had the bronzed complexion of Silane, though, or wore the checked weave of Affiran. Even a few of the waterfolk and stonekin wandered through the crowd.

When Branwyn had come to Heliodar, she'd wondered at its size and the sheer variety it contained. Then, knowing the city's potential fate, she'd feared for it. Leaving the conversation with Lycellias, her first thought was of how many threats such a crowd could hold.

Easy, said Yathana. *A tight string will sound clear, but one too badly stretched will snap.*

Zelen hadn't taken her arm this time, leaving them both free to draw weapons quickly, but he matched her pace closely. It was a pleasant sensation to have that side covered, since she knew he could defend himself well.

It also meant she didn't have to raise her voice when she'd gathered enough composure to speak. "A mage, even just for one spell, and a set of professionals wouldn't be inexpensive. Am I wrong?"

"I don't think you are. Not that I've ever tried hiring killers, granted, but I'd wager it's a sight more than most people could manage, even as a small group. I doubt there are a dozen shop-keepers who dislike you or your mission that much." They left the temple square by the east, walking onto a broad road full of soberly dressed people bustling about on errands. "There are a handful of respectable merchants who could swing it, one or two less respectable—might get a discount, for that matter—but I think we should focus on the nobility. They've seen the most of you, for one thing."

Branwyn nodded. Then the individual words struck her, rather than the overall meaning. "We?"

"No question about it," Zelen responded immediately. "For one thing, it comes off as rather atrocious for Heliodar if a diplomatic envoy gets killed here, and even worse if she's in the company of a noble house. Even I've picked up that much of the principle. This is my city, as little as some might believe the sentiment from me, and I'd rather not have it disgraced."

"Understandable," she said, remembering what he'd said about Thyran and Heliodar when they'd first walked together. "And I'm grateful for your help, even though you didn't have much choice in the matter."

"That's the second part, isn't it?" Zelen asked. He grinned as charmingly as ever, but there was a hardness to it that Branwyn hadn't seen before. The edge didn't quite seem new, though. What had there been in his life before to bring it out? "Nearly getting killed quite spoils the evening. I'm inclined to bear a grudge in that category."

"By that logic," said Branwyn, only mostly joking, "I'm the one you should bear a grudge against. If you hadn't been with me, you'd have had a pleasant night elsewhere, and a dead foreigner would just have added interest to the local gossip."

"No." Zelen stopped, so that Branwyn had to as well, and turned to face her. The crowds flowed around them, but for a moment they were both as still as temple pillars.

Then Zelen raised one hand to touch the side of Branwyn's face, gloved fingertips light behind her jaw. "You're my third reason."

There was no light answer to make now, no way to dismiss his regard as a passing fancy, and she was too much Tinival's creature to pretend under such circumstances. "Zelen—"

"I'm not asking for anything." The smile appeared again, softer and rueful. "Gods, I don't even know that I'm *saying* anything. There's been no time, and neither of us are our own creature, are we?"

"No," said Branwyn.

"But you're a bloody sight more than a temporary distraction. I know that much." His eyes shone. "I'm not a young idiot. If I'd woken up tomorrow and heard you were dead, I'd have lived, but it would've left quite a scar. The sort that never quite stops hurting."

The breath she let out was a feeble thing. It left a great weight in her chest, good and bad mixed. "I wouldn't have precisely walked away unmarked if you'd been killed back there," Branwyn said. "The choice is yours, but I know things I can't tell you. And I don't want to draw you in, unwilling, to a matter that doesn't concern you."

"You and I both know it does. Or it will."

"You aren't wrong," she admitted, and considered practicality even as she took comfort in Zelen's palm against her chin. "I have another meeting with Yansyak tonight. I doubt there'll be much information there, but the job remains, assassins or not."

"I'll make some discreet inquiries," said Zelen. "My patients might know a few facts the upper crust doesn't. Are you free tomorrow night?"

"Kolovat, I'm afraid." The older man wasn't bad company: he kept a good table, his husband had an excellent sense of humor, and their three heirs were youths of boundless and refreshing enthusiasm. Still, it didn't compare to the possibilities of an evening with Zelen.

"Then I'll see you at the ball." He leaned in and brushed his lips across hers. The kiss, light as it was, made Branwyn's body hum with sensation, but the gentleness of it caught at her as well because there was nothing patronizing in it, no assumption that she needed protection or reassurance. *We're in this together*, it said. *We have meaning to each other.* "Save a few dances for me."

"You can depend on that."

Chapter 15

THE STAR PALACE GLOWED WITH LIGHT, AND FOR THAT ONE evening, none of it was magical. The legends said that Irinyev had carried only a torch to the mountains and back when he'd brought the cure for the summer plague. In his honor, the only light within any well-to-do house that evening would be flame.

Candles burned in colored-glass sconces in the hallways and in the gold-and-crystal chandeliers hanging over the ballroom. Beeswax and smoke mingled their scents with those of perfume and humanity. Flames stretched out shadows, hid faces, and picked out a sparkling eye to illuminate one moment, a lock of silky hair the next, a sly grin the second after.

Zelen was already beaming as Andras announced him, and there was nothing sly about it. As the tune from the harpists and pipers in the corner swirled into his ears, he moved into the crowd around the dance floor, greeting those he knew and being introduced to those he didn't. There was nobody he dreaded meeting: Gedomir would no more make an appearance at a ball than would Marton and his brood. A few among the others might be tedious or awkward, but all were amiable, and all were there to enjoy the evening—and with that in mind, it was easy for Zelen to overlook other faults.

He knew Branwyn before she turned toward him. There was a particular set to her shoulders and a slow, generous curve of her mouth when she smiled that Zelen was beginning to think he would've recognized even if she'd worn a mask.

Formal dress was quite nearly enough to test the case. The

simply dressed woman who'd presented herself in court, or the one in doublet and breeches who'd joined Zelen in the streets, was a very different image from the vision greeting him in the ballroom.

Her dress was dark gold, embroidered all over with deep-pink roses. Long-sleeved, with a long, straight skirt, it was nonetheless far from modest: barely far enough past Branwyn's shoulders to keep the dress on, the neckline plunged down to her stomach. Thick rose-colored ribbons that laced the dress tightly to her waist, revealing shimmering pale skin in the spaces between them. A line of roses bordered each side and curved up around her breasts. Zelen was instantly sure that only a petal or two concealed her nipples, and instantly very desirous of testing his theory.

Politeness and a vast effort of will brought his gaze upward again, past the bare column of her neck and back to her amused face. "Madam Alanive," he said, and sank into a deep bow. "I'm very glad to see you."

"It's a pleasure to hear it," said Branwyn, the pins in her braided and upswept hair sparkling as she stepped forward. For a dizzying moment, she was only an inch from him, and her breath was hot against his ear. "But I have to wonder which part."

———————

"Don't ask me to choose," Zelen whispered back. "Hardly a fair question for a stunned man."

"Why, thank you," she said. "It's good to see you too."

It truly was.

Zelen was wearing brown—fawn-colored for his trousers and darker above—and there was nothing plain about his clothing. The doublet was high-collared in back, cut low in front to expose the firm, flat muscles of his upper chest, lightly dusted with dark hair. Gold trim ran the length of the collar, around the hem, and circled the armholes, while buttons of polished amber

fastened the garment tightly against Zelen's slim waist and hips. The velvet of his doublet was thick, but the silk trousers clung to every line of his thighs and calves. The topaz was back in one ear, and his rings were cat's-eye and amber, not overwhelming his hands but enough to catch the light with every gesture.

His smile said that he knew exactly what Branwyn was looking at and how much she appreciated it.

"Do you dance?" he asked.

"Possibly." She looked around for a place to set down her goblet. A passing servant made a signal, and Branwyn handed it over with relief. "You may have to inform me of the specifics."

"Gladly," he said. The musicians ended one song. In the pause before another began, the two of them walked out onto the crowded floor.

———————

Only a very little explanation turned out to be necessary, and almost none for the basic steps. Branwyn mirrored Zelen's movements with a skill that would have surprised him if he hadn't witnessed her fighting. That glimpse hadn't foretold the light grace with which she moved across the floor, though, nor had battle conveyed her ready, fluid response to him.

"Have you done this before?" he asked.

"Once or twice, somewhat," said Branwyn, passing under his arm and coming back to settle her hands at bicep and shoulder. "There's a form in Silane, but it's slower and without as many of the flourishes."

"Ah, you've spent time in Silane?"

"A little. My duties take me on the road often."

"Do you enjoy it?"

"For the most part," she said. "There are always rainy evenings where I'm outdoors more than I'd like, or bad food, or"—silk

rustled as she shrugged—"unpleasantness, but I suppose that happens in many lives, wandering or still."

"I can't argue with that," he said. Even he'd encountered his share of wet feet and dubious dinners, and he had some idea of how those who came to his clinic lived.

"Do you enjoy this?"

"The festival, yes. Very much so." The hint of a question in her eyes prompted him to go on—or perhaps he just made up an invitation to do so. "Irinyev was one of my heroes when I was young."

"He is an inspiring figure, if…" Branwyn paused, clearly searching for the tactful word.

Zelen chuckled. "A bit mortification-of-the-flesh for my tastes, yes. That was part of the appeal, though: he wasn't always. Before the plague, before he had the vision of the healing spring, he was a Mourner, but a young one who liked his comforts." The Dark Lady's more common priests, the ones who healed the sick and burned the dead, didn't have nearly the strictures or the frighteningly single-minded purpose that her Blades did. "He gave all of that up to save his people, and when bandits took all his belongings at the foot of the mountain, he kept going."

"And you always wondered if you could do the same?"

"Oh, I always knew I couldn't," Zelen said, letting more laughter flow around the old bitterness. "That made him even more admirable, you see. The unattainable always looks best from here on the ground."

"I suppose you're right," Branwyn said, "but you underestimate yourself. I've seen many people do what they'd never prepared for when the time came."

They turned a corner on the floor, and Zelen spun her around again, watching her shine. "Do you like it?" he asked when she was back in his arms. "The festival, I mean. Are you liking it, I suppose, since you haven't experienced the whole yet?"

"Oh, yes. Like most of my stay here, it's been considerably

more luxurious than I'm used to, and I do like the new experience. More than I should, some would say," she added, but without any hint of serious concern. "More than that, I've always enjoyed holidays, even the ones that are no more than a honey cake with dinner and a song in the evening, even when I wasn't in a position to have either. They…they're like points that the year can hold to, as though they're different enough that everyday life can mold around them."

"You make them sound like temple rites."

"Rituals," Branwyn agreed, mouth tilting in a contemplative half smile. "But distributed among everybody, without the stakes that they have in the temple and with more license."

"I'm fond of license too," said Zelen.

Branwyn's laugh made the tops of her breasts tremble above her gown. Desire, held at arm's length by the music and the need to remember steps, advanced in a rush. Zelen didn't stumble, but dancing, or indeed walking, was going to present certain difficulties before long.

It was still early in the evening; nobody had likely snuck off to the garden or up to the private rooms yet, and it wouldn't have been wise if Zelen and Branwyn had been the first pair to do so. Given that, it was technically fortunate that the music drew to an end, but it was no kind of good fortune that Zelen welcomed.

———————

Duty called, and it was hardly arduous. Drinking wine and eating small savory pastries in a warm room, dry and well dressed, while making mostly interesting conversation with people who weren't immediately trying to kill her, was physically an immense improvement on all of Branwyn's previous tasks. True, at least one of them might want her dead, but they weren't trying to accomplish the goal then.

She admired the clothing of other people, including Lady Galcian's shimmering gown of sea-blue taffeta and the yellow-and-orange medley that Starovna's eldest son wore. That admiration, expressed as slightly envious praise—"we have no such clothes where I'm from, particularly now"—was a seed. She planted it early and let it grow, allowing the others to ask about the war, then making a point or two and changing the subject. This was a night for nibbling around the edges, and charging ahead would do more harm than good.

With her dance partners, she took the same approach. General Mezannith, the leader of Heliodar's mostly idle army, joined her on the floor, and so did Kolovat in time. Both admired her dancing, and Mezannith actually speculated on how akin the skill might be to fighting, which saved Branwyn the better part of a segue. Between them came a wide assortment of well-dressed men, from a couple barely out of their teens to one nearly Lord Rognozi's age, and a few in between who were quite attractive.

None held Branwyn's attention as Zelen did, though. What had already passed between them—not only pleasure, but fighting at each other's side—made a foundation that raised him far above any other man in the room. While discussing wine with Lady Yansyak or dancing with one of the young guardsmen, even while she kept her attention politely on the subject and the partner, she was aware of Zelen as long as she could see him. When she could manage it without being rude, she scanned the room for dark hair and amber buttons.

It was later in the evening, after the Rognozis and many of the older guests had departed, that Branwyn had no pressing engagements and saw a clear path. Zelen was standing by one of the long banquet tables at the edges of the room.

"Dance with me again?" she asked, slipping up to his side.

"I'd like nothing better."

Branwyn believed him, and not only out of vanity. Proof was

in the glow in his eyes as he turned toward her and the closeness with which he held her when they danced, not very much more than was customary but enough that she noticed. She doubted she was the only one.

"I'm not sure assassins are my worry tonight," she said. "At least five women and two men may simply try to throw me out of a window after this."

Zelen laughed, clear and melodious. "You'll make me blush."

"I can try."

The hand at her waist tightened.

"I know you have your mission, and I wouldn't want to interfere," Zelen murmured, "and if the setting's wrong for you I'll understand, but after this, there are places we could go. It's almost a tradition."

Branwyn drew in a long breath, and even that motion felt sensual, making her aware of the slide of silk against her skin. "I think it's practically mandatory," she said, "that I experience the local customs."

Chapter 16

"I COULD THINK," SAID BRANWYN, IN A TONE OF SPECULATIVE amusement that ran straight from Zelen's ears to his swelling cock, "that you've done this before."

Lanterns behind polished glass cast pools of colored light around the gardens, illuminating bare trees, giving color to statuary, and picking out the occasional couple—or group—who weren't guarded enough in their desire. Zelen had led Branwyn past the blue-tinged rosebushes, which were discreet but hazardous to tender regions, and a spot in back of a hedge where interruptions were frequent. The next trysting place they encountered was in back of a statue portraying the wizard Gerant, one of the heroes from Thyran's War. The ground there, Zelen recalled, tended to be damp.

"Knowledge is the most valuable treasure a man can possess, my nurse told me," he said, as they passed the wizard.

Branwyn brought Zelen to a dead stop by dropping her hand to the front of his trousers and squeezing the bulge there—lightly, but more than enough to get his attention. "At the moment, I might disagree."

"Ah—" Zelen exhaled sharply. "If you'd prefer this place, I'm rapidly becoming very fond of it."

Peering up at the statue, Branwyn shook her head with a laugh that Zelen didn't understand and she didn't explain. "No," she said, "I'd rather he wasn't so close. Lead on."

Around a corner, near the back of the palace, yellow light illuminated the marble features of a woman on a horse. Fewer people made the journey back there, and since the horse only had one leg off the ground, the earth behind it had been sheltered from rain. Zelen started toward it, then hesitated. "Do you object to statues as a general rule," he asked, "or—"

Branwyn leaned in far enough to kiss his neck. He felt the light imprint of her teeth before she pulled back, and he shivered pleasantly. "No objection at all," she whispered into his ear.

The night air carried harpsong out from the palace across the gardens, the shoulders Branwyn gripped were covered in velvet, and Zelen's fingers brushed over silk as he cupped her breasts. Although they were outside, she thought that she might be having the most high-class assignation of her life.

It was also shaping up to be one of the most enjoyable ones. Zelen's mouth and hands were as skilled as they'd been outside of the Rognozis' house, and if more urgency animated him now, the same was true for her. Deliberate exploration was all well and good, but desire had been building for days, not to mention thwarted several times. Branwyn arched into Zelen's touch with no particular need for leisure. They could go slowly later.

Zelen slid his hands into the neckline of her dress—thank the gods that was low—and teased the stiff peaks of her nipples. His breath was quick and hot against her neck, but he never fumbled. As Branwyn moaned and rocked her hips against the ridge of his cock, he deftly stroked, lightly pinched, and managed to pull the dress aside enough to free one breast.

The sheer hunger on his face was arousing by itself. "Gods," he said hoarsely, "I could look at you like this all night."

"I appreciate the sentiment," Branwyn panted. Now that she had room, she began to address his shirt. The buttons were harder to work than the neckline of her gown, but as she captured one, she employed her other hand well, cupping the firm muscle of Zelen's arse beneath his doublet and pressing him toward her again. "But I'd really rather you took a different path."

"All sorts of them," he said. "Starting with this one."

Dropping gracefully to his knees, he closed his mouth around her exposed nipple, and Branwyn went molten with pleasure. She leaned back against the statue's marble, only managing not to close her eyes with the sheer sensation because the sight of Zelen's dark head at her breast was too much to pass up. As he used his tongue in warm swirls and little tantalizing flicks, gasps worked their way up her throat, then rapidly became moans, and not subtle ones either.

She would have been more disappointed when he raised his head save for two things: first, he moved to her other breast, and the contrast of his tongue through the thin silk was itself intoxicating, and second, his hands found their way beneath her skirt.

There was no way Zelen could have believed her unmoved even before he felt her wetness: it would've taken a far better actress than Branwyn had ever seen to counterfeit the desire that she'd experienced from their first dance and that had all but overtaken her as soon as they'd entered the garden. Still, when his fingers brushed against her sex, the ensuing groan sounded as though he hadn't quite been prepared for what he felt, and the sound stoked Branwyn's passion even further. She thrust forward, begging without words for more: she wouldn't have hesitated at using words if she could have spoken then.

She didn't need to. The initial gentle brush of fingertips quickly became firmer, a stroking rhythm that still teased but built as well, taking her further and further into lust as Zelen learned what pleased her most and adjusted to give it to her. Branwyn was writhing before long, everything between her legs turned to pure need.

Zelen was quick. When he took his hands away, Branwyn had only just noticed the deprivation before he'd lifted her skirts and pressed his mouth against her sex, and then she was in no mood at all to protest. He tasted her thoroughly, with more moans that vibrated against her and drove her even closer to the edge.

When he shifted his attention to her swollen clit, Branwyn shot toward that edge like a flaming arrow. A few circles of his tongue and she was crying out over and over, incoherent as pleasure racked her. She was conscious of her hips jerking in Zelen's grip, but otherwise sensation was all.

She was leaning against the statue when she came back, legs like jelly. Zelen's head was still between them, but his mouth was gentler on her sex now, lighter.

"Well," she said when she had both breath and brain for words. "That was extraordinary. And I should see if I can manage its equal."

Zelen pulled back and rose. When he wrapped his arms around Branwyn, she felt his erection, hard as ever, press against her, but there was no forcefulness about his touch and no trace of impatience. "I have complete faith in you," he said, and exhaled hard. "Though not quite in my own willpower. Should we—"

"Willpower's useful in many situations. This isn't one," Branwyn said. "Besides, my legs won't hold me much longer."

She started to kneel, watching his face as she did and savoring the way his eyes widened and his lips parted slightly. Branwyn grinned. This was going to be *most* enjoyable.

Under the circumstances, she could almost have dismissed the screams she heard in the next moment—but she had too much experience to think they were cries of pleasure.

Chapter 17

WHEN BRANWYN FROZE AND PULLED BACK, ZELEN AT FIRST worried that something had gone wrong between them. He hadn't spoken coherently enough to offend, he was sure of it, but had he moved the wrong way and caught her with a knee? Had the posture itself brought bad memories to mind?

"Are—" He started to ask, ignoring the ache in his groin and extending a hand to help her up.

But she was already on her feet, her speed uncanny, one finger pressed to her lips. A second later, Zelen heard the reasons.

"Oh what is it? What is *that*?" someone asked, sounding terrified.

"Letar defend us!" came another cry, from a different part of the garden, and then, "Someone *help*!"

Mostly, there were screams. Zelen's frustrated arousal quickly dwindled.

Branwyn pulled her dress back over her breasts, but the motion was clearly an afterthought: she didn't even look down. A casual observer might have thought her idle, but Zelen saw the taut lines of her muscles, the flare of her nostrils, and the too-regular way her breasts rose and fell. She wasn't idle; she wasn't frozen in panic; she was hunting.

Zelen tried to follow her gaze. Out in the darkness he saw flickers of…he wasn't sure what. It was darkness on darkness, darkness that sank and rose, and it tugged at the corners of his vision like a fishhook. The ground seemed to waver beneath him.

A scream became a shriek of pain. He was a healer. The sound had come from their left. Zelen started that way, only to have

Branwyn seize him by the biceps with more strength than any human should have exhibited.

"*Not* unarmed and not unaware. You'll do no good."

"I have no weapon. Nobody here… The guards out front, I suppose…" Zelen corrected himself, but feebly. There were two guards, and while their swords weren't exactly dull, they'd been made more for show than fighting.

"Not quite." Branwyn reached into the side of her gown, the place where bone and steel stays had pushed her breasts high and blocked Zelen's touch. She wiggled, hissed, then pulled out a dagger. It was long, thin, and razor-sharp, the hilt mostly a flat place on the blade. "Here."

Zelen took it, noting the pattern of runes twisting down its length. "These are from the stonekin."

"They're good at magic." Branwyn was pulling a matching dagger from her gown's other side. "Throw, if you can, and don't engage if you can avoid it. We'll get the civilians into the palace and work from there. Closing with these things is a bad idea."

"What are they?" he asked as the two of them started toward the nearest source of screaming.

Branwyn didn't turn her head. Zelen saw her profile as she spoke, painted red by a lantern they passed. "Demons."

The darkness was full of shapes. Some were human.

Branwyn watched them dart across her vision or run past on its edges. Many were half-naked, a few were bloody, and all were terrified. Other things followed, too many for her and Zelen to intercept. Her hands ached for Yathana, but the sword was far away, barred by rules of etiquette regarding blatant weaponry at the ball.

A couple burst from behind an ash tree and stared at her and Zelen. "What's happening?" asked one.

"We're under attack," said Zelen. "Best get inside, and quickly."

One of the pair might have been inclined to ask questions, but the other yanked him away, into a run toward the palace. None of the fleeing people acted as if they were confused about where to go. Branwyn blessed the human instinct to run for the biggest structure when in danger.

There was no chance to ask pardon or blessing aloud: Branwyn hoped the tree, or Poram beyond it, would understand. She leapt up and grabbed two long branches near each other, letting her weight help her break them off on the way down.

"Here." She handed one branch to Zelen, took hold of the other, and started running again, making for the nearest of the demons. "Life disrupts them. Range might save you."

———————

A man lay screaming on the grass, and above him the world was torn open.

The demon was tall and thin and…*flat*? It floated in the air like paper laid on a table, and Zelen couldn't work out how—not just how it was doing so, but how that could even *be*. He had the impression of a manlike shape, with a rudimentary, elongated face and not so much arms as a set of jagged edges at its side. Around it the night puckered inward, like skin around a fresh cut.

To view it was to feel the world tilt beneath his feet, not out of terror—though he felt plenty of that—but out of his mind's effort to reconcile what he was seeing with any part of the world he'd been born into and understood.

If not for its victim, Zelen might have frozen there, or fled. The years of his training and those at the clinic took over, though, and said: *There's a wounded man here.* That was familiar. That was knowable. And if Zelen needed to treat a wounded man, he'd need time and space to do so. The nature of the obstacles to those didn't need to matter.

He forced himself to look long enough to aim, raised the dagger Branwyn had given him, and threw as hard as he could.

He'd never know whether he hit squarely, whatever that might mean for such things, or whether he'd only nicked it and the knife was simply that magical. There was a flash of blue light, a sound like papers sliding together but far louder, and the demon was gone.

Its victim, Zelen found as he dropped to his knees by the man, was missing chunks of flesh from half a dozen places. The shoulder was the worst, with almost nothing left but bone. There was very little blood, though, and it wasn't flowing nearly as quickly as it should have been. "Do you think you can stand?" Zelen asked.

"Wha... Verengir?"

Zelen vaguely recognized his patient. They'd joked together at dances, gambled and hunted in the same parties. He had no time to recall names any more than he did for gentleness. "You need to run, if you can. Back to the palace. There are more of those things. Can you stand?" he repeated.

"I think so."

The wounded man managed with help from Zelen, if a sort of braced shove upward could be called helping, and then stared at Branwyn. She was standing, facing the darkness with knife in one hand and branch in the other, her hair falling tangled down her back. She didn't look as though she even noticed the existence of the men behind her, and yet Zelen knew that she was alert for the slightest hint of matters going wrong.

"Gape later," he suggested. "Move now, or are you that tired of life?"

That suggestion got through. The man started moving, limping in a way that made Zelen want to turn and assist—but he wasn't the only one out there. Branwyn was already moving, tracking the next set of screams, the next writhing human form.

"Not nearly enough blood," said Zelen, catching up to her. "Do they drink it?"

"No, but they're very cold. That's why they're here, I wouldn't wonder. The heat of living things draws them. Many people in one place, particularly people exerting themselves, would have been a beacon as soon as they broke through."

Her grip on the branch was different than the one she used on her sword, and the contrast made Zelen think of the blade. His mind, clarified by nearness to death, seized on the great jewel in the sword's hilt and snapped it into place. It was the missing detail, the feature that made a portrait recognizable as a person.

The sword.

Branwyn's strength and speed, more than any human could have possessed.

Her knowledge of demons and how casual she was about it.

The blow, fighting assassins, that should have left her dead and yet she'd shaken off easily.

Her comment afterward: she hadn't killed people before.

No detail alone would have been enough to draw conclusions, but now Zelen saw the whole portrait before him. "You're a Sentinel," he said.

Branwyn didn't even turn. If she blinked, Zelen missed it. "Yes."

———————

She didn't have the time or energy to make up a good denial. Honestly, Zelen would more than likely see through any lie she did put together, even a painstakingly crafted one. The man was perceptive.

He said nothing in response to her answer, but that might have been simply a lack of opportunity. The demons, aware of their fellow creature's forcible return to the outer darkness or attracted by motion and greater heat, were moving toward Zelen and

Branwyn. That gave some of their victims a chance to escape, but it also required a certain amount of focus.

The first to approach caught Branwyn's branch hard on the side of what passed for its head. Yellow-green light flickered through its pallid form, webbing out from the point of contact, and it reeled. Branwyn ducked low, past its guard, and plunged her knife into its chest. As the demon dissipated, the magic buzzed through her fingers and up her arm.

To her side, Zelen fended off two others, wielding the branch he carried like a quarterstaff. She noticed flashes of motion as he blocked and dodged, then a more vivid burst of yellow-green as he caught one of the demons with a fatal blow.

They kept moving, killing when they could but mostly trying to keep clear of lashing claws, heading toward any human bodies they could see or screams they could hear. To Branwyn's mild surprise and distinct gratitude, they met with others on the same errand: one of the palace guards wielding a gold-hilted sword and an older man who carried a fireplace poker in his remaining hand.

Branwyn threw her knife to destroy a demon and buy them time while Zelen picked up a young woman with her right leg in tatters. The guard helped a man with a badly clawed face to his feet and propped the man's shoulder under his arm while Branwyn and the man with the poker smashed down the appendages that flailed toward them.

Their mission became a fighting retreat soon enough, when Branwyn stopped seeing human figures in motion. The demons massed around them, seeking the remaining prey outside the walls. By Branwyn's estimate, at least six remained when the small group of rescuers and rescued made it to the side door.

It was the man with the injured face who hammered on the oak and shouted. Branwyn didn't even make out what he said, for she was thrusting the sharp end of her branch into the middle of a demon, and the rustling sound of its death was overwhelming up close. She pulled her weapon back and ducked another creature's strike, aware that the door behind her was opening and Zelen and the guard were going through with the wounded.

Cold brushed against her neck, feeling wet even with no substance. Branwyn ducked before the demon's talons themselves made contact. They sliced open one arm of her dress from shoulder to wrist. The skin below was only scratched, but it felt as though she'd plunged her whole arm into an icy pool. She hissed and brought the branch upward. Close range made it awkward, but the blow took nonetheless, slamming into the demon's "head" and bursting it apart.

A hand closed around her other shoulder—fingers, not talons, so she didn't wheel and strike immediately—and yanked, pulling Branwyn back through the open door. She grabbed the handle on the way, slammed the door behind her, and then stumbled to a stop.

Unsurprisingly, it had been Zelen who pulled her in. Now he and what looked like everyone in Heliodar stood, in fear and formal clothing, staring at her.

Chapter 18

CLAWS MADE OF NOTHING SCRAPED AGAINST THE DOORS and tapped at the windows. Those inside had done what they could by way of overturned tables, but the palace had never been made to withstand a siege. It showed, and all knew it. Zelen, doing what he could for wounds that didn't bleed but also appeared too dead ever to heal, fancied that he could hear the press of demons even over the moans and the weeping that filled the room.

He, Branwyn, and their recent allies weren't the only ones who'd rallied, though. Small groups stood at every possible entrance: guards with broken table legs, servants with long kitchen knives and platters, even one person who'd tied their sash around a heavy crystal vase and was swinging the result idly as they guarded their window. Near every two or three of the armed sentries stood one other. They held no weapons, but Zelen recognized a few and knew they were wizards.

Near the center of the room, Mezannith stood, draped in sunset-pink taffeta and carrying a jeweled sword. It was a relic from the portrait gallery, and neither the edge nor the balance was probably much to speak of—but Zelen had been fighting with a tree branch, so he was in no position to complain.

"You say you know these things?" she was asking Branwyn.

"Not socially, but yes. You might call them scavengers, bits of the darkness that were left over when Poram made the world. They're not very bright—they don't even properly exist as separate beings when they're not drawn here—or much sturdier than a human, but they don't feel much pain, and they can do a great deal of harm, as you've seen."

Zelen had seen them dancing earlier. With an artist's eye, he'd noticed the pleasant contrast between Mezannith's curls, still more pepper than salt, and the bright gold of Branwyn's hair. Now the pairing reminded him of patterns in temples: light and dark, fire and ice, air and earth, each deadly on its own and more so when balanced.

Either that or he was babbling to himself out of terror. He could believe it likely. "Fire?" Mezannith asked.

Branwyn shook her head. "They consume heat. Iron, silver, magic, or things that had life in them are good. Failing that, hit them hard enough and they'll leave the world—though I suppose that's true of most things, in a way."

"We could wait for the city guards, in that case," said Mezannith, tapping her fingers against the skirt of her gown, "but I'd just as soon not. Too much danger of the demons getting bored and seeking other prey, or of some poor soul wandering in unsuspecting. How many did you leave out there?"

"Five was my count, assuming they all converged on us. I'm reasonably certain we could handle them if we have that many to go out as a purely fighting force."

"Count magic in that number, and we certainly do. You and I should take point—"

The conversation turned into a discussion of tactics. Others entered into it—one of the nearby mages and the guard who had joined Zelen and Branwyn's party among them—but many of those in the ballroom simply stood well away and gawked. Branwyn was the center of their attention, and that held as much fear as it did admiration.

"...Criwathi woman," said someone, only slightly hushed and more than a shade accusatory. "Made no secret of being a soldier, but..."

Zelen didn't search for the speaker. No response on his part would help Branwyn's cause. He had other matters at hand.

He tied the last knot in a tablecloth-turned-bandage, then checked his patient's heartbeat. It was steady enough. They'd probably live, though their arm would always be missing a patch of flesh.

A mage who wasn't guarding doors or windows was holding some of the most badly injured in stasis until a Mourner could arrive and repair them. Her skin was paper white, and beads of sweat ran down her forehead to her cheeks.

Nobody moved to assist. By doing so, they might break her concentration, with horrible results. They, like Zelen, knew just enough to realize their own uselessness.

His skills had limits. He'd never fought hard enough for the path that would have lifted more of them.

"It's hardly how I'd hoped the evening would go," Branwyn said from behind him.

Zelen's heart responded *Branwyn* before his mind could focus on *Sentinel* and all the questions that raised. "I wanted to join the Dark Lady's service when I was younger, you know," he said, turning toward her. "As a Mourner, of course. Even then I was too frivolous for a Blade."

"I've never met a person outside the Blades who wasn't," said Branwyn. "What changed your mind?"

"My family wasn't having any of it. Bad form for a son of nobility to become a jumped-up undertaker, even a holy one," Zelen said. Years later, he could still remember his father's words, right down to every exasperated pause. "Makes it look like we don't have enough property to go 'round too."

"I wouldn't have thought of that, but then, I don't spend much time thinking about property."

Zelen nodded. Sentinels were taken from the ranks of the unwanted: the orphans, the foundlings, the bastards. Their training, from what stories he'd heard, also tended to be light on courtly graces and aristocratic customs. Branwyn, he assumed, had been given special instructions for…well, for whatever purpose drove her.

That was a subject he should probably inquire about, he knew. Gedomir would likely want him to, and perhaps rightly so. The woman had been keeping more secret than Zelen had suspected.

"If you'd taken the vows back then," Branwyn said with a little who-knows hitch of her shoulders, "you might not have been here tonight. That is, Mourners aren't specifically prohibited from dancing and so forth, but the ones I've met have had to be on duty at all hours, and they're usually dead tired when they're off. It's not a life that lends itself to balls—which is probably why we don't have any here now, damn the luck."

"Well. Yes," said Zelen, because she *was* right, from what he knew. A few of the younger Mourners had attended the ball, but they had, in fact, all gone back to the temple long before he and Branwyn had slipped out to the garden.

The guilt didn't vanish. That was always a part of him, only aching more or less at times. Branwyn's words pushed it back toward *less*, though. The circling *If I'd chosen differently, I'd have fixed this* ran into *Or not even known it happened until too late* and was shaken out of the pattern.

Branwyn pushed back a strand of hair, leaving a streak of dirt on her forehead. "I should explain…many things…" she said, uncertainty apparent for the first time since Zelen had met her, "and I should be more tactful about what comes next, but I'm tired and we're going to go deal with the rest of these creatures soon. And, as you now know, I'm not really a diplomat. Therefore"— she squared her shoulders, confidence returning as she went on— "your family sounds like vile people, the sort that make me glad I don't have relatives, and you have my sympathy. I think you turned out…splendidly…regardless."

Weariness and danger were as good as wine for breaking down her guard, but Branwyn knew she wouldn't regret speaking. Watching Zelen's face soften out of its expression of tight pain would have been worth it alone, even if she hadn't known she'd been the cause.

Whatever he thinks of me when he has a chance to rest, I've done him a bit of good now.

"I'm too weary to do the filial-spirit bit and protest," he said in return, "so I can only thank you. You're…going, you said?"

"A half dozen of us. You'd be an asset, but"—she surveyed the room—"if you'd do more good here, as a healer and a familiar face, say so. I'm inclined to trust your judgment either way."

"I'd rather…but I might be able to keep people calmer here, and if one of the demons slips past you all… No, I should stay." Zelen quirked a grin. "Besides, it's hardly as though you'll need protection, is it?"

"Or you," she said. They were too much in public for her to risk kissing him, but Branwyn squeezed his shoulder quickly. "Be careful, all the same. I'd like to see you again soon."

That was true, and not merely because she wanted to go to bed with him. It would have been easier if that had been the only reason. Branwyn headed out quickly. She wouldn't wait to hear if he echoed her sentiment, or to try to figure out whether he was only being polite if he did.

Those in the Order knew its reputation long before they chose whether or not to be reforged. Zelen struck her as an open-minded man, but the most open-minded of men had their unexpected blind spots.

And Branwyn had lied to him.

It had been in a good cause. She didn't regret it. Where other members of the court were concerned, she might have said, and meant, that she hadn't lied—she *was* a military envoy from Criwath—so much as left out certain information. Thinking of Zelen, thinking of herself, she couldn't wish she'd chosen otherwise, but she also couldn't couch it in terms other than *lied*.

Killing the remaining demons was brutal, clumsy, cold work. With five companions, all armed and focused on fighting, it wasn't particularly dangerous by Branwyn's standards, but the creatures were unpleasant to see, even for her, and a fight was a fight, demanding concentration. *Even a rat can get lucky* had been one of the first lessons she'd learned, and *Your enemy's luckiest when you're the most confident* another.

It still wasn't enough to take her mind off Zelen for long, not completely. In the thick of battle, her vision narrowed, but once the demon shattered and vanished, Branwyn wound up wondering whether Zelen was all right back at the palace, recalling how his hands had felt in those moments behind the statue, or wondering whether that evening had ruined any chance for another such encounter.

She slammed her branch into the final demon's head with perhaps unnecessary force and found little satisfaction in its death. It would only dissipate, returning to unconscious scraps of creation from a "life" it had never sought and perhaps didn't welcome, unaware of the trouble it had caused.

"The problem is," said Branwyn when they stood surveying the aftermath, "as I said, these things don't exist unless they're drawn to our world."

"How do you know?" asked a palace guard who'd come with them. "Made a study of demons, have you?"

Darya would have responded sharply. Emeth would likely have punched the man. The Adeptas, and Olwin, had sent Branwyn for more than one reason. She reminded herself of that and replied calmly, with another of the half-truths she could comfortably tell everybody but Zelen. "We thought it might be useful, when preparing for war, to know what it might draw, or what our enemy might summon."

"Masses of people?" Mezannith asked. "We've had these festivals every year, though, and never with this result. As far as I know, there's no stack of corpses nearby either."

"Life does it as well as death, once they're here."

"Ah," said a third of their companions, who'd been out in the gardens when the demons attacked. He coughed. "Well."

"Once they're here?" Mezannith picked up on the crucial point.

"It's very rare for them to come through naturally. When they do, it's usually because there's been enough death or life in one place, at one time. I doubt this qualifies."

"So this was deliberate?" The general's question was swift and intense.

Branwyn wished she had a more certain answer. "Probably in part."

"Give me the least troubling option first."

"Badly done magic makes the world weaker," said the wizard with them, a pale-haired youth, either uncertain of themselves or of speaking up. They gulped and went on when Mezannith jerked her chin at them impatiently. "Maybe an apprentice tried a thing they didn't ought to have."

"Right," said Branwyn. She'd been called out to handle one of those incidents. It had ended even worse for the wizard in question than it had done for those around her, and that was saying a great deal. "Nastier spells bring them forward too, even when cast properly, and those who cast them generally don't care. And specifically, if somebody summons a large demon, the small ones can slip through behind it."

The mage winced. "So—"

"It's possible that there's a major demon roaming Heliodar, yes." Mezannith gave Branwyn a hard bit of scrutiny. "Should I hold out hope, Madam Alanive, that one day you'll bring us a piece or five of cheerful news?"

"The world is large," said Branwyn, "and life hard to predict, and hope is always valuable."

"No, then."

"No, not really."

Chapter 19

"You've done well here," said the Mourner, magic glowing reddish-orange as her chair lifted her up and away from her final patient, the young mage who'd spent so much of her strength stopping time for the worst of the wounded. Now the badly injured lay, asleep but stable, on makeshift beds, and the wizard was slowly sipping a goblet of heated, watered wine.

City guards, wearing more severe uniforms and carrying less ornamental swords than the ones who'd been at the palace, checked the gardens. A Blade went with them, vast in their black clothing, and a knight in polished armor.

Zelen couldn't feel glad about it; he didn't have the strength to feel much except a dull relief. The night was over. Nobody had died.

Nobody in the ballroom had died, he corrected himself, and that did spur him to approach the Mourner. "Pardon, but do you know if the people who left here are all safe?"

"The people who left here?" She raised coppery eyebrows.

"The ones who went to get help, I mean. I don't think any of us bolted for it."

The correction helped. "I would hope not. I didn't witness the rescue party myself, but this is the only place where the temple has received an unexpected summons tonight. I expect, if any of them *had* been badly injured, we would've known of that before I was sent here."

"Thank you," said Zelen.

It had been foolish to worry, he thought. Branwyn would

naturally be all right. Sentinels were more than human, weapons of the gods. If the stories were right, they were practically unkillable—though the stories had never really mentioned what happened when they didn't have soulswords, and "practically" wasn't "entirely."

Still: Branwyn was all right, and he'd been an idiot to worry. He suspected he'd been an idiot about quite a bit.

He watched the Mourner turn her chair, skimming across the floor as if she were sailing a boat over a very smooth lake, and move off. All of it seemed a long way away.

"Here," said a youth in undyed robes, one of the Mourner's apprentices. They pushed a goblet into one of Zelen's hands and a slice of bread into the other. "Sit down, eat, and drink. Just because the demons didn't get you doesn't mean the evening didn't leave a mark."

Zelen managed a smile. "I've said the same thing myself a few times. Or similar. Without the demons."

"Then you know it's true," said the apprentice, and disappeared into the crowd again.

The stairs were empty. Zelen sat on them and obeyed orders. The wine was good—not high-quality, but well-spiced—and combined with a few bites of bread, it took away a bit of the numbness.

He'd expected the evening to go differently. He'd very much *wanted* it to go differently. But it could have been worse.

The voices around him merged into a soothing, low hubbub. Zelen closed his eyes. Soon, once the wounded had been moved to more comfortable surroundings, he'd get up and seek his home. A bath would be good if he could stay awake long enough—the demons' nature meant that he hadn't gotten bloody, though he was conscious of dirt now, and sweat—but otherwise he'd fall gratefully into his own bed.

Talking with Branwyn would have to come soon. He'd go to the Rognozis' house in the morning, or whenever he woke, and seek a private meeting, and not only to discuss her identity. Perhaps her mission was really no more than she'd said, and she'd only kept her true nature silent because she didn't want it to be a distraction.

If the person behind the assassins had known they were targeting a Sentinel, did that make matters worse? Zelen wasn't sure, but he could hardly see how it would improve the situation.

The bread was almost gone, the goblet nearly empty. Most of the unwounded guests, save the guards and those with some experience at healing, had left the palace. Word of the night would spread quickly—hells, half the city likely knew by now—and there'd probably be no few guesses about Branwyn's involvement, since she was an outsider as well as the one who'd known how to fight the demons. Zelen might not be the only one to work out the truth.

The truth was probably the precise sort of thing Gedomir had asked him to watch for.

Zelen was too tired to think much about that.

He would figure out what to tell his brother after he spoke with Branwyn.

At twenty, that change in loyalties would have bothered him more. Twenty was many years gone.

———————

Branwyn wasn't sure when the Rognozis' house had started to feel comfortably familiar rather than intimidating and alien, but she suspected that the aftermath of two attempts on her life had something to do with it. It also contained a bed, which was a significant asset then.

One of the guards, not the one who'd asked how she knew about demons, had offered to walk her home, but she'd declined. In the very unlikely event that another crew of assassins came after her, she didn't want to get another civilian harmed, least of all one of Heliodar's guards. She was reasonably sure that would be a diplomatic incident of some sort.

Thus, she dragged herself up the stairs alone and fumbled for the key Lady Rognozi had given her earlier that evening. "There's no reason to keep the butler up late on a festival night," she'd said, "and we certainly don't want to make a young woman like you keep our early hours." She hadn't quite winked.

Branwyn cracked the door, slipped inside—and stopped.

At the bottom of her vision, the floor had looked out of place, an inch lower than it should have been. Branwyn blinked, and it was normal again.

Carefully, she closed the door, and the sound of it shutting echoed many times and too lightly. *Clack* became *click-tick-tickticktick*. Then that, too, was gone. The hallway was silent. The mirrors showed the dark shapes of shadows and her own form, wavering and unclear—but that might have just been mirrors, particularly those made more for ornament than accuracy.

The rest? It had been a long night, and she'd been fighting demons. Viewing them took a toll, even for her. They were not supposed to be in the world, and even reforged vision could only cope so much with their presence. Aftereffects might well have started to show up, in which case the cure would be a good night's sleep.

Her shoes slid over the wood with serpentine sounds when she walked, and the skirts of her gown rustled. The material of both was unfamiliar, and the hall far quieter than usual. That might have been all.

There could be a major demon roaming the city. She'd said as much herself.

Weariness or warning? Branwyn didn't bother trying to decide. Overthinking would be of no use at all. If her exhaustion was leading her astray, she'd feel foolish, but not for the first time, and she'd always survived before.

She didn't bother picking up her skirts either. The night had given her plenty of experience moving with them at their full length, and she wanted to keep her hands free. Crossing the dark hallway quickly, she aimed herself like an arrow for the stairs, her room, and Yathana.

Part II

Call: What is justice?
Answer: *A shield for those in peril. A wind that sweeps away deception. A sword against those who choose evil.*

Call: What are its tools?
Answer: *Patience, forswearing judgment until all is known. Proportion, that retribution may balance misdeed. Protection: above all else, to guard the weak against the strong.*

—Litany of Tinival's Knights

The mistake here is thinking that affection and preservation are one. Gizath once ruled over those forces that tie the world together. He does still, in many senses. Hate is as much a tie as love. In sparing Heliodar from the worst of the general destruction, I don't necessarily suggest that Thyran acted out of fondness for the place. He may have had a far worse fate in mind for it.

—Gwyrn of the Red Tower, at the Midsummer Debates

Chapter 20

"Lord Gedomir's here to see you, sir," said Idriel.

Zelen tried to open his eyes, made it about halfway, and muttered a curse. "Later." The bed was warm. His muscles ached. He saw no need to be conscious a minute sooner than he had to. Without any idea what hour it was, he knew nonetheless that it was too damned early.

"My apologies, sir," the valet said, "but he's most insistent about it. He says it's urgent, and I'm afraid I couldn't prevent him from entering."

That was a polite way to say *I can't have the footmen throw the heir of Verengir out on the street as though he were a dishonest peddler.* On that particular morning, Zelen would have loved to disagree, but thoughts of the clinic and of family surfaced before he could actually move his mouth enough to do so.

He managed to lift his eyelids on the second attempt. By the light that escaped his drapes, it was midmorning. "Show the plague in, by all means," he said. "And bring some very strong tea, please."

"Very good, sir," said Idriel, and vanished. He'd known Zelen too long to suggest that his employer try to dress before receiving that particular company, or even that he get out of bed.

If Gedomir wanted to invade Zelen's house, he could take Zelen as he was.

He stepped through the door just as Zelen sat up. "You won't have heard the news, naturally," said their father's heir, looking disdainfully over Zelen's tousled hair and bare chest. "It's only fortunate that I find you without…external company."

"Fortunate for you, me, and the hypothetical lady. The general rule for gossip, by the way, is that one issues an invitation. And generally provides wine. Cakes are—"

"Lord Rognozi and his wife are dead."

The words made no sense for a second. Then they took Zelen's breath away as thoroughly as any of his mother's lectures or the beatings his father had ordered. Gedo wasn't putting in nearly as much effort as had gone into the other incidents: he was either very talented or very fortunate.

"When? How?"

It would have been unsurprising for Lord Rognozi to have perished quite naturally and uneventfully, and dimly possible that his wife might not have survived the shock and sorrow of it, though it would've run counter to what Zelen knew of the lady. That wouldn't have brought Gedomir to his bedroom.

"Murdered. Butchered, in fact, late last night. If you want the more sordid details, I'm afraid I didn't ask for an anatomical report. I'm given to understand that the servant who found them is in a state of shock." He smoothed an imaginary strand of impeccable hair back from his brow. "And your…envoy…has vanished. As has her very large, very likely magical sword."

"She'd *never*—"

Zelen lunged forward, with no notion of what the motion might achieve. Denial simply demanded action.

As he'd so frequently done in their past, Gedomir smiled with lofty derision, not to mention a share of pity. "She *has*, I'm afraid. You're welcome to try and convince me that a burglar broke into one of the best-warded noble houses in the city and did nothing but slaughter the inhabitants, or that a servant with years of service suddenly went unstoppably berserk in a manner that didn't rouse the attention of the others in their quarters."

Colors faded from the world. Zelen sat silently and Gedomir fell silent as well as Idriel stepped in, carrying a tray of tea and cakes. He put it down in front of Zelen and glanced between him and Gedomir: *Shall I pretend you have another engagement?*

Zelen shook his head. Even that motion took an almost unsupportable amount of strength. "Thank you, Idriel, that will be all," he said by rote.

"Very good, sir."

"It may not be entirely her fault, granted," Gedomir said. "I can perceive no motive for the action, regardless of what others may think, given what you've told me of her nature. The Criwath court, or even subversive agents there that Olwin knows nothing of, may have placed a spell on her for this purpose. Or her experiences in the war may have caused damage that hid until now."

"*If* she did it," Zelen said, "I'm certain that it wasn't of her own will."

"I'm certain that you're certain. And Father and I are prepared to take that into account," Gedomir said, spreading his hands. The ring with Verengir's crest, his only ornament, gleamed in the pale light of the autumn morning. "Honestly, the information she can provide is more valuable than any vengeance would be—the Dark Lady can wait on her claim. Father thinks the rest of the council might even see a case for clemency, if the circumstances are right."

"Does he?"

"Would I speak falsely?" Gedomir's lips tightened, but then he relaxed. "I understand that you're…biased, but for once your proclivities may have been useful. There's clearly more here than simple murder. Father and I are prepared to investigate it and to argue as much in the face of all opposition—once you retrieve the woman, of course."

———

There was rock under her cheek and blood in her mouth. Her arms were sticky—probably more blood—and a net of pain wrapped her whole body, fiercest around her right knee and her left eye. Branwyn was fairly sure her nose was broken too.

All of that was comparatively minor. She'd been injured more severely in the past, though not often, and the healing of a Sentinel was already doing its work, pulling bones and muscles back into place. Even the knee, which would likely have crippled a normal person for life, would give her only a few days of trouble. Branwyn knew as much, and none of her wounds troubled her.

She had no room in her mind to worry about them anyhow. As consciousness returned, she searched her memory for the fight that must have taken place and found only blankness, then paralyzing fear.

After the ball, she'd felt uneasy about the Rognozis' house. She'd gone to get Yathana. From that moment, she remembered nothing concrete: she had a dim recollection of the world spinning, of a sword in her grip and the smell of blood and death, but that was all.

Now she was—her eyes focused, one considerably slower than the other—in an alley, in the early morning, wearing the blood-soaked remains of her ball gown.

Yathana was gone.

Her memory had an enormous hole.

There was blood on her arms, up to the elbows, and she couldn't feel any cuts there.

What happened? was her third question.

Where's Yathana? came in second.

The first was *What did I do?*

―――――――――――

"We do have guards," Zelen pointed out. "The city and the house. They're trained for this."

"They're trained to subdue drunks and disrupt fights, and they have a good deal of that to contend with already. They also know much less about Madam Alanive—or whatever her name truly is—than you do." Gedomir paused, which told Zelen nothing good was going to follow. "What they do know is that she's likely a murderess. Their duties are much simpler than ours. It's not likely that they'll try to get to the bottom of the incident. Were I the gambling sort, I'd wager that they'd stick her full of crossbow bolts, dump the corpse at the burning grounds, and congratulate themselves on a job well done."

The image painted itself across Zelen's mind with scorching clarity.

Next he thought of the knights, but didn't even try to bring that option up with Gedomir. Tinival's servants would be very thorough, but they too had other duties, and little or no experience of political intrigue. Branwyn was dangerous, particularly armed, and they knew that.

If her actions were due to insanity or magical control—or, he forced himself to speculate, if she had genuinely murdered the Rognozis out of her own free will—she was very likely to fight. She would probably kill a few of her opponents, and at that point if no other, they would certainly and justifiably turn to lethal force.

Carefully, so he didn't disturb the tray whose presence was still an alien weight in his lap, Zelen sat back against the pillows. Gedomir observed with his arms crossed over his chest, impassive and tolerant. "I can't make any promises," Zelen said to him.

"We would expect none. You failed to probe deeply enough past her facade to predict this, after all—the house is aware that your knowledge is far from complete."

Zelen wanted to have a bitter, flippant riposte, or at least not to flush like a lectured schoolboy. He failed at both.

He did manage to keep meeting Gedomir's gaze, which grew regretful. "That, however, was at least partly our fault," said Gedomir. "We asked too much of you, particularly considering the situation in question. You have my apologies, and I'm confident that I can extend Father's as well."

"There was no sign of any of this," Zelen managed, "and what could I have asked? If it was a geas—"

"No, no," said Gedomir, "I quite understand. And if you don't succeed at this, then I don't doubt there will be very good reasons for it. Only do your best, for the family's sake and the city's. And the woman's, too, of course."

"Of course."

"If you require assistance, send a message to the estate. You have the full support of Verengir in this." Gedomir bowed. "I wish you luck, Brother."

"Thank you," Zelen said, and even kept from gritting his teeth.

Chapter 21

THE WORLD AND NECESSITY BOTH BROKE DOWN IN BRANWYN'S state, becoming a series of very small observations and steps that weren't much larger. It was part instinct, part training; it let her push aside panic and manage events. Questions of Yathana's whereabouts, of her memory, of her potential actions all faded, becoming the stones her more urgent thoughts walked on, there but unnoticed.

First step: Assess the damage. Pain had done a large portion of that job for her, but Branwyn went back over the situation with more attention to detail as well as the future. She wasn't dying. She didn't need help to avoid dying. That situation wouldn't change if she tried to move.

Second step: Assess the circumstances.

Branwyn slowly surveyed the alley. She'd never been in a pleasant or a scenic alley, and this one was no exception. It smelled—even through her probably broken nose—like garbage, heaps of which lay against the walls behind her. A pool of what she would have liked to believe was water, but probably wasn't, lay a few inches from her face. Beyond that, the remains of barrels and a spectacularly broken table had probably shielded her from discovery.

It wasn't a bad temporary hiding spot, but it wasn't exactly good for recovery, and it wouldn't last forever.

The temples, the guards, and the council itself were all out. If—Branwyn braced herself and met the worst possibility head-on—if she'd actually committed some manner of unspeakable crime, she'd throw herself on Tinival's mercy and then likely on the Order's, which didn't really exist. But if she was innocent, she had no way to prove that. Without memory, whatever she said to Tinival's knights would only be an opinion, with no weight toward truth or lies.

A person with wealth and, likely, power had sent the assassins. If that person was responsible for her current state, turning herself over to the authorities might be the worst path Branwyn could take—not just for herself, but for the city and possibly the world.

"Tinival's balls, you look bad," said a high voice. "You need a healer?"

It was a measure of Branwyn's injuries that she hadn't heard footsteps, though the new arrival didn't have much weight to make noise regardless. A child, one arm in a sling and a cast, eyed her from a gap between the barrels.

"No," Branwyn rasped, which gave her more information: attempted strangling had been part of her evening. She tried to clear her throat, winced, failed, and went on. "Thank you."

The child didn't leave. "What happened?"

"I'm not sure."

"Ah." The child looked to be in the ambiguous stage that came after toddlerhood and before apprenticeship. They showed no trace of shock or more than idle curiosity. "Drinking, huh?"

"Not precisely." The pressure on Branwyn's side was becoming too much. She pushed herself cautiously upward.

"Hey!" said the child, poking their head further through the gap. "You go around with the healer from the clinic, don't you?"

"Hunh?"

"Zelen, at the clinic with the squidface. My cousin dances down at the theater, before the shows and all, and she says she saw you two there. You want me to get *him*? You look like a house fell on you."

"No!" said Branwyn, so quickly that the child darted backward but didn't run. "No, thank you. This is…" She pulled her thoughts together, breaking midway to spit blood. "You should go. It's dangerous to be around me."

"Everything's dangerous," said the child, who glanced down and kicked a rock, but didn't flee. "Bet you couldn't get to me before I could run."

"I'm not the danger," said Branwyn, and hoped that she was right, or that the child was.

The child peered behind them warily, then around. "You running from the law?" They returned to the gap in the barrels, their voice lowered. "I know a place you can hide."

"Not just the law," said Branwyn. "Ruthless people." By shifting her weight carefully to her good leg and putting a hand on the wall, she was able to claw her way up to a standing position. She stood there briefly, panting.

"What's 'ruthless'?"

"It's—" She thought, which was not the easiest task in her current state. "People who don't care who they hurt if it gets them what they want. Or what they think is best," she added, not wanting to define the word too narrowly to include herself.

"Huh," said the child. "You want me to show you that place?"

Branwyn's head swam. Were she the only one at stake, she would've refused—or so she liked to think—but her death or captivity would likely mean her would-be killer went unhindered. That in turn had a decent chance of endangering the world, which included Heliodar and the child waiting for an answer.

"Please," she said.

"All right," said the child. "Wait here. I'll be back as soon as I can get you a cloak. Maybe you shouldn't have stood up."

"No," said Branwyn, leaning against a wall, "no, it's better I get used to it now."

She watched her would-be rescuer depart and thought the thing she hadn't said: that if the child brought back lawmen rather than a garment, she'd need to be on her feet. It wouldn't do her very much good, but at times like that, the principle counted. It was really the only thing she had left.

"You've…heard, m'lord?" said the Rognozis' butler, looking more mortal and less certain than Zelen had ever seen him.

"I have. My deepest sympathies." Zelen eyed the half-open doors with no great enthusiasm. "I've come to see if I might be able to find out more than the guard," he went on. "Different perspective, you know."

The butler nodded. "If you can help find that…woman," he said, clearly longing to finish on an obscenity but brought up short by his training, even in such circumstances, "then gods bless you."

The house was a strange shell of a place. Zelen's footsteps didn't echo, but he felt as though they should have. "Are you expecting…" he started, and then hesitated, consulting a mental chart to try and remember the Rognozis' heir. Their marriage hadn't produced children, he knew that much.

"His lordship's niece," said the butler. "Within a matter of days. Certainly she'll be here for the burning."

"Yes," said Zelen, a memory coming back to him. Marior: a short, dark woman, fond of horses. He'd seen her off and on, but they'd never talked much. She seemed an unlikely choice to secretly be the actual murderer, even were he grasping at straws.

He couldn't allow himself to do so.

The floor was gleaming. "You've cleaned up the tracks, I'm sure."

"There weren't any, m'lord," said the butler. "It's quite likely the creature went out the window after committing her…deeds…or simply took great care to clean her boots."

Either was possible: Branwyn was careful, and a Sentinel could manage the climb from a second-floor window easily, particularly when there were trees outside. "I don't want to keep you," said Zelen.

"No, no, but—well, I'd as soon not see it again, m'lord, if it's all the same to you. We'll clean the bedchambers out properly tomorrow, and we've gotten the…the worst of it away, but otherwise we've kept things as they were. *Her* room included. It's the second door on the right, upstairs. My lord's was at the end of the hall, my lady's next to him."

"Much obliged," said Zelen, and began his trek through the house.

Branwyn's room was neatly arranged, the bedclothes smoothed, all curtains and chests closed. Nothing there gave any sign of a murderous rampage or indeed of any other use. Zelen found clothing, two pairs of boots, and three books: *The Triumphs of Aeliona*, a small volume of poems about the seasons from a Criwathi-sounding name he didn't recognize, and a philosophical treatise that he did, albeit from many years ago.

The belongings spoke of an active mind and a woman who traveled light, who never really settled in any one place—but Zelen had known as much already. He searched the boots for concealed keys or knives or messages, but discovered only leather.

One of the maids was watching him. "Sorry," said Zelen, "but nobody found a ball gown in here, did they?"

"No, m'lord."

"No. She's likely still wearing it, then. Or was." That argued, strongly, for the theories Gedomir had suggested and Zelen wanted to believe—or at any rate against cold-blooded, deliberate murder. Nobody, much less a warrior, would of her own volition go kill people in a floor-length gown, then climb out a window to get away, not when she had plenty of time to change clothing. "What about a sword?"

The maid shook her head. "Must've taken it with her."

"Yes, just so," said Zelen absently.

She'd gone to the trouble of getting her sword but not of changing her clothing.

Nobody would have needed a sword, let alone a mystical one, to kill the Rognozis. Branwyn could have done it barehanded. Half the servants probably could've managed as much.

Barehanded murder would probably have been considerably less brutal than what had happened. The servants had, as the butler said, done their best to remove the worst remnants of the crime, but a certain sense of events was still very, very obvious from the Rognozis' chambers.

The human body held a great deal of blood. In Lady Rognozi's room, the stain spread not only across the floor near the threshold but up the walls as well. One small, distinct handprint stood out from the rest, clear against the gold-figured paper.

In Lord Rognozi's room, the gore was more contained: a darkness that spread over the sides of the bed and trailed in rivulets down to the floor.

Zelen closed his eyes there and braced himself against the doorframe. He'd seen people die, yes, and blood itself had long ceased to unnerve him, but this was too close to showing the exact circumstances of their deaths, their helplessness and terror.

They'd been his friends.

His heart was hot iron, shrieking on the anvil. If Branwyn had done this—if Branwyn had been forced to it—if she hadn't—

None of that means a thing, he told himself in the cold inflections that were the closest he could come to his mother's rebukes. *Your duty is to evaluate the situation as it is, not as it might be. That's the whole of your responsibility just now.*

He forced himself to make a closer inspection.

The mattress where Lord Rognozi had lain and died was soaked with blood and torn in several places, and the hangings on one side of the bed had been shredded, but nothing else in the room was damaged.

Lady Rognozi's room was a very different story. Many of the small glass windowpanes had been shattered. So had the iron bars of the frames, in several places. The mirror on the dressing table lay in shards, and the table itself had practically been cleaved in half. Her bed-curtains had suffered as well, though not so badly as her lord's—a few wide cuts, as if in passing.

Most notably of all, the wall on one side of the room had a great hole in it. Zelen could look, carefully, past splinters half a foot long and into the study on the other side.

There was no blood there, he noticed, nor any near the window. And while the broken part of the window was large enough for someone Branwyn's size to crawl through, the edges were treacherous with broken glass and metal.

If the legends were true, a Sentinel might have had ways of getting through unharmed or might simply not care.

Nothing in any of the rooms provided a clue as to where Branwyn might have gone—and the more Zelen found out, the less sure he was of what had actually happened.

Chapter 22

WALKING WAS A TRULY HELLISH EXPERIENCE. NOT ONLY DID every part of Branwyn hurt, but the cloak that the child had brought her was barely large enough to provide any concealment. She had to walk bent over, which didn't help her spine at all—although it did let her lean on the child more easily, which, to her embarrassment, she had to do often.

"You sure you don't need a healer?" they asked, after they'd tugged Branwyn off the wall and put their good shoulder under her arm. "You don't have bones sticking into your organs?"

"No," she said, "thank you." A few staggering steps later, it occurred to her to ask, "How do you know that can happen?"

"I listen to things."

Evidently they also watched, and watched well. Their path didn't take them through any main street, but rather into a maze of narrow, twisting alleys where buildings cast shadows even in the morning light.

The smell of salt water mingled with that of garbage, meat, and human refuse. They were near the docks, Branwyn suspected, and likely a tannery or two. She couldn't narrow the location down any further. At times, particularly after a misstep jolted her or the light got in her eyes despite the cloak's hood, she barely knew where she was even as far as "the back streets of Heliodar."

"Here," the child eventually said, and Branwyn looked up, dazed, at the blackened wreck of a building. "Caught fire a while back. Nobody's going to go in there now. It hasn't fallen down yet, though."

"Yes," said Branwyn, realizing the child had mistaken her confusion for reluctance. "That…good idea. Thank you."

She grabbed the doorway and pulled herself in. Beneath the mostly intact roof, the world was mercifully dark, and while the floorboards were bare and hard, at least they weren't wet. She focused on a corner out of sight of doors or windows and staggered in that direction, holding onto the wall for balance.

"I'm going to go now," said the child once Branwyn had managed to lower herself to the floor. "Mam will be worrying."

"That's wise," Branwyn said, rasping out the words. Now that she was sitting again, she had enough strength to explain more. "You should stay away. Whoever did this…" Her voice, which had been sliding away toward a whisper, gave out. She gulped and tried again. "Might want to hurt people who help me. And their families. I'll be all right. I heal fast."

"You'd better," said the child. "That must've been some fight."

They didn't bother saying goodbye or reacting to Branwyn's warning. Or maybe they did: Branwyn thought she only closed her eyes for a moment, but when she opened them again, she was alone in the abandoned house. There was still some light outside, but between her vision and the shadows around the building, she couldn't tell how much or how long she'd been unconscious.

She still hurt, which was no surprise at all.

Slowly, she grasped what remained of her skirt and ripped off a wide piece of silk, then pulled the remains up to bare her right leg. The knee was monstrously swollen and livid purple. Touching it, even gently, nearly made her scream, and she battled to keep from vomiting, which would only increase her pain.

Probably broken, Branwyn said to herself when she could manage words again. She bit her lip, squinted with her good eye to compensate for her bad one, and began to wrap the silk around the joint as tightly as she could bear.

Zelen would have done it better, she thought, for many reasons.

She tried not to wish him there. As she'd told the child, it was too dangerous. The reforging meant that his skills as a healer, while useful, weren't vital, and the comfort of his presence wasn't worth risking his neck. Branwyn had spent most of her life alone. Another few nights wouldn't kill her.

It didn't occur to her to wonder if she'd fought him, or worse, until it occurred to her to wonder why that hadn't occurred to her. She froze then, and her vision went blurry.

No, don't panic, she told herself, speaking the way Yathana had done more than once in Branwyn's youth. Thinking of the sword made her throat close up, but she clung to the silent words anyhow. *Follow the lines of your thoughts. Why didn't you assume he was your enemy? Because you're fond of him?*

Yes, but it was more than that, and there was a point there, one more important than reassuring herself that Zelen likely still lived. Branwyn started wrapping her knee again, giving her body a task so that her mind could work.

That must have been some fight, the child had said.

Zelen was good in a fight, but he would have used a weapon. Branwyn could find no cuts or scratches: all of her wounds were from impact. She'd assumed, probably rightly, that she'd transformed.

There was no chance at all that Zelen could have caused that much damage to her metal form. No human could have managed it. Blows could bruise, and monsters had done more, but Branwyn had been kicked by a horse when she'd been metal, and it had done no more than leave a vast black-and-blue spot across her side for a few days.

If she hadn't transformed, her opponent hadn't fought with steel. Large men with blunt instruments might have managed her injuries, but in that case she would have changed. Even if she'd been out of her mind, Yathana would have done it for her: the power was actually the soulsword's.

Branwyn's wounds suggested that she *had* changed, that she'd been metal for a time and still been hurt almost too badly to move.

And that, in turn, suggested a foe far more fearsome than any she'd known Heliodar to contain.

She'd spoken of possibilities to Mezannith after the ball. Now the worst one of all struck her as quite likely.

―――――――――――

Murder or not, life went on in certain ways. The clinic was one. Zelen knew that Gedomir wouldn't have understood or approved. He hoped the Rognozis would have done both, and believed that the lady would at any rate.

They were dead. Nothing worse could happen to them. Others still lived, and it was important to make sure that they could keep doing so, especially while Zelen tried to find another path to follow toward Branwyn. He poulticed a woman's burned arm, cleaned and sewed a large gash on a man's cheek, and sent another woman to Letar's temple, as the rattle in her chest was beyond his power. It might well be beyond the Mourners', too, for disease was a tricky matter, but she was strong and otherwise healthy, which gave her a decent chance.

It was good to have that sort of work to do. Burns and cuts were straightforward. Illness was different, but even there he had a rough idea of its shape. There were no hidden agendas, no swift turns to yank his footing away when he'd assumed it was smooth.

Altien asked no questions. The work unrolled under Zelen's hands, putting a small amount of order back into the world. After he'd given a child spiced tea for a cold, he felt enough like himself to have a meal, or at least bread and cheese with a glass of wine.

Three bites in, he heard the outer door open. Altien was seeing to another patient, so Zelen put down the bread and cheese and poked his head around the corner of his office.

Tanya stood in front of the door, sling and cast considerably more grimy than they had been but still intact. Her good hand plucked restlessly at her skirt.

"Hello," Zelen said gently. "How's the arm?"

"All right. Um." She peered around the outer room, which was empty, and then behind her at the door.

"We can talk in my office, if it would help," said Zelen. That was all the invitation Tanya needed to dart inside.

"Um," she said again, once she'd shut the inner door securely behind her. "Did the woman from Criwath really kill the high lord and his lady? My sister's beau just came back from the tavern, and he said—"

"Nobody's certain." Zelen fought to keep his reply steady and gentle. "They are dead, sadly, and she's gone, but that's all that's known right now."

Tanya looked down at the carpet. "So she's a bad person?"

"We don't know that either"—and oh, it hurt to say, as did what followed. "If she did it, if she could control herself when she did it, and if she knew that she was killing helpless old people rather than monsters, then yes."

"You mean she might not have meant to do it or known she was doing it? Like a spell?"

"That's one possibility."

His heart was beating faster and his stomach had closed up again, but still Zelen sat calmly, not pressing the girl for answers. Carefully, he arranged the assortment of quills on his desk, then brushed imaginary debris off the surface.

"Can you follow me?" Tanya finally asked.

Chapter 23

"AH, DAMN IT TO THE LOWEST OF THE HELLS," THE SHAPE IN the corner said, in a croak that half resembled Branwyn's voice. "Child, I specifically told you not to tell him."

"Yeah?" Tanya tilted her chin up, shook off the reassuring hand Zelen tried to place on her shoulder, and riposted. "Well, you *didn't* tell me who you killed. So you're lucky I didn't go to the guard right away."

"You did well," said Zelen, not using Tanya's name in case Branwyn really was as bad as the worst possibilities. He stepped forward, ready to meet her wrath, lightly gripping his sword.

The shape shifted again and he knew he wouldn't need it. Even through the shadows, he could make out a broken nose and a swollen eye and could mark that every movement was bought with pain. And when Branwyn rasped a response, there was no anger in it, only bitterness. "Yes. With the information you have, doubtless I'd have made the same choice." She paused for a labored inhalation. "Who did I kill?"

"Lord and Lady Rognozi," said Zelen flatly, and waited for a response.

Her laughter, hoarse and cheerless, took him by surprise. As he stepped back, as Tanya let out an indignant and wordless noise, Branwyn found words. "Gods rest them, then. And gods help us all, because I'm not the one you have to worry about. You knew the Rognozis better than I did, Verengir—do you think they'd have fought back this hard? Against me?"

With that, she dragged herself into the dim light from the boarded window. Zelen forgot Tanya's presence and muttered an oath.

One entire side of Branwyn's face was swollen and purple-black, the skin scraped away in places. Her nose was indisputably broken, and one of her cheekbones might have been too. Dried blood covered much of her skin, so Zelen couldn't tell for certain, but he was fairly confident that her lips had been badly split. Above the ruin of her ball gown, huge black bruises spread down her neck and shoulders.

Someone, probably Branwyn herself, had wrapped pink silk roughly around one of her knees, but the fabric didn't disguise the swelling there or the joint's unnatural angle.

He rushed to her side. "Gods, don't move. What happened?"

"Don't know." Closer, Zelen could see bruises along her temple and her jaw. It took very little force to kill people with blows there. Branwyn was a Sentinel, of course, and that was said to help, but... Zelen dropped to his knees, immediately beginning a gentle investigation as Branwyn went on. "I got back after the ball. The house felt...off. I went for Yathana. Then I woke up in an alley. Your friend brought me here."

"Yathana?" asked Tanya, who'd remained where she was and was watching avidly. Zelen considered telling her to go home but suspected it'd do no good. "Who's that?"

Only brief hesitation betrayed what was likely Branwyn's silent profanity. "My sword," she said, outwardly casual. Her quick inhalation as Zelen touched her cheek was good camouflage too.

"You've got a fracture here," he said, retreating as far as he could into the abstract. "Not as bad as it could be. Your nose too."

"I'd thought as much." She lay still beneath his inspection, gathering strength for her next question. "The Rognozis...how did they die?"

"A blade," Zelen said carefully, mindful of Tanya. "Or blades."

"They say there was blood everywhere," Tanya added helpfully, "and Lady Rognozi was practically cut in half, an' the lord's head was just about clean off."

Zelen swallowed. He kept on with the task at hand, passing his fingers lightly over Branwyn's scalp. There were several sticky places, and one lump behind her right ear that made her wince.

"Stupid," she hissed, quickly shook her head, and then just as quickly cursed. "As was that. And I didn't mean either of you, but why would anybody use such force or be so obvious? They were practically beyond the Veil of Fire as it was."

"Hatred," said Zelen, "or madness. You may have been hit very hard right here."

"Most likely, but I won't fall over dead from it," she said, and although the bruises made it hard to tell, Zelen thought she gave him a significant look.

She had a mystical Sentinel sense of her own physique, then, or a mystical Sentinel assurance that she wouldn't die from a swollen brain. Either way, Zelen was glad of it, particularly as he'd have no way of telling how badly the blow had hurt her. He'd learned to be alert for bruised eyes and bleeding from the nose, but external forces had already given Branwyn both. As for lack of coordination, a broken knee was more than sufficient.

"So maybe you went crazy and did it, and now you don't remember it?" Tanya suggested. "Or you say you don't. That's what I'd say if I got mad and killed people."

"It's possible. I'd say my state argues against it, but...*nnnngh*"— she broke off as Zelen examined her knee—"I know the counter... *sssss*...the counterarguments too. I could have killed them and then...fallen down the stairs, or fought a troop of guards while making my escape."

"None of the guard have mentioned fighting a woman of your description, and I'm sure they would have," said Zelen. "Robbers, on the other hand, are possible. Either way, my family is inclined to believe that you weren't under your own control. I'll take you to Letar's temple, send word to them, and we can start—"

"No." She grasped Zelen's wrist. "It's not safe to tell anyone."

This was the part Branwyn had feared. She'd hoped to heal enough to walk and fight, then to find a disguise and start searching for clues to what had truly happened. In a day or so, she likely could have left the abandoned house, stolen clothing, and blended into the street. It would have been a start, and it wouldn't have put others in danger.

Now her mission and her life depended on convincing Zelen. She was in no condition to run or fight if she didn't get through to him—she wasn't in much condition to *talk*, which didn't help— and she'd likely be putting him in more danger whether or not he listened.

He and the child were both silent. Branwyn's vision was too hazy for her to read Zelen's expression. She went on. "Assassins, remember? The person who sent them had money." She stopped, got her bruised windpipe to work again, and kept going. "Power. Temple will make sure I don't die, then turn me over to the guard. Easy to bribe jailers to look the other way, send a thug with a knife. Or use the knife themselves."

"But the *priests*—" said the child.

"Are busy," said Zelen slowly. "If there were enough of them to take care of everybody in the city, there'd be no need of the clinic."

"Mortal too. Think I'm a killer. Know there's a system. Probably will trust it, unless the Dark Lady sends a vision." Branwyn smiled, which made her lips start bleeding again. "Wouldn't count on that. So…they follow rules. Like they should. Mostly."

"'He makes treachery of bonds, and bonds of treachery,'" Zelen quoted.

"Gizath?" Branwyn said, though she'd never heard the line.

"Yes. A poem by… It doesn't matter." He sat back. "Go home," he said to the child, "and don't mention this to a soul."

"She said it would be dangerous. If I talked."

"She's right. One way or another, this is nothing you should be part of." He turned and fished some coins out of his pockets. "But you did right to help her, and right to get me. Thank you."

"Thank *you*," said the child. They pocketed the coins quickly but didn't leave right away. "And I hope you didn't kill the high lord and lady, and I hope people don't kill either of you."

Then they darted off, or at least Branwyn didn't see their shape beyond Zelen's shoulder any longer.

"I don't want to leave you here until nightfall," said Zelen. Branwyn could read the consternation about him even when she could barely see straight. A portion, she knew, was his calling as a healer, a portion suspicion of what she might do, given the stories about Sentinels, and a third portion might be personal fondness, but Branwyn didn't want to make any assumptions. "But there's no damned way of moving you until then without standing out, and if I come back with supplies, I'm as likely to be followed as not."

"How long?"

"Five hours or so. Thank all the gods that it's autumn."

"Go," said Branwyn. "I'll be all right. And I won't be in any state to escape. You can bind me if you want."

"No!" He actually drew back at the idea, a supple motion she'd have appreciated more if she hadn't been a bloody mess. "With your knee as it is?"

"It'll heal. And you have no reason to take my word."

"The offer is a fair reason," he said. Then he took off his cloak. Bronze gleamed from his torso in the weak light, and Branwyn noticed the embroidery on his doublet as he leaned over to slip the folded wool under her head. "I'd give you more, but the aim is not to attract attention, and a shirtless man near winter would do plenty of that."

"Wouldn't ask for more," Branwyn said. She felt a dim urge

to object even to the cloak, but her sore head overruled pride. "Thanks."

"Don't move more than you have to," said Zelen, "and for the sake of…everything…don't die."

Chapter 24

BRANWYN DIDN'T DIE, THOUGH THERE WERE INTERVALS throughout the next few hours when it would have seemed like a reasonable option, if not for her mission, her larger duty as a Sentinel, and, surprisingly, the knowledge of how shaken Zelen would be if she did.

She slipped in and out of consciousness. Out was better, far better, but the pain kept waking her up. She fought back screams at those times, aware enough of her surroundings to hold back, and stared mindlessly at the ceiling, practically unable to breathe from the agony. Pain that severe meant she was healing, she knew: life was returning to the broken parts of her. The knowledge was no comfort. She endured in a white haze until exhaustion took over and she passed out again.

The Forging had hurt, maybe even as much, but that had been in a clean, shining room, with the Adept to help with the worst of the pain and Sentinels-in-training bathing her brow with cool cloths. She'd been able to scream when she needed to.

Now all the world was pain and filth and the smell of her own dried blood. And the Rognozis', possibly.

She'd been an honored candidate during the Forging, a weapon-to-be against the darkness, not a possible murderer. That had been different too.

And there'd been Yathana at the end. Branwyn hadn't known the soulsword, then, of course. She hadn't known what she was missing.

Nobody had ever been able to destroy the blades or the spirits in them.

That didn't mean nobody could figure it out.

Branwyn would have wept, but she couldn't manage tears, and she was already taking the kind of gasping breaths that went with sobbing when she tried not to scream. The ceiling swam in front of her, faded to blackness, appeared again, and vanished in turn.

Eventually, it was no longer duty or consideration keeping her alive, only her inability to act. Ending her life was not even a question. The magic of her reforging would heal her as long as she did nothing drastic, and she couldn't have moved enough to manage that. She became pain itself, pain and shapes and light that slowly faded.

"Poram's blood, Branwyn."

Zelen was her fourth or fifth thought. First she had to recall concepts like words and voices and other people—like herself as a person, separate from pain.

Slowly his features became clearer. So did the worry.

"No," Branwyn choked out. "Mostly mine."

How badly off was she? Zelen had seen people die. She wasn't dying; she knew that much. She'd never thought to ask what it looked like when she healed. Perhaps it was disgusting beyond measure.

His expression softened when she spoke, and Branwyn read relief there. Her vision was getting better. "Do you know who I am?"

"Zelen."

Relief grew stronger. Then he was holding something cool and metallic against her mouth. "Drink. Slowly."

She recognized the strong, pine-sap taste of dragon-eye syrup, and the knowledge itself made the pain seem fainter—a little. It didn't take the edge off, but that edge wasn't rusty and jagged any longer.

Zelen removed the flask after a while. His face disappeared, and she felt his touch on her ankle.

"You were bloody far away when I came in," he said from the vicinity of her feet. "I'm afraid this will hurt, but try and stay with me."

New pain swept over her leg when Zelen lifted it. Branwyn went rigid to contain her scream. Her hands clawed at the stone beneath her, which didn't help, as they hurt too, but then her leg was straight and resting on a board. As the fresh pain ebbed, she recognized that this was a better state of affairs. There was pressure around her ankle, then her thigh, as Zelen bound board and leg together. The immobility was soothing.

"Still here," she whispered when she could talk again.

"Good. Good."

The darkness beyond him spoke in cultured tones and a voice like rustling leaves. "The horses are standing, and I'm ready to assist."

"Wha—" Branwyn said. The syrup was starting to take effect in earnest, and she wouldn't have had the strength to be alarmed anyhow, but confusion was entirely possible. She blinked at the darkness. It became one of the waterfolk, who regarded her dispassionately out of amber eyes and folded supple legs to kneel down by her feet.

"A friend," said Zelen, moving to her head. He slid his palms under her shoulders. "He's not wealthy or noble—not as the council sees it—and I trust him with my life."

"Oh," said Branwyn. That would have to be good enough for her. Perhaps it was the painkiller or her injuries, but she had no difficulty convincing herself that it was. The waterman's touch was soft on her good ankle. His hands had fur like a rabbit's.

She didn't see the signal that passed between Zelen and his companion, nor did they speak. Branwyn was on the ground, and then she wasn't. The world was moving.

Outside was dark. For a little while it was cold. Then they lifted her again. She heard horses, shifting their weight and snorting, and she was passed onto the seat of a large carriage. Zelen knelt beside her, one hand at her shoulder and one on her thigh.

Branwyn didn't look at his face. It would be just as painful to find faith in her there, when she herself didn't know if she deserved it.

The world had developed fuzzy edges and was fading fast away from her.

That was all right. That was good. As the carriage started to move, she let her consciousness go with it, rolling like a small boat on large waves.

———————

When Branwyn's eyelids closed and her breathing faded into the deep steadiness of drugged sleep, Zelen muttered quick prayers of thanks to all the gods: Letar for the healing, Sitha for the craft of the syrup, and Poram for the plants that had gone into it. Neither justice nor battle seemed terribly relevant, but he thanked Tinival regardless—best to leave nobody out, and the words kept him busy.

Branwyn's sleep would spare them both. She wouldn't feel the drive—Altiensarn was careful, but the streets were never perfectly smooth, particularly not in the slums where Branwyn had been hiding, and they included a number of sharp turns. For Zelen's part, he wouldn't be tempted to ask her questions that he knew she couldn't answer, even if it had been at all wise for her to speak.

He makes treachery of bonds, and bonds of treachery. Zelen had read plenty of theological poems in his youth, when he'd still aspired to the priesthood. That one, on Gizath's nature, had been truly disturbing. The Traitor God didn't just rule over flagrant backstabbing or the magical process of setting a thing's nature against itself, but the dark side of all the ties mortals had to each other—the ones he'd truly and, some said, wisely ruled before his fall. Under his guidance, faith became fanaticism, love obsession, and loyalty slavery or blindness. The priests said as much, but few put it with such frightening clarity.

Darkness hid Branwyn's face, but Zelen remembered it well enough. It had still been bruised and bloodied when he and Altiensarn had carried her out of the building, but already far less swollen than he would have expected after a few hours, even a day. The cheekbone was almost mended.

Sentinel, he thought, and stared at her.

There were plenty of stories. The Sentinels were necessary in all of them, but in the best they were still ruthless and alien, living weapons without the divine guidance or the almost ascetic focus of the Blades. Grimmer tales spoke of berserker rages or said that the soulswords needed to kill a living creature every month to keep their powers.

Once Zelen had passed the age when being able to scare friends over wine was a mark of prestige, he'd never really listened to the tales.

Branwyn slept in drugged peace. Nobody would have mistaken her for fragile—even when she'd been curled in the corner, her eyes heart-stoppingly distant, there'd been a sense of endurance, rather than helplessness, about her—but her face might have been gentle beneath the damage.

There'd be more convenient prey for a blood-drinking sword than the High Lord of Heliodar and his lady, whether animals or people whose deaths wouldn't attract the whole city's attention. Berserker rage fit the scene but didn't pair with the premeditation that getting Yathana would have implied, or the damage to Lady Rognozi's room but not her lord's. The lady might have run, might have fought, but a struggle that put holes in walls and shattered furniture? That would have been difficult for a hulking dockhand in their prime. Branwyn could have destroyed the room out of rage, but why that one and not Lord Rognozi's?

Zelen knew he couldn't trust his judgment for any sort of ultimate decision. He knew what he wanted to be true, and he knew how badly he wanted it. There was no getting around that.

The carriage sped on, darkness inside and out.

Chapter 25

EVEN IDRIEL AND FEYHER HAD THE NIGHT OFF. THAT WOULD arouse suspicion before very long, but if the gods were kind and Zelen was competent, he'd have more idea what Branwyn had or hadn't done by then, not to mention a shred of real evidence. If not, they might all be dead regardless.

Branwyn added more fuel to that fire when she woke halfway up the stairs in the front hallway. She came back to consciousness in total stillness, looked up at him, and said, "There might be a demon. I didn't want to alarm the child. They couldn't do anything if there was. And then…couldn't talk."

Even then her voice was slurred, the faint roll of her *r*'s exaggerated and her words punctuated with seemingly random stops and starts. Her eyes were glassy in the dim light, but Zelen didn't believe for a heartbeat that she was only rambling from the pain and the drug. "A demon," he said, keeping her weight steady. "Like the ones we fought? Don't move your head."

"No. Th…"—she took a few breaths—"those were small. Kind that slip through the cracks when there's magic. Or when a big one is summoned."

"And such a demon could have killed the Rognozis," said Altien. The three of them turned off the landing and onto the second floor. "Demons have not been my study, but it seems likely that it could have broken you in the process."

Branwyn flinched. Zelen's impulse was to comfort, but squeezing her shoulders would not help, to say the least. "Temporarily broken, I should say," he said. "Considering."

"Yesss. Even…even me. Even armed. Even—" She glanced over at Altien. "Ah, intrigue's gone out the window. 'MSnetinel. Sentinel. Order of the Dawn."

"They are also not my area of study, nor my people's," said Altien after many silent steps down the hallway, "but they seem to serve a valuable function and to do it well. I take it that would have given you no small advantage in combat, madam."

"You take it c'rectly. But a demon, a real demon…might've been a match for me. Especially if it was fresh and I wasn't. Of course, tha's what I'd say if I was a murdererer hoping to get away with my crimes. So noted. But if I'm right"—she was fading again—"we have a considerably difficult situation."

"Their bodies vanish," Zelen put in hopefully. "You might have killed it. In here, Altien, please," he added, jerking his chin toward the spare-room door.

"Would be nice if I had," Branwyn agreed, "but the problem is, we don't know. That is…a significant number of our problems here, Zelen. Funnnnnnamental uncertainty. 'Sgonna get us killed."

"You are," Zelen said, "in some ways the most well-spoken drunk I've ever met, if also the gloomiest."

"And the most correct. And it's the situation. And I'm not drunk."

"Technically speaking," said Altien, "the lady is correct."

The spare room was large and dark, the bedclothes dim white shapes. Without needing to discuss it, Zelen and Altien turned so that Branwyn's head was in line with the pillows, lifted her gently, and laid her on the bed. "Be careful," she said, dazed and small in the sea of white.

She didn't speak harshly, but Zelen still winced. "I'm sorry. Are you all right?"

"Wha—yes. Or, relatively. Why—oh. No. Not because of me," she said, clearly believing she explained the obvious. "You should be careful because there could be a demon."

"When couldn't there be?" Zelen muttered a few phrases, and

the magical lights shimmered faintly into existence. Pure and clear, they painted Branwyn's wounds in unforgiving detail. "Gods have mercy."

Darkness had blurred lines and taken the depth from colors. In the light, her face and neck were a study in red and purple: deep bruises, patches of missing skin, and dried blood. Blood had matted her hair in places, too, near where Zelen had felt the swellings on her head.

"They already have granted as much as you'll gain from them by invocation," said Altien. "Where does one obtain water and basins in this household? And do you have an adequate supply of female clothing?"

"Shockingly," Zelen said, retreating into the joke, "no. Water and basins are in the kitchen."

"I'll go for them."

"Really," said Branwyn. She spoke with the slurred single-mindedness that Zelen had seen in many patients and more drunks—that he'd probably displayed a time or two, as the latter—but more desperation than was usual, "it's not unlikely. And I can't be of any assistance. I used my knives, and I've"—Zelen saw her eyes shine with more than the haze of the drug—"I've mislaid Yathana, and if I've failed so badly as to leave the demon alive—"

"Hush," he said and, forgetting the last few days, took her hand. "If you went after a demon and took on all of this"—he gestured to the length of her body, with its broken skin and shattered knee—"as a result, that's not failure."

"It's not success," she said grimly.

"It's a bloody lot more than most could've done." Very gently, painfully aware of the places he shouldn't even graze, he pushed a lock of hair back from Branwyn's forehead. "I know injuries, mmm? Yours weren't from a single blow. Whatever you fought, I'd lay odds it's not feeling in peak condition just now itself."

"Might still come after you, peak condition or not. 'M in your house."

"And I'm not a Sentinel, but I'm not helpless. I'd be insulted that you thought so, except that I've drugged you."

"Against a *demon*—"

Branwyn wasn't exactly wrong. The small demons at the ball had been bad enough. The notion of a larger one out there, shambling its way toward him… Zelen grimaced but didn't turn away from Branwyn. "There are a few things around here that'll be better than steel, and some magical defenses as well," he said. There were chests in the cellars. Winter hadn't hit Heliodar as hard as other lands, but it, and the monsters that had come with it, had demanded a response. The great houses preserved their artifacts well. "Tomorrow, I'll go to the temples and the mages for more… Don't worry," he added, seeing her stifle an objection. "After the ball, I shouldn't wonder if they've got half the city asking for extra protection."

Wire-tight muscles eased in Branwyn's neck and shoulders. Zelen stroked her hair again and inwardly cursed all that kept him from doing more—the uncertainty of their situation as well as her injuries. As if reading his thoughts, she said, "I wouldn' trust me too extens'vely, either, were I you."

It wasn't a quip, and Branwyn wasn't seeking reassurance. Both of those were clear. She spoke bleak truth in a slurred, cracked voice, closing herself around the pain to do what was useful.

And it *was* truth she spoke. If she'd been possessed, she could be again. Spells didn't necessarily only work once. Madness, or conditioning, was unpredictable. Zelen couldn't say he should trust her or even that he did.

He'd done so not that long ago. When they'd been fighting the demons, he'd put his faith in her as unquestioningly as he'd done in Altien when a particularly complex bit of healing or a large and thrashing patient—or a possible murderer in an alleyway—required two of them. He'd never thought to doubt. It had been a brief feeling, but its absence hurt all the same. Worse, it meant that he could offer no reassurance.

"You deserve better than all this," he said.

———————

Gentleness called forth the tears that Branwyn had been too over-whelmed to shed from pain. Her body still lacked too much water for them to do more but prickle at the back of her eyes, but they were there. Zelen had known her for all of two weeks, knew that she could've killed two people brutally, and still his hand around hers and his fingers in her hair were the gentlest touch she'd known since she'd become a Sentinel and a weapon.

She swallowed and welcomed the pain. It centered her.

Did she deserve better? The Rognozis aside, she'd killed people, gotten others killed, and chosen her path. She hadn't had very many choices, but who did? The farmer's child and the wheelwright's apprentice didn't exactly make mindful choices about their future. Neither had Zelen, gentle and deft and barred from his calling for stupid reasons of status.

Hazy, slurred, she formed words. "Ever'one deserves better than all this." She gestured to indicate the world. It hurt, though not as badly as it would have a half hour earlier. "It's…" A quota-tion drifted up through rapidly thickening layers of mist, a passage from a book she'd read on some road. "'A web's pretty 'nless you're a fly.'"

"And she quotes Cosnian while drugged," Zelen remarked. At first, Branwyn thought he was talking to her and pretending to have an audience.

No, his friend was there, setting down large basins of hot water and thick, folded towels. She remembered bathing as a thing normal people did and liked the idea, then looked at Zelen and quickly away. They'd almost been lovers. Now, given what she might have done…

"My name is Altien," said the third person in the room, "and with your permission, I'll assist you in bathing while Zelen acquires clothing. I know that a female attendant is usual, and I'm male, but I promise you that while I'm sure you're comely by the standards of your people, I don't have such exotic tastes."

Branwyn blinked, then giggled, from the formality and the drugs but also from relief. "Yes," she said, "an', Zelen, get weapons. Wards."

He gently set her hand down and rose. "Quite so. I'll be back soon—can't imagine the family's left any very lethal guardians in the cellars."

"I'll listen for screaming," said Altien. "Madam, I suggest that you let me sit you upright, if you have the strength."

She did, barely. The door closed behind Zelen, and Branwyn looked after him for a long moment. "*He* deserves better," she said.

"You would each say that you survive in a satisfactory enough fashion." Altien began cleaning her wounds with the careful, impersonal precision that Branwyn was used to from healers. "I would say that you're both correct, in both senses, but I'm not infatuated with either of you. I'm going to cut this garment off. The strain of removing it will do your muscles no good, and any value it once possessed is certainly gone." His tentacles twitched in distaste.

"We're not infatuated," Branwyn said, barely noticing as Altien produced a pair of small scissors from his garments and made short work of her now-filthy dress. "Just…pleasan' company."

"Nonsense." Altien returned to the task at hand with an occasional sibilant noise when the cleaning process bared a particularly hideous bruise or swelling. Branwyn supposed it was the waterfolk equivalent of *tsk*. "Your attempt to deceive either me or yourself is impressive, however, given the sedation. I'll credit your nature. On your stomach now—I'll brace you."

After a second of pain, during which the dragon-eye and will-power managed to keep Branwyn from screaming, she changed position and found herself very glad that Zelen wasn't the one ministering to her, suspected murder aside. She'd been bathed by healers before—Sentinels, like all weapons, needed the occasional cleaning and repair, and the knee wasn't her first broken bone—and had come to accept the temporary helplessness, but being taken care of would have weighed on her far less easily when it was a lover doing it, or an almost-lover, or the subject of infatuation, if Altien was right.

Branwyn suspected that Yathana would've agreed with him. She expected to hear the dry, sardonic voice doing so in her head, and the silence hurt more than the skinned places on her spine that Altiensarn was attacking with soap.

You can't help that. Don't dwell on it.

"Drugs work on us," she said to give herself another focus for her thoughts, "jus' takes a lot. Mostly. A friend of mine's completely immune, but that's..." She shrugged. "I'osn—idionsa—" She knew the word, but it was a corkscrew that her tongue couldn't follow.

"Idiosyncratic? Hmm." Branwyn felt cool salve on her back, then bandages being wound around her torso. Altien eased her backwards, which didn't hurt as much as the reverse motion had done. Propping her head on the edge of a basin, he began washing days of filth out of her hair. "An interesting order, the Sentinels. I would avoid pressure on your right shoulder as much as possible. The bone isn't broken, and I don't believe you've torn the muscles significantly, but it's a near thing."

"Oh," said Branwyn, and a thought floated up in an increasingly thick fog. "How'd you find Zelen? Or other way?"

"He provides healing services to those who can't afford professionals, thus taking some weight off the Mourners. I came to these lands to study humans, specifically their physiology. Our meeting was natural."

"Of course," said Branwyn. She closed her eyes.

A little while later, the basin moved. "There," said Altien. Branwyn was aware of motion in the region of her shoulders and hips, of being turned and lifted slightly. The world was all mist now, but she was clean and the pain, though present, was remote. Relaxation stole over her, and a set of blankets settled more concretely about her. "Sleep is called for now. We can address the matter of your clothing later, with less awkwardness."

Branwyn made what she meant as a noise of assent, and then asked, "Zlen?"

"I'm certain he's well, but I'll make sure of it. Sleep."

She'd never obeyed orders so readily.

Chapter 26

WAKING, BRANWYN WAS AGAIN UNSURE WHERE SHE WAS. THIS time she was in a bed, though: warmth above her, softness beneath, and a pale-blue canopy before her slowly focusing eyes. She *could* focus her eyes, which was an excellent sign. She remembered why that pleased her, which brought the rest of the immediate past back, though her memory of those crucial few hours remained a blank.

She inhaled slowly, evaluated, and exhaled again. Pain was still in residence around her knee and one side of her head, and was a fainter presence along her backbone, but it was maybe a quarter of what it had been. She could reason around it. She could simply live with it, as long as she had to, the way she lived with the silence in her mind and the worry, beneath her conscious thoughts, about whether that would ever end.

Moving was still difficult. Branwyn sat up gradually, with an occasional hiss of pain when her knee became too involved in the process. The bruises she could see—she was still naked beneath the blankets—were faint purple-yellow, and the places where her skin had split from the impact had healed over to pink lines. A few of her muscles, particularly those in her back, were still healing, and her knee was swollen and disinclined to flex.

Judging from what she knew of her healing rate, and the faint light through the windows, she'd slept at least twelve hours. She wondered how badly her reputation had suffered in the process.

There was nothing she could do about that.

A small table by her bed drew her attention before she could start earnestly brooding. Branwyn saw a clear flask of wine, its pale color likely a sign that it was heavily watered. A plate beside it held sliced brown bread, pears, and a wedge of pale-violet cheese. Next to that sat a heap of folded white cloth with a note on top.

I didn't want to wake you just to have you dress. The shirt should fit until one of us finds better clothes. I should be back within a few hours of whenever you read this. Please don't leave the room, for everyone's safety. The servants won't come in, but I can't keep them out of the house without rumors starting.

There was a blotchy mark, where the writer had clearly considered adding more, but then only a signature: *Zelen Verengir*.

"Gods love you, Zelen," she muttered to the empty room, "for thinking I could even try."

All the same, she smiled, the first time she'd done so out of anything but the darkest of mirth since she'd woken up in the alleyway. Zelen was alive and well enough to write: that was good news.

He also trusted her enough to leave her unrestrained. Logically, Branwyn wasn't sure whether that was good or not, but it was pleasant to know.

All three of the occasions when Branwyn had put her faith in him had been out of her control: the assassins and the demons had attacked them both, he'd guessed about her being a Sentinel, and she hadn't been in any state to try to escape, or to fight, when he'd found her in the burned-out house.

None of that weighed on her as heavily, or as uncomfortably, as she suspected it should have. Zelen was almost certainly her friend, definitely not her enemy, but neither a Sentinel, a priest militant, nor part of her mission. His aims might be different than hers, and if they weren't, he still might give the game away through lack of training. Officially, the man was a useful liability.

All of Branwyn's teaching said that she should have been dismayed by having to rely on him, and by having him know so much about her, but she felt no inclination to worry. Perhaps she had enough to worry about as it was.

Yathana would have been a source of reason, one way or another. She would also have been another person to trust, one that Branwyn wouldn't have even theoretical doubts about. The soulsword was buried in the rubble of another abandoned building, maybe, or on the belt of a half-skilled brute who'd spotted a good blade on the ground, or being sold cheap in some second-hand weaponsmith's.

Those were the pleasant options.

Branwyn ate. She dressed, with a moderate amount of cursing. Zelen was near her height, so the tunic he'd left only fell to midthigh, but she wouldn't be walking around scandalizing people in the very near future.

She considered the room.

Exits were the door opposite her, a smaller one in the side wall that Branwyn guessed led either to a closet or to quarters for a personal servant, and a set of large windows, not entirely hidden by thick silver drapes. An enemy might be able to come down through the chimney of the small fireplace, too, but Branwyn certainly couldn't get up it.

Potential weapons were scarce. The lights were magical, which meant there were no candlesticks. A small eating knife went with the food. Branwyn supposed she could damage a foe not made of bread with it if she used her entire strength and went for an eye. There weren't even tongs near the fireplace. She wondered if the servants carried them from room to room, if stirring up fires without touching them was another of the prodigious ways people used magic in Heliodar or if Zelen had removed the tongs while she slept.

If he had, Branwyn couldn't fault him.

She sat back and inspected her hands. They were by no means

unmarked—as bruised as the rest of her, with swelling beginning to fade near her right wrist—but the marks were no map of what they'd done.

For the first time, her mind was clear enough to really think of the Rognozis, her kind and caring hosts. They'd been innocent as far as her mission went, though neither of them had been as naive as the word implied. A man didn't serve as High Lord of Heliodar for decades without awareness of the world, and Branwyn would've wagered his wife had shared that quality, in her own fashion.

No, not innocent. Not naive. Only good-hearted, and not prepared for the scope of the forces that moved across the world now—or the depth of their evil.

Whether or not Branwyn had struck the blows that killed them, she might have been at fault for that lack of preparation. She didn't think the enemy, whoever it was, had targeted them for hosting a Sentinel, or even knew that facet of her identity, but if the Rognozis had known, they might have been more careful, or not made the offer at all.

If she'd come to the city openly as a Sentinel, her enemy might have gone deeper and her contacts refused to talk to her. That had been the Adeptas' argument. It had been King Olwin's, it had been Vivian's, and it had been the one Branwyn had believed. She still thought it was, and she *thought* that she thought that not only to assuage her guilt.

Thyran would kill far more than two people if he got his way. War exacted a red toll. Branwyn had known that since long before Oakford.

"Dark Lady, take the pain of their deaths from them," she said, the old litany for those who fell in battle coming easily after years of use. "Lord of the Scales, let them know their own courage. King of the Wild, make a place for their mortal remains in your creation. Queen of the Golden Webs, give them the thanks of the civilization they died upholding."

"May the Four so grant," said Zelen, stepping into the room.

The day, which was barely more than half over, had already been long: long and cold.

Branwyn had still slept deeply when Zelen had left clothing and food. One shoulder had poked out of the blankets, still bruised enough to inspire concern rather than lust. Her gold hair had spilled across the pillow above it, reminiscent of the webs that decorated Sitha's temples in silk, metal, and stained glass.

A web's pretty unless you're a fly. He thought he'd always hear Cosnian's quote in Branwyn's drug-slurred voice from then on. The words of the Southern Kingdoms' greatest cynic sounded both odd and oddly appropriate from one whose entire life was duty.

He'd left before he could let himself think about how much he wanted to stay with her.

Work had been slow at the clinic. That had let Zelen slip out and ask a few questions of people he knew: former patients, men he'd drunk with after the day's labors, and Tanya, who'd been playing a few streets away and come to investigate. He'd asked all of them if they'd heard about a big fight a few nights before, if they'd seen anyone looking as though they'd been in one, if any of their acquaintances had disappeared lately, or if a gold-hilted sword with an opal in the hilt had turned up.

He hadn't actually had to ask Tanya. "Haven't seen *anyone* hurt as bad as they'd be if they'd tangled with your lady," she said. "Not nearly, not assuming she gave a little bit as good as she got."

"She would have," said Zelen, trying to ignore both *your lady* and his idiotic impulse to beam at the phrase.

"She all right?"

"She will be. You did well," said Zelen, and Tanya smiled more at that than at the silver he slipped her.

His other conversations had been less straightforward but revealed as little. Nobody had gotten worse than a black eye and a split lip in a fight, or for most any other reason—except a set of crushed ribs, but that had been an accident loading a barge, in full view of witnesses. Missing people were harder, since many took to the road when love or money turned sour, without informing anyone they left behind. There'd been only one disappearance that really puzzled Zelen's contacts, though, and he'd been fifteen and bookish, a clerk's apprentice.

That was worrying itself, on top of the previous missing child, but Zelen doubted that a stripling would've been able to land a punch on a maddened Sentinel, much less leave one too badly injured to walk.

Nobody had seen a fancy sword. They certainly would've remembered that.

Until he reached the room, carrying the day's letters, and heard Branwyn's prayer, he still hadn't been sure whether or not to tell her. There was still plenty he didn't know. She *could* have killed the Rognozis and met with an accident or a fight later. She could even have been in league with the demon, then turned on it.

Then her voice had reached him, hoarse with injury and cracked with grief and regret, in the words of a prayer Zelen had once learned but never had cause to use.

He could have kept his silence as easily as he could have stopped breathing.

When Zelen closed the prayer, Branwyn turned to look at him. Most of the bruising had faded from her face, leaving only a faint shadow around one eye. With her grave expression and his white shirt for clothing, she had an almost holy air about her, and a very solitary one.

"Nobody's seen anything," he blurted out. It was all he could offer in the face of her somber regard. "No fights. No injuries. One disappearance, but hardly the sort who'd give you trouble. And you're not the sort to fall down stairs. I've seen you move."

"That argues for a few possibilities," Branwyn said, "and

only one of them is entirely good, even as little as *good* is possible in the situation. I *could* have killed the demon and staggered away blindly, either to escape the authorities or because"—she shrugged—"blows to the skull don't exactly inspire clear thinking. But I might not have."

"True. I've set up wards around here in case." The paraphernalia in the trunks had been carefully packed away, oiled and censed by an unknown hand but one that appeared expert to Zelen's decidedly inexpert judgment. Sigils in twisted silver and copper wire, set with gems, now hung from the doors and windows in each room, and braziers burned in the front hall.

Visitors would be nonplussed. Zelen suspected the servants already were, though, as he'd told Branwyn, the ball provided more than adequate justification. "I haven't heard stories about a demon either. People would notice that, wouldn't they?"

"If it were independent and the mindless rampage sort, yes. It could be controlled, or smart enough to scheme and hide, though the Rognozis' death argues somewhat against the latter." She sat back on the bed with a grimace of pain.

That drew Zelen's notice. "I'd like to check how disturbingly fast you're mending, if I may."

"Yes, thank you." She arranged the shirt carefully to expose the knee while maintaining modesty, and her expression became, briefly, both wry and a touch sad.

Zelen understood. Above the shirt was nothing he hadn't touched, licked, gotten to know quite thoroughly—but that had been *before*. The last few days were a gulf like the western sea. He perched on the bed, placing the sealed papers to one side, and turned his attention strictly to Branwyn's knee.

The improvement got a low whistle from him, and that made her chuckle. "I'd give my right eye to study how you do that," Zelen said.

"Oh, don't. You're much better off with both, and I'm certain we have copious notes in one of our chapter houses. About how long do you think I'll still be incapacitated?"

"If the current rate of healing continues?" He prodded gently, feeling heat and swelling but not the break that had been there the previous night. "You'll be able to walk in a day, if you're careful. Run, or fight, in three or four. It's bloody amazing."

"Our makers do good work," said Branwyn. That called Zelen's attention to a part of her leg he hadn't noticed before—it had always been too dark, or he'd been too concerned with her wounds. A thin bronze line, perhaps the width of her fingertip, ran up from her anklebone on each side.

He had to check, and yes, the lines were on her other leg too, like welded seams in metal.

"And they sign their masterpieces," she added from above him.

"I'm sorry—" Zelen said, sitting up quickly, but Branwyn was grinning faintly. She pushed back a sleeve to show him the same pattern on her arm, starting close to her wrist.

"I'd have had the same curiosity in your place, and given that you've healed me and let me stay in your house, I don't have much grounds for complaint. Besides, I don't hide them as a rule—only when I'm playing spy, which I didn't do until a few weeks back."

The lines were astoundingly straight, the contrast with her skin subtle and fascinating. Zelen wished he'd had paper and pen handy, but he wasn't sure any oils could have come close to the shift in color or the metallic gleam. The healer in him took over from the artist, then, and he asked, "Do they feel different?"

"Not from the inside, not usually. I can turn to metal—could, with Yathana." Her expression was briefly very controlled. "It ripples out from those lines, and when I was first reforged I was much more aware of the process. I'm used to it now. As for the outside, somewhat. Would you like to—"

Awareness hit them both as she held out her wrist, Zelen thought, in what he even then knew was a spectacular display of rationalizing, that turning down the offer would only make the moment more awkward. He set his fingers lightly on Branwyn's arm.

The line did feel precisely like polished metal, slightly cooler than the rest of her skin. Zelen thought it thrummed faintly with her pulse, but that might have been his own heartbeat suddenly picking up speed and volume.

You've already had your hands all over her, fool, he told himself, *no more than a day ago.*

But this was different. This was exploration rather than duty, pleasure rather than simply relief of pain. Was the pulse beneath his fingers, if he did feel it, speeding up like his own?

She's possibly a murderer, but she likely wasn't.

Zelen lifted his gaze. Branwyn's eyes were dark, her lips faintly parted, and her breasts rose and fell quickly, making his shirt far more interesting than it had ever been. He envied the fabric, sliding against her firm body like that.

She's injured, and she's trapped in your house.

That got through, cold water enough for the moment. "Thank you," Zelen managed. By force of will, he laid her hand gently back in her lap. "I shouldn't pry."

He reached for the pile of letters as though the scraps of paper might lend him stability and tore one open seemingly at random.

"You seem popular," said Branwyn. Zelen tried to tell himself that her voice was only throaty because of her injuries.

"Most of the council gets more, I'd think. I—" He blinked down at the message.

"Not more bad news, I hope."

"It could be worse, but it couldn't have come at a worse point. At least the food will be horrible." He met Branwyn's questioning look with an explanation. "Gedomir wants me in the country tomorrow."

Chapter 27

LEAVING HELIODAR PROPER BEHIND, ONE APPROACHED THE Verengir house across a long stretch of flat land: tree-studded plains that rapidly gave way to marshes. In summer, these were a hell of insects, but now they were, if gloomy, at least subdued. Slim, dark cypress trees clumped sociably together above brown cattails and water that reflected the flat gray of the sky overhead. Zelen's carriage rumbled along steadily, but with squashy enough noises to make him occasionally nervous—as though he didn't have plenty to worry about.

Fields of barley and other plants Zelen had never learned to recognize punctuated the landscape occasionally, all in clumps like the houses that went with them. Solitude had never been the death sentence in Heliodar that he'd heard it was in Criwath and the other kingdoms that hadn't had sea or southerly positions to keep them from the worst of the storms, but living too far from one's neighbors was still a bad idea.

A high fence marked the boundary of Verengir lands. Orderly rows of trees began to line the road after that. Passing between them had always made Zelen feel as though a harsh hand descended on his shoulders, pulling his back rigid against the carriage seat, and a cold voice pointed out every wrinkle in his doublet and bit of dirt on his boots. This time, he was acutely conscious of the secret he carried as well and wondered how obvious it was.

He was still thinking it over when the carriage pulled up at the front door.

The Verengir house was dark wood, plain but large, with four stories and chunky, sprawling wings to either side of the square central building. What few windows it had squinted out suspiciously from the upper floors. Standing stiffly at the large double doors, footmen in livery regarded the carriage with the same lack of reaction they showed everything.

Zelen got out, nodded politely and received polite bows, and passed through the doors, miniscule in their shadow.

Inside was as he remembered: high hallways and tapestries in sober colors. Duty, Purity, and Prudence lined the front hallway, each one a maiden with pale skin, rosy cheeks, and a sickeningly earnest expression. Duty had her head bent over a cradle, Purity was holding one hand out in front of her in a warding gesture, and Prudence was closing the door on a well-stocked larder.

As he'd done twenty years ago, Zelen crossed his eyes and stuck out his tongue at them. It felt embarrassingly juvenile but extremely satisfying, and nobody was likely to box his ears now.

"Brother."

Zelen's ears actually did tingle at the greeting, and the swish of skirts that went with it. He turned to meet Alize with far less composure than he'd hoped.

She kissed him on each cheek, her lips cold and dry. Her hair, white blond like Gedomir's and their mother's, was twisted into a tight bun, as always. She probably hadn't been wearing the same all-concealing black wool dress since she'd been fifteen and Zelen six, but he couldn't have told the difference between one gown and another.

"It's good to see you," he lied.

"And you. You look…" She scanned his clothing, taking in every bright color and scrap of ornament. "Well. Gedomir is in the library."

"Much obliged. Mother and Father?"

"Getting ready to go to the city, naturally," she said. Immediately Zelen wanted to look away, sheepish for having asked. "It's hard on them, particularly at their age, but for a state funeral…well. There's no point objecting to duty."

"No," he said. "And Ilesen?"

"Overseeing our estates." Alize's husband was a washed-out and rather chinless man, who gave the impression of being a petty tyrant in his own home but obeyed Lord Verengir's suggestions as soon as he heard them. That quality had probably recommended him as a match as strongly as his impeccable bloodlines had done. "I'll give him your regards."

"Much obliged," Zelen said, realized that he'd repeated himself, and coughed. "Well. I'll just duck in and have a word with Gedo, shall I?"

"You'd best do so. He's quite busy. I'll see you at dinner," she added, and then swept off on some errand immeasurably more important than talking to him.

"How much pain would you say it gives you to stand?" Altien's tentacles waved idly as he observed Branwyn, and his fingers tapped his legs in the same rhythm. Branwyn suspected it was a barely repressed desire to take notes.

"Only a little now," she said, closing her eyes to better concentrate her other senses. "I've had worse after a day of hard training. But I'm keeping my weight on the other, mostly. If I shift—"

She did so, not entirely but evenly. The pulse of discomfort made her grunt. "No. I couldn't maintain that for very long."

"Then don't," said Altien, and waved her back toward the bed. "Progress will happen faster if we don't get in its way. I will provide you with mild exercises. They should be helpful, insofar as I understand human musculature, which I do. You're not as dissimilar that way as you are skeletally."

"We must have some advantages," said Branwyn, sitting back down and not disguising her sigh of relief. Sitting in bed and reading the books Zelen had brought her had left her restless, especially with her half knowledge of the situation outside, but four turns around the room—one for each of the gods, Altien had said—had left her sweating and sore.

"As a people, yes. You excel at violence, and you're paradoxically quick to form attachments, both of which can be useful qualities. We did not, you note, construct an Order like yours after the storms."

"You weren't facing the kind of attacks we were, from what I heard."

"That's true as well, and not a fact many humans have cited—though you're the first I've spoken to about the issue."

"I spent a month or so working in partnership with another of the waterfolk, out in Kvanla. They'd studied as a mage, and I was hunting an oviannic."

"The name is unfamiliar to me."

"They're a malicious sort of a house spirit, mostly a nuisance until they get enough power. Then potentially very nasty." Branwyn remembered dozens of eyes in an elongated face and fire hotter than a smith's forge springing up in a circle around her. "They're also extremely difficult to track, or to keep in one place long enough to fight or banish, without magic. Anyhow, Vemigira and I spent a fair bit of time together."

Altiensarn nodded. "That name is also unfamiliar, but my brood was raised far from Kvanla. The sea is much colder there, I hear."

"Most places are, in my experience." Branwyn hesitated over the story and then said to the other outsider what she wouldn't have said to Zelen. "A few of the Adeptas, the Order's scholars and leaders, used to debate whether Heliodar got off lightly because it was farther south to begin with, and near the ocean, or because Thyran still couldn't bear to strike his home too hard."

"I would be very much inclined to believe the former," said Altiensarn.

"Me too. Practically speaking, the spell never exactly worked as he intended—he got stuck in time before he could build it up and direct it as much as he wanted, or so say witnesses."

"The general who I hear has come back?"

"Him, and the soul in my friend Darya's sword." There was a long and involved story there, one that Branwyn didn't entirely know was hers to share. Besides, she was trying to keep her mind off of soulswords. She moved on. "From all I've heard, Thyran had no reason to feel at all fondly toward the city either. I'd have expected it to be his first target, really, or the most severely hit one, if he'd had things entirely his way." Branwyn laughed without humor. "I should've made that argument to the council while they'd still listen to me."

"You may yet have their ear," said Altien, calm as ever. "But I wouldn't be certain, myself, in your estimation of Thyran."

"Gods know I'm not overly familiar with the man, and glad about that, but how so?"

"People's sentimental attachments very rarely obey common sense, in my experience. I have often found it surprising to witness what one can still be fond of, or want to believe, even in the face of hostility."

———

"Thank you for joining me," said Gedomir, standing up from behind his desk and bowing quickly before waving Zelen to a seat in one of the hard horsehair chairs facing him. "I hope the roads are still adequately maintained. We've had workers out, of course, but haven't been able to properly supervise them this year."

"The ground's what it is in winter, but they did a good job," said Zelen, not wanting to expose the laborers to his brother's notion of proper supervision.

"Good. Good. Your journey was a pleasant one then?"

"Fairly, thank you."

There were always more pleasantries here, where Zelen was the visitor. Until a few years before, he'd assumed Gedo was busier in the city. Eventually he'd come to see the truth: a matter of territory and control, points awarded based on who could get their business over with first.

Asking about the reason for his summons would annoy Gedomir, and Zelen needed his goodwill just then. Besides, he had the entire evening, and it wasn't as though there were more congenial places in the house than the study.

A few changes had taken place in that room: a couple new books stood in the cases against the wall behind Gedomir, their covers catching the yellow magelight with more of a shine than those of the other, more weathered volumes. The portrait of their great-grandfather had been reframed, and the man's hawklike features peered out from a border of dull gold, ugly but expensive. The heavy curtains were the same, and so were the dark desk and chairs, but while the bookcases themselves hadn't changed, the shadow one of them cast was subtly different.

"Has the council discussed the succession?" Gedomir asked.

"Not in any useful way," said Zelen, "or I would've written."

"You've had a great deal on your mind lately."

"Nonetheless." He let the point go. "The obvious heir is Kolovat."

Var, said a voice: high, female, and familiar, though Zelen couldn't for the life of him have said who it was. He blinked and glanced behind him.

Nobody was there. That, after a second, was no real shock. The voice hadn't sounded like it came from anywhere in the study.

It had been inside his head.

Verengir.

"Zelen? Is everything all right?"

"Ah. Yes, sorry. Thought I heard a fly."

Gedomir frowned. "If you do, I'll have words with the servants."

"No, no." Zelen hastily waved off the complaint. "You're right. I've had too much on my mind lately. I'm afraid I'll have to ask you to repeat yourself."

The way Gedomir smirked was also familiar. Zelen had seen the expression when he'd fallen off his first horse and started wailing. "I was saying that Kolovat is the obvious heir, if one measures simply by duration in the post. Starovna was bred and raised to nobility, so it would come far more easily to her."

Zelen had never noticed either of the councillors struggling with their duties. Gods knew that Kolovat, who'd been an army officer before a few uncles had died childless, acted far more sure of himself than Zelen, "bred and raised" to his status, ever felt. He didn't make the argument, both for the same reasons that had kept him from speeding the conversation and because he knew it would make no difference. "I'm not certain she wants it. She's a great one for her studies, you know."

Verengir, said the voice again. It was clouded and cracked, as though coming to him through a wind-filled tunnel. . . . *ind. The*. . .

He tried to appear interested in the matter of Starovna versus Kolovat, and only in that.

"It hardly matters what she prefers. She knows—" said Gedomir, and then there was a knock on the door. "*Yes?*"

His anger was icy. He'd come to sound entirely like their father at such times. Zelen's back twinged with memory.

It wasn't a hapless servant standing at the door, but Hanyi, the younger of Zelen's two sisters. She usually had more of a friendly word for Zelen than his other siblings did, but just then didn't even seen to see him. "I'm sorry," she said, "but you're needed."

"Incompetence," said Gedomir, in the same tones other men might have used to curse. "Wait here, would you? With the gods' favor, I'll be back before too long."

"Of course. Can I help?"

"No," Gedomir said, and vanished out the door.

Zelen closed it behind his brother. Later, he would say that the hallway was drafty, which wasn't entirely a lie. He stood in front of it, listened to the footsteps as they receded down the hall, and, for lack of other ideas, opened his mind the way he did in prayer.

Bookcase, said the voice. It was clearer, but still not nearly conversational. Zelen got the impression that every word took effort.

More words weren't really necessary, though, because he knew what the speaker meant. He'd seen the shape, the way the shadow of the bookcase had changed from what he remembered. Zelen darted over to the spot he'd seen, where a gap of a few inches ran on two sides between the case and the walls.

An object was changing the shadow, a long, thin object that someone had wrapped in dark cloth and shoved behind the bookcase. Whoever it was had done a decent job of hiding it back there—even the shadow wouldn't have made Zelen catch on if not for the voice—and had wrapped it well.

He knew what it was all the same. The words wouldn't come, but his stomach roiled when he saw the shape, his body recognizing what his mind couldn't yet. Listening for returning footsteps, Zelen only had the nerve to unwrap the top of the object, but that was all he needed.

Dark blood had dried on gilt, leaving the outline of three fingers clear, though slightly distorted. Above it, the magelight shone off a huge fire opal, the same one that Zelen had seen over and over again in the hilt of Branwyn's sword.

Chapter 28

PART OF HIM HAD KNOWN. PART OF HIM MUST HAVE KNOWN, Zelen realized, because he didn't collapse from shock, or vomit, or shout in rage. He didn't so much as pause before wrapping the sword back up again, as tightly as Gedomir or Alize—it would have been one of the family, no point going through names—had concealed it before.

I'll come back later, he thought at it, and stumbled to his seat. There was the shock, manifesting after the initial urgency had pushed it aside. He knew such things. He'd read the books and trained with the priests, even when his father had forbidden him to actually enter the Dark Lady's service.

He would come back to that fact later too.

At first he toyed with the idea that his family might have been framed for the attack, thinking, *They're my blood. I owe them at least the same courtesy I gave to a Sentinel*, but it wouldn't wash. None of the household had been staying with the Rognozis. Except for Zelen, none of them had been in the city.

If, by whatever freak chance, they'd come across the sword innocently, it wouldn't have hurt them at all to take it to the guard or one of the temples. They'd even have been praised for it, perhaps, as providing a valuable clue.

Why hadn't they?

Because their story would raise questions, and they couldn't swear to the truth of it in front of Tinival's altar. Because at least one of the Verengirs had been involved in killing the Rognozis, and possibly in framing Branwyn for the murder.

And why had they done that? What would they get out of it?

Thinking even briefly of that question was like taking the bandage off a wound where blood poisoning had set in completely. There was nothing to find in any direction but putrescence.

If Zelen flubbed what came next, there would be no chance to discover how far the rot went or to heal whatever was left.

He sat upright in the chair and thought hard at himself: *Nothing happened, you're bored, you're talking about the succession, you want wine and dinner. You want wine and dinner, nothing happened, you're talking about the succession, and you're bored.*

By the time Gedomir came back in, Zelen had almost managed to make himself believe it.

"House not on fire, I hope," he drawled.

"Hardly," said Gedomir, in the same we-take-care-of-ourselves-better-than-that manner that had always irritated his brother.

Now Zelen just hoped he'd go on being superior. Superior might let him overlook enough.

———

"Do you know much about the wards Zelen put up?" Branwyn asked.

The morning had dragged into afternoon. Interesting as her book was, the urge to be taking action had crept back up after the exercises. She supposed talking magical theory could serve as a stopgap.

"Not a great deal," Altien said. "Zelen mentioned that his ancestors had left belongings in the cellars here, and that a few of those had been warding disks." He closed his notes and made a thoughtful purring noise. "He did mention a few more complicated ones that he hadn't been sure how to activate. Do you believe you might know?"

"Maybe." She'd never been a wizard, but the basic magical

principles had been part of all Sentinels' training. Branwyn had been interested enough to study more now and again. "It's worth a look, at least, if you don't think he'd object."

"I doubt very much that you could do a great deal he'd object to," said Altien, and went on before Branwyn could react in any way aside from an embarrassing blush that her bruises no longer camouflaged. "And he's never been particularly sensitive about his family's belongings. I'll see if his servants will allow me access."

Ten pages of poetry later, he returned with a small armful of metal and wood, and set it down on the table where Branwyn's food had been.

"A few of these resemble the protections our mages use," he said, "but not many, and not a great deal. Then again, it was never my area of expertise, and we have different symbols for the gods."

"Sitha is a tower for you, not a spider, yes?" Branwyn picked up the first ward, a glyph formed of delicate silver links, and tried to remember what Vemigira had told her about waterfolk religion, as well as what she knew of magic. "This one might need to have a censer in the middle, though you'd have to ask an actual wizard what to put in it, or maybe a priest."

"It's true. We're not overstocked with spiders, and our cousins"—he flared his tentacles indicatively—"spin no webs, so the metaphor's less apt. And the sword is Talleita, not Alcerion, as it is for you. Neither flames nor tears have much meaning for us, you understand."

"Underwater? Makes sense to me." The next item was a wooden statue, with a hollow cup in front and the back curving up into a series of patterns. All were abstract, and none suggested any god to Branwyn. She suspected this one was meant to channel magical power directly. It probably needed a wizard to work, but it was hard to know for certain. That cup in front, for instance... With wine or blood, depending on the spell, a decently skilled amateur might manage some protection.

She picked it up, meaning to check if there was any residue of one substance or the other. An unevenness near the back caught at her fingers. "This could have been better maintained," she said.

"It was thrown in a trunk with a number of others," Altien confirmed. "I suppose the family wanted a good number of such things out of their way. Is it badly broken?"

"No," she said slowly. Branwyn realized she wasn't feeling splintered wood but a straight line, slightly raised. "I don't think it's broken at all. Pass me the fruit knife, please."

An old catch was unlikely to be trapped, but one never knew, especially in this city, and Branwyn didn't have Darya's gift for ignoring poison. It was more frustrating springing it with the knife but less potentially deadly, so she was willing to take the time and bite her tongue when she wanted to swear. Altien closed his notes and watched.

The catch popped open at last. In the compartment beyond was a wad of old paper: a tightly wound scroll that had been folded in half before being jammed into the hidden niche.

"Old love letters?" Altien suggested. "It would seem an incongruous place, but any port in a storm, as the saying goes."

"There's a poetic sentiment about love chasing away demons," Branwyn said. She smoothed out the paper. It wasn't as old as she'd believed at first—this ward had been put away considerably after the storms had ended, likely in her own lifetime—but there were ragged places already, and the ink had blurred in spots. "But no, I don't think so."

Third month, second week, fifth day. Unusual appetites continue as expected. R. can no longer enter the ceremonial chamber, as her presence—or more likely the babe's—disrupts the established magic there, and it takes hours to repair. Inconvenient, but the best evidence that she truly bears the Vessel of the Sundered Soul.

Health otherwise robust. No emotional upset: she is radiant,
rather, in the knowledge of her Great Purpose.

"I don't know what they were doing," said Altiensarn, bending over
to read the cramped script, "but I suspect that I wouldn't like it."

"No," said Branwyn. "Anybody who uses capitals like that has
nothing good in mind."

———————

Dinner was a bad dream.

The food was plain as always, and there was no wine, but for
once that didn't matter to Zelen. He didn't taste a thing, though he
ate as heartily as he could make himself.

Father sat at the head of the table, a gaunter, taller version of
Gedomir except for his eyes, which were very pale blue, a color
he'd only passed on to Alize. He spoke very little, but Zelen knew
that he heard all that the others said and was noting it down for
future use. Mother, at the other end, was his dark counterpart,
shadow to his ice, and she did speak.

"Zelen, what have you been doing with yourself?"

"Oh, this and that," he said, weighing his options. Mentioning
the festivities in town would have gotten him a rebuke for frivolity
when the Rognozis hadn't been dead a week. "Keeping fairly busy
with the clinic, you know."

"Charitable," she said, and the approval still pleased him. "I
hope they have a proper sense of gratitude for what you do. Alize,
how are the harvests this year? More rice than last?"

So it went on, a tutor's quiz about their own lives, with sparse
smiles as the reward. Zelen and his siblings didn't talk to one
another at the table; they ate and waited for questions until the
meal was finally over.

"I will retire now," his father finally said. "Zelen, on your return to the city tomorrow, ensure that all is ready for our visit. It will be a painful enough occasion without chaos."

"Yes, Father."

He'd be going back the next day, then. That was just as well—it meant less time in which to give himself away, not to mention less time he had to spend in the house itself. Zelen would have liked to have been asked, but had long since given up expecting it.

After another interminable hour in the parlor, while Alize played well but somberly on the harp, bedtime arrived, and Zelen went thankfully to that as well.

He didn't sleep, of course.

He did take his boots off. That would help. Then he lay on his bed for an hour, alternately reading a scandalous novel and wondering what Branwyn was doing in his house, until he was fairly certain that the rest of the household had sought their own beds.

Sneaking had served him well as a youth. Through learning to move quietly and blend decently with the darkness, he'd often been able to get food after hours and books he wasn't supposed to read, not to mention pursuing a liaison or two with local girls when he'd gotten a bit older. He hadn't thought to use the skill as a grown man, but it came back fairly quickly. He reached the scullery without waking the half-grown boys sleeping on the hearth.

A spare broom handle served his purpose admirably. The weight was very different from that of Yathana, of course, but Zelen doubted that any of his family was going to try to wield the thing. He held it close to his chest as he crept back into the hallway. The crash as one end knocked into a pitcher, or he tripped over a table leg, echoed endlessly in his mind but never actually came.

The library door sounded like an avalanche when he closed it. Zelen froze shortly beyond, listened for footsteps, and for a moment couldn't make himself believe he heard none, or shake himself into action when he was sure. The enormity of what he was going to do, of what it all meant, descended on him. He was only glad that dinner had been hours in the past.

His feet felt too large as he headed toward the bookshelf. His hands were blocky, clumsy as they'd never been when healing, but he withdrew Yathana without breaking anything and quickly substituted the broom handle, wrapped in one of the old cloaks that had still been in his wardrobe. It looked enough like the sword's wrappings to fool a casual glance. A more-than-casual one... He hoped to be well away before that happened.

Back, said the sword in his mind. *Good.*

If that's the word for it, Zelen thought in return, and left the library.

The servants' staircase was unlit, and without any carpet to soften the wood, the stairs were inclined to creak. Zelen descended one careful, measured step at a time, in dark silence bound by narrow walls. When he heard voices near the first-floor landing, he nearly jumped.

"...contained...Hanyi," Gedomir was saying. Dim light came through the wall from where he spoke, so Zelen sidled carefully closer, making sure that Yathana didn't bump into any of the surrounding wood, and peered through the minute crack. The view was too restricted for him to be certain, but from the direction, he thought Gedomir was on the first floor in the east wing. Voices did carry; that went with the drafts, particularly in the servants' quarters.

"She knows what she's about," Mother replied calmly.

"But refreshing the wards is going to take another expedition."

"And? There's no shortage of supply."

"It'll draw attention." Gedomir sighed. "Damn Sentinels, and damn Zelen. If he'd done his task competently—"

Zelen's immediate wince, ridiculous given what he knew about Gedomir but as inevitable as his next breath, turned into startled paralysis at the sound of a hard slap.

"Watch how you speak of family." Mother pronounced every

letter in every word, and all of them were ice-edged. Behind the wall, Zelen blinked, and his grip on the sword tightened. He hadn't anticipated hearing any of them take his part. Then Mother continued. "Furthermore, this is the second time you've forgotten your brother's place in our plans. I might begin to believe it willful."

"I assure you, Mother, I know his role."

"Do you? Perhaps we were insufficiently clear in your youth. The youngest is a necessary distraction. In case you don't comprehend both words, 'distraction' means he's ill-suited to be your spy, and 'necessary' means he's not collateral damage when you want somebody dead. We'd have to call up your tiresome cousin to fill his place, for one thing, since Hanyi's far past being able to take on the role. There's no end to the disruption that would cause. Particularly now."

"Yes, madam," Gedomir said, contrite or putting on a reasonable show of it.

"Seek your bed, Gedomir. The god has laid many tasks ahead of us for the next few days, and we must all remember our rightful positions."

There was a silent moment. Zelen thought Gedomir was nodding and possibly bowing. "Good night, madam," he heard again, and then footsteps.

Zelen started down the stairs again. The effort of it, the care involved in moving so that no step creaked under his weight, wasn't exactly soothing, but it was a place to put his attention, which was almost as good. He wished it had taken more work.

Distraction.

The god.

The air of the stable yard was cool against Zelen's face when he opened the door. That and the solid weight of Yathana were all that convinced him that he was solid and material, that all of the last few hours had really happened.

It had. He had to act on it.

As he made his quick, covert way across the yard to the coach house, Zelen felt the sword in his mind. There were no words this time, but he got a general sense of encouragement: a rough clap on his mental shoulder. It made the stones steadier beneath his feet.

Grooms and stable hands slept close to their charges, but the coach house was set off a little way in the stable yard and offered no half-comfortable bed of hay. Zelen was fairly certain that nobody saw him approach his carriage. The seat took some effort to pull up, and the ripping noise when it did come loose made Zelen hiss, but he created enough of a gap between the cushions and the wood to slide Yathana into. Fortunately, winter was coming on, and carriages weren't overly warm. Furs hid a multitude of defects.

He was reluctant to leave the sword, not only because of fear that it—she, he supposed—would be discovered, or because she was the first sympathetic presence he'd encountered in the house. Power lingered about Yathana in a way that Zelen, no mage, could sense once he'd touched her. It was a refreshingly hot, clean force.

His mother's words came back to him as he snuck back to his room. They hurt, but pain was familiar, even if not in that particular form, and secondary. She'd said Zelen was a distraction. He was afraid that he knew what he'd been distracting people from.

Chapter 29

"I'VE HEARD OF THE 'SUNDERED SOUL' BEFORE, I BELIEVE," SAID Altien. He closed the door behind him and took his seat, fur golden-brown in the afternoon light. "The memory occurred to me while I was putting the clinic in order. If I'm correct, it's a story from the stonekin, and it concerns one of the gods, though I couldn't provide more details. How is your knee recovering?"

"Quickly, thank the gods," said Branwyn, and flexed it to show him. "Walking around the room only hurt a little today. The exercises have been helping. Have a look."

Altien sat, peered, and then pressed in several places. Only three hurt, and only one drew a yelp from Branwyn. "Yes," he said, finally, "excellent improvement. I'd give your physiology equal credit, though, and perhaps more."

"The Adeptas will be flattered if I survive long enough to tell them. How would you say I'd fare in a fight?"

"I expect you've done your own assessment."

"Yes, but two points are more stable than one."

"Poorly, then, if you were up against a skilled opponent, or more than one. The knee wouldn't collapse immediately, but it would hinder you badly. I suspect a day or two more before you're at your full strength and speed. Do you anticipate combat?"

"Well, there's at least one force in this city that wants me dead. I'd like to think secrecy and Zelen's wards will help, especially given the ones you put up yesterday, but I liked to think I'd have quick and uneventful success here." When Altien left the bed for his customary chair, Branwyn picked up the scroll of formerly hidden papers again. "I've been considering these too," she said. "Did Zelen ever mention his family conducting magical experiments?"

"He rarely speaks of them at all," said Altien, "except to tell me when he has to depart the city and pay a visit to the country estates. His elder brother occasionally arrives to deliver news, or orders. It's not a warm family, even by the human standards with which I'm familiar."

"It doesn't sound that way even by the human standards *I've* observed. Lady Rognozi said there was a tragedy when Zelen was three or so, a mother and child both perishing. That would have been around the time of these notes."

Altien's tentacles rose, then fell. "We can guess, though we shouldn't assume, that the procedure went badly."

"True. Especially since there's no god-powered youth running about. This story you heard, do you happen to remember whether it had the soul in question as a force for good?"

"No," said Altien regretfully. "I never even heard the entire story, only read a mention or two of it." He paused. In the silence, Branwyn heard footsteps approaching the door. It was probably Zelen returning, but she tensed anyhow, and reached under her pillow for the knife Altiensarn had brought her. "I believe it was about the primordial battle, the one between Talleita and—"

"Gizath," said Zelen, opening the door.

In dress and grooming he was as impeccable as ever, but his face was gray, and his eyes were shadowed. He carried a cloth-wrapped bundle that immediately filled Branwyn with hope, though it was matched by equal parts worry. Zelen moved like a man with a knife in one kidney.

"My family worships him," he said numbly. "Some of it. Possibly all. I'm bloody certain of Mother and Gedomir. They were the ones who killed the Rognozis. Here," he said, and pulled the wrappings off the object in his hands, revealing Yathana's gilded-for-Heliodar hilt and fire opal. Zelen thrust her toward Branwyn, hilt-first. "I brought her back for you. It was the least I could do, after... Given what we are."

———————

The sword took the strength in Zelen's legs with her. He fell as much as sat on the bed, the world blurry and colorless.

He knew that the questions would come soon. He owed answers—owed the story, in fact. He was thinking of how to begin when Branwyn put an arm around him and he looked up, startled.

"Your sword—"

"Yathana and I can speak just as well without touching," she said, and her hand was warm on his bicep. "Thank you for returning her. She thanks you too."

Altiensarn was kneeling in front of him, peering from face to body and back. "You don't appear physically wounded," he said. "Are there injuries I don't see? If not, I'm going to get you a cup of tea. Nourishment won't solve our problems, but it will help a great deal."

"I—" Zelen didn't seem able to finish a sentence. They trailed off, boats loosed from their moorings. He made an effort. "No. No, I'm not injured. I don't—"

"Think that you can eat," Altien finished for him. "I'm perfectly aware, and we've both seen these circumstances before. I'm going to go extract the necessary provisions from your servants."

Zelen watched him leave, more because it was too much effort to move his eyes than out of any real attention. There were next steps. There were steps that came next. Branwyn was beside him. He turned his head, which felt as though it took a year, and observed that she was beautiful.

It hurt.

"Gedomir asked me to get to know you," he said, laying the

words down between them, "then to tell him what I found out. I'd been reporting more or less faithfully up until the ball."

Branwyn didn't pull away. She didn't move either. Zelen waited, deserving what came next.

"Did he know I was a Sentinel?"

"No. Neither did I."

"I didn't think so," she said, in the same calm voice he'd heard when they'd been preparing to fight the demons: evaluation, instruction. "You seemed surprised. You might have been a very good actor, of course."

"I might still be."

"There's no advantage in it for you, none that I can work out. I don't suppose you stopped reporting for any reason other than circumstance."

"No," said Zelen. He didn't know that he would have, and it wouldn't have mattered.

"Did he tell you why he wanted the information?"

"Only that you were a foreign agent."

"Well," said Branwyn, after a minute that stretched out longer than Zelen's entire carriage ride back, and he'd thought that had lasted an eternity, "that doesn't seem unreasonable. If I were a noble family, even if I didn't worship the Traitor God, I'd want to learn as much as possible about me, too, since I'm trying to get you involved in a war."

Zelen, who'd been expecting rage of either the hot or cold variety, and hadn't known what to say to either, found himself at even more of a loss for words than he'd predicted.

While he sat staring and, he feared, resembling a frog, Branwyn started to speak, stopped, actually flushed, then asked, "Was that the only reason you...took an interest in me?"

"No!"

He spoke with more passion than he'd felt in days, more than he'd known he was still capable of, and clasped the hand on his arm gently with one of his own. The skin was smooth under his fingers, save for the sword calluses that had been there as long as he'd known Branwyn—that had been there most of her life, if the stories about Sentinels were true.

"Well," she said, still blushing. "Then here we are."

"Yes," he said, and then, "You've healed bloody well in my absence."

"Good," said Branwyn. "I wish there was a better way to put this, but—"

"You expect you'll need to be in fighting form soon? So do I." Zelen stopped. "That is to say, fighting other people. Who I'll also be fighting. That did sound a bit like a threat."

He'd missed her chuckle, which was as comfortable as a hearth fire on a winter day. "Don't worry. I don't think you're stupid enough to bother threatening me if you wanted me dead. There are a number of things we each need to tell each other, but I doubt you'll be in any shape for talking about them for a little while. Have you eaten today, at all?"

"I don't think so." He'd left the country house before breakfast, claiming the desire to get an early start on preparations. The journey had been gray and endless. Zelen thought he'd have remembered food. He wasn't sure. "Are you a healer now?" He tried to joke.

"Only in the direst need, but I've seen any number of people in various states of devastation. It goes along with the calling."

Was he devastated? He supposed he was. The way he felt certainly went along with pictures of crumbling buildings and blackened fields, all that had been familiar suddenly gone.

"Stupid of me, really," Zelen said. "It isn't as though we ever got on."

"It strikes me that there's a fair amount of difference," said Branwyn, "but I lack expertise." She paused again and tilted her head in a way that Zelen had only seen glimpses of before: listening to her sword, he realized, and now not bothering to conceal it from him. "Yathana says she could talk to you because you're both devoted to Letar, by the way. Neither of us are sure if that's helpful information, but there it is."

He'd thought himself incapable of being surprised any more. "But I'm—"

"Not a priest, no, and she hasn't been a priestess as such in a hundred years. The gods leave their mark on their followers, even when they can't work through...official channels."

"Oh," said Zelen, and a band or two around his heart loosened.

"You've improved," said Altien, coming in with a tray like the world's oddest valet. "A minuscule improvement, but there it is." He poured a cup of tea, added a liberal dose from a bottle by the side of the kettle, then handed the cup and a plate of seed cakes to Zelen. "Drink this while you eat a cake. Pace yourself equally. I suspect you can't afford intoxication now."

"Is that my brandy?"

"It's nobody else's." Altiensarn added brandy and tea to the other two cups on the tray as well, passed one to Branwyn, then took a cake and sat back in his chair. "I have no story to tell. You have one, and Branwyn, or Yathana, has another. I suggest we share information, and quickly."

"Let me start," said Branwyn, sitting forward. She kept her arm around Zelen, though, and her hair brushed against his cheek. "You eat."

———

I sensed the demon when it entered, Yathana said, and Branwyn relayed that to the others. *It wasn't long before you returned.*

Experience both in a human form and out of it had rendered her calmer than any living person, but Branwyn still got a trace of horror when Yathana spoke, and no wonder. She'd lain unable to act, sensing the presence of not just a murderous juggernaut but one of the creatures she'd dedicated herself to fighting, in life as well as death. Most people would've been driven beyond rationality.

Branwyn wished it were possible to pat a sword's arm or give it a drink.

Nothing to be done, said Yathana, *now or then. You came back. I told you as soon as you got in hearing distance.*

The demon had already finished with Lord Rognozi by that point, likely slaughtering him in his sleep. Lady Rognozi had been awake. Branwyn hadn't heard her scream. Neither, by Zelen's account, had any of the servants who had been in the house. Maybe the lady had been too scared: fear could lock the lungs.

She had tried to run, though by that point she'd already been fatally wounded. Branwyn had kicked down the door and found the demon dragging her back toward it, one taloned hand around her ankle. Blood was pouring out of the lady's back, drenching her nightgown and the floor beneath her.

Her gaze had fastened on Branwyn.

"She thought I was coming to save her," Branwyn said. Her memories were secondhand, from Yathana, but one or two of the facts the sword recited called answering notes from the darkness. She remembered Lady Rognozi's expression. "But I was too late."

"All the same," said Zelen, "she knew you were there at the end. That'd be worth a fair amount, were I in her place."

Smart boy, said Yathana.

Branwyn tightened her arm around his shoulders. "Well. We fought, of course."

The demon had been nearly as tall as the room, and the Rognozis didn't believe in low ceilings. Its arms had been too long for its torso, its hands too big for its arms, and its jaw vast and permanently open, perhaps because the spike teeth inside couldn't fit in a normal mouth. It had been cold and glutinous when Branwyn cut it, and there had been orange-gray eyes studded all over it.

Branwyn stabbed through what passed as its body a few times. Its maw had yawned wider in a roar on those occasions, though no noise had emerged—neither she nor Yathana knew whether it was mute or whether its voice had been bound.

Some are void-silent, Yathana said. *But I think its orders were to make it seem like you'd killed the Rognozis, then yourself. I'd have kept my demon quiet in that case, if I were the sort of bastard who'd do that.*

Eventually, Branwyn had seen what she'd thought was an opening. She'd leapt up and in, striking for the head—and the demon had peeled back its face.

"It was like the things in Oakford," Branwyn said, "the creatures that made men stand still while other abominations slaughtered them, but more so. The Sentinels could resist those. This one, even with Yathana—no."

The soulsword didn't give her those memories, only the words. Branwyn still had to pause and drink from her cup of well-fortified tea before she could go on.

"If I hadn't been a Sentinel, it could have put a knife in my grasp and made me slit my own throat. And if it hadn't had orders, it could probably have crushed my neck while I stood there like a stunned ox—being metal doesn't prevent that."

Instead, the demon had wrenched Yathana out of Branwyn's grasp, then tossed Branwyn out the window, and returned to the Verengirs with its dubious prize.

It knew what I was, said the sword, *and so did Zelen's siblings. They didn't want to touch me more than they had to. Neither did they want to bring me into the place where they conceal most of their work. There are enchantments there that mine might disrupt. So they covered me, and stuck me in a place where they figured I'd do no harm but they could still be sure I remained in their possession.*

"Which of my siblings, my lady?" asked Zelen, once Branwyn had related Yathana's words.

"Gedomir," said Branwyn, after consultation with Yathana,

"and Hanyi. They referred to telling a sister about the results, though. I'm sorry, Zelen."

"As am I," said Altien, "though I also, forgive me, wonder how it is that you turned out differently, and why they didn't raise you in the faith, so to speak."

Zelen grinned bitterly. "Easy enough to answer that one. The council invokes the gods to close each of our sessions. They needed one of the family who could do that without being struck down. I'm sure it also helped to have one of us who really didn't know a damned thing the rest were doing. A distraction, as my mother said."

He told his story then, quickly but leaving out no detail, staring straight ahead. The tall form beside Branwyn might have been a marble pillar, and the shoulders under her arm were taut as wire.

"You had no knowledge of their actions or their allegiance," Altien said at the end. "We all know better than to say you can't blame yourself, but I can state certainly that you *shouldn't*."

"No, and yes, and…" Zelen set his empty cup down on the table, every movement very careful. "I didn't know, true. But I've no doubt that they got away with more because of me than if I hadn't given them cover. Now I do know—and I have to act. Surely you understand that."

Chapter 30

"Yes," said Branwyn immediately. "I can clean Yathana quickly, and you can wrap my leg in case we're wrong about it being healed. That'll take perhaps half an hour. Do you have any armor?"

"Afraid not," said Zelen. He still wasn't feeling at his best, but a quick ride would sober him up. "I can't imagine it'll end in much of a fight, though. The demon's contained, and only Gedomir's really... Well, there are our household guard, but—"

He'd never stopped to consider which side the men would be on. It had never been a question before. He realized, with a sinking heart, that it wasn't truly a question now. If they didn't know the family's ties and Zelen or Branwyn could prove them, that would be one thing—but otherwise, between their liege and a younger son making wild accusations, it would be no contest.

The guards might well be in on the whole affair too.

"How many would you say there are?" Branwyn asked. Her arm dropped away from his shoulders, but Zelen felt no insult. She was beginning the hunt. "And how are they disposed?"

"Both of you," said Altien, getting smoothly to his feet, "would do well to stay where you are and not rush off as though you're the only people in the world who can wield weapons, or the only ones interested in seeing this matter brought to a just conclusion."

"Generous of you, Altien, but it's my—" Zelen began.

"Are you proposing to go on your own?" Branwyn asked at the same time. "I'm sure you fight well, but—"

"I'm proposing," Altien said slowly, breaking down the word into its separate syllables, "that I go to the temple of Alcerion—Tinival, as you have him—tell them of the situation, and bring back one of the knights to let you both swear to the truth of your stories. *Then* I'm proposing that they, who have a multitude of armed and trained warriors who have neither been severely wounded nor suffered great shocks in the last few days, take the measures that I assume they—or the guard—are prepared to take against murderers and traitors. I've never wielded a weapon, Sentinel, and I'd predict I would do so very badly, though I thank you for your misplaced confidence."

The air of great purpose left Branwyn, replaced by one of considerable embarrassment, which was a comfort to Zelen, as he was sure it matched his. "Oh. Yes," she said. "I should probably have thought of that first."

"You're not the one who lives here," said Zelen. "Much obliged to you for stepping in, Altien. Don't know what I was thinking."

"You were thinking with guilt, exhaustion, and the aforementioned shock," Altien replied more gently, "and you're both too close to the matter to see clearly. Just try to remember that while I'm gone, I beg you."

"I suppose," said Zelen, "that now I shouldn't say that I can go to the temple myself and save you the errand."

"And yet you have said it. I'll choose to ignore it and trust that neither of you will have set yourselves on fire until I return," said Altien. "Remember that I would mourn deeply if you managed to harm yourself, please."

"Oh," said Zelen. Unable to find anything to say, he sat still, got a pat on the shoulder from a furred hand, and let Altien depart.

"He's very fond of you," said Branwyn, relaxing back onto the bed.

She wasn't sure how the waterman regarded her, though she thought they'd reached a tentative understanding over the last two days, but she was glad he'd intervened. Neither she nor Zelen needed to be running into a fight then.

"I know," he said, "I just…didn't know, if that doesn't sound too idiotic."

"No." Branwyn put an arm around his shoulders again. "Some ties are assumed when you work closely enough with another person. Neither of you feel the need to speak of it until you realize the other might not always be there."

Zelen's eyes were on a level with hers, and light had begun to come back into them. "The situation's one you know, hmm?"

"It's happened a few times. Teachers, comrades-in-arms." Branwyn hesitated.

Hell, girl, there's a war on, said Yathana.

"And you," she finished.

She caught a flash of joy on Zelen's face, not banishing the shock but lightening it until it was only a shadow, and her own heart lifted in response. Then he wrapped his arms around her and brought his lips to hers, seeking urgently what she gladly gave.

Just as Branwyn leaned in, her mouth opening at the touch of Zelen's tongue, he pulled back, panting. "You can tell me to stop. I won't take it amiss… You still have a place here if I've misinterpreted—"

"No," said Branwyn and took him by the shoulders, guiding him back toward her. "You have it exactly right."

And now I'll take my leave for a bit.

Desire was an avalanche this time, abrupt and completely overwhelming.

What intellect Zelen had left recognized the response in part—the body's way of celebrating survival and releasing tension—but that wasn't all of it with Branwyn. Kissing her, slipping his hands under her borrowed shirt to fondle her breasts, hearing her breath quicken, he could completely let go. There were occasions for wit and seduction, but this wasn't one, and it didn't need to be.

She was as eager as he was, and as ready to be lost in the moment. When Zelen brushed his fingers over her stiff nipples, Branwyn made a sound between a gasp and a growl low in her throat. Her own hands moved quickly, deftly busy with his belt buckle, then the buttons of his trousers. At the pressure of her fingers on his erection, Zelen gasped, thrusting up into her touch, and when she freed his cock, closing her palm around the rigid heat of it, he groaned her name, desperate and broken.

"Yes," she said, breathless, and started to swing a leg over his lap.

"No." Zelen was amazed that he'd said it—that he caught her hips and actually postponed their union. He was aching, lust pulsing through every vein, but stronger than that were duty and caring. "Your leg," he explained.

"Damn my leg."

"Branwyn," he managed again, despite her hand stroking up his shaft, then over the head, in a way that made him choke on the second syllable. "Let me…" He nudged at her shoulders, not quite pushing, only offering suggestion and guidance. "This way. If—"

"Ah. Yes."

Branwyn stretched herself backwards to the bed and pulled Zelen down with her. Her soft breasts nudged up against him, even through the layers of their clothing, her neck curved beneath his mouth, and his erection slid against the junction of her thighs, rubbing against smooth skin and silky hair.

Zelen was sure he spoke then, but what he said didn't pass anywhere near his brain. It might not have been words. When he slid a hand between them and found her wet and ready, he was sure words didn't enter into his reaction at all.

Branwyn wrapped her legs around his hips as Zelen guided himself in, and the first thrust made his vision go white around the edges. The heat of her was overwhelming—the hunger—and beyond all else unexpected, the feeling again of solid ground, of sense in a world that made none. He raised his head and looked down, rearing above her.

In all his life, surrounded by art and making an amateur effort at some himself, he'd seen nothing as lovely as Branwyn was at that instant. Her gold hair made a corona around her flushed face and her eyes were wide, showing more black than blue.

Her gaze went straight through Zelen. Every inch of his body flared into almost-unbearable sensation. At the same time he had the feeling that he could let go, that a fall with Branwyn would only be a dive, or even flight.

That was when she started moving, rocking her hips up and back with short, quick motions that spoke of desperate need. Her thighs were tight around Zelen's, and he could feel her nails digging into his back even through his shirt and doublet. If he hadn't been clothed, he'd have borne her marks for days. The notion of that aroused him even more.

Against all those things, he couldn't have controlled himself on his best day, and this was far from that. There was no question of holding back. He was surging to meet her immediately, burying himself in her clinging heat. Branwyn's moans in his ear became deeper, quicker, and her whole frame tensed around him. They were chasing each other around the spiral, retreat or delay impossible, unthinkable.

All the same, when Branwyn threw her head back and cried out at her peak, Zelen knew a satisfaction that went past the rippling pleasure and rush of warmth. As he arched and groaned, as Branwyn shuddered beneath him, pulling him closer, he felt for the first time in a long while that he wasn't alone.

Chapter 31

AFTERWARD, BRANWYN HAD EVEN LESS DESIRE TO MOVE THAN was usual following bed sport.

Actually being in a bed, and a fairly luxurious one, was no small factor there—most of her previous encounters had been, at best, on lumpy mattresses in dubious inns—but it wasn't that alone. Zelen's warmth, the clean smell of his sweat and their mutual satisfaction, and even the weight that he managed to keep mostly on the elbows were all far more welcome than such things had been with previous lovers.

If she'd had her way, they'd have curled up together under the blankets to doze, broken by talking and more vigorous activities, while the cold late-autumn rain fell outside.

Branwyn sighed, mostly in resignation, though she appreciated how Zelen shivered at her breath on his neck. "I'm afraid," she said, "that you'll have to find me another, more complete set of clothing before Altiensarn returns with the knight."

"You mean he won't take our oaths like this? We could simply pull up the blankets…" Zelen teased, and it heartened Branwyn to hear him capable of joking again.

"Depends on the knight, I suppose," she said. They weren't a celibate order, but they tended to be more romantic than the Blades. Certainly the ones Branwyn had met were more restrained than the Sentinels. "You'd know better than I would."

"True," said Zelen, and rose from her with a wordless grumble, stopping at the edge of the bed to run his fingers down her cheek. "The word 'splendid' rather comes to mind again."

"Takes one to know one," said Branwyn. She watched him

leave, looking more rumpled and more alive by far than when he'd come in the door.

He came back with hot water and cloths later, as well as a new shirt and a pair of gray trousers. "No need to hurry yet," Zelen said, as Branwyn started to clean up. "We've got ten minutes at least, and that's if Altien had an audience right off."

"You know the timing very well," she said, lifting her eyebrows.

Zelen laughed. "I wasn't taking it into account at all when I threw myself at you, I swear. But I do often go to the temple district." That was a trifle more serious. Branwyn was silent in respect, pulling on the trousers carefully and searching for the right words.

"I feel the same," Zelen said, surprising her. "About you, that is, as you said you felt about me before. I suppose that might have been a bit obvious, but I wanted to say it."

"I'd hoped," said Branwyn, "and I thought I might have reason to hope. But it's good to hear it for certain."

She pulled the shirt on and crossed the room, kissing him warmly enough that his newly donned doublet was disheveled again before she was done.

"Despite," Zelen added when he stepped back, "the disastrous effect you have on my wardrobe."

"I do owe you half a tailor's shop by now, don't I?"

"Something like. I'll let you consult with my valet on the specifics—oh." He frowned. "Speaking of, it might be best if he witnessed the oathtaking, and the rest of the servants as well, particularly if you're going to stay here…"

His voice trailed off. Both of them knew there was no point in trying to follow up with more specifics. Branwyn had the duty she was made for. She'd stay until her mission was done—and how that would react with Zelen's own duties, or how either of them would want it to, was a discussion too sharp and definite for that moment. "For a while," she finished. "It's a good idea."

"I'll go have an entirely awkward conversation then," Zelen said, and added quietly, "though it'll probably be the easiest of what I need to tell them in the next few days."

In other circumstances, Branwyn would have offered to go with him, but she didn't think her presence would be an asset, to say the least. At worst, one of the servants, doubting, might decide to try to avenge the Rognozis with a paring knife. Branwyn met Zelen's eyes and knew he realized the same thing.

"Good luck," she said. "I'll be here."

He kissed her, lightly and softly. "Knowing that will make it much better."

It did. So did the better part of a bottle of brandy. Zelen, who had a decent head for drink, was still glad Altien had brought up cakes as well. That way he was only feeling insulated, not actually slurring his speech.

There weren't many servants assembled in his little-used parlor. Idriel and Feyher stood at one end, authoritative in dark clothing. Three maids, two grooms, and Barthani, his cook, fanned out around them in a semicircle facing Zelen. Despite the drink, he knew that they were trying not to gape at him. A few minutes of pleasure with Branwyn had lightened the weight on his shoulders, and their conversation afterward had made him more able to bear it, but none of that erased the marks of strain and sleepless nights, particularly to people who already knew he had a mysterious announcement to make.

At least one of them likely thought he was dying. Another probably leaned more toward an announcement of marriage, or had until they'd seen Zelen. He wondered if they'd had a chance to place wagers.

Blunt was better, he decided, and cleared his throat. "Hello.

Altiensarn will be here soon with one of Tinival's knights. Then Branwyn of Criwath will come downstairs and join us." He'd expected the gasps and murmurs, and raised his hand before they could get too loud. "She didn't kill the Rognozis. She and I have discovered who did, and we'll swear to that. I'd like you to hear the oaths. In return, you'll swear those that the knight asks of you. They'll likely want you to keep silent about this for a few days."

"Of course, my lord," said Feyher. He looked startled, which Zelen had almost never seen from him, but there was neither hesitation nor question in his answer.

"Will she be staying here, m'lord?" asked Barthani.

"Yes. Do you object?"

"If her word's good enough for Tinival, it's good enough for us," said Idriel.

Zelen nodded his appreciation, then added, "If you hear what we swear to and feel you can't stay here any longer, I'll understand. You'll have a good character and two weeks' pay."

They all exchanged glances at that, even Feyher, but there was no time for questions. A quick knock came on the study door, followed by Altien's voice. "Is everyone prepared?"

"As much as possible," Zelen said, opening the door.

Altien stepped quickly into the room and to the side, taking up a place by the youngest housemaid. Behind him came Branwyn, as respectable as she could be in bare feet and what all the servants would recognize as Zelen's clothing, and Lycellias behind her. His silver breastplate shone in the light, and the silver work on the sheath of his sword put Yathana's ornamentation to shame, more so because it was genuine.

He tilted his head a little when he saw the assembled servants. "Good afternoon to you all," he said. "I am Lycellias. How many are swearing?"

"Only me," said Zelen, "and Sentinel Branwyn."

A third murmur went around the circle. Zelen knew it wouldn't be the last.

"Well enough. Sit as you feel comfortable." When Branwyn and Zelen had taken chairs, and Altien and the servants had dispersed themselves as well as they would fit on couches, Lycellias walked over to stand in front of Branwyn. "The lady first," he said, barely hinting that he recognized the person the city'd spent the last few days searching for. "Do you know how this proceeds?"

"I do."

Lycellias nodded. One long-fingered hand went to his brow, then out to the east, first two fingers upright and the others folded down. "Tinival, you hear and see past all artifice. Yours is the wind that scours away falsehood, yours the knowledge of justice, yours the eyes that pierce every veil. Grant that I, your servant, may share in your gift, for the good of your world."

A small breeze blew through the closed study, bringing with it the smell of roses and rain.

The knight touched his fingers lightly to Branwyn's lips. "Speak your piece to me and to the gods, child of creation."

Her story left out most of the gory details, but it was bad enough. One of the grooms covered her mouth at the description of Lady Rognozi's death, and when Branwyn described the demon, the immovable Feyher shuddered. Lycellias himself grew graver and graver as he listened.

"You tell no lies," he said at the end, "though I could almost wish you did, Sentinel. My temple, and the Healer's, will have much work to do tonight."

"More than that, I'm afraid," said Zelen.

His story, once he'd taken the oath, wasn't even really a story. "I found Branwyn's soulsword, with a bloody handprint on it, yesterday," he began, "behind a bookcase in my family's country house." There wasn't much else to say about that, save to describe the conversation that he'd overheard while he was smuggling

Yathana out, and the sword's secondhand statement about Hanyi. "So," he finished, "it seems that the rest of my family worship the Traitor. I don't. I can take further vows along those lines, if that would help."

"No," said Lycellias, "that won't be necessary." He regarded the servants, who had moved on to looking different versions of stunned. "I'll take all of your oaths, good people, that you'll let four days and nights pass before speaking of this matter. After that"—he glanced back to Zelen, Branwyn, and Altien—"the four of us must hold conversation."

<hr />

It was a relief when the oath taking was done, the servants went about their business, and Branwyn was left in the study with Zelen, Altiensarn, and the knight. She was eager to learn what would happen to the Verengirs for the sake of her mission as well as Zelen's peace of mind. She was also tired of being stared at.

The servants were likely quite nice people, particularly the valet, who'd taken Zelen aside to ask if he was all right, and the cook, who'd given all of them a keen glance and then declared that dinner for four would be ready before very long, assuming none of them minded a simple meal. Branwyn couldn't even blame them for being curious. Sentinels were rare and strange. A Sentinel who had also been a suspected murderer, but now wasn't, and had come face-to-face with a greater demon... Yes, Branwyn would likely have stared, and not done half as good a job hiding it as even the younger of the grooms.

Still, they and Lycellias were the first people other than Zelen and Altien she'd seen in days, and their regard was wearying. When the door closed behind the last of them, she was glad to be in a room with only familiar people and the preoccupied knight.

"How many armed guards do you believe your family has?" he asked Zelen, exactly as Branwyn had an hour or so before. "And what do you estimate their training and disposition to be?"

"A half-dozen professional guards," said Zelen, seating himself on the couch next to Branwyn. "I'd say they're about as well trained as any of the patrolmen in the city. Two watch each of the outer doors every night, and when I was growing up, they changed every four hours. The grooms and the coach drivers can likely pick up clubs if they need to, so that's another half dozen, and Gedomir's decent with a sword."

Lycellias, who'd kept his feet, paced as he thought. His armor flashed in the light. For the first time in a while, Branwyn remembered Olvir. The two men were different in almost every way, but they were both knights, and preparing for battle made everyone kin. "And he, as well as at least one of your sisters, is a wizard," the stonekin went on.

"I'm fairly sure." Zelen spoke without inflection. "Could easily be all the rest."

"That could be so," said Lycellias. "We aren't without defenses in such matters, but we might do well to involve the Blades. You mentioned that the others are coming to the city in the next few days?"

"For the burnings, yes. It'd look damned odd if they didn't. Unless they find out what I've done with Yathana..." Zelen frowned. "And you know, I think they'd still come and try to brazen it out. Could always claim I'd taken leave of my senses, after all, or misinterpreted matters. They don't know I'd met up with Branwyn again, or what I overheard."

"If they do decide otherwise," Lycellias said, "they won't meet with clear passage. There's only one road from your family's estates, and I sent messages to the Temple just now. It will be blocked."

"What should we do then?" Branwyn asked.

"Only what you've been doing. You've given us your knowledge, and the Sentinel has fought one dire foe already. Until the traitors are in our grasp, or that of the Shadow Queen, the duty is ours. But you"—Lycellias turned to Altien, his blue-and-black eyebrows slanting inward—"asked for me by name. Why?"

"We didn't quite get to explaining this," said Altien to Zelen, and produced the folded sheaf of notes that Branwyn had found.

The story was simple there as well, though it baffled Zelen when he heard it. "Judging by the date, R would've been Roslina, my aunt. She died when I was three. A number of the family did—there was a fire in one of the old wings. All damned suspicious now, of course, but I've no idea exactly what I should be suspecting."

"I do, somewhat," said the knight, and moved from the window to perch on one of the chairs. He sat lightly—even in plate mail, the stonekin couldn't really sit any other way—but he passed a hand over his brow wearily before he began. "The story is old, mark you, and not one that I have ever heard as other than a legend, but in simple terms it is this: when the Traitor killed his sister's beloved, out of spite and pride and unbrotherly jealousy, a piece of his essence split. There are tales that say it fell to the ground, unnoticed, when he struck the blow, and those that have it cut off by Lethiannar later, in the greatest of battles. One seems as likely as the other."

"And my family was trying to incarnate it," said Zelen. "Why? What would that…fragment…be, really?"

"That, too, depends on the story. It could be the power Gazathar needs to reach his full might, in which case he might be able to treat the Veil of Fire as a courtesy and manifest fully in this world. It could be all that was still good in him—the god he once was, and still could have been, up until his final decision. Or it could simply be power, and the one who took that into themselves would make Thyran look like a child kicking over toy blocks."

They sat silent, contemplating that possibility, as night came on outside.

Chapter 32

DESPITE EVERYTHING, THEY MANAGED A DECENT DINNER. Barthani served up spiced rice cooked with sausage and squash, and dried fruit in syrup to follow—as simple as they'd promised, but a satisfying meal all the same—and Feyher brought around a hearty red wine with it. Zelen enjoyed it but didn't drink much, mindful of the earlier brandy.

Thus fortified, though, they turned the conversation to relatively lighter matters. Branwyn told funny stories from her travels, including one about overhearing an arguing couple in a shoddy inn.

"…and as I was lying there right on the other side of the wall, she threw the water jug across the room and yelled 'How many times must you stab me in the heart, Brendan?' I felt my professional opinion was relevant at that point, so I called back: 'If it takes more than one, get a priest!' They were quieter after that."

Lycellias compared notes with her about their early training and mentioned that the blue streaks in his hair were how he'd known that his destiny lay with the gods. "It's ever been so among my people," he'd explained, when the other three looked curious. "Blue for the divine, red for a warrior's life—though I admit there's some common ground there—white for magic or scholarship, green for hunting or farming, and so on."

"It would make missions like mine difficult," Branwyn said, "but then, so does the Forging for most of us," and she pulled back one sleeve to display her wrist.

The evening went on in that fashion, and while the darkness

gathered beyond the windows and the rain pattered against the glass, the room was warm and bright. For a few minutes at a time, Zelen managed to forget what he'd learned over the last few days and what still lay ahead.

Lycellias was the first to leave, headed back to his temple with a bow and a return to his solemn demeanor of the afternoon. "Be sure that I'll send word of any developments," he said.

Not much later, Altien departed. "You both should make an early night of it. And, Zelen, if you'd rather—"

"I'll be at the clinic tomorrow," Zelen said, "as usual."

"It seems rather pointless to argue. Get some sleep, then."

Sleep did sound like a wise idea, but Altien's departure left Zelen alone with Branwyn, standing next to her in the hall and noticing how much better she looked in his clothing than he'd ever done. Her hair fell loosely over the shoulders of his shirt, which clung to her breasts in a most diverting way, and the firm curves of her hips and thighs greatly enhanced his trousers.

"Ah," he said, suddenly uncertain how to start when before he'd simply acted.

"Your valet mentioned a bath to me before we came in to dinner," said Branwyn, "and I believe I'll take him up on that. Afterward, um." She didn't look away, but Zelen could tell that she wanted to, and was surprised by her reticence until she spoke again. "I don't want to impose, but if you'd... I'd rather not sleep alone, if you're inclined toward company. I understand if not. It's been a day."

"It has," said Zelen. He took both of her hands in his and kissed her gently. "And I believe my bed would feel empty without you there, since you mention it. We can even actually sleep, if you'd rather."

She chuckled, self-assured once more. "Eventually," Branwyn said, with a gleam in her eye that took his breath away.

You've chosen well, said Yathana, as Branwyn was scrubbing away the last traces of her wounds.

"Thank you, but it wasn't only my choice." She sank down in the tub and groaned with satisfaction. Quarters were a little more cramped than in the bathhouses she'd been used to, but she had the basin to herself—and a full bath for the first time since she'd woken up in the alley. "Given the circumstances, it might even have been his wretched family's doing."

They didn't ask him to seduce you.

"He didn't."

There you are then, Yathana said.

"I'm not sure what you mean, but I've missed you." Branwyn hesitated. "If you'd rather stay around, we really *can* sleep. I'll let him know."

Don't be an idiot. I'll be here when you're done, and you're not likely to have many chances like this once you go back on the road, you know.

"I know," said Branwyn. It was another matter she preferred not to give very much thought. "And thank you."

She took Yathana's physical form with her regardless, caring little for how she looked carrying the sword while wrapped in one of Zelen's velvet dressing gowns. The servants knew what she was, and despite the wards, Branwyn didn't want to take chances.

Then, too, she was oddly nervous as she approached Zelen's room, just as she'd been in the hall. Falling asleep by chance next to a lover was no new experience, though it hadn't been terribly common for her, but deliberately choosing to spend the night was a different matter entirely. It was good to feel the weight of Yathana, to be reminded of who and what she was, of what she'd done and mastered and was capable of now.

She pushed open the door to find Zelen sitting on his bed, wet hair and dressing gown a mirror to hers, though he wore plum-colored velvet rather than her black. He looked up from his book, and the welcome on his face banished Branwyn's nerves instantly.

"The robe suits you," he said, "and I should've offered it before. My apologies."

"No need. You had a number of things on your mind." She laid Yathana down gently by the door. "It's very comfortable," Branwyn added, crossing the room until she stood by the bed, only a few inches from Zelen, "but I admit I don't plan to wear it very long tonight."

His gaze, already intent, sharpened further as he looked up the line of her frame. "I'd better be a gentleman then," he said, reaching for the knot in her sash, "and help you with that."

Kissing him didn't make the untying process easier, but Branwyn did it regardless, gently tangling her hands in his hair as she bent toward him. It was languid at first, teasing, and the distance between their bodies became pleasurably frustrating as Zelen worked at the knot. Branwyn caught his oaths in her mouth, and his short cry of triumph when the sash parted as well.

She pulled back reluctantly so that Zelen could push the robe off her shoulders. The path his hands took tingled in their wake. Branwyn felt no cold when she finally stood naked, especially not when she saw the light in Zelen's eyes.

"Gods, you're perfect," he breathed.

"Thank you," she said, without enough modesty to argue the point. It wasn't objectively true—but perfect for Zelen was the only sort Branwyn was interested in being just then. She placed her hand in his and let him pull her onto the bed.

Even there he was careful, not only watching the way her breasts bobbed or her thighs flexed, but studying her face, alert for signs that her injuries still pained her. Stretching herself out beside him, Branwyn smiled at his concern and stroked his cheek before kissing him again.

This time she could try and melt into him, bare breasts

crushing the plush fabric of his robe, arse tense in his cupped hands, the ridge of his arousal hard against her thigh. For a while, Branwyn held mostly still, letting the sensations spiral outward to run through her whole frame, learning Zelen's body as she'd never the chance to do before.

Then she pushed him away. He retreated promptly, though with a curious expression that verged on worried until Branwyn sat up and started undoing his robe. "You should hold still for a while," she told him, slipping her hand down from the undone sash to trace over the substantial tent in the fabric.

"That'll be a challenge," he half gasped.

"Yes, but you enjoy those." Branwyn parted the robe and sat back, taking in the view.

It was a magnificent one. Zelen was all lithe firmness, long and compact and without a spare inch of flesh. His chest was thickly covered with dark hair, which became a narrow trail, crisp under Branwyn's trailing fingers while the muscles beneath tensed and Zelen made a choked noise. She followed it down to the point where it widened, becoming a backdrop to the erection that arched, straining and flushed red, to almost meet his flat stomach.

She didn't touch that yet. Branwyn let her hands wander instead, stroking up Zelen's chest and making small circles over his nipples, then down over his thighs, in, and up—but not too far.

The way he looked, fighting not to writhe or grab for her, was a caress in itself. The way he groaned as her fingers approached the top of his thighs was another. When Branwyn finally did wrap her fingers around his cock, lightly squeezing the hot, hard shaft, Zelen said her name in a breathless plea that went straight between her legs.

"That's me," she said, and bent, touching her tongue to the head, licking at the moisture there, and finally taking his cock into her mouth.

For a while Branwyn teased him, pulling away whenever Zelen got too tense, her hands firm on his thighs while her lips and tongue were busy. Her hair fell around them. Branwyn felt it brushing her breasts as she moved, adding to her excitement, just as she was a thousand times more aware than normal of the feel of the coverlet against her wet center when she shifted position.

"Branwyn," Zelen said again, deeper than before and even more ragged. "Please—"

She lifted her head. "You could mean two things by that," she said, meeting his wild eyes. "Which one would you prefer?"

"Cruel woman," said Zelen. "Come back here, I think. I want you with me this time."

"On account then," said Branwyn, and gave his erection one lingering swirl of her tongue around the head before sliding up beside Zelen.

He turned on his side to meet her, kissing her deeply while he parted her legs with one hand, stroking her aching sex until Branwyn was squirming against him, showing as little hurry as she'd done with him. Then, when she was arching her back and moaning, Zelen guided her good leg over his hips and slid inside her.

It felt even better than it had before, and that without even the fuel of pent-up fear and grief. This was pure pleasure, delight in each other, with no urgency save what gradually built between them as they rocked in rhythm.

"I could stay here for a year or two," she said, even as Zelen's fingers on her nipples were quickening her pulse.

"Medically unwise," he said, the words hot against her earlobe, "but I'd do it with you regardless."

And Branwyn laughed and let herself flow toward him: toward his touch, toward the pleasure of his cock thrusting deep inside her, and in due course, toward a climax as overwhelming and as inevitable as the summer sun at midday. She basked in it, and in

Zelen's answering release, rejoicing in every line of his arching body and every pulse of heat inside her.

Eventually, in the morning, the rest of the world would exist again. It could take its damn time.

Chapter 33

"Sir."

Idriel's voice was quiet but insistent, reaching through exhaustion and satiation both. Zelen's instinct was still to ignore it. The bed was soft. He felt less dead than he had on his return to the city, but he wasn't ready to bound out and greet the day yet. Moreover, Branwyn was tucked neatly against his side, her breath light on his neck. If he was going to rise for any reason, it would be because of her, and in the more anatomical sense.

But a matter that sent Idriel in to wake him, especially when Zelen had company, was not trivial. Events of the last few days made it even more likely to be urgent. Zelen opened his eyes and grunted.

It wasn't dawn yet. Idriel carried a candle rather than activating the magical lights, and the flame picked out shadows in his craggy, lined face. "Sir," he said, seeing Zelen awake, "we've caught a boy breaking into the house."

"Lgh."

"He was armed, sir, if you can call it that, and seems to be seeking other children. I wondered if you wanted to speak with him before I summon the guards."

"Oh gods," said Zelen, managing actual words with considerable effort, "what's happened *now*? Yes, put him in the study and give him a hot drink and a tea cake. I'll be in directly."

"Yes, sir."

"Why in the world," Branwyn muttered as Idriel closed the door, "would you have one child here, much less a number?" She slid away to let Zelen get up.

"I've no idea. I helped look for that one earlier. Maybe the boy came to ask for my aid again? Or demand it, given how he arrived."

"Or he suspects you, though I don't know why he would." Branwyn sat up, lithe in the moonlight, and swung her long legs over the side of the bed.

"You should stay here," said Zelen, wrapping his robe around him. "Not that I wouldn't be glad of your company, but it'd likely make the conversation more tricky, so there's no reason you have to get up."

"You never know," she said. "Two sets of ears—three in this case—can pick up on details that one might miss. I won't come in, but I'll lurk outside and listen, unless you object."

"Not at all."

Only two of the servants were awake at that hour, which proved to be four after midnight: Idriel and the maid who'd collared the boy as he'd broken in through the kitchen. She clearly noticed Branwyn's presence, and the fact that she was wearing Zelen's robe, but showed neither surprise nor any other emotion. Their sleeping arrangements, Zelen reflected, were probably no secret, and other events had taken their place as the latest excitement.

He left both of them and Branwyn behind at the study door and slipped past it without letting the boy who sat on the couch see who was in the hall.

The boy was rigid, the tea and cake untouched before him. Zelen thought he was between eight and twelve, but poverty made that hard to tell, as did the boy's too-large black clothing and the soot he'd smeared liberally on his face and neck. Either Idriel or the maid had scrubbed him as best they could before sending him into the study, but mortal power only went so far.

"You bastard!" He was on his feet as soon as he recognized Zelen, then running forward headfirst with tiny fists upraised. "You lying son of a whore, you—"

Zelen caught him by the shoulders, breaking the charge. The

force as the boy struggled spoke of his desperation, but even his flailing arms couldn't do much damage. "Easy now. I don't doubt you've got a good reason for thinking I'm everything you claim, but I swear I haven't knowingly hurt anybody. Tell me what's wrong, and let's see if we can't sort it out."

The flood of expletives cut off. The boy froze, staring at Zelen as tears of rage made cleaner lines down his cheeks. "Sort it out? Like you did before? With my brother, Jaron, and Cynric, and pretending to help us? Acting like you were a friend to our sort, like—" He choked off whatever he was going to say next and lunged for Zelen again. "Where's *Tanya*, you godsdamn liar?"

Branwyn didn't know who the boy was talking about. Her mind immediately leapt to the child who'd found her in the alley, but she couldn't trust her judgment on that. There were more than a few street urchins in the city. The disappearance of one might have nothing to do with another's inclination to help strange wounded women.

She kept listening, not bothering to hide that fact. The valet had waved the maid back to her bed and was standing a discreet, or plausibly deniable, distance from the door. Branwyn had tried to wave him back in turn, but he'd simply shaken his head. Branwyn couldn't blame him. Oath or not, she was an unknown quantity with a sword.

There was silence for a while, and Branwyn's lesser gift enabled her to truly know that it was silence, not whispering.

Likely Tanya's name took your boy by shock, said Yathana, *and likely the child observed as much. Wasn't what he was expecting. Children like that get good at reading people.*

"I don't know," Zelen eventually said. "I had no idea she was gone until you spoke. I'll take any oath you want on that, in front of any priest you want."

"You... But...she..." The torrent of rage had turned into confusion and despair.

"Sit down, won't you? Have a sip of that tea and a bite to eat." Branwyn heard footsteps, then Zelen opened the door a crack. "Bran—Oh, Idriel, good. Get me clothes and a sword, would you? And rouse Jander and Lena. This might take a bit of force."

"Right away, sir," said the valet, glancing past him toward the boy, who was holding his mug like he wasn't sure what to do with it. "Are you sure?"

"He wouldn't do this on a prank," Zelen said, "and if it turns out to be all a misunderstanding, I'd rather look foolish than otherwise. Thank you."

He returned to the room.

"What are you going to do?" Branwyn heard the boy ask.

"Go and find her, of course. Any bit of information you can give me will help, but not until you've drunk at least half that and eaten three bites of the cake. You'll be more harm than good talking until you get yourself steady. Gods help me, I know that."

Branwyn heard the muffled noises of eating and drinking, as well as footsteps. Zelen was pacing, she guessed.

"When you've finished," he said, "and not before, let's start with the obvious question. Why did you think I was the one who'd kidnapped Tanya—or all of the missing, going by what you said earlier when you were trying to break my jaw with your head? By the way, old man, excellent effort, but I'd have thrown the tea at me first off, were I in your place."

The boy laughed nervously, but almost immediately began. "We were playing before dinner. In an alley. I wasn't daring her to do nothing dangerous, not after she broke her arm, so we stuck to ground. I was hiding and she was looking for me, that was all. Except she didn't find me by time, so I headed back to the start... and I saw her. She—" The flow of words sped up and became ragged. "There were two men dragging her into a carriage. One had his hand on her mouth so she couldn't scream. The other was a man I'd seen before. With you. When you said you were trying to find my brother."

———————

No wonder we didn't find a damned thing was Zelen's first thought.

His second thought wasn't really a thought at all. It was pure rage, unfiltered by words. His family was the immediate target, but he himself wasn't far behind. The connection between the missing children and the demon, not to mention Gedomir's talk of "expeditions" and "supply," was obvious in retrospect. If he'd reflected on it more...

That didn't matter. The boy—Mitri—was staring at him, waiting for a response. Tanya was in his family's grasp, waiting for a response as well.

"Well," Zelen said, "trying to stab me was basically sound. Just a tad misdirected, and you weren't to know." Mitri blinked. "Never mind. I've found out a few things about my family recently. This is one more. Finish up the rest of the food. I don't suppose you'll wait quietly here while I take care of matters?"

"Like Sitha's arse I will!"

"The right spirit, I must say." Zelen went to the door again. "Idriel, if—"

"He's just coming back," said Branwyn. "Get me a paper and pen. I'll write a message to Lycellias while you're getting dressed and having the horses saddled. I dress very quickly when I need to, and your grooms won't listen to me quite as well as they will to you. You don't think she's in the city, do you?"

"No," he said. "They wouldn't have brought a coach, and"—he glanced over his shoulder at Dimitri, who was staring past him at Branwyn—"the situation's at the house in the country."

Zelen did the math as he turned to retrieve writing implements, calculating how long it would take to get out of the city earlier in the evening and the speed of a laden coach compared to that of fast horses. "We might make it," he said quietly, handing parchment and pen to Branwyn, "but not if we wait for others—not even if they act at once."

Human sacrifice required specific times, didn't it? Or was that merely a device of plays, which said that all murders must take place at midnight, preferably in thunderstorms? Zelen could only hope that the truth was in their favor, but he couldn't count on it.

"I know," said Branwyn. She was writing quickly, steadying the paper against the wall and covering both wall and wrist with ink as a result. "Twelve guards might be a problem, even for both of us, and magic will be worse."

Idriel came back down the hall then, the two grooms trailing behind him. Zelen considered them as possible allies, then rejected the notion. Lena was strapping enough, and Jander nimble, but they had no real training in armed combat. They might have done for hunting down a few criminals, but he couldn't in good conscience take them up against the guards of Verengir, let alone whatever magical tricks Hanyi might pull.

"I'll need Brandy and Jester ready to ride as soon as you can get them saddled," he told the grooms. "Idriel, take this to Tinival's temple as fast as you can." Zelen passed over the folded message as soon as Branwyn handed it to him. "And bring the boy along. He's an important witness."

That would make Dimitri less trouble, gods willing.

He took Idriel's armload—tunic, trousers, boots, and belt, complete with sword—and began changing then and there.

"Come along, lady," said Lena to Branwyn. "There's a set of my clothes that'll fit you."

Zelen only realized then that he'd either been expecting Branwyn to have clothing ready or to go fight armed men while wearing his dressing gown. He would have been embarrassed about that oversight as well, except that he had every confidence she could have done exactly that and triumphed under most circumstances.

———————

"You've got two guards on the front," Branwyn said, swinging up onto the roan mare that Lena had provided for her and looking to Zelen on his brown gelding, "and two at…what, the servants' entrance?"

"Outside the stable building, yes."

"Any chance we can catch the carriage and waylay that?"

"Not much. Might catch them as they arrive."

"Tactically sticky."

Zelen, who knew the city better than Branwyn, nudged his horse into the rapid start that the young animal seemed eager for, and they were off as fast as they could go. Heliodar's streets slowed them down, though, so they made plans while the horses jogged.

"Could take two, even four guards on my own," Branwyn said. "Would have to leave the horses and sneak up, I'm guessing. Or they'd all be ready."

"Right." Zelen turned down an unexpected alley, and his words came back to her as they rode single file in the narrow gap between the houses. "Hoping some will have left for the city already, but can't count on it."

Half of the force waiting for them wouldn't be professional, and most of them wouldn't have seen a Sentinel. That might help. The grooms and footmen—maybe the guards as well—might break and run when she turned metal. It had happened before.

On the other side of the scales, the Verengirs had at least one wizard, maybe more, and maybe a demon. The possibilities were too wild to predict—and then there was the chance that, if pressed, the traitors would slit Tanya's throat then and there.

232   ISABEL COOPER

Only way a hostage situation can get worse, Yathana agreed. *Bring the bloody mages into it.*

"I'd love a distraction," Branwyn said. "Fire, maybe?"

"Too wet to burn well."

They emerged from the alley practically at one of Heliodar's lesser gates and slowed as the lone watchman there came forward to peer at them. "Name and business?"

He was young and alone, but the halberd he held was sturdy, and Branwyn didn't doubt that he had a companion with a crossbow covering him from a nearby building.

"Zelen Verengir," said Zelen, holding up the hand with his signet ring on it. "Urgent family matter."

The guard didn't even examine Branwyn closely enough to make out her form under the cloak or her face under the hood. "Gods speed you, m'lord," he said, and stepped aside.

Amris would have had the man mending armor and chopping wood for a month for that, Branwyn thought, but Amris was commanding on the front lines, not in a rank-bound city. She followed Zelen through the gates and then drew alongside him on the narrow road beyond.

"You know," he said, "I have a notion of how we might do this."

Part III

Call: Who are the children of Sitha and Poram?
Response: *They are three.*

Eldest is Letar, the Queen of Shadows, lady of desire and death, healing and vengeance. With her, the elder gods gave mortals the gift of fire.

Second is Gizath, the Traitor, the Forger of Chains. Once he ruled over the ties between all things. Now he is the enemy of creation.

Youngest is Tinival, the Silver Wind, the Lord of the Scales. He holds in his hands true justice, that to which high and low alike have a right—and that which low and high alike should fear.
—Litany of Sitha, Part IV

The question remaining is this: Where did Thyran get his knowledge? We grant that the slaughter of his household sealed his pact with Gizath. A chance does exist that he acted simply in murderous rage and that the blood so spilled weakened the Veil of Fire enough to allow a direct connection or a demonic intrusion. It's far more likely that he knew precisely what he was contacting. That suggests a teacher. And that in eighty years, we haven't identified a likely candidate for the role...that worries me greatly.

—Letter from the Blade Caden to his superiors

Chapter 34

RAIN STARTED FALLING AGAIN AS THEY WERE RIDING AWAY from the city. It wasn't a hard downpour, but the wind blew it past hoods and it kept the ground too wet to really push the horses. Zelen bent low over Jester's back, wiped his brow with his sleeve until the skin chafed, and did his best to remind himself that they'd be later yet if an all-out gallop turned into a broken leg.

Even the comfort of having Branwyn beside him, an anonymous shape in the darkness but one he could have picked instantly out of a crowd, was mixed. He was taking her into danger, not two days since she'd been unable to stand on both feet for more than a few minutes. Zelen's mind could repeat endlessly that she was fully healed now, that a Sentinel was worth any four or five normal warriors, and that Branwyn had thrown in with the plan before he'd so much as hinted at her coming along.

His gut, and his heart, were having none of it.

The darkness was full of demons and magic, evil sorcerers wearing familiar faces, and foul pictures from his imagination and memory both. He remembered Branwyn lying huddled in the alley and knew too well that her powers didn't protect her against all threats. He considered how fragile the human body was, especially a child's, and thought of all the methods of human sacrifice he'd heard of in lurid tales.

Zelen also thought of Hanyi, who'd occasionally looked the other way when she'd caught him sneaking back into the house, or brought him hot drinks when he was sick in bed, and who summoned demons now. No such memories of Gedomir came to mind. Perversely, that was itself painful—the man was his brother, and if there was nothing to mourn for on finding out where his allegiances lay, Zelen couldn't believe the fault was all on one side.

He wasn't divinely inspired. He hadn't preternaturally sensed that Gedomir worshipped the Traitor. They'd just never liked each other, and Zelen had never had quite enough family feeling to overcome that.

The ride would've taken forever, even if they hadn't been in a hurry.

No lights shone from the house's windows. It was a great black hulk in the darkness. Fans of white magelight shone from either side of the doors, though, giving the guards a good view of the road.

Shortly before they'd come into view, they reined in the horses. Branwyn came close enough to lay a hand on Zelen's arm and bent toward him, talking as softly as she could manage while making sure he could still hear her over the rain. "I'll be as quiet as I can, but I'm not a Blade, and I'll be noticed eventually. Be prepared."

"I will," he said. "Come back to me."

"I'll try."

He kissed her with the rain falling around them, her lips the only warm part of the world. He couldn't take her in his arms because of the horses, and they couldn't linger.

Letar, he prayed as she turned Brandy away from the road, *you lost your lover to your brother's evil. Have mercy on me.*

Then he rode hell-for-leather, or as close to it as the mud and any consideration for Jester would let him, toward the house. The hood of his cloak fell back, and the rain lashed his face, but Zelen didn't bother to pull it up.

He knew full well how he appeared as he crossed the edge of the magelight. The cloak was black, his hair black and straggling now that it was soaked, his eyes dark in a face that was pale by comparison. With Jester equally dark and wet, the pair of them could have come from a scene from a ballad about highwaymen.

The men who stood guard in the nighttime, wielding axes and spears, were not romantic figures. They stepped forward in challenge before recognition dawned.

"My lord Zelen?" asked Kostan.

"I need to speak with my brother at once," he said, trying to sound as arrogant as Gedomir ever had. "Is my family still here?"

"Some, sir," Otto replied. He was older and hadn't come to "help" Zelen in his search for Dimitri's brother. "Your lord father and lady mother have left for the city, as has your elder sister. The others depart tomorrow."

"Good," Zelen lied, and swung down to the wet ground. "Give my horse to one of the grooms and see that he's well tended. I've ridden hard tonight, and I may have to do as much tomorrow."

All but the most dedicated men, when told to leave what shelter they had and take care of a wet and likely out-of-temper horse, would hesitate. Verengir's guards were mercenaries, not knights or Blades, and not the best of them at that. The long glance between them spoke of a complicated negotiation of seniority, favors, and potential blackmail, one that Zelen would've found deeply funny under other circumstances.

"It'll be done, sir," said Otto, and took the reins.

That would occupy his attention and then at least one groom's. If Zelen and Branwyn were lucky, that groom might not be in a good mood on being woken. An argument would be a fine thing. Kostan, the lone guard left at the front, would be less likely to go investigate mysterious noises, or even respond to yelling.

So far, so good. Zelen strode up to the doors and hammered on them. After six hard blows, he heard quick footsteps and muffled swearing from the hall beyond.

Now he just had to make a scene.

There was a great deal to be said against the Verengirs. They were certainly traitors and, given the missing children, likely murderers as well. What little Branwyn had heard about the way they treated Zelen made her furious, even with her own limited experience of normal families, and at least one of them wrote excessively pretentious ritual notes.

They did let trees grow fairly near the wings of their house. Branwyn considered it a significant point in their favor.

She admitted that few people without a Sentinel's gifts or other inhuman enhancements would have been able to perch in the highest branches of the ash tree nearest a second-story window. Fewer still would've been able to throw rocks from that position hard enough, and with enough accuracy, to take out the wooden separation between the panes and then the leaded glass itself. Branwyn did it in three throws, then leapt, grabbed the sill, and pulled herself in. Glass scraped her fingers and her back, but she'd had far worse injuries.

One day, Yathana observed, *you've got to stop jumping through windows.*

"I'm not jumping, I'm climbing," Branwyn whispered, "and I'd love to. Furthermore, you're the reason I can't go in the normal way, you know."

They'd thought about trying to bring Branwyn in as Zelen's "captive," the reason he'd come back in such a hurry, but there'd be no way to keep Yathana with her, and the soulsword gave her too many advantages to risk for the deception. Once Zelen had said his family likely conducted their rites in one of the disused wings, the window had struck her as the best choice. Branwyn could have wished for a quieter way, but perhaps distance and rain would be on her side.

She'd landed in a room without distinguishing features. It had likely been a bedroom, and the windows suggested it had housed family or guests, not servants, but the furniture had been moved out long ago. Now it was dustless but anonymous, only a dark square of walls and floorboard.

There was no obvious threat there either. Nothing any of the five senses could detect seemed off. The room was as bare of skulls or the smell of old blood as it was of furnishings. All the same, Branwyn felt her stomach start to coil, and a sour taste crept up the back of her throat. It might have been her mind, since she had a broad idea of what happened in the house, but she'd learned to trust her instincts, all the more so since the night at the Rognozis.

Deathmistress, give us a good ending, said Yathana. If a sword had a stomach, she would have been three seconds from losing an entire week's worth of meals. *This is what I sensed all along.*

"It's not just me then," whispered Branwyn, drawing the sword slowly.

If you feel like the entire building is made out of flyblown meat, then no, it's not just you. Gods, how long have… How did we…

"I know," Branwyn said, "but speed is of the essence here."

Yes. The sword-spirit gathered herself together. *Sorry, girl. I should be able to guide you to the worst of it, at any rate. That's probably where they're keeping the kid.*

"Silver lining, I suppose."

Branwyn opened the door slowly, which didn't keep it from creaking, and stepped carefully out into a dark hallway. The walls held brackets, but no torches, and they were bare of any ornament that might provide either color or warmth.

Darya, Branwyn's friend and fellow Sentinel, spent much of her time hunting in ruined cities. Now Branwyn recalled her stories with a new perspective, one that let her understand them much better. She didn't *think* any of the rooms would contain the restless dead Darya had talked about, but neither guards nor cultists were an especially pleasant alternative. As for monsters, one never knew.

Down, said Yathana, *and I think on the left. Hard to say from this distance.*

Regardless, Branwyn opened the doors up and down the hallway, gave each room a quick inspection, and left when they contained neither a child nor, in most cases, any signs of use. One end of the hall was boarded up, and scorch marks stretched long, misshapen fingers out onto the wall in front of the boards on either side.

"With any sense," Branwyn whispered, "they'd have given up being cultists after all of this."

Nah. Probably made them try harder to be worthy. That's how fanatics work. Yathana chuckled. *I should know. But my cult's right.*

"Is this the time for existential philosophy?"

In a desecrated building, right before we might die? Absolutely.

Branwyn opened the last door, found nothing, and then followed a winding, narrow staircase down to the ground floor.

There, a reasonably skilled and fairly unpleasant person had carved murals into the wood. Most of them showed a giant head— presumably Gizath—glowering at people in different states of vice: a man in a gutter with a bottle of wine, a woman in a low-cut gown, a mob at the gates of a castle. Another scene met with its evident approval, one in which a well-dressed family accepted the obeisance of three soldiers and a peasant couple.

Oh, for a picture of a waterfolk orgy.

The first door Branwyn opened led to a small room with a table, a chest, and a bookshelf. She didn't spend much time investigating, but at least one of the books looked like it was bound in…

Well, it could, in theory, have been goatskin or pigskin, undyed, but Branwyn wouldn't have been confident about saying it was either.

New plan. We get the girl, the knights execute every damn one of these people except Zelen, and then we come back with a squad of Blades and set fire to the place. Sorry about your young man's house, but…

Branwyn doubted he'd mind.

Chapter 35

IT'S AT THE END OF THE HALL, SAID YATHANA, AS BRANWYN crept forward. *At least, that's where the corruption is strongest.*

"Do you know if they've still got a demon?" Branwyn asked under her breath. The door opposite the study had only been a linen closet, though why cultists conducting rituals in an abandoned wing would need linens…

Well, she did know. Or she could guess, little as she wanted to. They were quite organized about the whole business; Branwyn had to give them that much.

No. After a certain point, degrees of corruption don't register. Once you've drowned, it doesn't matter if you tried to breathe twelve feet of water or only ten, does it?

"No," said Branwyn, and the neatly stacked linen took on a new connotation. "How long would you say they've been worshipping the Traitor? Sacrificing to him?"

Generations. Maybe since before the storms.

For a second, Branwyn could see darkness overlaying the whole hallway—not the shadows that had been transparent to her since her reforging but the grime of old filth, spreading and clinging to wood and rock. She shuddered, and had the mission not been so urgent, would have paused before opening the next door, perhaps found a cloth to wrap her hand in. The handle felt as though it crawled underneath her palm.

She pushed it open regardless.

"Mmmmmmfffff!"

The muffled, desperate, angry sound came from one corner of

a small bare room, not much more than another closet with the linen taken out. There was a shape there, a small version of the comma human beings became with their limbs tied together. As she hurried over, Branwyn recognized the face that she'd dimly seen through her injuries. It was bruised now, with a large purple lump near one temple.

"Easy," she hissed. "Be still, be quiet. I'm going to get you out."

Tanya looked in her direction but didn't focus on her, and it took a moment for Branwyn to realize why. Mortals didn't have the Sentinels' vision in the dark. She'd been navigating fine, but there was no light in the hallway, and none in the room.

The girl had been in there for a few hours, and that was bad enough.

How long had they kept the other children in darkness? It seemed almost worse than what had followed. Should Branwyn let them live long enough—which she had no intention of doing—a cultist could perhaps argue that the sacrifice itself was necessary from some twisted viewpoint, but the bonds and the darkness spoke of either cruelty or horrible indifference.

Tanya flinched at the sound of Branwyn drawing her belt knife, and her body was rigid until Branwyn cut the rope binding her ankles to her wrists. Then her sigh of relief mingled with a muffled yelp of pain as feeling began to return to her limbs. The girl did her best, but there was another yelp when Branwyn freed her arms and legs individually.

"Shh," said Branwyn before she untied the gag. "We're going to wait here until you can walk again. Then I'm going to lead you out and put you on a horse. Can you ride?"

Tanya shook her head.

"Then just hang on to it. If I've pleased the gods lately, Zelen and I will be there the whole time. If not, climb onto the saddle, hang on, and nudge the beast in the sides. Don't kick. It should take you to a safer place than this, at any rate." Branwyn passed her knife over, hilt-first. "If anybody who isn't me, Zelen, or one of Tinival's knights lays a hand on you, cut them and run. Run first, if you can."

"But Zelen..." the girl croak-whispered. Branwyn wished she had water, but there was none. "His men were the ones what did this."

"His family's men. He didn't know, I swear it."

Tanya hesitated, and Branwyn let her. The girl would have to get the feeling back into her hands and feet before they could go forward. She could get it back into her mind as well, as Branwyn would have had to after such an experience—as she had done, when she'd found out what had really happened in the Rognozis' house—and decide whether she trusted Branwyn and Zelen, or at least whether she figured they were the best she was going to get.

Meanwhile, Branwyn asked. "When was the last time you saw another person?"

"A–a while ago. Hard to tell time. They dumped me in here, and then a woman in white came in and looked at me like I was a cut of meat from a butcher. Did everything but ask to see my teeth." Tanya managed a weak grin. "I showed 'em to her anyway."

"Good."

"I guess that wasn't too long ago. I haven't gotten hungry yet, or had to piss, though I've been sweating enough that maybe that doesn't matter."

"Hunger might not either," Branwyn said absently, "if you're scared enough."

"I'm scared, all right."

"Sensible."

Tanya rubbed at her wrists. "What'd they bring me here for? I thought maybe"—she shrugged—"men, you know, bad ones, but nobody's touched me except to grab me and tie me up, and one of 'em belted me for biting, and there was the lady in white."

"Human sacrifice, probably, to keep a demon under a modicum

of control," said Branwyn, listening with her gift. There were people coming down the hallway from the main part of the house, at least four of them, but they were far away yet. She pushed the door closed, in the vague hope that they'd be on other business and walk right past. "It seems that Zelen's the only member of his family who doesn't worship Gizath. It's a complicated situation."

"You're not bloody kidding!" said Tanya, wide-eyed.

———————————

"Master Zelen," said the footman, as disapprovingly as the difference in their rank allowed. "Are you well?"

"I am," he said, flinging off his cloak in a dramatic gesture that also spattered the walls with rain. "There's much else I can't say the same about."

He was cribbing wildly now, drawing from every play he'd ever caught glimpses of on a drunken evening, and there was no time to tell if it worked. Zelen had the notion that he might lose his nerve if he tried, as though he raced across a bridge and dared not let his weight rest long enough to look down. "I *must* see my brother now. Lives are at stake, do you hear me?"

"I—"

"Tell him that. Tell him that I've been about his business and discovered a darker secret than either of us had ever dreamed existed. Tell him I'll await him in his study," Zelen finished, feeling that was considerably anticlimactic.

To make up for that, he stalked down the hall and was glad that his boots weren't too wet to rap on the stone floor.

The study wasn't locked. The study was never locked. The servants knew what would happen if they went in the family's rooms without orders. As far as Zelen knew, none of them had ever taken the chance.

As he kicked open the door, relishing the wet print of his boot on the wood, it occurred to him that he didn't actually know what the consequences of disobedience were. Being turned off without a reference or pay had always been his assumption, and it had seemed bad enough, but the new and terrible information of the past few days made Zelen reconsider.

Servants left rarely, but when they did, they simply vanished.

Surely, he thought, they couldn't all have been sacrifices. Surely that would have excited too much comment. But he actually *couldn't* be sure, and the very need to consider the possibility was chilling.

Gedomir didn't keep wine, brandy, or whiskey in his desk, or Zelen would've poured himself a stiff drink, oncoming battle or not. Holding it would have conveyed the proper mood, for one. Lacking that, he picked up a series of carved stone paperweights on the desk—cats of different sizes and colors, all rather charming and one of the few remotely human touches in the place—and then dropped them out of order, in between pacing from the door to the window and back.

It didn't take much pretense at all.

He was by the desk, toying with a gray-blue sitting cat the size of his palm, when he heard the door open.

"Gedo, thank the gods," he said, turning with the figurine still in his hands. "This place is torment for a sober man, you know."

"Zelen." The delay made sense. Despite the hour, his brother was impeccably dressed: gray tunic, black surcoat, breeches, and boots, silver-buckled sword belt and silver-hilted sword in a sheath worked with the same metal, not a hair out of place. "You choose the most interesting hours."

This time, he wouldn't rise to the bait. He'd let his emotions carry him away when Gedo had told him about Branwyn—had told him what he wanted Zelen to believe about her—and Gedomir would believe that the same would be true when Zelen heard any particularly important news about the matter.

He didn't bother putting the figurine down, just summoned as much wide-eyed alarm as he could. "I'm sorry for waking you, Gedo."

"You could've saved me the interrupted sleep, and yourself the time and the strain on your horse, most likely," said Gedomir, stepping inside the door. "I expect to be in the city by tomorrow afternoon. Mother, Father, and Alize are halfway there already."

Lord and Lady Verengir, and their elder daughter by virtue of traveling with them, didn't spend more than three hours on the road at a time. There was a small inn between the estate and the city, one that Zelen suspected made its entire profit from his family's infrequent trips and the ability to use their name.

"It couldn't wait. You'll understand…" He passed his free hand across his mouth, letting it shake, and watched Gedomir watch the motion. "I hope you'll understand. You're not going to believe what I've discovered—"

"No," said Gedomir.

He took a few steps further into the room, but Zelen now noticed that he stayed carefully far away. Behind him, the shadows in the hall grew more solid, developing harsh faces and broad shoulders, dark armor and bared weapons.

"No," Gedomir repeated, "I don't think I would."

Chapter 36

GEDOMIR HAD NEVER REGARDED ZELEN PARTICULARLY fondly, but now his gaze was brimming with contempt. "I don't even want to know the lies you've come up with," he said. "It would only insult us both."

"I don't know what you mean." Shock and fear were appropriate. Zelen gave them free rein and yanked back hard on guilt, or hoped he did. "I came because—"

"You found the…woman's…sword." Gedomir ticked off points on his fingers as he stood, square-shouldered and upright as a statue, eyeing Zelen as though he were a maggot in meat. "You didn't bother consulting with me, our parents, or even the girls about it. Instead, you practiced a rather shoddy deception with a broom handle."

The last word was the kick in the stomach. Zelen didn't respond. The guards moved in, each taking one of his arms in a none-too-gentle grip. The cat statuette fell to the floor.

They knew. Yathana hadn't counted on Gedomir's paranoia about having the sword around outweighing his distaste for it, or some event had made him decide to check on it, or, hell, Gizath had given his faithful a vision. It didn't matter. They knew.

He thought that as hard as he could, hoping that Yathana would pick up on it across the house and through their barely existent bond: *They know. Get Tanya and run for it.*

"I suppose I shouldn't be shocked," Gedomir went on, "by your lack of any family feeling. You've constantly demonstrated that you have no regard for the ties of blood any proper gentleman should feel—and yet, you manage to disappoint us again. Tell me, Zelen, didn't you even think of consulting us?"

The question, and his brother's genuinely wounded manner, startled Zelen into a cawing laugh. "Consulting you? What in Letar's name would you have said if I did?"

Now that he was alert for it, he saw Gedomir flinch at the mention of the goddess. It wasn't much, only a slight twitch near his left eye, but it put to rest any ideas Zelen might have had about the whole business being an awful mistake.

"Or am I wrong?" With nothing to lose, he pressed his point. "Has there been some horrible error? Did the demon that killed the Rognozis not bring Branwyn's sword back to you, like a good dog returns game to the hunter? Do you and our parents, and even the girls"—Zelen imitated Gedomir's delivery—"not worship the Traitor?"

The blow was openhanded, but full strength. Zelen's teeth split two of Gedomir's knuckles open, which was a small bright point in the whole wretched evening.

"You shouldn't speak of truth that's beyond you," Gedomir said, shaking his wrist. "Our lord knows more of loyalty and order than any of his degenerate sister's favorites, as feeble an example as you may be."

"Oh, lovely, a theological debate." Zelen glanced toward the guards. "And you gentlemen? Faithful to the Backstabber? Blackmailed? Don't care as long as the money spends?"

It was possible that the eyes of the guard on the right, a relatively new arrival whose name Zelen hadn't learned, shifted. The one on the left, Nislar, opened his mouth, but Gedomir waved him to silence.

"Don't bother with any of your tricks, Brother. Their fealty is far more certain than your honor."

"Honor, off 'er." Zelen grinned with bleeding lips, falling into the accent of the docks. "Depends on the night, doesn't it?" That got him another blow, this one to the right eye.

"I'd hoped there was more sense and less filth in you," said Gedomir. "Foolish of me."

"Absolutely. You do know that I told Tinival's people about you, don't you? Swore in front of a knight and all that? And by the way, I'd start hitting with the other hand soon. You're apt to sprain a finger at this rate."

"I'd have expected nothing else," said Gedomir. "But it won't matter."

"No? Going to take over the world before they can act? Flee west and join up with Thyran?"

Gedomir didn't switch hands, but he did make a fist and aim for just under the rib cage that time.

"Don't speak that idiotic upstart's name in this house. If not for his…whims, your strumpet would have no war to drag us into. We could proceed to our goal in an orderly fashion, as He always intended."

There were several points of possible debate there, but Zelen was trying to breathe.

Gedomir continued. "I'm certain you did swear. I'll be just as certain that you honestly believed what you were saying, you poor fool. After all, the Sentinel doubtless has many wiles, and you were never the most…stable…young man. Returning home to drown yourself will only prove that you realized, too late, where your madness had led you."

"You"—Zelen gasped out—"think they'll believe it?"

"They won't have the power to do otherwise. The high lord's dead, no heir has been selected, and the knights don't rule the city, much as they may wish it. Our parents and Alize honestly will know nothing of what's happened here. By the time a suitable candidate takes the seat, your woman will be dead, and you'll be no more than an unfortunate footnote to the whole messy business. Take him to the lake," Gedomir said to the guards. "Hold him under before you throw him in. I don't want any busybody saying that he didn't *look* as though he'd drowned."

"I can't blame you for your ignorance," he told Zelen, "but I had hoped you'd have more regard for your own blood, even so."

Zelen drew himself upright, despite the sickening pain in his stomach. "The rest of us have four gods to your one, Brother, and the Dark Lady isn't known for forgiveness. If I were you, I'd worry less about what's in my veins and more about what's on my hands."

That time, Gedomir didn't even bother to hit him. He just addressed the guard on the left. "Make it last awhile."

For a wonder, the footsteps outside did go past the door, while Branwyn waited with bared sword and Tanya hid in the corner behind her. They slowly grew fainter. A heavy door opened down the hall, then closed, and Branwyn, even with her gift, could hear no more.

"Can you walk?" she whispered, and Tanya nodded.

Good, said Yathana. *Things are moving here.*

"Moving how? I'm a Sentinel," she added to Tanya, who was looking confused. "I talk with my sword."

"Oh."

Getting worse. A wizard could explain it better. A wizard could understand it better.

"But?" Branwyn asked, opening the door. She glanced in either direction and spotted no threat, so stepped quickly out into the hallway, beckoning for Tanya to follow.

But it has the feel of a tower ready to fall. Too much balanced on too little foundation, or too many supports knocked out. Could be both.

Branwyn, who didn't want to risk speaking now that they were in the hall, nodded and grimaced.

More good news, Yathana added. *Unless you saw a door that I didn't, we're going to have to go in that direction to get the child out.*

If silence hadn't been important, Branwyn would have cursed.

There was nothing to be done about it, though, nor would there have been if she'd known. Branwyn started down the long hallway, opening one door after another in the hopes of finding an exit and listening all the while to make sure Tanya still followed.

The girl stuck close, walked quickly despite her long immobility, and kept as quiet as she could. Little weight and bare feet helped there. So, Branwyn suspected, did a childhood spent on the wrong side of the law at times, and not only when sheltering dangerous fugitives.

None of the doors led outside, nor to another hallway. One room had chairs and tables draped with dark cloth, as carefully cleaned but as bare of activity as much of the rest of the wing had been so far. Another, equally lifeless, had a series of cords hanging down off one wall, limp and dark.

That was how you called servants, said Yathana. *Pulling on those would ring bells in their quarters, or make sounds through enchanted jewelry if your family was rich enough. House servants on the right, grooms and guards on the left.*

Branwyn closed that door slowly, feeling as though she were putting the lid back on a coffin.

Finally she saw their salvation up ahead, obvious without her even having to open a door. The hallway branched into a lopsided T shape. A sharp right turn led down a long hallway, and a short stub of the path she was on ended in a thick set of double doors.

They looked normal enough, those doors. Underneath them, though, and from the tiny crack between them, Branwyn could see dull orange light, faint but definite. Even if she hadn't known better from what Yathana had said, she couldn't have mistaken the light for flame, sun, or even more innocent magic—not the way it squirmed.

Branwyn didn't know what else might be beyond the doors, but the room was full of Gizath's power. It leered at her from around the wood, only light but capable of knowing her, of remembering.

Despite her gift, and although she was looking directly at the doors, it almost caught her completely off guard when they opened, and it was a genuine relief to see two human figures come out.

One was a young woman in high-necked, long-sleeved white, likely one of Zelen's sisters. The other was a tall man in dark clothing who drew a broad-bladed shortsword with admirable speed when he spotted Branwyn.

He clearly knew what he was doing and had the strength to back it up. The sword would be more useful in close quarters than Yathana was, and Branwyn had used all of her enchanted knives on the demons at the ball. The sorceress would be a complication too.

Still, Branwyn did feel relief, not only because they were mortal. In an instant she thought of the filth she'd crept through and the windowless room where the Verengirs had kept Tanya bound. She remembered the Rognozis, murdered in their own home, and gods knew how many children taken for sacrifice. Then she added Zelen's pain and the wounds that had left her nearly dead. Branwyn gazed at the figures and the light behind them, and felt a grin stretch her lips as the transformation came over her.

"Stay well behind me," she told Tanya, "and stay watchful."

The man charged. Branwyn stepped forward to meet him, practically with a song in her throat.

Sneaking was over for the night.

Chapter 37

WITHOUT LETTING GO OF ZELEN'S HAND, NISLAR PRESSED THE point of a small knife right against his carotid artery. "Hold very still," he said tonelessly, leaving off any title.

"I assume you'll kill me if I don't," Zelen said dryly. All the same, he didn't move. He had the usual foolish mortal combination: the body's reluctance to move against a certain threat, and the mind's speck of idiotically persistent hope that death would become less certain if he waited.

Searching him and taking him to the lake would also take longer than simply killing him, and that would give Branwyn and Tanya more opportunity to flee. He wished that more of his obedience had been that selfless but, really, the other factors flooded over his will.

The new guard pulled Zelen's sword from its sheath and tossed it to the floor. It clattered loudly. Obviously none of them were worried about discovery, and why should they be? Nobody would come to Zelen's aid.

"Won't it look odd if I drown myself with an empty sheath?" he asked.

"We'll give you the sword back," said Nislar. "After."

"Good thinking. Very well planned. Whatever my brother's paying you, he should double it, especially since he's damned you."

"Shut up," said Nislar, but without any anger in it. His voice, like his gaze, stayed flat.

The other guard searched Zelen with a probing, efficient thoroughness, starting at the feet and working upward. Two boot daggers joined the sword on the floor. Zelen guessed they wouldn't bother replacing those, or the knives in his sleeves, though they'd likely put back his eating knife.

Suddenly he saw an image of himself: cold, blue, and beginning to be waxy, as drowning victims generally were, with the guards sliding weapons back onto his unresisting corpse. Zelen's throat closed up. If it hadn't, he might have started begging then, knowing that it wouldn't help at all.

Then the new guard, patting Zelen's chest, slapped his palm against the teardrop amulet. "Here, what's—" he began, and pulled it out by its silver chain. The onyx and rubies glimmered up at him, brighter than they should have been in the dim room.

The flicker that had been in his eyes earlier returned and stayed. "Nislar," he said, glancing back toward the closed door. Suddenly he was confused, hesitant, and yet more *there* than he'd been before, like a sleepwalker roused. "What's…"

"Best drop it, Hidath," said Nislar. He stayed less emotional, less present, but even he hesitated. "It's probably not important. Leave it."

The amulet thumped back against Zelen's chest. The guards became almost as they were, but now Zelen realized how little of that state had come from training, payment, or a natural lack of morals.

"Binding spell, hmm?" he asked, as Hidath stepped back. "The Traitor and his servants do have interesting definitions of loyalty. Here I always thought it didn't count if you forced it, but…" Zelen shrugged. "Clearly I haven't heard from the right sources."

"Doesn't matter what you think," said Nislar. Lacking the passion that would have made it a threat, it was only a statement of fact. What Zelen thought didn't matter. Nothing mattered. "Come on, Hidath. We have our orders."

Hidath took one of Zelen's wrists again. Nislar was too much of a professional to lower the knife as he went for the other, but

Zelen, watching him with all the focus he'd learned from drawing and healing, glimpsed the slight relaxation there, the dropping of his guard, if only minutely. The prisoner was disarmed. Whatever he tried would be little use against two armed men.

If Zelen had a chance, this was it.

"Can I wipe my face?" he asked, looking between the guards. "I give you my word, by all of the four gods, that I won't try and hurt you." Now he tried to reverse all the arrogance he'd displayed on his way in and to sound humble, shaken, and fearful. It wasn't nearly as difficult. "I–I don't want to die with blood running down my chin. Please."

Nislar took in Zelen's split lip and swelling eye, then Hidath's grip on his other wrist. "Fine. Be quick."

And Zelen was.

His strength was only human, but the chain around his neck was ornamental. One desperate yank and it broke, releasing the pendant into his hand. He was spinning as he pulled, going *toward* Hidath, which neither of the guards expected and which used the other man's grip against him. Zelen might have been able to break free then. He didn't test it.

As Hidath yelled his alarm, Zelen brought his hand up, palm first. The blow itself was light, no more than a slap, but what hit the guard's forehead wasn't just Zelen's skin. It was the pendant, shining red and black, that pressed into the space between the guard's eyes.

"Help me, please," Zelen said quietly, and not to the men at arms.

The grip on Zelen's wrist dropped away. Hidath stood entranced a heartbeat. Then he screamed.

He didn't stop. The sound kept coming while he stood there. It was high, wavering, strange from a large man but not womanly or childlike so much as inhuman, the noise that metal or wood might produce just before it snapped if people could hear it.

How long, Zelen wondered, had the man been making that noise inside his own head?

That horror didn't bear contemplating, not least because there wasn't time. Zelen dove, barely ducking Nislar's clumsy, half-stunned grip, and grabbed his sword from the floor. He kicked out as he rolled up, catching the guard in the ankle, but didn't take him down. The other man was a professional. He stayed on his feet, alert enough even to take a swing.

Zelen blocked hastily on the way up. His sword stopped Nislar's, a heavy but keen-edged short blade, an inch away from his neck.

Once more, Zelen struck out with the pendant, but missed Nislar's forehead. The guard blinked, then slapped Zelen's hand away, sending Letar's sigil clattering to the floor. Zelen used his sword for momentum and pushed himself hastily backwards.

Hidath was still screaming.

Around came Nislar again, sword slashing down as Zelen leapt sideways. A chair splintered beneath the blow. Zelen took a step back and found himself against the desk. "We could always *not* do this, you know," he said, sidling along its surface. "You leave, find a nice tavern, come back when all the evening's festivities are over. I'll put in a good word for you if the subject arises."

He blocked another swing. This one didn't come as close, but he still felt the strength in it. Nislar's face was blank, intent, and the pendant was gone.

That meant Zelen had a free hand.

A second of groping on the desk brought his fingers into contact with the largest of the cat statues, a white marble piece the size of his palm. Zelen backed away from a thrust, grabbed, and threw the thing directly into Nislar's face.

It hit him in the nose. Zelen the healer heard the sound of rupturing cartilage, noted the spray of blood, and winced in sympathy, knowing precisely how much trouble and pain it would cause to fix that. Zelen the swordsman saw his moment and took it: a step inside Nislar's range, a slash to the inside of the sword arm that cut a tendon, then one to the back of the leg, and the man was down on the floor, groaning and bleeding.

"I'm sorry," Zelen said. "I can't stay and fix those."

Sword bared and dripping blood, he turned and ran out of the room. He didn't know where Gedomir had gone, or where the other guards were, but with Branwyn and Tanya both likely still in the old wing, he didn't want to take any chances.

Compulsion, Yathana said after the guard's blade had met Branwyn's. The man had shifted his stance to work with the close walls, taking advantage of his shorter weapon. He was good, and thus still alive. *On him, not her.*

Yathana's speech was faint, a sign of the effort she was using to hold on to the world after Branwyn's transformation. *Been on too long for me to undo it in battle.*

That was just what Branwyn needed to hear: a reason to try to leave the man alive. She growled. It was pure frustration, but the guard, who'd evidently heard a few things about Sentinels, gulped.

"Fine," said Branwyn, and swung inward, grabbing the guard's arm with her other hand. She'd use the swords as a lever, dislocate his shoulder while she kicked his legs out from under him, and then be on the sorceress before she got clever.

That was the idea. The guard was too smart by half for a man under compulsion, though. He dropped his own arm as Branwyn moved, sending her weight further forward than she'd wanted, and slammed a fist into her kidney. It hurt his knuckles—he cursed practically in her ear—but it hurt her more, despite her metal form.

Mercy had very few rewards.

Branwyn spun back around, striking out with her fist in a

punch that hit the guard in the shoulder and carried him a clear foot back down the corridor. He fell onto his back, arm at an angle that didn't bode well for his chances of using it in the future.

The sorceress took a few paces back as well. Her eyes were wide with fright. They looked very much like Zelen's, but Branwyn couldn't care. It was the setting that mattered, not the gem. Branwyn saw the woman's fear, grinned, and went after her.

At her first step, the stone of the floor reached for her. Fleshy tendrils coiled around her leg, gray like the stone they'd been but with the coiling litheness of serpents.

"Now you learn, abomination," the sorceress said. "Your masters aren't the only beings that can reshape the world."

Behind her, the light pulsed in rhythm with her words. Branwyn, alternately kicking and slicing at the tentacles, couldn't be sure, but she thought that it might be brighter—if brighter was the term.

You're not wrong, said Yathana. It was almost a moan now, as Branwyn had heard from wounded soldiers calling out for water or Mourners or simply an end to pain. *She feeds it. Tears the world. I don't know. It's worse. She's making it worse.*

"Of course she is," said Branwyn.

The tendrils were persistent, but yielded easily enough to her feet or Yathana's edge. While Branwyn dealt with them, Zelen's sister showed a speck of good sense and darted back toward her room and her god. That was fine. Once they got Tanya out, Branwyn would come back with a pack of priests and deal with them all. The Verengir girl could run while the running was good, and it warmed Branwyn's heart to know that her fear earlier had been as much reality as ruse.

"Come on," she said to Tanya. The guard was getting up, his arm still dangling uselessly. Branwyn still didn't feel any need to confront him again, not with the sorceress at his back and the whole place now resting, if she'd understood Yathana correctly, on a magical house of cards. "Let's—no, dammit, go back!"

Footsteps, at least four sets, were running toward them from down the hall.

Tanya, who'd started forward, yelped and made a dive for the back hallway again. "What do we do?"

"Back down the way we came," Branwyn said quietly. "You'll find stairs." The guard was moving toward her again from one side. From the other came another man with a sword, two other figures—one with a pitchfork, *wonderful*—and a fourth behind them that she couldn't see clearly. The mage was doubtless up to no good in her room too. "There's a broken window. Knock out the rest of the glass, then get to the tree outside."

"What are you gonna do?"

Branwyn glanced to either side of her. She was metal. She was armed. There was a wall at her back.

"I think," said Branwyn, "a bright girl like you can draw some conclusions."

Chapter 38

"HALT!" ONE OF THE ONCOMING FIGURES ACTUALLY YELLED. HE was carrying a fireplace poker—they were becoming a constant in Branwyn's fights, which she supposed was what happened when she went around battling cultists in cities—and doing so with no confidence whatsoever. Branwyn suspected that he was a footman who'd gotten dragged into the fight with no notion of what his employers were doing in this part of their house.

"You first," she replied, and had no chance for more.

The real guard among them was on her, then. He looked uneasy, likely at her shining metal skin, the uncanny light, or both, but that didn't stop him from charging and chopping at her knees with a hard blow. Branwyn hastily sidestepped. She'd had enough broken knees for one lifetime.

Moving to the side put her in jabbing range of the pitchfork, which the probably groom stuck straight through her tunic. It made a *ting* as it hit the metal skin against her ribs. The groom stared. Branwyn yanked the pitchfork away and threw it down the hallway at the guard with a broken arm. He ducked easily. At least it was a distraction.

She turned back, leapt over another slash of the guard's sword, and kicked the groom neatly in the ribs on her way down. He fell back into a slump against the wall. Branwyn couldn't tell whether he was bleeding from the mouth or not, but she didn't try very hard. There was only so much effort that she could put into sparing her enemies, under the circumstances.

The footman with the poker moved up to occupy the vacant

space in the hall. He'd learned his lesson, since he didn't hesitate at all before trying to smash her skull in. It was admirable, in a way. Branwyn blocked the poker with Yathana.

Agony abruptly swept over her. Branwyn had known pain since the first days of her training, but this was breathtaking. Through watering eyes, she saw her skin ripple, saw the dull orange sparks dancing across the gleaming bronze, and knew the horrible magic that she was fighting.

Gizath's power could have turned an unprotected victim inside out, or crushed their organs from the inside as their body betrayed them in the most fundamental way. Branwyn, reforged with the power of the gods, gritted her teeth and held on to Yathana's hilt, keeping herself in one piece and her head intact.

The pain didn't stop. She stepped forward through it, raked her nails across the footman's cheek, and stuck Yathana into his side when he staggered backwards.

Someone grabbed her neck. Branwyn spun and struck upward, heard the guard's jaw crack under the blow, and caught sight of the sorceress. She stood with one hand outstretched, her brow furrowed. Clearly she expected Branwyn to be a whimpering heap on the floor, if not dead.

It was some pleasure, even through the pain, to disappoint her. It was even better to see the puzzlement turn to outright alarm when Branwyn charged, forcing herself past sensation to a speed that the daughter of Verengir didn't anticipate.

No spell had compelled the sorceress's actions. Yathana pierced her gut, with Branwyn's full, desperate strength behind her. The other woman's face became a mask of torment, even as Branwyn's pain ceased. For a moment it was as though the spell had doubled back on its caster. Then Branwyn's backstroke took out her throat. It was reflex rather than mercy, but it served the same purpose.

"*Hanyi!*"

It wasn't a familiar voice, but it was enough like Zelen's to rattle her for a heartbeat. The same reflex that had sliced open Hanyi's neck carried Branwyn back to her previous position in the hall, where she put herself in the way of the man with the poker before he could go after Tanya. The iron smashed down on her upraised arm, which hurt like hell. It was a known pain, though, not one that meant her body was trying to destroy its own organs, so she took it with almost a sense of gratitude.

"I'll watch you die for *days*, you harlot," said the person who had cried out.

Branwyn turned to bat his sword away with Yathana. From the platinum hair, the dark eyes, and the better quality of clothing and weapon than the others, she guessed that the man was Gedomir. From the quick way he recovered, she knew that he was good in a fight—better than his guards, perhaps, in these close quarters. There was open fury in his expression, offense mixed with honest grief, but he didn't strike recklessly or push too far forward.

She hated it when they were intelligent.

Dodging the next blow from the poker, she started to flick a cut at the footman's unprotected arm when the earth moved.

Branwyn stumbled backwards, catching herself on the wall. Both of her opponents reeled with the quake too, and both looked stunned, which was some comfort.

"What—" the footman started.

"Kill her," said Gedomir. "One thing at a time."

Branwyn regained her footing quickly enough to meet the next strike with steel, not flesh. A punch to the stomach left the man doubled over. She saw steel flash from the corner of her eye and shifted her weight backwards.

Gedomir's sword sliced a shallow line from her shoulder down her side, neatly splitting her tunic. The skin beneath only opened a little, a scratch rather than any kind of significant wound. In another fight, Branwyn wouldn't even have noticed the sting, or the hot kiss of blood.

The problem was that both existed. Gedomir had cut her, and that meant her transformation had worn off. From now on, it would be flesh against flesh.

Zelen ran.

He'd do no good if he arrived exhausted, or if he tripped on a footstool and brained himself. He hated knowing that. Restraint chafed him. Caution bound him, just at the moment when no turn of speed would have been enough. He silently cursed every inch of the floor that he had to cross, every turn of the corridors and door that took a second to open.

The dark house would've been eerie under any circumstances. As Zelen ran, it was a nightmare landscape around him. Every doorway was a yawning mouth, every chair a misformed ghost.

From the study to the main hall, his path led into the back of the house. A right turn took him to an old door, which he'd been prepared to open and which he found already ajar. That was no real surprise, but the sight dismayed him—though it did save him a moment or two, as he dashed through without pausing.

Below him, the floor changed from smooth wood to stone, only slightly rougher after generations of residents and the efforts of many servants. The walls had no ornaments, and the light was much dimmer.

Up ahead, around a corner, that light became dull orange. Something about its color, or the way it flickered, raised Zelen's hackles right off, but he had no opportunity to think it over. He was running, and then the earth shook beneath him.

He stumbled, fell roughly to his knees, and managed to hold onto his sword without cutting himself in half as a result. Solid rock shook like a frightened horse beneath him. *What in all the hells have they done?* He was already getting to his feet while he framed the question, pushing himself up despite the world's unsteadiness.

Zelen went slower for the brief time that the shaking lasted, and so it stretched out much longer in his heart and gut. In a way, it was no more than he'd expected. He'd never been in the old wing, and particularly knowing what he did, he was not surprised to find it a dark place, where even the ground was untrustworthy.

Soon after, he began to hear the noises of combat and to smell blood in the air.

Gedomir's order echoed through the hall, cold and furious. Their father had often sounded that way, and nothing good had ever followed. "Kill her. One thing at a time."

The insults he'd tossed at Branwyn earlier had left Zelen unmoved. They were tiresomely typical of Gedomir: of course he'd pick at how many beds he thought she frequented. Of course he'd think that mattered. Zelen hadn't felt any urge to defend her honor, only to roll his eyes.

The command sent a flood of red across his vision. When he rounded the corner into the long hallway and finally caught sight of his brother, the metal on Zelen's sword hilt was etching bloody patterns in his palm.

"You're going to regret that," he snarled, and didn't recognize his own voice.

Gedomir did. He didn't turn away from Branwyn, as Zelen had been hoping he would, but he looked back for a breath, disbelief warring with spite. Never one to let an opportunity get past her, Branwyn thrust past his guard, but the footman next to Gedomir knocked Yathana to the side with his poker.

The unnerving light didn't reveal very much about anybody in the hallway. One of the guards was slumped against the wall, cradling his bleeding side. He was still breathing. It was harder to tell about the groom, who lay faceup between Zelen and Gedomir, but eventually his chest did move. Branwyn knew about the compulsion, then; he couldn't imagine her sparing their lives otherwise.

For the second occasion in his life, tending to others' wounds wasn't Zelen's priority. He dashed past both wounded men with a muttered apology, similar to the one he'd used for the guards in the study, seeing them only dimly. Gedomir and Branwyn were the center of his vision.

She wasn't metal, which suggested either careful hoarding of resources or that she'd been fighting for a while. She also wasn't moving with the normal superhuman speed she demonstrated in a fight. That and a slight favoring of her left side made Zelen think she was flesh out of necessity, not tactics. Gedomir, fresh from trying to have his brother killed, was moving nearly as quickly and using the footman's amateur-but-desperate efforts with the poker to decent advantage. Zelen picked a spot with anatomical exactness and lunged forward.

Gedomir spun, catching the strike on his blade, and uttered three words Zelen didn't understand.

Branwyn, who had just laid the footman low with a sweeping kick to the ankles, staggered back, clutching her neck. Gedomir actually smirked as he advanced on Zelen.

Their swords met again. Zelen blocked his brother's strike that time. He disengaged and stepped sideways, seeking an opening and finding none. Gedomir's hair shone like fire from the light in the room beyond. Behind him, Branwyn made choking noises. She'd dropped to the floor and was crawling back the way she'd come, nails scrabbling against the stone.

The air around her was wrong. Not poisoned, or not that Zelen could smell above the blood in the hallway, but simply *wrong*.

Maybe Branwyn could get out of it. He didn't want to take that risk.

Other risks were better.

Chapter 39

HE LOWERED HIS BLADE AND RETREATED, LETTING GEDOMIR'S next slash almost hit. "Please," he said, taking another step backward. "Let her go. You can do what you want with me."

"It's too late to repent," said Gedomir, with a thrust that truly came close to Zelen's ribs. "Your woman's killed Hanyi. Was that your intent all along?"

"No!" He'd thought that might happen, but hadn't known it. "Please, Gedomir, I'll say whatever you want. I'll take back my oath, say I was mad—just let her go. I'm begging you."

Zelen took a deep breath, then dropped his sword and fell to one knee, an inch or two outside Gedomir's range. The fallen guard stretched out beside him, complicating the terrain, but that wouldn't stop Gedomir for long.

His brother paused, but not out of mercy. He lifted his chin, the picture of righteous justice. "You can't buy her life," he said, "though you might have bought her an easier death than I'd planned. But you attacked your own brother. We won't need you alive to show madness."

Gedomir stepped forward again and swung his sword down toward Zelen's neck.

It was a quick blow, with all Gedomir's force behind it. It would've severed Zelen's head, had he not already been rolling forward. The sword sliced a hot line of pain down the side of his back, but he kept going, tumbling inside of Gedomir's range.

On the way up, he stabbed. The guard's knife, which Zelen had grabbed from its sheath just before launching himself forward, sank into Gedomir's thigh. It wasn't a vital spot, and the knife wasn't particularly sharp or well made, but Zelen, like his brother, was using all of his strength. Gedomir dropped his composure, not to mention his sword, and howled.

Beyond him, Branwyn drew her first real breath in too long. The dragging sound of it echoed through the hall, over Gedomir's screams, and got Zelen's heart beating again.

He couldn't pause to savor the victory. A knee to the groin seemed a good way to follow up the initial attack. Then, when Gedomir doubled over, his head was at the right height for Zelen to punch him in the temple.

"You were onto something," he said, shaking out his knuckles. "It's worth a bit of pain."

Gedomir, lying on the floor by the guard, didn't respond. His eyes were still open, and he tried to glare despite not being able to focus them.

"I can dispatch him now," Branwyn said. Her voice was back to gravelly hoarseness, but she was upright, holding her sword. "Or we can take him back to the city. The choice is yours."

"He'll see the house disgraced before he faces the Dark Lady," said Zelen. "That's fitting. Only, if we leave him alive, will he be able to cast more spells on the way back?"

"Not if we leave the knife where it is," said Branwyn. With speed that was even more impressive given how recently she'd been struggling to breathe, she sliced the tunic from one of the fallen guards and twisted it into a rope. "Once Yathana comes back to us, she'll be able to manage a longer-lasting, less awkward solution, but iron works in a pinch, and so does pain."

Zelen rolled his brother onto his back and pinned Gedomir's arms behind him. It was far easier than he would have ever expected, even given the other man's condition. As a child, he'd have looked on this moment with pure wonder that his hands didn't blister, or that the earth didn't open beneath his feet.

It did tremble again. That didn't stop Branwyn, who was winding the fabric tightly around Gedomir's wrists.

"She killed Hanyi," said Gedomir. His speech was slurred, but the words came out clearly.

"I did," said Branwyn. She jerked the knot tight. "It was the best course of action at the time."

The body lay in the hallway, her white dress drowned in a pool of red. "Then," Zelen said slowly, "I'm sure it was. We can talk about it later. Tanya?"

"Upstairs. Hopefully she's either made it out the window now or hasn't tried at all."

"I'd bet she's better at climbing than she'll be with either of the horses. We'd—"

The earth shook hard enough to send Zelen staggering, grabbing for the wall. He was glad that they'd tied Gedomir already, and looked back to his brother to make sure that the bonds still held.

They did. But a smile was on Gedomir's lips, one Zelen had long since learned to dislike.

"What?" he asked.

"I didn't tell you hoping for proper remorse, Zelen. I'm long past hoping you'd act decently. Your woman killed Hanyi. Hanyi was a wizard, casting a spell, and the Sentinel killed her here."

"Oh, gods have mercy," said Branwyn.

"Why? They never have before. And the Deathmistress," Gedomir spat the honorific like a curse, "isn't the only one who knows vengeance."

The next quake hit, and with it came the roar of rending stone. Nothing fell in the hallway around Zelen, but still it took a minute to locate the center of the sound. The snarl that followed, equally as loud but clearly a voice—and clearly not a human one—did it for him.

"There," said Gedomir.

It was his last word. His jaw split with the syllable, falling away into gray-orange fire. The flame had eaten away his face before either Zelen or Branwyn could act, and moved quickly to devour the rest of his frame.

Even if water would have worked, Zelen had none. All he could do was bear witness as his brother became sickly radiance, all vestiges of human form melting away into a conflagration that never touched the rock.

It streamed away, instead, into the room beyond.

And the creature there snarled louder.

Branwyn hadn't heard the roar before. She knew it meant nothing good and hastily turned to face the ritual chamber. A moment's sight gave her the impression of a large room with niches cut in the walls. Skulls looked out of them in most cases. Three still had skin attached.

The floor was crumbling in the center. Stones fell away into an expanding rift. As Branwyn watched, trying to figure out what the next step was, a hand the size of her chest reached out of the hole and grabbed onto the edge. She knew those spindly, many-knuckled fingers, studded with gray-orange eyes. Not long ago, she'd felt their grip.

She'd almost thought they'd get out alive.

Branwyn laughed while she charged into the room. It was a waste of air, tactically speaking, but she couldn't stop. They'd come so close to getting away. She was only flesh, with Yathana still at least minutes away from consciousness and likely hours from full power. She faced a greater demon, one that had nearly killed her when she'd been in metal form.

She whipped Yathana down and across. The sword sliced cleanly through three of the seven fingers, which twitched like dying worms while the demon's blood painted glowing rime on the stones. The other four strained, but held. As Branwyn raised Yathana again, she saw another hand grip the rift's edge.

Zelen was there then, and stabbed with several quick, precise jabs into the eyes dotting the hand. The grip wavered. The demon roared. Nobody was there to keep it silent now, just as nobody was there to restrain it.

Still it held on to the hole's edge. The top of a head, hairless, gray, and lumpy, rose from the pit. It was larger now. Branwyn wasn't sure that the room would hold it.

As had been the case in the hallway, size wasn't always an advantage.

"Don't look at its face," she reminded Zelen.

She struck again, rending the demon's strange flesh. Glutinous blood oozed from the wound, but this time she'd hit closer to what passed for its wrist, and her strength didn't suffice to take it off.

"Back," she said, trying to give the impression of fear.

Zelen, bless him, didn't argue. He retreated as she did, barely more than a shift in weight. Branwyn was coiling herself, tensing her muscles. If the demon had any reason or perception, it might assume it had the advantage.

Or it might just see prey.

Either way worked for her.

She watched it rise from the abyss below Verengir. First came the vast tumorous expanse of forehead, then the half-circle of eyes, various sizes and all blazing with Gizath's power. Below them, the wide triangular maw began to emerge.

That was all she dared to look at. It was all she needed to see.

And there was no point asking the gods to give her strength: they'd given her all they would when she'd been thirteen.

Branwyn shut her eyes and sprang forward.

The demon's substance gave way before Yathana's point. Backed by the full weight of Branwyn's body, every sinew launched toward her goal, the sword sank hilt deep. Cold jelly brushed against Branwyn's knuckles, and she heard, with great satisfaction, a gurgling scream.

The demon started to fall.

The force of Branwyn's charge didn't lend itself to reversal. She scrambled backwards, desperate to pull Yathana free before the vast weight on the other end of the blade could break her.

She yanked, overbalanced, and teetered on the edge of the rift, sword free but feet unsteady, even her reflexes failing her at the end. Gulfs yawned below her. Branwyn knew that they weren't empty. She knew that she was going to fall.

Zelen tugged her backwards, his breath hot in her ear. "Careful! That place is even worse than this house, hard as that is to imagine."

"Thank you," said Branwyn. She couldn't let herself rest against him, much as she would've liked to, but snapped her eyes open and shook the demon's gore off Yathana. "We should move back more."

"Why—oh." A few more stones had fallen into the hole in the world, eaten away by the power there. "Silly me. I'd assumed it would close when the demon died."

"I doubt if it's really dead, just licking its wounds. Discouraged if we're lucky. But it didn't make the hole; it was only first in line. I hope the next one will be smaller."

"What's our task then?" he asked, as steady as any comrade-in-arms she'd ever had.

Branwyn wished she had better news.

"The knights should get here eventually, particularly if we don't return for a while," she said. The tip of a dead-white tendril wavered above the rift, not out enough to strike yet. "They'll bring one of Letar's priests if they have any sense. Mourners and Blades both know how to fix these rips. The longer we hold out, the easier they'll find their job."

"Ah," he said.

"Yes. I'm sorry."

"We all die one day," said Zelen. "You're the best company I could've hoped for."

She blinked away tears—clear vision was important—and smiled. "Love and death, hmm? You'd have done the Dark Lady proud, from what I can tell thirdhand."

Other tendrils were winding their way to the rift's edge now, wide but oddly flat in the same way that the demons at the ball had been. Finding her balance again in the few seconds they had, Branwyn suddenly heard Yathana.

Switch weapons, said the sword, faint but distinct. *Quickly. There might still be time.*

Chapter 40

ZELEN DIDN'T CATCH THE WORDS, BUT THE SENSE OF WHAT Yathana was saying filled his mind. He switched his grip so that he could offer Branwyn his sword hilt-first, and took the soulsword in return.

All swords were different in small ways, matters of weight and balance. Yathana was as unlike them as one of the knights' great warhorses was unlike Jester, and Zelen couldn't have reduced the difference to one physical aspect. Like the steeds, she gave off an overwhelming feeling of being able to destroy without effort, even completely by accident. He had a second to wonder if the Sentinels ever sparred using their swords, and if so, how any of them survived.

Then the voice was in his head again, still with the sense of shouting from a long way off or over other noise.

Are you still hers?

In shock, he looked to Branwyn, utterly confused that the sword would pick that moment to ask about their affairs, and that either Yathana or Branwyn would have chosen the language of possession.

You didn't have the choice. Now you do. Are you hers? The sword went on, and as the white things crawled over the rim of the pit, Zelen realized that he'd heard the pronoun wrong: not *hers* but *Hers*. No mortal woman, not even Branwyn, was the subject of discussion here.

Once he'd worked that out, the answer was easy. "Of course."

Say your full name. Hold on as well as you can.

Not understanding, not needing to understand, Zelen began, "Zelen Sienatav Catalzin Verengir—" and it felt as though he should go on, say more, but first there was no more to say and then there was no *him* to say it with.

It was as though Yathana had pulled aside a set of drapes, spilling radiant midday light into the dark room that had been Zelen's entire being. The speck that remained of his consciousness cringed, but marveled too: pain was only a small part of what he sensed, even of the fraction that any mortal could have put into words.

There was a presence and a pattern.

They emerged from each other and became each other again. Maybe they were never different. Was a flame different from the fire?

They were flame and fire. They were blood, tears, seed, and sweat, purification and destruction and birth, all the tides of rage and pain and desire that ran bone-deep in most mortal life.

Letar was the name he knew. Any name or gender seemed inadequate in the face of that flood, though—a lantern to contain a midsummer bonfire—even if the being overwhelming him had once put on both. There were traces of that self in the presence, as there were flashes of the features Zelen had seen on stained-glass windows, but traces were all they were.

The pattern was all that lived, from Branwyn to the moss on the outside of the wall to a scuttling creature far beneath the ocean. Zelen couldn't approach that understanding, but he sensed for a second the depth of the god's knowledge. It encompassed all lives— their choices, their changes, their deaths, all winding around one another and shaping each other, even from leagues and years away.

There was a beauty to that pattern that would've blinded any mortal. There was, within and around Zelen, an utterly shattering love for that creation and each part of it, for every bit of life that did the best it could in its own way and thus took part in the great, ever-shifting splendor of the world. The god could only make a few adjustments, minor in the scheme of things, but they did what they could to heal, to protect, and to shelter at the end. They always, eternally, loved.

With that love came hatred, unbounded and implacable, for whatever would harm any part of that creation—whether a segment that turned against the whole or a force from outside. Life could make many choices. Most balanced. Some did not. Some splintered the beings who'd made them, destroyed their better selves, and rotted their surroundings. For those decisions, for those threats, there was no mercy.

In that awareness, Gedomir and Hanyi were scabbed wounds, loathsome but already closing.

The rift was different. The rift was abomination.

The god didn't use Zelen's vision to view it. He doubted his eyes could've handled such use. Instead he was an anchor, an opening, a lens. He felt awareness move through him, or around him, in the direction of the pit, and knew the dim echo of anger that could split the world in half.

If there had been words, they would've been in a voice like the crackle of flames and the gush of blood, even-toned but with each syllable carrying a mountain of hatred.

That should not be would have been the closest a mortal could come.

It was speech, thought, and action all at once.

———

The rift wavered.

Branwyn wasn't sure what that meant. Her initial response was to take a step back and raise her sword, or Zelen's sword—not Yathana, but a decent blade for all that—in case the hole was growing again. She nearly grabbed Zelen's shoulder to pull him backwards as well.

A finger's width away, her hand stopped, as if she'd reached unknowingly for new-forged steel and felt the heat. This sensation wasn't quite heat, though, or pain. Branwyn couldn't name it. She knew it was nothing to meddle with.

The tendrils acted then. One whipped down toward Branwyn, while another lashed at Zelen's head. Branwyn lunged, striking the white filament out of the air in front of Zelen. It fell smoking to the floor. The other one snapped across her right shoulder and down her side, leaving a long trail of stinging venom.

She choked off a scream, wanting neither to distract Zelen nor to give the creatures in the pit any satisfaction.

In pain, she reverted to the routines she'd practiced: strike and retreat. Branwyn's weight fell back onto her rear foot, her shoulders rose, and she turned again to the rift, ready for the next enemy to emerge.

The hole in the world was shrinking.

Gray-orange light above a small part of the rift lost the gray. The orange then deepened to red, then winked out, leaving solid stone behind it. The change spread from there, one patch of radiance shifting and shrinking at a time, forcing the remaining tendrils backwards, closing the gap.

She dared to glance at Zelen for more than the second she'd spared to establish his whereabouts before. He was standing perfectly still, holding Yathana before him in a trembling grip, although he was more than strong enough for the sword's weight.

A faint glow came from the opal in the hilt. At first Branwyn thought it was reflected in Zelen's eyes, but when she looked closer, she saw it was no mere reflection. His dark irises gleamed with sparks, like the night air above a campfire.

That light felt a thousand times better than the other: where Gizath's power had left Branwyn nauseous, viewing the brighter radiance stiffened her back and put new life into her weary muscles. She sensed that watching too long would be a bad idea, though. There was a difference between warming her hands at a fire and sticking them into the flame—and the power coming off of Zelen was a conflagration.

It wasn't familiar, exactly. Still, Branwyn hadn't been reforged or spent years with Yathana for nothing. She raised her sword in a salute.

The Deathmistress wouldn't want her to kneel, then.

It seemed as though the rift closed slowly, while Branwyn kept an eye on it, but she knew not how much time passed. The tendrils retreated, back, then below the surface. That surface rippled, red light flowing and swirling around the gray-orange patches. Branwyn saw Zelen clench his jaw, the muscles in his arms standing out as he gripped Yathana's hilt.

She wanted to embrace him, but she suspected that would be a distraction—and thus a disaster—rather than a source of strength. It was always a delicate balance when mortals dealt with the gods. Without knowing precisely what another weight on the scales would do, it was far better not to risk it.

The pit closed inch by inch, the orange light struggling with the red but always pushed into a smaller and smaller space, until finally Branwyn heard a cheated, bubbling roar and Letar's power lit the room like a sunset. Green and pink specks danced in front of Branwyn's vision when it faded, but through them she saw smooth rock where the rift had been.

She let her sword fall at that instant, ignoring all the irate shouting of past teachers, and spun sideways with a speed she hadn't known she was still capable of. Before Zelen had done more than sag to his knees, she was down on the ground beside him, one arm around his shoulders and the other catching Yathana as his grip loosened.

Red specks still shone in his eyes when he looked up at her. Those eyes were practically the only color in his face: he'd gone the shade of old parchment. "Thank you," he said, and smiled, utterly weary and completely serene. "That was a very timely loan."

Chapter 41

FOR A VERY LITTLE WHILE, ZELEN HAD ALL HE COULD IMAGINE wanting, partly because he was too tired to imagine much. The demon was gone, the rift was sealed, and Branwyn's arm was tight around him. He could've stayed there for quite a while, given a chance. He let himself indulge for a few heartbeats.

Letar had vanished with the rift, which was just as well for Zelen's capacity to live as any sort of thinking being. The world had mostly taken on its normal proportions again. A shade of Her—the name and pronouns came back now, out of habit, though they'd never fit quite as well again—lingered in the back of his mind, though. Perhaps it always would—perhaps that was how devotion worked. He'd have to ask the priests.

Yathana had gone silent. That didn't worry him, and not only because Branwyn acted calm. Zelen could feel part of the soul still residing in the fire opal. His wounds hurt no more than they would've otherwise, or troubled him more, but he could've named each one, and when he touched Branwyn's arm, he could've done the same for hers, from the cut down her side to the aching soles of her feet.

Had he not been so exhausted, he could've healed either of them.

That brought duty to mind, and he groaned. "Your side," he began. "I'm afraid we've no bandages here, but if we can get back to the house—" Zelen tried to remember. "The stillroom."

"It'll be fine before then. Can you walk?" Branwyn used the arm around his shoulders to help him up as she rose herself.

"As much as I need to."

One of the footmen was dead when they got to him. The one with the wounded side was still breathing, though, and Zelen bound his wounds while Branwyn checked the other two injured men. He was going to have no sleeves at all if this sort of thing went on. He ardently hoped it didn't.

"He alive?"

An unfamiliar voice slurred the words. Zelen turned, reaching for his sword as he did so but not very quickly. For one thing, speed was beyond him. For another, the speaker sounded as tired as he felt—and far more human than any of the guards or the servants had before.

"Yes," he said.

The man who'd tried to hit Branwyn with the poker was pulling himself up to a sitting position against the wall. There was a hell of a lump coming up on his forehead. Branwyn stood over him, Yathana bare but not leveled at him.

"Is that…good?" The footman was more coherent than Hidath had been, gods knew, but his eyes had a trace of the same horror, and his hands were shaking. "He… They…they told me to do things, and I couldn't *not*. I tried. Forgive me. Forgive me."

"I know," said Branwyn, standing bloody in the darkness and speaking lullaby-gentle. "You were their prey as much as the rest of us. There's nothing to forgive. Do you know if everyone who served here was afflicted in the same way?"

"I think so, mistress," said the footman. "We…couldn't talk about it."

"I understand."

Zelen finished with the sliced-up guard and got to his feet. "At least one of them was," he said, "and he took it badly when the spell was broken. Finding the rest might be a good idea, and I'll gladly…" That was a lie. He wanted nothing more than to leave the house and never see it again, but that wouldn't help. "Gladly go with you for assistance."

"I'll go," said Branwyn. "You find Tanya. Gods willing, she's made it to the horses but not ridden off yet. Will you be all right to search?"

"Better than, thank you," he said, and didn't try to conceal how much he meant his gratitude. "Nothing's broken, I just have to remember how to move."

"That was… What was that, my lord? What you did? I didn't see very much, was getting my breath when all hell broke loose— really so, I guess," the footman added with a nervous laugh, "but then…what happened?"

"We stopped it," said Zelen, "and I might be a priest."

Saying that, feeling the shadow of Letar within him, and remembering the moments when he'd been overshadowed by Her presence seemed to push the walls further apart and let light into the hallway. He took Branwyn quickly in his arms and gave her a light kiss. That helped, too.

They were both here, even if "here" was still a wretched place. They were both alive.

He might wish for more—a large floating bed, for example— but it would have been greedy to ask. Zelen knew the gifts he'd been given.

———————

It was a long journey through the house. The place itself was oppressive, more rigidly bare than half the peasants' huts Branwyn had seen, despite the Verengirs' wealth. What ornament existed seemed designed to show off money and emphasize virtue. Comfort wasn't only an afterthought; it was as widely avoided as possible.

Branwyn, who had little to do with children, pictured four growing up in that atmosphere and found her lip curling up like an angry dog's. She could almost feel sorry for Gedomir and Hanyi.

The idea of Zelen's youth made her want to take Yathana to the furnishings, particularly to a series of cold and disapproving portraits in one of the hallways.

There had never been much cheer in that house, but there was far worse now.

Two other guards were in the study, as Zelen had said there'd be. One was in a corner. He'd stopped screaming when his throat had given out, then curled into a ball and stared blankly into space. The other lay on his side with shoddy bandages around his arm and leg, cloth he'd slashed off the curtains. He struggled to get up when Branwyn and the footman—Mandyl—came in, but only managed to raise his head.

"What happened?" he asked.

"They're done for," Mandyl replied.

"The child?" The man was pale with more than blood loss.

"She's alive," Branwyn answered. "And well, I'm guessing."

It was really more of a hope at that point, since she wasn't disposed to count on either trees or horses, but Tanya had acted like a capable girl, and Zelen was nothing if not diligent. "Don't try to move," she advised the man, glad to see the worst of the dread leave him. "Help's on its way."

Similar scenes played out in other rooms, though with no wounded in those cases. There was a death, though: in the kitchen, the cook had deliberately fallen on one of his own knives. Branwyn shut his eyelids and muttered a prayer to Letar, asking that the man find healing in death for the horror that must have been his last moments of life.

Three of the newer, younger maids and grooms were in better condition, though still shaken. Branwyn deputized them to take care of the others. That group included two more huddled, speechless figures, a constantly weeping butler, and the senior housemaid, who had clawed raw lines down her cheeks but otherwise was coherent enough.

"The others will have gone back to the city with Lord and Lady Verengir," said Mandyl. "Their personal servants. I don't know if… Do you think they got free when we did?"

"I don't know," said Branwyn. "If they aren't now, they'll be so soon. There are plenty of people in Heliodar who can take off that spell, once they know what to look for. It won't be as sudden or dramatic as it was with you, that's all. And maybe it did vanish on all of you at once."

She imagined that: the personal servants, the ones closest to the cultists, who'd probably been under the tightest control, suddenly having their bonds snap. For the sake of getting any information from the other Verengirs, she hoped that the knights had put them under close watch by the time that happened.

Slowly, they got most of the others into the study, leaving Mandyl to wait with a huddled old man—the steward, possibly—who refused to be touched or moved. There the servants stared at each other like strangers. Branwyn supposed they were, having hardly met or spoken as themselves. Horror was all that united them.

She'd seen similar groups in Oakford and elsewhere, strangers except for one or two awful commonalities, but they'd never been like this. The servants *had* known each other, for years, they just… also hadn't.

Branwyn wanted Zelen's touch at her back, or Yathana's no-nonsense presence in her head. Failing either, she wanted a hot bath with plenty of soap and a brush with good hard bristles, which was equally unlikely. Only the winter wind helped, once she'd gotten everyone secure and stepped outside into the cold night. Rain spat into her face, and Branwyn welcomed it.

Hoofbeats approached. Branwyn turned toward them, though she didn't raise Yathana. She'd be no good against a mounted foe in her condition, and she didn't think there were any nearby.

She'd hoped for Tanya and Zelen, but seeing them on Jester, the girl hanging onto the saddle and Zelen's arms sturdy around her, was as good as the bath she'd been longing for. The six mounted knights in armor, and the two shadowy figures in leather who rode near their sides, were the gravy on top of the meat.

"We'd feared we came too late," said Lycellias, pushing open the visor of his helm, "and rejoice to know otherwise. What can we do to assist? What do you still need?"

"Sleep, for the most part," said Branwyn. "Anywhere but in this house."

Chapter 42

IF NOT FOR TANYA, ZELEN WOULD LIKELY HAVE LOST THE struggle to keep his eyes open on the way back to Heliodar. The rain and wind wouldn't have sufficed, nor would his own sense of self-preservation. He'd never been so weary—not only from lack of sleep and physical activity, he recognized, or even from the aftermath of Letar's presence, but as a result of days of tension that his body now recognized it could let go.

Looking back at the house, unable to see it against the darkness but knowing it was there, he corrected *days* to *years*.

His lids kept drifting closed as they rode, Jester's steady walk lulling his mind deeper into the silence that had already started to fill it. Tanya was perched in front of him, though, her whole form stiff with wariness about large smelly beasts as a method of transportation. If Zelen fell, he'd almost certainly take her with him.

That, and occasionally biting the inside of his cheek when matters got too dire, kept him awake until the familiar structure of his own home emerged out of the darkness.

Feyher was there among the grooms, helping Tanya off Jester and handing her over to one of the maids—gods, had the entire household turned out?—and then standing nearby as Zelen practically oozed out of the saddle, ready to catch him but not being too obvious about it. "Bless you," Zelen said, or intended to say.

Very little was clear after that. He was fairly certain he got to his rooms under his own power, and even that he stayed in motion long enough to wash off the blood and the worst of his sweat. For one instant, he saw his hands clearly, and the water in the basin below them turning red.

That was his blood, Gedomir would have said, Verengir blood on Zelen's hands, a sin and a crime.

The presence in his head examined it and said, without saying: *All blood is blood.*

And he'd never seen a family crest in it, he had to admit.

Zelen laughed and swayed backwards with the motion. Branwyn caught him. She smelled of soap, and her hair was wet. "Be easy," she said, "or your people will have to carry both of us to bed."

"I don't much care how I get there," said Zelen. "The floor's seeming quite hospitable, to be frank."

They made it, though, through force of will and the allure of feather pillows. All became darkness of an extremely welcome sort.

Occasionally he woke, prompted by his body's needs, but only for as long as it took to stagger down the hall and back. On other occasions, after the initial long spell of sound sleep, he dreamed. He saw blood in the hallway and Branwyn on her hands and knees, struggling for air, or the demon seizing Tanya in its massive claws, or Hanyi's bloody mouth forming his name.

He held Branwyn tighter following those moments. At other times, as he dozed, he heard her quick inhalation and felt her turn toward him, burying her face between his shoulder and neck. Zelen stroked her back gently.

We're here. We're both still here, he said to himself, and they both slid back into sleep.

Branwyn wasn't in bed with him when he woke fully. She was sitting by the window instead, sipping wine and eating small things out of a porcelain dish. As Zelen focused, he saw that they were candied nuts, and that she was reading *Five Years in Semele*. She closed the book before Zelen had made a sound, though. Yathana's fire opal sparkled in the sunset light.

"This," she said, glancing down at the small red-leather volume, "is either desperately inaccurate or written by a man with more leisure than I ever had. Wine?"

"Please." He couldn't remember his throat ever feeling dryer, and he gulped from the glass Branwyn poured in a way that did no justice at all to a good vintage. "How long were we out?"

"You've been asleep for the better part of two days. Me? Half a day less, or roughly." She watched him rise with an appreciative eye that Zelen felt his collection of bruises and sore muscles didn't merit. He wasn't going to object, though. "I'm not surprised. For one thing, I didn't play host to a goddess."

"I'd have presumed you would, out of the two of us," Zelen said, shrugging on a robe and then taking a chair across from her. "More in the way of firsthand experience and so on."

"Not with Letar. Her brother and mother, yes, but even there…" Branwyn shook her head. "They lent their skill to my reshaping, but that was acting from the outside, and if it touched my soul, it was by way of my body. The opposite happened with you. From what Yathana says, the two don't blend particularly well."

She has too many lines to break along. The sword was clear now, and he blinked. *She might have closed the rift. She wouldn't have survived. I was pretty sure that you could, and that you might live through it.*

"I can't fault your logic," said Zelen, reaching for his wine again. "Tanya?"

"Cleaned, fed, and back with her family."

"And—" He tried to frame a more specific question, found that words failed, and fell back on vagueness. "Everything else?"

Branwyn set down her glass. "The knights intercepted your parents and your sister on their way here," she said, and her voice became gentler, though still matter-of-fact. "Your father was badly injured, your sister somewhat so, and your mother got off lightly. Their coachman was freed at the same time as the other servants. Their personal attendants were in another carriage, which is likely all that kept them alive."

In the silence that followed, Zelen heard Hidath's screaming again. "Yes," he said, "yes, I'd bloody well think so. Are the servants... recovering?"

"As well as the ones back at the house. Lycellias says Tinival might be the best god to tend to them, since his domain is generally affairs of the mind. He also requests our presence at the temple when we're 'feeling sufficiently restored.'"

"That should only take a year or two," said Zelen, but he finished his wine and rose with a groan. "Can you give me any advance knowledge?"

"I think," said Branwyn, "that your father's agreed to talk."

———————

Behind the outer room of Tinival's shrine, hung with blue silk and shining with silver, plainer hallways led back to rooms where the god's less showy work was carried out: barracks, armories, offices, and, up a long, winding set of marble stairs, a tower open to the sky and caged with intricate silver bars.

There, three knights stood in a triangle, armor polished to a mirror sheen, swords and heads both bare. Behind them was a Blade, tall and gaunt in a black robe.

Janayal Verengir, lord of his house, distant ruler and occasional terror of Zelen's youth and more distant dictator of his adulthood, traitor to humanity and the gods, knelt in the center of the triangle. He was bald, thin, frail-boned with age, and wearing the plain garb of a prisoner, but his eyes were as cold and superior as ever.

He watched his son walk in, side-by-side with the Sentinel that he'd tried to frame for murder, and his upper lip curled in a sneer that Zelen knew very well. It mixed a complete lack of surprise with a maximum of weary contempt, and it had never before failed to make Zelen either ashamed or angry, often both.

For the first time, he felt neither.

"I should have expected this," said Lord Verengir. "The distraction was always a necessary weak point. Most of you sensibly pursued self-destruction, but…" A shrug raised his bony shoulders for a fraction of a second. "I should have watched more closely, even so."

"You'll speak when you're instructed," said one of the knights, "or we'll gag you, *my lord.*"

"It's all right," said Zelen. "I hadn't hoped for…" He tossed aside both *affection* or *remorse*, as both seemed too much even for what he hadn't let himself desire. "Anything else."

"We're here to witness a bargain, I believe," said Branwyn. "Has the prisoner sworn his oath already?"

"The lesser," said Lycellias. "Now comes the greater."

He raised his sword, point straight up in the air, and the others followed. None of them showed fear of what their prisoner would do now, without weapons leveled at him. Faith was on their faces, and confidence, and nothing to mar that clarity.

"Traitor," said the Blade, stepping forward. They kept their empty hands at their sides and were somehow more menacing than any of the armed knights. "You stand in the shadow of the Dark Lady. The smoke of your own burning curls about you. The Fifth can give you no aid now, and She has no mercy. Save yourself, if you can."

At a distance, Zelen sensed power stirring, turning attention to the scene in the unhurried way of eternal beings.

"I offer knowledge," said Lord Verengir, "true knowledge. You and your masters can use it, if you let me pass without torment."

The thin voice didn't crack. The expression of scorn didn't waver, especially on the word *masters*. All the same, Zelen thought: *Gedomir wouldn't have taken the bargain.*

It was no better to be a fanatic than a pragmatist. Maybe it was worse. But Zelen faced the man who'd talked endlessly of family loyalty, of duty and purity and obligation, and saw that he might not, in the end, value anything more than his own skin. He hadn't gotten the chance to stab his father as he'd done to Gedomir, not even to strike him or shout at him, but he knew why he'd regarded him with so little feeling earlier.

There was nothing there.

"You who speak for Letar's brother, for the Lord of Truth," said the Blade, turning to Lycellias, "do you take his bargain?"

"I do so accept these terms," said the knight, glittering eyes grave, "and I ask that the Deathmistress stay her hand, for the love she bears the brother who remains to her."

Zelen perceived stillness. He thought it was consideration, but he could only dimly sense Letar now and was very far from knowing Her intent. Despite his devotion, he was glad of it. He only knew when the sense of impending power faded.

The Blade bowed their head. "She gives her assent. Speak, traitor. Buy your final mercy with the truth."

The western wind blew through the tower, bringing with it the scent of rain and roses again. When it passed the silver bars on the sides, they rang like chimes, and the note went on for far longer than it should have.

Lycellias waited until it died, then, sword still held upright, he told the prisoner, "Begin with names."

Lord Verengir wet his lips, opened his mouth, and spoke.

He mentioned a half-dozen names in all. It was more than Branwyn had expected, with her limited experience hunting human monsters, and fewer than she'd feared. She recognized most of them, though not well, from her stretch at court.

"Ranietz?" Lycellias asked at the end, the name unfamiliar to Branwyn until the knight clarified. "We know of your wife already, of course."

"Then it's no matter. She's the only one of the bloodline left," said Lord Verengir, but as Lycellias bent his attention on the old man and Branwyn, a cold wind blew past them. Verengir grimaced. "Her father served, though he was never particularly dedicated. His wife didn't, but she died before that could be a complication, as did her other...issue."

There was a nasty story there. Branwyn could guess most of the details, whether Zelen's mother had been old enough to take part or not. Zelen himself, she observed, was taking all of the information in with a complete lack of expression and a straight back that would've done credit to most of the soldiers she'd encountered.

Lycellias nodded. "And those are all of Gizath's servants that you know?"

"All I know. There are far, far more. You know that." The old man's thin, wormy lips turned up at the corners. "You all know that."

"Our knowledge is not your concern," said Lycellias. "What of enchantments?"

"None exist now," said Lord Verengir, and sighed. "Hanyi and Gedomir were competent enough for temporary matters, but those with the truly intricate skills perished years ago. Roslina was weaker, or less pure, than we anticipated. A pity." He did look truly sorrowful, though Branwyn wouldn't have laid odds on it being out of human caring rather than regret over lost resources.

"Yes," said Lycellias, tilting his head slightly. "How was it that she and the babe perished?"

"She burned. Her and those around her. From inside." Branwyn, who'd seen Gizath's fire at work, shuddered. The wind blew past her again, ice edged and implacable. Verengir's face twisted in effort, but his mouth opened again, and he said, in a voice not entirely his own, "But the boy lived."

"*What?*" Branwyn and Yathana spoke at once.

"Explain," Lycellias commanded.

"The boy survived. Alive, in a heap of ashes. There was great potential there."

"Where is he?" the knight asked.

Verengir laughed, dry and thin. "We've been trying to discover that for years." He didn't try to resist this time. "It was before we'd learned to ensure the servants' loyalty. We assumed them schooled enough in the proper order not to interfere. The child thrived. Alize and Hanyi tended him, as was proper. Then our manservant vanished, and the boy with him." The old man hissed at the memory. "We found the man and dealt with him, but he never said what became of the babe."

Branwyn silently made the sign of the Four for the butler. However long it had taken the man to see the truth, he'd done well at the end, and died for it—likely in torment. She saw Zelen gulp and Lycellias's sharp-angled features grow harder.

"And you seek him still?" the knight asked.

"Of course. If he can be...taught...he's valuable. If not, his death will release the crucial element to go elsewhere. Now, likely, it'll be into the nearest biddable host, not one trained and prepared as we would have done." Verengir shook his head. "Thyran was always a hasty idiot. I'll never know why my great-uncle told him as much as he did, but..."

Lycellias raised his hand. "We have no more need of your speech, nor of you," he said. The other two knights stepped forward, each taking the man by one shoulder. "Go now, and reflect, if you will, on what you've done in this world."

He might. One never knew. But Branwyn didn't have much hope. From Lycellias's tone, she doubted that the knight did either.

Chapter 43

THE COUNCIL DELIVERED THEIR DECISION A WEEK AFTER Lord Verengir confessed, after the executioners had done their duty and the bodies had been distributed in pieces to the four quarters of Heliodar, after an entire flock of rumors had flown about the city.

Branwyn stood in the chamber where she'd come on her first day, wearing the same blue wool gown she'd worn then, and the same bronze-and-opal torc around her neck. She bore Yathana openly at her waist now, though, and the council didn't treat her as if she was a new problem or a foreign curiosity. A few regarded her with admiration. Others looked at her like an omen of doom: the Skull card in a fortune-teller's deck, the black dog at the crossroads.

Two who'd been there before were simply absent. Marior Rognozi sat in her uncle's place, though without his rank on the council, absorbing the goings-on.

Verengir's spot had vanished, without even an empty chair to mark it.

"The rot went too far," Zelen had explained a few nights before, as Branwyn lay beside him in bed. "I'm the only immediate heir who survived, and…well, I'll be surrendering my title soon enough, won't I? Hardly the sort to sit in judgment for the city. Best for the council to go down a member, until some other house works its way to prominence. It won't be long."

"You don't sound as though you regret the loss of your position," said Branwyn.

"I can come up with more enjoyable ones," he'd replied, and kissed her.

Recovery, and delay, had had their benefits.

Now Branwyn waited with her hands clasped in front of her and tried not to speculate. The decision would be what it would be. She and Yathana—and the Sentinels, as a whole—would have to make their plans from the next moment onward, and she could do nothing until then.

High Lord Kolovat came forward to the edge of the dais, the circlet still a trifle small on his brow. "Madam—Sentinel Branwyn," he said, "the council has heard your request, and that of your Order and Criwath behind you."

"And I thank you, all of you, for so hearing," Branwyn replied.

Winter light shone in from the stained-glass window behind the high lord, casting patches of green and yellow on his white robe. They were very faint, however. The sky outside was overcast.

In the corner, a scribe lifted their pen from parchment and waited. Now there would be notes. Later, perhaps, a formal proclamation.

"Given recent events," said Kolovat, "we can't deny that our ancient enemy is at work again, nor that the power behind him endangers us all. For that reason, and in retribution for the suborning of Heliodar's nobility, we do here and now declare that we join Criwath and the Sentinels in the war against Thyran, against his reprehensible patron Gizath, and against the forces that seek to destroy what mortalkind has worked so hard to rebuild."

Lady be praised, said Yathana. *I could kiss the old walrus, if I had flesh.*

Branwyn felt the floor grow more solid beneath her feet as a number of potential futures suddenly joined into one that she could count on. She was glad, but not joyous—given the sober, measured fear in Kolovat's face and the red rims around Yansyak's eyes, she didn't think joy would have been right then. Even Yathana had spoken mostly in relief.

Marton looked joyous, which made Branwyn briefly doubt the whole endeavor.

That didn't matter. She knew her response and gave it: a low curtsy, skirts held out and leg drawn back, then the words she'd rehearsed. "Councillors, you have my thanks, those of the Order of the Dawn, and those of the Sentinels. When this business concludes, the world itself will owe you its gratitude."

The sound of the pen began again. It filled the chamber, because nobody else wanted to make a noise. Perhaps they, like Branwyn, were afraid that *if the world survives* would come out the instant one of them opened their mouth.

"It's snowing," said Starovna, who was standing by a clear part of the window.

They didn't murmur, nor did they all go to see; there was discipline in nobility, at least in this part of it.

"It's winter," said Kolovat. "That's all."

Nobody argued because they wanted him to be right. Nobody spoke again for a long time because they couldn't quite believe that he was.

Snow was falling when Zelen left Letar's temple—not heavily, but steadily. The Mourner and Blade who'd been examining him had glanced out the window when it had started and said nothing. People outside weren't nearly so composed, not with the tales going around the city.

"Been snow in the Oak Month before," said a young man in brown laborer's clothes, paused on the street corner with a cart of wood.

"Once in a while," said his bearded friend. "It's not *common*."

"But it doesn't mean—"

They didn't even glance Zelen's way as he passed. He wore no circlet of office now, nothing to distinguish him from the common man he was.

It was a pity, in a way. He could have done good on the council once, if he'd ever really been a member, but his family had prevented him in both life and death. Best to let the role go to someone who could truly act in the city's interest, with no hereditary ties binding their hands.

He could serve better elsewhere.

"You know," said Branwyn, suddenly at his side, "it takes a while for me to pick you out of a crowd without your finery."

"Altien said the same." Zelen turned to face her, brown cloak flaring with the motion. "I think you're both exaggerating. It's not as though I've gone completely drab."

With Gedomir in his memory, Zelen doubted he could ever do that, even when he did put on the Mourners' official regalia. He wore a scarlet wool tunic rather than velvet, though, with long sleeves and a high neck. It kept him warm, now that he'd abandoned most of the magical heat at his house, and it was less effort to take care of, freeing his servants to take over some light duties at the clinic.

A few of those from his family's estate had joined them. Nislar had a talent for setting bones, it turned out, and the senior housemaid had learned a bit of herbalism in her youth. The pay wasn't wonderful, drawn as it was from Zelen's own accounts and the proceeds of selling his jewels, but they didn't give any indication of caring.

"That would be physically impossible," said Branwyn.

"Much obliged, madam." Zelen noticed that she was pale inside the hood of her cloak, but that her cheeks were flushed. "What news? Are we acting?"

"We are... You are. Kolovat will announce it by sundown."

"Good," he said, and then made a rueful face. "Well, better than the other options."

Don't worry, said Yathana. *Neither of us thought you were going to fling your hat in the air over it.*

"I'll save that for when the war is over. When Thyran is gone. And when I have a hat to throw."

"Touch steel when you say that, and not about the hat," Branwyn said. Her short laugh was underlaid with solemnity, and Zelen wasn't entirely joking when he tapped the hilt of his knife.

"What now?" he asked.

"Kolovat said I'll receive more information within a day or two, and then"—Branwyn hesitated, but not for long—"I'll need to inform the Order."

"But that's tomorrow, if not later," Zelen said, and offered her his arm. "Now I'd say we both could use a meal."

"I can't argue with your professional opinion."

Branwyn's grip was light on his bicep, sure and easy now. She'd gotten used to him, if not the custom. Briefly, Zelen stood beside her, not yet walking, taking in the street he'd known most of his life.

Half the young people around them would likely go to fight. The others might join the army as well, as scribes or laborers or healers, or know the agony of waiting at home for bad news. None of them knew yet. None of them had known, for all the past weeks, what fate was approaching through a series of small rooms.

"If you don't object," he said, "let's not head back to my house. I'd rather be out when the word gets around."

"No," said Branwyn, turning the word over, "no, you're right. Show me to that place you'd mentioned before, then, and let's see if we can manage it without assassins this time. I'll even pay."

"My circumstances aren't that reduced."

They weren't what they had been. Zelen had sold every stick and stone of the country house and given the proceeds, along with what his father and brother had left him, to the families of the sacrificed children. Idriel had delivered it: Zelen hadn't wanted to see the reaction.

That left him what he needed for the clinic, as well as enough for clothing, a few rooms of his city house, and food—much of which the Temple of Letar would provide him before too long.

"How was the lesson?" Branwyn asked as they headed off into a moving curtain of snow.

"Surprising for everyone, I'd wager." Zelen grinned at the memory of the Blade's expression of shock during the magical inspection and the Mourner's pithy phrasing. "But they've begun to teach me a good deal already, and they say my training will help. I should be ready for the front lines in a week or two."

"The front lines?" Branwyn stared at him.

Zelen nodded. "They'll need healers. You know I'm decent with a sword. It seems the best choice."

"I don't think the city's armies will be ready to march in less than a month."

They won't. Don't ask for more than one miracle in a season.

"Lucky for me, I have one decent horse left, and I won't need to wait for the army." Zelen didn't stop walking. He felt as though he would've lost his balance if he had. He focused on Branwyn's profile, and took the last mental step forward. "If you'd like me to come join you, that is. Wherever you end up."

Now Branwyn stopped walking. She turned, and the hood of her cloak fell back, letting snowflakes fall on her gold hair. "Zelen—"

"If you don't, I understand."

He'd try, at any rate.

"No. Yes." She flushed. "I would like that. Very much. But you're aware of what I am, what I do, the risks I take... Are you certain?"

Zelen put both arms around her and drew her off to the side, giving people room to pass. Some were pausing to observe the scene, he was sure, but he didn't give a damn. "Nobody's safe these days, and it wouldn't matter if they were," he said, looking down into the strong, noble face he'd come to love. "I still can't think of anyone whose company I'd rather die in, and if we both end up living, I'd rather do that with you too."

"I—" Branwyn's mouth was open for a minute, but no more words emerged. She didn't need them. Her eyes told Zelen all he needed to know, and then she confirmed it by kissing him.

They stood like that for a long time, not caring who saw: two tall figures clinging together in the midst of the first winter snow.

Epilogue

"IT'S KATRINE NOW, ISN'T IT? BONDED TO THE SOULSWORD Coran? I'm Rolf... I don't know if you remember me."

"From Silane," Katrine said with an attempt to hide her shock. Rolf had been half her age in Silane, barely starting to learn the sword when she'd been reforged. In a properly made world, he wouldn't have been remotely old enough to be a full Sentinel.

Twelve years since then would make him nineteen, said Coran. *One does get used to time eventually.*

"Yes!" Beaming, he showed small silver fangs that proved his status, along with the citrine-adorned rapier at his waist. Rolf also had big puppy-like eyes and came up a little higher than Katrine's shoulder, neither of which helped mitigate the impression of youth. "You were very helpful about teaching me to ride. I was quite grateful on the way here, in fact."

"Was it a long trip?"

That was a polite question. Getting north of Oakford, to the last set of fortifications that had been built in the mortal world's few months of respite, was always a long trip. Still Katrine asked, just as she broke off a piece of the meat roll she'd been eating and offered it. Small politenesses had value, especially at the end of the world.

Rolf nodded and accepted the food, eating with the blinding speed of the young. "I've come from the chapter house in Affiran," he said, producing a sealed message from his belt, "but my news comes from beyond that—from Heliodar. They said I should take it to you or Vivian, though I wouldn't know her on sight."

"There's no time like the present for introductions," said Katrine, and got to her feet.

A short trip took them among the tents: the Sentinels, knights, and Blades all mingled, with the Mourners, Sitha's priests, and the wounded in the protected center of the camp. Katrine pointed out what landmarks they had, while Rolf goggled.

The camp was a bustling place at midday. Guards were changing shifts while warriors practiced or built up the earthworks with the help of Sitha's priests. The smells of sweat and horses blended with the scent of herbs as the Mourners prepared remedies and the wizards got other concoctions ready for their hour of need. A few talked over the snow: the inch or so on the ground, the flakes that were falling. It wasn't unusual, as late fall turned to early winter, but everyone was apt to see omens.

Vivian's tent was larger than most, a wood-ribbed circular structure made for meetings in foul weather as well as simple shelter. Like those of the other commanders, it was marked: the Sentinel sigil, a sun with an open eye inside, flew on a red pennant outside.

The woman herself emerged while Katrine and Rolf approached.

"Katrine," she said, spotting her second, then noticed the young man. "Sentinel. Have reinforcements arrived?"

"A few, Commander," said Rolf. He bowed quickly, then offered his letter. He was too young to recognize the air of purpose about Vivian, or too eager to wait for her to read the message. "And more to come soon. Heliodar's come in on our side!"

"Good," said Vivian, but her dark-skinned face was a mask. She took the folded paper and broke the seal with a flick of one thumb. "We'll need them."

"The wards?" Katrine asked.

"Crossed just now. In considerable force. I'm off to talk with the other commanders."

"I'll get our forces ready."

"Thank you," said Vivian. She focused on Rolf for the first time. "Welcome to the front lines. I'm afraid we won't be able to send you back soon."

Rolf was young, but not stupid. "How long do we have until they arrive?" he asked, touching the hilt of his sword for reassurance.

"Not nearly long enough."

**Don't miss the epic conclusion of
the Stormbringer series**

COMING SOON!

Part 1

The attacks resumed today. This first was only a test of our guard: a score of twistedmen and five of the trance-birds. We drove them off handily enough—the spell that Hanyi and your Gerant came up with at Oakford shields our minds well, and our mages have been diligent about applying the sigils. Injuries were light, comparatively, casualties nil, and the new fortifications hold well.

Still, the air here has changed. None, not the Order nor the soldiers from Criwath nor even the reinforcements from Heliodar, fresh as they are, can mistake the meaning of this attack, or be in any doubt of what will follow.

We have discussed, for eight months, what deviltry Thyran might be up to out in the forest, where we have no strength to reach. We have come to no conclusions.

I suspect we're about to find out.

—In the Order's Service,
Vivian Bathari

The Traitor, Gizath, murdered his sister's lover, they say, because he thought it a disgrace that a goddess should lie with a mortal. Over the centuries, his hatred for mortal life has expanded far beyond that.

Then one hundred years ago, Gizath's servant Thyran slew his wife and her lover out of jealous rage, and then his own servants to seal a pact with Gizath. Jealousy swiftly became spite: anger that the world did not give him what he believed was his by birth and blood.

In the north, when he called those of like mind to him and merged them with demons, perhaps they too wished to order the world by their standards. Perhaps even then Thyran did likewise.

After a hundred years, and two losses, I suspect his desires may have shifted.

He may strive still for conquest, if such a mild word can describe a world ruled by him and his twistedmen.

If he is thwarted in that, I think he will turn his sights to annihilation. And he will do so quickly.

—Lycellias, Knight of Tinival

Chapter 1

THE DREAM LEFT HIM COLD IN THE DARKNESS. SWEAT COATED his limbs, cooling rapidly in the spring night. He tasted blood in his mouth: he'd bitten his lip again.

None of it was new, but it was worse this time. His heart was thudding between his ribs and his chin, the images danced evilly in front of his open eyes, and not even the sound of three other knights snoring could make the memories seem as unreal as Olvir knew they were.

Dreams, he told himself, as Edda had told him when he was far younger. Nightmares had been different then: shapes outside the window, ghouls behind the house, the sort of stories youth repeated and parents could generally dispel with warm milk and a few words.

Olvir doubted that soothing words would've helped completely. He'd long since grown to prefer whiskey to warm milk, too, and a liquor-mazed head was the last thing he'd need the next day, particularly considering the quality of whiskey that went around the front lines.

It was a myth that Tinival's knights never surrendered. The training was very clear about recognizing lost causes. Sleep, right now, was among them.

He disentangled himself from his sweat-dampened bedroll as quickly and quietly as he could manage. None of his companions stirred. It was funny: their alertness was legendary, but a knight—or any trained warrior, Olvir suspected, though he hadn't exactly asked—grew accustomed to certain sounds. In camp, these included both snoring that could shake the earth and the noises of a tentmate trying to make a stealthy exit in the middle of the night.

Tinival hadn't given them heroic bladders, after all.

Putting on armor would be more likely to rouse his tentmates, so Olvir simply tugged on his breeches, then picked up his boots and tunic in one hand. He carried the belt with his sword on it in the other. The camp was relatively peaceful, no attack expected, but there was no point tempting fate.

Edda had taught him that long before he'd entered the Silver Wind's order as a page.

He stumbled outside into a chilly gray predawn. The remains of fires made the camp a little brighter but, at that hour, mostly just added smoke to the air. A flash of Olvir's dreams sprang from fading memory to vivid detail with the odor, and he sat down hard on a rock.

Vomiting would only waste rations, and the army had a strictly limited number of those. Screaming would only wake soldiers who had too little rest as it was. Olvir scrubbed his hands hard across his face, wishing that he could do the same to his mind, trying not to look too long at his hands themselves. They had been the worst part, and that was new.

If your thoughts are sour, turn to deeds. It was another of Edda's sayings. And he was already sitting down.

Olvir pulled on his boots, listening to the sounds near him. The camp was mostly still abed, but not entirely. Out of the three thousand or so souls who defended that part of Criwath's border, fifty-odd were assigned to patrol the fortifications. He could look up and see two of them walking behind the wooden palisades, looking through cracks too small for arrows to spot any activity beyond. He could certainly hear their footsteps, regular drum-beats behind the more irregular noise of snoring sleepers and shifting horses. Their presence was reassuring, but he'd have been a fool as well as an oaf to distract them.

A few rows of tents behind the defenders, the wounded slept restlessly. The Mourners, noncombatant servants of the Dark Lady whose domain included healing, kept their own vigil among them, watching for sudden declines. Letar's priests were good company as a rule, but Olvir didn't want to disturb the Mourners on their duty either.

There was always practice. The few sets of pells were barely holding together after rounds of recruits, so by common agreement nobody used them except those who truly did need help hitting the target. Fighting the air, however, required only space. Olvir stood up and turned to retrieve his tunic.

A woman stood a few feet away from him.

That itself wouldn't have been a surprise, or a problem—a relief, though he wouldn't have wished it, to find another who couldn't sleep—but Olvir hadn't heard her approach. Coming on top of his dream, it was more than he could reason through calmly. Before his brain caught up with his body, he'd hissed in a wary breath and reached for his sword.

"It's a shade early for a duel," she said.

As usual, Olvir recognized her voice before her face. He knew the tone in particular: soothing amusement. The words beneath the words were *we can laugh about this, we're laughing already, we wouldn't be joking if it was any great matter.*

He'd used that tone before, when the minutes before battle bit into the throat like wire, but he'd heard it most often in that camp from the woman in front of him: Vivian Bathari, commander of the Sentinels who held the border.

As was usual with the Sentinels, her clothes—dark, plain wool beneath a mail shirt—gave no indication of her rank. The gold-worked hilt of a greatsword over her shoulder, and the eye-sized sapphire set in it, made a striking contrast.

That was Ulamir, the soulsword that made her a Sentinel, and the stone housed a spirit hundreds of years old.

Vivian wore the other marks of the Order of the Dawn on her face: a half-circle of bloodred tears beneath each gray eye, glowing against her light-brown skin. The gods had reforged her, like they did all of her order, turning them into weapons, and none who'd been through that process ever looked fully human again.

None ever were.

Many feared the Sentinels, even as they relied on them, believing them too close to the monsters they killed. Olvir was too familiar with them, and with Vivian in particular, to feel the slightest alarm at her presence once he recognized her.

Embarrassment was a different story.

───────────

How easily he startles, said Ulamir.

"Everyone's jumpy right now," Vivian replied, "and no wonder."

She spoke in the half-voiced murmur that she'd spent eighteen years using with her soulsword, and which most people didn't hear.

Olvir nodded, then contrived to look even more awkward than he had before. He carried it well, as always. Being tall and square-chinned with big hazel eyes helped. "Not talking to me, were you? Though you're right. Or Ulamir is."

"I forget I have to be careful around the knights," she said with unspoken acceptance of his equally unspoken apology. "I'm still too used to people with normal hearing."

Should your memory slip around any of them, he's the safest, Ulamir put in. *What could you say to him that you didn't say in the Myrian lands, when that undead sank its teeth into your leg?*

"You didn't insult me," Olvir echoed, "and you didn't reveal any dark secrets." Relaxing, he glanced down at the sword in his hand, then at the scabbard he'd drawn it from.

That and the rest of his belt lay behind him on the large rock where he'd been sitting, with a folded bundle of sky-blue cloth beneath them that Vivian assumed was his tunic. "Er. I should either put this down or on, shouldn't I?"

"It seems like it would be easier on your wrist," said Vivian.

She began to turn away as he put the sword down and picked up his tunic. It was a shame to do so, with rippling biceps and a flat stomach on full display—she was middle-aged for a Sentinel in the field, and weary, not blind or dead—but it was best to avoid lingering awkwardly, particularly when she'd be working with the man. Getting breakfast going early would win her some favors, Vivian thought, and starting a fire came easily, even two years past her journeying days.

"You weren't looking for help, when you came across me, were you?" Olvir asked, making her turn. The tunic slid down over his broad back and narrow waist, concealing his head for a moment before his close-cut chestnut hair emerged. "If you'd be able to use an extra hand with any task, I'm more than willing."

"No, but I do thank you for offering. I woke up and couldn't get back to sleep, so I hoped a tour of the camp would help."

"You too? Not that it's so unusual, given the circumstances."

"I'm surprised there's not a crowd of us. Ample hard work or rotgut must be effective for the others."

Olvir turned toward her. His belt was fastened, and his sword on it—"girt to his side," as the old stories had said—and he mostly looked the picture of an upstanding knight, but with a far less certain expression than tapestries generally portrayed them having. "Forgive the question, but you haven't been having dreams, have you?"

"I have," she said slowly, "but only what you'd expect. And you sound like you mean another sort."

"I'm afraid I'm not sure what I mean. I've never been a prophet, so I doubt it's that, and yet they repeat more than any dream I've ever had."

The name and the face were both starting to niggle at her. She'd heard of him before, not just as her past sometime-companion on missions or another friend in the camp. The mention had been more recent, more official. "I don't want to pry," Vivian said. "Or, rather," she added, because she was talking to a servant of Tinival, whose dominions included truth, "I do, but only as far as it might be tactically significant. Tell me more?"

Olvir squared his broad shoulders, a man facing up to an unpleasant duty. "I'm in different places," he said. "It was the village where I grew up in this dream, but in the last one I was at the chapter house where I trained. It's always a place that I'm fond of. And it's always burning. The smell of smoke is very vivid. The screams are too."

"I haven't studied the mind," said Vivian, "but that doesn't seem so out of the ordinary to dream about, given all of this." She gestured, indicating the campfires but also the palisades and the army, and by extension the war. "It sounds like you put it a few degrees away rather than using memory straight out, but...minds do that, probably."

"So I thought. But"—he swallowed—"tonight I saw where... I saw that I was lighting the fires. My own hands were piling up the wood, spilling the oil." Olvir held them up and out in unnecessary illustration, or perhaps to try to get them as far from himself as he could. "I tried to stop. It didn't make any difference."

Chapter 2

TALKING DIDN'T ACTUALLY HELP VERY MUCH, WHICH CAME AS no surprise to Olvir. Knights were trained to meet fear boldly, both when it came from outside and when the source was inside their own heads. If he'd only needed to confront his dreams to make them stop, he would've done so months before.

He'd harbored a small hope, as he began describing them to Vivian, that putting words to the images, the crying and the odor of smoke and flesh, would define them and thus trap them. That didn't happen either—the dreams remained, as nebulous and unnerving as ever. Olvir sighed, then waited for Vivian to state the conclusion he'd already turned over, and still believed possible: worries about command, or about the war in general, and nothing more.

She stayed silent. While the fires smoldered around them and sentries' footsteps thumped out the moments, Vivian frowned, stared, and didn't speak a word. She didn't move either, adding to the sensation that gripped Olvir, a feeling of being looked not just over but *through*.

Vivian didn't resemble cheerfully profane Emeth and her earnest lover Katrine, who Olvir was most familiar with, or any of the other half-dozen Sentinels he'd met more casually. In that moment, facing her clear gaze, he experienced a little of what the uninitiated must have felt in a Sentinel's company. Training helped him not to look down or fidget, for which he was profoundly glad.

"You were at Oakford," she finally said. "You played a major role, unless I misread the reports."

"I was." That line of reasoning had also suggested itself. "But the dreams started long after that. I've only been having those for a handful of months. There could be a correspondence, I suppose, but—" He shrugged.

"It's not a clear connection," Vivian agreed. "If you don't mind, I'd prefer to hear what happened in your own words. You know what reports are."

"It was late in the siege," he said, remembering a different set of walls, other sets of companions who likely wouldn't all survive the next few days. Had it been more desperate? Perhaps, but a different sort of desperation. "Thyran himself came out to face us."

Nightmare had spawned nightmare then. They'd all heard that Thyran—the most famous servant of the traitor god Gizath, the man who'd locked the world in winter for years when his previous attempt at conquest had failed—had somehow returned. Olvir had thought he'd faced that fact until he'd seen the bone-crowned figure on his walking throne of corpses and looked into the rotting inferno of his eyes.

"I didn't know him," he told Vivian, a year later and not a great deal wiser, despite a fair amount of scholarly effort. "Not the way people mean that phrase. I grasped his…frame, his pattern. A familiar tune, but not the whole of the song. I tried to find out more," Olvir went on, gesturing to the badge on the shoulder of his tunic, where a blue sword signified Tinival, "and saw blackness, shining blackness in pieces, before I lost consciousness."

"The contact disturbed him too. Did I read that correctly? Darya, I think, said he seemed pained."

"If Darya said it happened, I believe her," said Olvir. "I was in no state to observe anything."

"That was all?"

"On that occasion. Later…" Olvir rubbed his chin, uncertain of the precise wording. Most of the magic he knew was the power Tinival granted his knights. Until a year before, he'd been content to let others attend to all else. "Gerant, Darya's soulsword, cast a spell to extend his protection to General Amris, and to let the three of them speak directly."

Vivian nodded, with a quick breath of resigned laughter. "It's a pity that the spell doesn't work outside of their circumstances, and that those are so unique. If I could give Ulamir's power to any lover I took…" She laughed again, a surprisingly light sound, clearly at a comment from her sword, then waved a hand. "Please continue."

"A few of us made a circle for them. We ended up connected. It was less intense for those of us on the outside, but I was aware of the others in a manner that I wasn't before."

"I take it that wasn't part of Gerant's goal."

"No. And Darya said it hadn't happened when the three of them had done the spell before."

"She and Gerant aren't—weren't—precisely used to having others nearby, to be fair. Even among us, she has an attraction to the remote."

"That's so," Olvir admitted, "and she said so. Silver Wind's truth, I have no idea how closely any of these incidents are related, except that the second and third almost certainly are, and Gerant said that he thought the third had to do with me. Forgive me… I'm getting ahead of myself."

A bell chimed in the distance: five slow, measured strokes. A fresh—relatively speaking—sentry headed to the wall, sparing a quick glance at Olvir and Vivian but no more. Their focus was already turning outward.

"At the end," Olvir said, "Thyran tried to kill General Amris and me with magic. I saw Gerant's protection taking a fraction of it. It wouldn't have been nearly enough to save us. I knew that. I…" He brought back a memory he'd repeated until the words had worn holes in what he'd once known. "I felt as though I was being torn apart. I don't recall what I was thinking, if I was thinking at all."

"Hard to be coherent at such times," Vivian agreed. "But you turned Thyran's spell back on him."

"I suppose so. All of us who'd been involved in casting the shield seemed to join in, but Gerant said my presence might have been the deciding factor." A year later, and it still felt like boasting to say it. "More likely it was the god's."

―――――――

"It's possible," said Vivian. She'd never heard of Tinival working like that, and she assumed that none of his priests had either, or one would have long since provided the clarity the god was known for. On the other hand, how often did a knight end up facing Gizath's champion, let alone with all of the magical complications Olvir had described? "He may be behind the dreams too."

Olvir looked politely doubtful.

Naviallanth wouldn't veil his message, Ulamir said, using the stonekin's name for the god, *nor would he have any need of obscurity with his chosen.*

Doubly reproved, Vivian switched angles of approach. "I take it you had yourself inspected by all of the correct people."

"As many as we could find, before the war called me away. The Dark Lady's Mourners said that my life force was normal, and her Blades couldn't find any corruption in me." Olvir made the fourfold sign of thanks, touching forehead, eyes, and mouth quickly with the fingertips of his right hand. "The mages said that my spirit had been altered somehow, shaped, but they couldn't tell why, or whether it'd taken place before or after Oakford."

One or the other need not be the only choice. All gems are cut before they're polished.

"Fair point," said Vivian, and explained, "Ulamir says the initial shaping could've taken place before Oakford, and then those events could have brought it out. Do you know when it might have happened?"

"No," he said, politely but promptly. Obviously he'd given the same answer a few times before. "I've had an active life, but no mysterious incidents with mages."

"And your childhood?"

"Infancy, maybe. I was only a month or two old when my mother found me, and she would've told me if it had happened since." His fond grin gave Vivian a little warmth in the chilly morning. "She was a dedicate of the Silver Wind herself. It had been many years since she'd held a blade, but the oaths don't vanish."

"No, they don't."

Vivian hadn't sighed, and she believed she'd looked suitably casual, but a trace of her thoughts must have gotten through. Olvir's large brown eyes briefly met hers in a moment of connection that had nothing to do with the war or his dreams. He was perhaps ten years younger than Vivian, but even he knew the point where a warrior, even one molded by the gods, had to see the ground shifting up ahead. Slower reflexes, fragile bones, and all the other frailties of mortal flesh were still mostly in the future, but not nearly as far away as they'd been at sixteen.

A soldier or a mercenary without a vocation might have started considering small farms, or inns, or ceremonial posts with nobility. The paths were different for the servants of the gods. Vivian had just begun to wonder about that when the war had really started. Now it was anyone's guess how many of them, god-touched or not, would see that terrifying age.

"That raises possibilities," she said, pulling the conversation back to practicalities, or analysis, which was the next best thing, "but only those."

It happens at times that my people bestow gifts on likely humans, said Ulamir, *but such favor is rare, and no land near here is missing a prince.*

Olvir shook his head. "No. If we'd had more time and could have consulted more mages, possibly, but I was more use with a sword than as a curiosity."

"You're right on that point."

"Thank you... and thank you for listening."

"I wish I'd been able to help more," said Vivian.

The camp was slowly waking up around them, with quiet groans and mild profanity drifting through the air. Those who hadn't had Olvir's dreams, or the more normal nightmares of the battle line, had to return to a world of unwelcome facts: they were still here, the war was still going on. *Bugger it* was a frequent response, with no effort to be more specific.

He shook his head. "I couldn't have expected it of you and been reasonable, any more than I'd have expected you to have the same dreams. I only thought, well, it's always worth asking."

"It is," said Vivian, and then heard footsteps behind her, less regular and more purposeful than the sentry's.

Olvir's gaze focused over her left shoulder. Olvir saluted just as Vivian was turning to see the newcomer. "Good morning, General. You seem to have a mission in mind. Can I help?"

"Morning." General Magarteach had a light, efficient voice. "Glad I caught both of you together."

"Glad to be of service," said Vivian. The general was broad of shoulder and bosom, with red hair running to gray in streaks. Magarteach was roughly her height, which was not inconsiderable, so that the general effect was of a moving wall. Right then it was a troubled wall. "What's today's complication?"

"Those clouds," said Magarteach, and gestured to the north, where the thick gray sky was taking on a darker shade. "I don't like them. More to the point, the mages don't either. I suspect we may have hoped in vain for spring, Sentinel, and I'm sure we'd best start getting the camp battened down."

Chapter 3

WIND SHRIEKED THROUGH THE NIGHT. CLOUDS BLOTTED OUT the stars, dumping snow by the bucketload onto the border camp, and the air was painfully cold, even when the wind didn't whip it into a sandstorm of ice. It had been spring two days before. Now it was midwinter again, hard and bleak.

Out beyond the walls, magelights shone stark white on the snow, bright enough to blind any watcher who didn't shield their eyes, but making sure that any figure approaching the palisades was visible right away. Thickly wrapped soldiers escorted the wizards out three times a day to keep them shining. It was a luxury that, like the spheres of heat surrounding the tents, had become the only way the armies opposing Thyran could hold the border through the winter.

Vivian watched the ground before her from the thin slit in her bonemask, blinked to clear her vision, and cast her gaze over every inch of the snow that she could see, looking not only for the obvious figures of twistedmen—Thyran's shock troops—but for movement that could mean tunneling.

The cold was fine. Poram and Letar had both blessed her at her reforging. Now Vivian could face the blizzard with no more than mild discomfort, just as she could hold her hand in a fire for an hour and come away with no worse than a nasty sunburn. The monotony of the watch itself was the danger, and the weather made it worse. Snow clouded the sharpest vision after a while. Visions appeared in the cold. Voices rode the wind. It would have been easy to lose herself.

She did lose track of the time, until another figure approached her position on the walls.

Only the Sentinels and the knights had the endurance to be sentries for very long in the storm, and not many of those had blessings to match Vivian's. Katrine was wrapped in wool and fur until she looked twice her size, and only the amethyst-hilted sword at her waist would have given her identity away if Vivian hadn't known who else was out there with her.

"All calm on your circuit?" Vivian asked.

"All calm. You make an excellent landmark, Commander."

"I do my best." She peered at the other Sentinel, observing what she could between fur hood, wool scarf, and bonemask. Katrine was pale, but she'd always been pale. The droop in her shoulders was more indicative. "You've reached your limit."

"So have you," said a voice from the stairs behind them.

Vivian didn't turn when she recognized the speaker. Nor was she surprised that she hadn't heard the approach: Emeth was the most silent-moving of the Sentinels she knew, particularly when snow muffled her steps. "Well—" she began.

"Well, you've been out here two shifts, and you'll be no damn good if you fall asleep on your feet. Katrine, love, you're damned near blue. Alyan's about ten steps behind me. We'll be fine while you two get some blood into your fingers."

"I'll ignore the insubordination, then," said Vivian.

"Good. Kat, Olvir said his tent'd have stew ready in a couple minutes if you want to stop in. I'm sure nobody'd mind if you brought our gracious leader."

Nor would I trust your fingers near a carving knife just now, Ulamir put in.

Vivian's aide was skilled in many things. Cooking was not one. "I'm told I make illustrious company," she said, and let Katrine take the lead.

Wizards took care of the inside of the camp as well as the

outside. Down off the walls, the wind was already less fierce, but a faintly yellow transparent shield a foot or so in, anchored by glowing yellow crystals every few yards, blocked the rest of it, leaving only adequate air to keep everyone breathing. A significantly larger transparent sphere sat further in, radiating heat to two circles of tents.

The wounded and those who cared for them got the closest spots. The healthy soldiers took the outside, supplementing magic with braziers, fires, and body heat.

Olvir's tent was large, with a glow from inside that hinted at the brazier. Those inside were singing as Vivian and Katrine approached. The smell of cooking food drifted out along with the music, making Vivian's stomach growl. It *had* been a long watch.

"Come in, please!"

She'd always admired Olvir's voice, which had the clear depth of a great horn. It was perfect for shouting orders across noisy battlefields. Now it cut cleanly through the wind. In its own way, it was as much welcome—as much shelter—as the light and the scent of stew.

———

Swords always gave Sentinels away, even when they were swathed in furs and wearing bonemasks. The amethyst in Katrine's Lothelas glinted in the brazier's light, and Olvir only took a moment longer to connect the sapphire with Vivian.

He'd seen her here and there since they'd talked, but both of them had always been very occupied with their duties as the camp prepared itself for the storm. As she pushed back her hood and unstrapped the bonemask, leaving her charcoal-rimmed eyes bare, Olvir found himself at a loss for words. Having spoken of weighty matters, it was hard to find his way to the lighter ones.

Fortunately, singing took care of it. There were five others in the tent, and two of them were silent, but Morgan and the two baritones with her were vigorously making up for the lack.

"O that my love were in my arms," the verse wound to a conclusion, the singers' low tones providing a comforting counter to the high shrieking of the wind beyond the walls, "and I in my bed again."

"Not that I'd insist on a bed," said one of the men, tipping Morgan a wink.

Vivian laughed. "That's the difference between twenty and forty, good man," she said. "I'd take the bed in a heartbeat right now, with love or without."

"So would I, if I'd been standing out for a day," said the other man who'd been singing. He dipped the ladle into the stew and held it up, offering the handle. "Come get 'round a bit of turnip and let's-call-it-bacon."

The two women stepped forward, but then Katrine stopped and turned, peeling off her bonemask in the meantime. She tilted her head slightly, in the manner of a hunting hawk, and looked at the men who hadn't been singing. "I'm afraid I need to ask who you are."

Olvir hadn't recognized them either. They'd come in with the others, back from refreshing the lights. Their faces looked vaguely familiar, but he couldn't place them, particularly as they'd kept their hoods up and were half-buried in piles of fur. He'd thought the cold must have lingered for them—some felt it more easily than others—and hoped they'd feel better after stew.

"Why?" asked one. He had a strange voice, low and clotted. That might have been his wrappings, or an earlier injury, but given the way Katrine was acting… Olvir rose to his feet.

"I'm Jan," the other said quickly, his voice similar. "He's Bres."

Morgan and the soldiers around the stewpot had been watching quietly, but now the man who'd winked at Morgan placed the ladle in the stew, shaking his head. "Nobody named that in our outfit," he said.

"It could be a simple mix-up," said Olvir, though he remained standing, and he was aware of precisely how far his hand was from his sword. "The storm confuses things. Which regiment are you from, gentlemen?"

The one who'd given names sucked a wet breath through his teeth. "Criwath."

"There's a lot of Criwath," said Vivian. "I think you'd better take those hoods off. A look at your faces could clear up a fair amount."

Olvir liked giving the benefit of the doubt, when he could, but he wasn't stupid, and Katrine's judgment was sound. His sword was out and in his hand when the "men" changed.

It only took a second. Their faces crumbled like the snow outside. Red muscle glistened beneath, apparently bare of skin. Faces and arms stretched too long, claws shot through leather gloves, and mouths gaped to reveal three rows of black barbed teeth. These were the twistedmen, Thyran's creatures, coming out of disguises that they'd never worn before.

Ignoring everyone else in the tent, they both rushed toward Olvir.

Acknowledgments

My agent, Jessica Watterson, and my editor, Mary Altman, gave me the opportunity to finally write the world I've been creating for years, and the entire Sourcebooks crew helped me get the Sentinels and their stories out there—my most profound thanks to them! I'm also indebted to my family and friends for their encouragement, and especially to my friend Sophia Khan, who hosted me while I was in the UK writing large parts of this book and kept me well fortified with Nando's, excessive desserts, and true crime.

About the Author

Isabel Cooper lives outside of Boston, where she spends her days editing technology research and her nights doing things best not discussed here. (Actually, she plays a lot of video games.) Her family is not an evil cult as far as she knows, though they do live in a town best known from an X-Files episode.

You can find her sporadically updated blog at isabelcooper.wordpress.com.

Also by Isabel Cooper